NIGHT CAP

JA Armstrong

PROLOGUE

Fallon shuffled the cards in her hand and chewed on the end of a cigar.

"How does she make that look sexy?" Marge whispered to Andi. "Lucky cigar. I'm not even a lesbian and I want to fuck her."

Andi spewed the whiskey in her mouth across the table.

"Hey!" Billie Steele yelled.

Andi kept laughing. "Who knew dating Dale would bring out your wild side?"

Marge shrugged and sipped her whiskey. "Tell me you weren't thinking the same thing."

"I'm trying not to think. And, you just caused me to lose my mind eraser," Andi replied.

"What are we betting on this year?" Billie asked.

"Riley thinks we should bet on Marge's love life." Fallon wiggled her eyebrows.

"You might want to be careful with *that* wager, Fallon," Andi said.

Marge shrugged and grinned. "Go ahead."

"Aw, shit! No way, you and Dale already…"

"No," Marge said. "I hope I haven't forgotten how."

Andi snickered. "Keep watching Fallon with that cigar; you'll remember," she said.

Fallon laughed. "Is that a compliment?"

"It's not an insult," Andi said.

Ida tossed back the whiskey in her glass. "Why do I come to this party?"

"Because you love it," Fallon said.

"It's disturbing," Ida made her reply. "Just deal the cards, Casanova."

"Not Casanova anymore," Deb Homan said. "Fallon's been whipped." She made the sound of a crack with her hand on the table.

Olivia picked up a cigar and lit it. "Must be a change of pace," she commented.

"What's that?" Fallon asked as she dealt the cards around the table.

"You're usually the one holding the whip," Olivia said.

Ida threw back another glass of whiskey. Andi did the same.

"This could get ugly," Billie whispered to Marge.

Marge coughed a bit from the cigar in her mouth.

Fallon took everything in stride. She ignored Olivia's comment and sipped her whiskey. "All right ladies and lesbians in waiting." She winked at Marge. Marge coughed again. Andi chuckled. "Five card stud—that's why I'm dealing."

Ida rolled her eyes. "Why do you all encourage her?"

છ ✖

"Riley?"

Riley turned to find Emily and Evan standing behind her. "I thought you two were in bed?"

Both kids looked at their feet.

"What's going on?" Riley asked.

"Can we stay here?" Evan asked.

Riley was perplexed. "Stay here? You are staying here."

"No, like forever," Emily said.

Riley sighed. *Oh, boy. How do you handle this one, Riley?* She threw the dishtowel in her hand on the counter and directed the pair to follow her into the other room. "How about we talk on the couch?" Riley took a seat and inhaled a deep breath. Fallon had shared a bit about her talk with Emily that afternoon. *Diving in.* "I know you both love visiting. You'd miss home and your parents if you stayed here all the time."

Evan shook his head. "I want Mom to stay here," he told Riley.

"I want to stay with Evan," Emily said. "Summer too."

You are way over your head on this one. Riley smiled gently. "You don't think you'd miss your friends? What about your dad... and your other mom, Emily?"

"They're not there anyway," Evan said. "Em sees Dad more than me."

Emily put her arm around Evan. "I don't know why we can't just be together," she said. "Evan's our brother."

"Yes, I guess that's true," Riley admitted. *No sense in dodging that.*

"And, Ma moved away. Mom is always working. We'll just end up at Aunt Beth's anyway," Emily offered.

Riley tried to take everything in. She had many conversations with her niece when she lived in California, and understood that kids often needed someone they regarded as an impartial adult with whom they could confide their feelings. The family that Evan and Emily shared was complicated. It didn't have to be. Riley didn't think so. Everyone loved the kids. Everyone wanted to be a part of their lives. From where Riley sat, Olivia had used her daughters as a pawn in a twisted game of chess. That not only unnerved her, it also disgusted her. They knew who their father was. All three children knew who was raising them, and yet it seemed that Emily and Evan felt incredibly insecure about where they belonged. They all clung to Beth and Fallon as anchors. It made sense. Riley had only just met Fallon's sister-in-law and she already considered Beth a friend. Beth Foster was easy-going, nurturing, and honest. She was a bit like Andi when Riley thought about it. She could see a lingering sadness in Beth's eyes. It was the ache that accompanied betrayal. In some way, the girls were a reminder of that for both Beth and Fallon. Ironic — they were the two adults that all three children trusted the most. For Riley, it spoke volumes about the woman she loved and Beth. It also told a story about who Olivia Nolan was. Riley thought it resembled a twisted fairytale; the original kind that ended in tragedy rather than glass slippers and pumpkin coaches. Her inclination was to end the discussion and tell Evan and Emily to wait for their parents. That would equate to a betrayal for them. They'd sought her out. They'd placed trust in her. She would need to navigate carefully through the rocky waters of childhood confusion and emotion.

"I'm sorry that your mom, and that your dad, Evan are both away right now."

"I wish we could be here," Emily mumbled.

Evan looked at Riley. "Are you gonna marry Aunt Fallon?"

Riley's eyes grew wider. She took a breath. "Someday, if she decides to ask me; I will."

Evan nodded. "So, Owen will be her kid, right?"

Riley's heart began to pound. She'd never heard that reality spoken to her. It threw her off balance.

"If you get married," Evan tried to explain his reasoning.

Owen already thought of Fallon as his parent. She was *his* Fallon. That's what he'd told Riley's mother and sister. Listening to Evan and Emily, Riley realized what Owen meant by that. "I think that he already is."

"But he doesn't call her Mom," Emily pointed out.

"No, he doesn't. He loves her that way. Just like you love both your moms."

"His dad is really far away, huh?" Emily asked hesitantly.

Riley smiled. "Owen's dad is in heaven. So, Owen can't *see* him, but I think he's still close by."

"How?" Evan asked. "That's so far. My dad is in another country and I only get to talk to him once a week."

"But you think about him; don't you?"

Emily and Evan nodded.

"Just like you think about Fallon and your grandmother when you are home," Riley said.

"Yeah."

"Do you ever think about them and then they call?" Riley asked.

Emily smiled. "Once, I was talking about Fallon and she called to say happy birthday."

Riley nodded. "Well, that's kind of what I mean. Just because you can't see someone or even talk to them doesn't mean they aren't missing you too."

"Then how come they leave?" Emily asked.

Oh, Emily, I wish I had that answer. "I don't know," Riley answered honestly. "They never leave here," she said, pointing to her heart. "No matter where you live."

"Riley?" Evan looked at Riley and then cast his eyes downward.

"What is it, Evan?"

"What if they don't?"

"What if they don't what?"

Evan pointed to his heart.

Riley thought hers would break. She pulled both kids close. "They do, Evan. Sometimes, people have a funny way of letting you know they love you. That doesn't mean they don't. I know that's hard to understand. You both have a lot of people who love you."

"Do you?" Emily asked.

Riley pushed back her tears. No child should ever worry about their parents' love. "Of course, I do."

❧

Andi was off-kilter. In other words, Andi was drunk. She was not alone in her predicament. Several poker games down, she'd lost track of the number of whiskey glasses she'd drained. Ida, Marge, and Billie had all slipped into a bout of silliness. It was a typical Cigar Club gathering that felt anything but ordinary to Andi. Olivia had spent the night making loosely veiled comments about Fallon and Andi's affair. Andi had noticed that Fallon measured her alcohol consumption. That was not for Riley's benefit. Andi guessed that Fallon was close to decking her ex-girlfriend. Olivia had also been a slow sipper all evening, hardly able to make an excuse that her comments were the result of inebriation. Andi slapped her cards down on the table. "I fold. And, I've got to pee."

"You should never have broken the seal!" Fallon called after her.

Andi waved her off.

"I'm out too," Olivia said, throwing her cards on the table. She stood and followed the path Andi had taken.

"You too?" Fallon asked Olivia.

"You know the drill, Fallon. We travel in pairs."

Fallon glared at Olivia's back as she walked away, knowing what Oliva had meant by that comment. *She'd better not start shit with Andi.*

Ida grabbed hold of Fallon's hand. "Andi can handle herself."

"I'm missing something," Marge said.

The table laughed. "The question for all of us, Marge, is how long you'll be missing it," Billie said.

Fallon sipped from her glass, feeling a sense of unease creep over her skin. *Andi can handle herself.*

⁓

Andi emerged from a stall and washed her hands. She startled at the feel of two hands on her waist and looked into the mirror. Olivia's eyes met hers. "What are you doing?" Andi asked.

"That's not obvious?"

Andi turned and pushed Olivia away. "Have you lost your mind, Liv?"

"Pining over Fallon is pointless, Andi."

"Oh? Who are we talking about?"

Olivia stepped closer. "If I had known that you were open to this, I might have made some different choices when I visited Whiskey Springs."

Andi laughed. "You are unfucking believable."

"I am." Olivia reached a fingertip over to trace Andi's cleavage.

"What the fuck?" Fallon's voice boomed.

Andi stepped away, and into Fallon's arms.

"What the hell are you doing, Liv?"

"Well, if you hadn't interrupted, I might have been doing something a lot more fun."

Fallon looked at Andi. "Are you okay?"

Andi nodded. She took a deep breath and put her hands on Fallon's chest. "Go. I'm all right."

"Andi..."

"Maybe you should leave, Fallon. Last I checked, you didn't have any claim to either of us."

Andi felt Fallon tense. "Fallon." She forced Fallon's eyes to hers. "Go. Trust me."

Fallon sucked in a slow breath. She turned slowly and left.

"She really needs to get over her Lancelot complex," Olivia said. "Where were we?"

Andi shook her head. "You have; you've lost your mind."

"Oh, come on, Andi. We're both adults, both single last I checked, and we both know what we like."

"Stop," Andi said. "Olivia, I would marry my vibrator before I would sleep with you."

Olivia chuckled.

"You think this is a game? You think it's funny?"

"Isn't it?"

Andi had sobered quickly. "You know, I used to think that you loved Fallon and you were so afraid to admit you fucked up that you did crazy things to hold onto her."

Olivia crossed her arms.

"Now, I think you're so in love with yourself you can't see anyone else. You left, Liv. In case you forgot, that broke her heart."

"How could I forget with all of you constantly reminding me?"

"She's happy. Let her be happy. If you ever loved her at all, let her go."

"Like you did?" Olivia asked. "Do you? Love her?"

Andi swallowed the lump in her throat. *More than I thought possible.* "I love her. That doesn't mean I belong with her."

"Do you know where you belong?" Olivia shot.

"No. I know where you don't." Andi stepped up and brought her face within an inch of Olivia's. "Watch it, Liv. You underestimate how many people have your number."

"What does that mean?"

"You know what? You do what you want."

"Thank you for the permission slip."

Andi shook her head. She was about to open the door when she heard a loud crash. She ran toward the sound. "Fallon!"

☙ ❧

Fallon sat in the backseat of Charlie's car without comment. Olivia stared forward silently. Carol looked ahead to where Riley was standing on the front porch. She wasn't sure if it was the right thing to do. It seemed like the only thing she could do. If the annual Cigar Club continued after tonight, Carol was confident it would be minus one of its founding members. She'd never seen Fallon out of control. Fallon had made the excuse she wanted to check on Andi because she was drunk. Carol knew that was bullshit when Fallon approached the bathroom. She and Ida had shared an exchanged glance that expressed mutual concern. Andi could hold her alcohol as well as anyone Carol had ever seen. Andi might've wavered in her stride; she was not one to waver in her senses because of a few drinks. Fallon had walked out of the bathroom and strolled to the bar without a word. Her silent walk had been the calm before the storm. Fallon gripped the bar trying to calm her anger. When that failed, Fallon swiped her hand through a line of bottles, sending several on a collision course with the floor and a few directly at the wall. Despite the distance between them, Andi had been the first to reach Fallon. Carol counted that a blessing. She felt sure that Andi was the only person in the room with the ability to calm Fallon at that moment. Even Ida stepped aside until Andi had managed to drag Fallon into the kitchen.

Carol's inner debate lasted less than a minute when she saw the blood dripping down Fallon's hand. She called Riley. More than a shitty hand of cards had made the night a bust. For once, Carol was glad she didn't have to be a fly on the wall in Fallon's house.

"I'll be down in the morning to clean the rest up," Fallon said evenly.

"Fallon, don't worry about it," Carol said. "Call me when you get up."

Fallon nodded and stepped out of the car. Olivia followed.

"What the hell happened?" Charlie asked when both women had closed their doors.

"Olivia happened. What else is new?"

"Fallon looks pissed."

Carol sighed. "I think it's a lot more than that."

Riley moved to the steps and greeted Fallon. She ignored the woman trailing a foot or so behind. Riley shook her head and wrapped an arm around Fallon's waist. "Come on, let's get you inside."

Fallon let Riley lead her to the bedroom. She said nothing, embarrassed and regretful for her outburst. She'd been simmering all night. Who was she kidding? Her patience had been slowly reaching boiling point for days. Olivia was famous for crossing all kinds of lines. Cornering Andi, trying to seduce Andi, thinking that Andi was an easy target—a way to hurt Fallon again, a way to distract Fallon from Riley—that was Olivia's fatal mistake. If there was one silver lining, it was that Fallon had only broken some bottles and not Olivia's nose.

"I'm sorry," Fallon muttered.

Riley looked at Fallon's hand. "It's not me who needs an apology. Good thing Billie is a nurse, huh?"

Fallon groaned.

Riley directed Fallon to sit on the bed. She sat beside her. "Talk to me."

"I can't have her in my life, Riley, and I can't kick her out of my life. She made sure of that when she had the girls with Dean."

Riley sighed. "No, you can't. They need you, Fallon."

Fallon looked at Riley curiously.

"Emily and Evan wanted to talk to me tonight."

"About?"

"Living here in Whiskey Springs, living with you."

Fallon threw her head back. "Fuck."

"What happened?"

"Carol didn't tell you?"

"Only that something happened."

"She tried to put the moves on Andi."

Riley was dumbfounded.

"Yeah. I can't believe it. I mean, I can understand wanting to be with Andi. That's not why she did it."

"No, I don't imagine it was."

"That's shitty to do to me, Riley. To Andi? I can't even…"

"I know."

"She just doesn't know when to stop."

"No, she doesn't. Fallon, she knows you've moved on. She's in a bind. Her partner left her. Dean's away. She's alone."

"You don't seriously feel sorry for her?"

"No. I feel for the kids. I feel for you. I feel for Beth, for everyone that she's hurt. And, unfortunately, you're right. As much as I want to tell you that I never want to see her in this house again, that would hurt all those people in some way. Because all of you love each other, and those kids need you, Fallon—whatever role you play for them, that much I do know."

"She can't stay here."

"Well, I might have a solution to that."

"Really?"

"There is an empty house a couple of miles away."

Fallon stared at Riley in disbelief. "It does have two bedrooms. Maybe it's time you set some different ground rules."

"She's here for another week, Riley. That will break the arrangement you and I have."

Riley nodded. "Well, maybe we need to talk some more about that *arrangement*."

"What are you saying?"

"Only that we need to talk some more about it," Riley said. "The kids made me realize something tonight."

"Oh?"

"You and I are the only parents Owen has ever known."

"Riley, I..."

"Just listen. He'll never know Robert. I don't know if he has impressions of his father. Robert is a face on paper, a story people tell him. You're real. You're *his* Fallon. When he says that, that's because you're not the fun adult friend who entertains him, you're the person he trusts to protect him. You're the person *I* trust to protect him. He's lucky, Fallon. He'll have loss someday. Right now, all Owen knows is that people love him. He's secure."

"That's because of you," Fallon said.

"Partly. It's because of you too. And, Ida, and Andi... and Carol, and all the people he *knows* he can count on. But most of all it *is* because of you and me. And, Fallon, that's also because he sees how much we love each other."

"Must've been some conversation."

"It was," Riley said.

"I'd better go talk to her," Fallon said.

"No." Riley kissed Fallon's cheek. "I will."

Fallon tipped her head.

"Did you mean it when you said you wanted me to consider this home?"

"Completely."

"Then she's in my home. You're my partner, Fallon."

Fallon grinned.

"What are you going to say?"

Riley winked. "That's between Olivia and me."

❦

"I'm glad you decided to stay here tonight," Ida said.

"Thanks for the offer," Andi replied.

"Are you okay?"

"I am. I wish I could say that I can't believe it."

Ida rolled her eyes. "I have a feeling she's not going to like where this all leads."

"Safe bet," Andi agreed. "Riley might seem naïve; she's not a pushover."

Ida chuckled. That was the truth if ever she'd heard it. She poured them each some whiskey. "I noticed Billie was casting a lot of glances in your direction."

"What?" Andi took a sip of her drink. "Billie? You're imagining things."

"I don't think so."

"Billie's not a lesbian."

"Neither were you a year ago."

Andi laughed. "I still don't know who I am."

"I like Billie."

"Oh, my God. Are you trying to play matchmaker?"

"You don't?" Ida asked.

"I like Billie."

"Do you think you might *like* Billie?"

Andi laughed so hard she coughed. "Are we in sixth grade?"

"After tonight, we'd be lucky to classify as kindergartners."

"Touché."

"Well?" Ida prodded.

"I don't fancy making a fool of myself — again."

"So, you did notice the glances."

Andi grinned. "Maybe."

"Just don't close yourself off."

"Alcohol makes people do strange things, Ida."

"Alcohol reveals the strange things people want to do, Andi."

Andi sighed. "I don't think I'm ready for that." The mere thought of dating anyone, much less Billie caused her to down her whiskey.

Ida sipped from her glass to keep from laughing. Andi still loved Fallon. She'd caught a few long stares between the affable nurse and her friend. No one was ever ready for love. Maybe it had been the haze of alcohol, cigar smoke, and innuendo. Ida had a strange feeling that something more was starting to brew between the pair. She'd suspected for years that Billie was a lesbian. She also guessed Fallon knew that. She never asked. As much as people liked to accuse her of being nosy, she wasn't. She simply paid attention. Andi wasn't attached to anyone, and while it remained something people murmured about, everyone was aware of her affair with Fallon. She looked at Andi with a devious smile. "You're not ready for *that*?" Ida asked.

"Anything," Andi replied.

Ida shrugged. "Well, not that anyone listens to me, but Billie is a thirty-eight-year-old single woman who I've yet to see involved with a man. You do the math. One plus one equals two."

"That doesn't mean it equals Andi."

"Never know 'til you jump into the equation."

Andi chuckled. "Pour the whiskey."

Riley made her way into the kitchen. Olivia was sipping a glass of wine.

"Come to read me the riot act?" Olivia asked.

Riley leaned against the counter. "No."

"Really?"

"Should I?"

"I figured Fallon filled you in."

Riley nodded. "What is it that you hope to accomplish here, Olivia?"

"Accomplish?"

"Yes."

"I'd hoped that my daughters could visit their family."

"Meaning their grandmother and their aunt," Riley said. "Yes?"

"Mm. You do realize that Fallon is their aunt; not their parent?"

"I think I would be aware of that."

Riley waited for a beat to continue. "Fallon cares about you, Olivia."

"Thank you for letting me know."

"Because you were a big part of her life."

"Were?"

"Yes, were." Riley sensed Olivia's desire to bait her into an argument. She remained calm. "The truth is, you'll always be a part of her life."

"And, that doesn't sit well with you, I'm guessing."

Riley smiled. "What doesn't sit well with me is seeing anyone I love hurting."

"And, I would be responsible for that hurt."

"I don't need to answer that. You just answered it yourself. Here's what you need to understand."

"I'm listening."

Olivia's sly grin made Riley want to choke her. She refused to allow her disdain to show. "I don't care if you like me. I don't care if you hate me. I don't care what you say *about* me. When you're here in this house; you're in my home."

"Is that so? Moving in already?"

Riley ignored the question. "The girls are Fallon's family. That makes you a reality. That's all you are to me. I know all the reasons this house was built. I know what every room was intended for. I know that a piece of Fallon broke when you left, and another shattered when you and Dean decided he'd father your children. None of that's a secret to me. It's also no secret to me that all of it, everything you do is to try and keep Fallon dangling on a line, just waiting for the moment you can reel her in."

Olivia grinned and sipped her wine.

"You'll be waiting on the shore until the end of time to catch that fish."

"Because you have."

"No. Fallon's not a prize to me," Riley said. "She's the person I share my life with. There's a difference. She's ready to send you packing. Tell you to go back to DC."

"I'm sure she is."

Riley nodded. "That's your choice."

"That's kind of you."

"Not really. I haven't given you the choice yet. Emily and Summer are welcome to stay here anytime. You are not," Riley said. "That presents an issue for you. I doubt very much that Beth feels like sharing her quarters with you right now. So, that leaves out Ida's. And, I don't need clairvoyance to know that you won't be bunking down with Andi."

Olivia's skin was beginning to flush.

"There is a house not too far away that will be vacant for the next week. You are welcome to stay there. As a mother, I know I would want my son close. There's an extra room if you want the girls to stay with you. That's up to you."

"You think I'm disrespecting you in your home?"

"I don't think you possess enough self-respect to be able to *respect* anyone. What I think isn't the point. You don't need to decide tonight. You can let us know in the morning." Riley pushed off the counter that had been supporting her and walked to the doorway. "And, Olivia?"

Olivia looked up.

"So, we're clear; Fallon and Andi are both a part of my family. I know what it's like to lose family. There isn't anything I won't do to protect mine. Just so we're clear. Goodnight." Riley left the room.

Olivia looked into her glass of wine before downing it in one gulp. *Shit.*

❧

Riley climbed into the bed and wrapped herself around Fallon.

"Well, you survived," Fallon said. "Did she?"

"She'll live to see another day."

"What did you say?"

"Nothing that wasn't true."

"I really am sorry."

"For what? Messing up your bar, cutting your hand, or the fact that you still stink of cigar smoke?"

"I'm sorry. I can shower."

Riley pressed her weight against Fallon. "You're not going anywhere. Neither am I."

Fallon took the first deep breath she had in hours. "I think Billie has a crush on Andi."

"What?"

"Yeah."

"Billie's not a lesbian."

"Yeah, she is."

Riley sat up. "You're joking."

Fallon shook her head.

"Huh. She's cute."

"She's cute? Thinking you jumped too soon?" Fallon teased.

Riley laughed. "Not a chance." She laid back down. "Evan thinks we're getting married."

"Yeah, I heard. I think my mother and Beth helped in that department."

"Crazy."

"Insane," Fallon said.

Riley closed her eyes.

"Is it?" Fallon asked.

"What?"

"A crazy idea—us married."

Riley smiled. "It is if you think we're doing it tomorrow."

"What about Monday?"

"Which Monday?"

"You pick."

"Fallon, if this is your idea of a proposal, I think you need to be getting lessons, not giving them."

"I'm not proposing."

"Glad we cleared that up," Riley said.

"But if I were to decide… You know, at some date in the very distant future…"

"How distant?"

Fallon chuckled. "Pick a Monday."

Riley laughed. "I'll look at the calendar in the morning." She yawned.

"You do that." Fallon closed her eyes.

"I will. Goodnight, babe."

"Riley?"

"Hum?"

"It doesn't have to be a Monday, does it?"

Riley kissed Fallon's chest. "Go to sleep, Fallon."

"I love you, Riley."

"I love you too."

"I really love you."

Riley gigged. Fallon was a bit intoxicated. "I *really* love you too."

"Okay."

A few moments passed.

"Are you really going to look at the calendar?" Fallon asked.

Riley shook with silent laughter. *This could be fun.* "If I can find one long enough."

"Okay. Wait… What does that mean?"

"Go to sleep, Fallon."

"Sorry." Fallon sighed. She started to drift off. "I have a calendar," she muttered before falling asleep.

Riley smiled. *I wonder when she'll pencil me in.* She closed her eyes and held on to Fallon. *Maybe on a Monday.*

CHAPTER ONE

ONE MONTH LATER

*I*t was going to be a long day. That thought passed through Fallon's mind repeatedly, and it was only noon. She'd been up since before the sun. Who was she kidding? She'd been awake all night. Nights without Riley were torturous. Riley's insistence on keeping a separate residence continued to perplex and frustrate Fallon. She kept reminding herself to take it slow; to give Riley as much time as Riley required, and not press the idea of living together. Fallon struggled with her ability to support Riley's decision more with each day that passed. It was far too quiet at home when Riley and Owen weren't there. Fallon had given up trying to sleep in bed without Riley. She'd spent years enjoying the comfort of her recliner or her couch. Even the familiarity of those places failed to lull her into sleep. She huffed as she wiped down the bar for what she imagined was the millionth time in a few hours.

"Are you trying to clean that or kill it?" Carol asked when she strolled through the front door.

Fallon groaned something unintelligible.

"Guess that answers that," Carol commented.

"You're early," Fallon said.

"And, you're grumpy."

"I'm not grumpy."

"Right, and I'm the Queen of England."

"Your Majesty," Fallon quipped.

"Ha-ha. What's up with you?"

Fallon flopped onto a bar stool and tossed the towel in her hands aside. "I didn't sleep much."

"Let me guess; Riley spent the night at home."

Fallon nodded.

"Fallon, why don't you just ask Riley to move in?"

"I can't."

"Why on earth not?"

"Because I don't want to push her."

"Well, she's not going to invite herself," Carol pointed out the obvious.

"We've talked about it."

"And?"

"And, Riley said she thought it was good for us to have a place to go to for a while—a separate place."

"When was this?" Carol inquired.

"I don't know; not long after we started—you know..."

Carol howled with laughter. She still found the way Riley transformed Fallon into a shy teenager amusing. "Not long after you what? After you kissed her?"

"No! After we, you know..."

"Oh, my God. You're like a twelve-year-old sometimes. After you slept with her? Is that what you are trying to say? Fallon, that was months ago."

"And?"

"Maybe you should raise the point again," Carol suggested.

"I can't."

"Why not?"

"I promised I would give her as much time as she needs."

"Yeah, well, call me crazy; I think that theory might be flawed."

"What am I supposed to say?"

"How about—Riley, I would really like it if you and Owen moved in."

Fallon groaned. It sounded so easy. It felt impossible. "I don't know," Fallon said.

"Well, if you don't, I might."

"Don't you think your husband might have something to say about asking another woman to live with you?" Fallon quipped.

"Very funny, Fallon."

Fallon gloated.

"I'm serious. Just ask her."

Fallon watched Carol disappear into the kitchen. "Just ask her?"

"Right," Carol called back. "Just ask her."

Riley couldn't seem to concentrate on anything. She scanned the words on the page in front of her and groaned. "What is wrong with me?" She was relieved when her phone rang.

"Hi." Fallon's voice came over the line.

"Hey," Riley replied.

"Am I interrupting you?"

"Not at all," Riley said.

"I thought you had a deadline?"

"I do," Riley said. "One that keeps moving."

"Are you okay?"

"Yeah. I just didn't get a lot of sleep."

Fallon took a deep breath. "Come home tonight, Riley."

Riley closed her eyes. *Home.*

"Please," Fallon said. "I know I shouldn't be asking you this on the phone. I can't stand it anymore."

Riley grinned. "What's that?"

"Being without you. I can't stand it. I can't sleep. I can't even sleep in the recliner! It's too quiet in the morning without Owen. And, it's just.... It's too..."

"Okay."

"What?"

"Okay, I'll come home."

Fallon closed her eyes and let out a sigh. "I don't want you to leave, Riley."

"Okay."

"Seriously?"

"Second thoughts?" Riley teased.

"What? No!"

"Did you expect me to put up a fight?"

"I don't know. I didn't expect to call you from the pub and ask you to move in. I dropped three glasses this morning, and I washed the same batch of dishes twice. I have no idea what I'm doing."

Riley giggled. She had no desire to protest. She had no interest in fighting the future. She'd begun to wonder why she'd insisted on any distance at all. She had to force herself to leave Fallon's. Owen was miserable when he had to leave. The one issue that nagged at her was that *home,* as Fallon referred to it, was *Fallon's* home. It was the house Fallon had built intending to share with someone else. That reality still unsettled a small part of Riley. Would she and Owen be enough to banish the ghost of Olivia Nolan? "I don't want to be apart either," Riley confessed. "I do think we should talk about it."

"I figured. We can talk all you want. Just come home tonight."

"To *your* home."

"To *our* home," Fallon corrected her. "In fact, don't wait. Just go home now. I'll be there in a few hours."

"Okay."

"I know something is bothering you," Fallon said. "We'll talk when I get there; okay?"

"Okay."

Fallon thought for a second that she'd never heard Riley say "okay" so many times in a few minutes. It left her wondering if everything *was* actually okay. Riley had agreed to Fallon's request. Fallon could tell that Riley wanted to agree. Something was bothering her girlfriend. Fallon could sense that as well. "I'll be home by six," Fallon promised. "We can talk about everything tonight."

"Okay."

Again, with the okay. "It will be, Riley," Fallon said. "Just come home."

⚜

Andi strolled through the front door of Murphy's Law and plopped herself on a stool.

"Hey." Fallon emerged from the kitchen, surprised to see Andi sitting at the bar. "I didn't think I'd see you today."

"Hey yourself," Andi replied. "No offense; you look like hell. Are you feeling okay?"

"Gee thanks, and no, not really," Fallon answered.

"Everything okay at home?"

"Depends on what you mean by home," Fallon said.

"Missing Riley, huh?"

"She called you, didn't she?" Fallon guessed.

"Should she have?"

"She didn't?" Fallon was surprised.

"Not since yesterday—no. Why? Did something happen?"

"I asked her to move in."

"Relax, Fallon. Everything will be fine."

"I get the feeling she's hesitant to make the move. I don't understand why…"

Andi's hand found Fallon's and gave a reassuring squeeze. "Tell her everything, Fallon."

"What does that mean? I don't hide anything from Riley," Fallon said.

"I know. Tell her what you want, Fallon—all of it."

"She knows."

"Yes, I think she does know," Andi admitted. "I wonder if you've had that conversation outside the comfort of pillow talk."

"It's not…"

"Fallon," Andi lowered her voice. "I know you. Don't hold back with Riley—at all."

Fallon's usual inclination was to argue, or at least, to banter with Andi. Oddly, she felt no desire to protest Andi's advice. The only person Riley was likely to confide in about her feelings or her misgivings where Fallon was concerned, was Andi. If that wasn't odd, it *was* ironic. Fallon imagined that having your former lover serve as your current lover's confidante was outside normal practice. Normal could be overrated. Andi was Fallon's best friend; she also played the role of a motherly best friend to Riley. There was no point in arguing with Andi. Andi was right; Fallon did hold back sharing her hopes for the future with Riley. She'd received similar advice from her mother. It was time that Fallon, "got out of your own way," as Ida had told her. Maybe it was. Fallon shook off her musings and focused on something else.

"Not that I'm not happy to see you, but what are you doing here?" Fallon wondered.

"Meeting someone for lunch."

Fallon grinned. "Would that someone happen to be a nurse I know?"

"Yes," Andi replied. "And, wipe that smirk off your face. Billie and I are just friends."

"If you say so."

"I do say so."

There were times that Fallon wished she carried a mirror in her pocket. Working behind the bar, she found herself listening to people's hopes and dreams, their woes, and to her amazement, their protests about being in love. Love wasn't easy to disguise. Fallon thought it was strange that often, the person falling in love didn't notice they'd been falling until someone else pointed out the obvious. She wondered if people's denials would survive if they were forced to look at themselves in the mirror for more than the time it took to brush their teeth. Right now, she'd love to show Andi her reflection. Andi's eyes flickered with admiration and excitement at the mere mention of Billie Steele's name. While Andi's answer had been honest; she and Billie had not slept together nor made any romantic declarations to each other; Fallon was sure that Andi's feelings were deepening by the day for Billie. And, Billie's feelings for Andi were as transparent as glass. Before Fallon could offer another thought, Billie opened the door. The expression on Billie's face the moment her eyes fell on Andi made Fallon chuckle. *She is cooked.*

"Sorry, I'm a little late," Billie apologized.

Andi's eyes twinkled. "I just got here."

"Hi, Fallon," Billie greeted her friend.

"How's it going?" Fallon asked.

"Can't complain," Billie said. "No one listens anyway."

"That's the truth," Fallon agreed. "What can I get you two?" Fallon looked at Andi. "Margarita?" She guessed.

"No, actually, I think I'll have a beer."

Fallon's eyes narrowed to a point.

"We are in a pub," Andi said. "Is that a strange request?"

"From you? Yes," Fallon replied.

Andi shrugged. "Billie's been slowly introducing me to her passion for…"

Fallon held up a hand. She was either about to burst out laughing or smack herself on the forehead. Come to think of it, maybe she should smack Andi on the forehead and knock some sense into her. "That's between the two of you," Fallon quipped. She noted the flash of red creeping up Billie's neck.

Andi glared at Fallon. "For beer, Fallon."

"Uh-huh. So, would you like that light or do you prefer something with a little more body?" Fallon teased.

Billie covered her face.

Andi's hand reached over and squeezed Billie's. "I'll take mine *full-bodied,* thank you," Andi deadpanned.

Billie wished she could shrink somehow, maybe become invisible. Invisible sounded good right about now.

"Same for you?" Fallon asked Billie.

Billie offered Fallon a strained smile and a nod.

Andi squeezed Billie's hand again. "Ignore her," she said when Fallon walked away. Her heart lurched slightly in her chest when she turned to look at Billie. "Billie," she spoke softly. "Don't let Fallon get to you. She likes to tease me."

"Yeah, I know," Billie said. She searched for a way to recover. "I'm sorry about running behind."

"Don't be sorry."

"I thought I only had a million things to do; somehow that turned out to be a million and one," Billie explained.

"Billie, we didn't have to meet today. It…"

"No," Billie stopped Andi's thought in its tracks. "No, I wanted to see you." Billie blushed at her admission and silently admonished herself. *Smooth, Billie, really smooth. Could you be any more pathetic?*

"I'm glad you were able to make some time for me," Andi said.

"I always have time for you."

Billie's words brought a smile to Andi's lips. Billie always made time for Andi. Lately, Andi had begun to wonder if she was requesting too much of Billie's time. Billie was the Nurse Manager, or as most people called it, the Head Nurse for the Emergency Department at a hospital in Essex. Billie worked long hours in a job that carried considerable stress. As their friendship blossomed, Andi found herself musing that Billie often didn't get enough rest.

"I know," Andi said. "But you need some downtime too."

"This is downtime," Billie replied honestly.

Fallon emerged with two mugs. She noticed that Andi still had hold of Billie's hand. *And, she calls me clueless?* She decided against teasing either of her friends. Instead, she placed a glass in front of each of them and smiled. "I give you a lot of credit, Billie."

"Why is that?" Billie asked.

"I've tried for years to get Andi to give beer a chance," Fallon said.

"Really?" Billie was surprised. It was no secret—least of all to Billie—that Andi had once been in love with Fallon. Her friendship with Andi Maguire had deepened over the months to a relationship of confidence and compassion. She'd had many late-night conversations with Andi about the past, about Andi's marriage and children, Billie's family, and, of course, Fallon. She would have guessed that Fallon could convince Andi to try anything. That thought conjured another rosy tint to Billie's cheeks.

Fallon bit her lip to keep from laughing. She didn't require psychic powers to guess where Billie's thoughts had traveled. Who could blame Billie? Certainly not Fallon. Loving someone new didn't banish memories of the past. Fallon would always recall her year with Andi with both fondness and gratitude. She loved Andi Maguire. Andi loved her. That love had changed. Their bond had endured — different, but stronger.

It had taken Fallon longer than she thought it should have to admit the truth. She *had* fallen in love with Andi. Oddly, it had been Riley who pointed that out. Healing from their separation had been easier for Fallon. She'd never expected Andi to leave her husband. That kept Fallon from allowing her feelings for Andi to transform into any meaningful expectations about their relationship. When Riley arrived in Whiskey Springs, Fallon's direction began to shift. It had taken Andi longer to recover from the end of their affair, even if Andi was the one who had ended it. Andi was incredibly selfless. Fallon was sure that many people guessed what drew her to Andi had been sexual attraction. That was only partly true. Andi's allure was rooted in her authenticity, her honesty, and her kindheartedness. Andi's beauty was anything but superficial. Fallon would always treasure the time they had shared. She understood Billie's predicament. Andi was easy to fall for, and Billie had fallen *hard*.

Fallon caught Andi's expression from the corner of her eye. It silently pleaded with Fallon not to give Billie a hard time. Fallon laughed inwardly. Andi might need more time to examine her feelings; Fallon felt confident that some part of Andi already knew Billie loved her. Andi would fight her feelings for Billie. Fallon knew that too. Funny how roles could reverse. It hadn't been long ago that Andi was the one gently pushing Fallon to acknowledge her feelings for Riley. *How things change.*

Fallon smiled at Billie. "Do you know what you want?"

Billie choked on the sip of beer she was taking.

Andi patted Billie's back.

Fallon couldn't help herself. She chuckled. *Oh, Billie, give her a little time. Just give her a little time. She might surprise you.*

❧

Riley closed her laptop and groaned. She'd hoped that following Fallon's directive and coming *home* would have helped her focus. No such luck. She silently pondered the word, home. What was home? Where was home? What was it that she needed from Fallon? She rubbed her face vigorously in frustration. Fallon loved her. She loved Fallon. Fallon wanted a life with Riley. Riley wanted the same thing. Why did she continue to feel that something held Fallon back? Maybe it wasn't Fallon who was timid about the future. Perhaps, Riley was the guilty party. "What the hell is wrong with me?" Riley felt a headache emerging. She needed to put her racing thoughts in some semblance of order before Fallon got home. And, there was that word again—home. *Shit.* She took a deep breath and reached for her phone. "Hi."

❧

"Are you sure you have time?" Andi asked Billie.

"To sit on your deck and have another beer? Absolutely."

"Believe me; I'm glad you're here," Andi said honestly. "I know you've been working a lot of hours and you probably have…"

"A million and one things to do?" Billie repeated her earlier mantra. "Yeah, well, there are always a million and one things to do."

"True enough."

"This is exactly what I need," Billie said.

"Beer?"

Billie was tempted to answer honestly. *You.* Instead, she answered, "beer is good."

"So, you continue to tell me."

"Still not buying it, huh?" Billie guessed.

"Oh, I don't know; I think I could learn to like it."

"Ah, but could you learn to *love* it?"

Andi smiled. *Maybe.* "You never know." She looked down at her phone as it rumbled against the patio table.

Billie caught sight of the name on the screen. "I'll go liberate a couple more of my beers from your fridge."

"Thanks."

"I don't give up easily," Billie said.

Andi winked. "I'll keep that in mind." She picked up her phone. "Hey, Riley."

"Hi."

"Are you okay?"

"Define okay?"

"Oh boy. What's going on?" Andi heard Riley's heavy sigh on the other end of the line. "Riley?"

"Fallon wants me to move in."

"I know."

"Why is that so hard for me?"

"I don't know; why *is* it so hard for you?" Andi asked.

"I don't know! What's wrong with me?"

"There's nothing wrong with you."

"I want to."

"But?"

"Andi, when I think about home, I just… It still makes me think about…"

"I know," Andi said sympathetically. "It reminds you of losing Robert."

"It's crazy; I know it is."

"Hardly," Andi disagreed. "Riley, what do you want from Fallon?"

"Everything," Riley muttered.

Andi smiled at the ache she detected in Riley's heart. "I'm going to tell you what I told her."

"Oh, God. I'm not sure I want to know."

"Tell her, Riley. Stop holding back."

"She knows."

"Yes, and so do you. You two keep making little comments about what you want. You allude to your hopes. You don't make that clear. Make it clear, Riley."

"Haven't I?"

"Have you?" Andi countered.

Riley combed her thoughts. *Have I?* "Shit."

Andi laughed. "It's scary," she said. "I understand that."

"It's insane. I *know* she wants the same things."

"It's not insane," Andi disagreed again. "Sometimes, we all need to *hear* it."

Riley wondered if Andi's observation might apply to more than Riley's insecurities about living with Fallon. *What's that about?*

Billie set a bottle of beer in front of Andi. "Not quite as full-bodied as the last one," she whispered.

"Thank you," Andi said.

"Andi?"

"Sorry, I'm still here."

"You're not alone; are you?"

"No. Billie's here."

"Billie, huh?"

Andi was ready to warn Riley not to start getting any ideas.

"Tell her I said hello."

"I will," Andi replied, grateful that Riley opted not to make any insinuations about her friendship with Billie.

"Listen, go enjoy your afternoon," Riley said.

"Riley, it's okay if you need to talk." She looked over at Billie and received the smile she knew she would. Billie was content to sip her beer and soak in the warm afternoon. Andi's heart fluttered slightly. She pushed it aside—again.

"I'm all right," Riley promised. "I guess I just needed to hear your voice to calm me down."

"You can call anytime; you know that."

"Yeah, I do. Andi?"

"Yeah?"

"I hope you know how much I..."

"I know," Andi said. *I do know.* "I love you too," she said. "Just be honest, Riley. Don't be afraid to say what you need to—all of it."

"Okay."

"Call me if you need to."

"Thanks. Tell Billie I'm sorry."

"There's nothing to apologize for. Let me know how it goes."

"I will. Love you."

"Love you too."

"Everything okay?" Billie inquired.

"It will be," Andi replied. "Fallon finally asked Riley to move in."

"That's good; isn't it?"

"It is."

"Andi? Are you okay?"

"Are you asking me if I'm okay because Fallon and I used to be involved?"

"I guess, maybe I am."

Andi took a sip from the beer bottle Billie had given her. "I love Fallon."

"Yeah, I know."

"And, I love Riley."

"I know. It has to feel strange sometimes."

"Not really," Andi said. "It did—at first."

"Riley and you..."

"Riley is the daughter I'll never have," Andi said. "I love the boys. I always hoped that I might have one more."

"A girl," Billie guessed.

"Guilty as charged."

"I get it."

"You do?"

"Sure. That just wasn't in the cards for me, I guess. Motherhood, I mean."

Andi nodded. Billie would have made a terrific parent. She was nurturing, and she was loving. "You never…"

"I never found the person I wanted that with, and I never had the guts to do it on my own," Billie explained.

"You never know what the future holds," Andi offered.

Billie took a long pull from her beer. "I don't think it holds *that*."

"Fallon said the same thing. Look at her now."

Billie's grin was laced with doubt.

"All I'm saying is that sometimes what you've always wanted comes when you least expect it."

"Speaking from experience?" Billie wondered.

"Not entirely," Andi admitted. "But I know it's true."

"Well, at least there is always beer."

Andi laughed. "Or margaritas."

"Give it time," Billie said. "I'll convert you yet."

Andi shook her head. *You just might, Billie.*

❧

"Owen was certainly wound up tonight," Fallon commented.

"He missed you," Riley said.

"I missed you — both of you."

"It was only one night."

"That's one night too many."

Riley nodded.

"We need to talk," Fallon said.

"We do."

"Wine?" Fallon asked.

"No." Riley patted the cushion beside her.

"Why do I suddenly feel like I'm going to throw up?"

Riley laughed. "I love you so much, Fallon."

Fallon looked a bit green.

"That's not what you thought I was going to say?" Riley guessed.

"I guess I'm not sure what I expect you to say," Fallon replied.

"Fair enough. So, how about I just say it?"

Fallon swallowed hard and nodded.

"I'm scared."

"Of what?"

"Of this," Riley said. "Of losing you, of being alone again, of losing my home again."

"Riley..."

"Let me say this."

"Sorry."

Riley forced herself to suck in a deep breath. She let it out slowly, hoping to steady her nerves. "It scares me because this *is* home," she admitted. "It scares me because I want everything with you, Fallon. I mean — everything. I want to see you every morning and every night; I do."

"Me too."

"I know. I want that to last forever. And, I know," Riley hesitated.

Fallon took Riley's hand. "Go on."

"I know that forever is as long as it lasts."

Fallon wished she could banish the pain of Riley's past. She couldn't. Riley was a strong woman. She didn't dwell on the loss she'd experienced. That didn't mean grief failed to leave its mark. Grief had made an indelible impression on Riley's life and heart. The anguish of unexpected loss always left remnants. Like love, loss shaped a person. Fallon accepted that. She held Riley's hand tenderly and endeavored to let Riley say what she needed to.

"I want it to last forever," Riley confessed. "I loved Robert, Fallon."

"I know."

"But the truth is I love you in a way I'm not certain I was capable of back then."

Riley's revelation surprised Fallon.

"Didn't expect that either, huh?"

"Not really."

"It's true. I was so young. Love was different somehow."

"I think I can understand that," Fallon offered.

"I know you can." Riley smiled. "Fallon, I don't want to talk in somedays anymore. That doesn't mean I'm ready for everything I hope we can share. I think you need to know what I picture for our future. And, the truth is, I'm not sure I've ever told you—just *told* you."

"You can tell me anything."

I know. "I want to grow old with you. I want to watch our children grow up and one day bring their children here to visit. I want to be the one there through everything. I want *you* to be my home." She closed her eyes. "And, sometimes I can't help that all of it terrifies me."

"Riley, I want the same things."

Riley opened her eyes and smiled.

"I can't make the past disappear. Believe me; if I could, I would take it all away. And, as much as I want to, I know that I can't promise you forever will be until we are both old and grey—although, I'll always be older and probably greyer."

Riley sniggered.

"I love you, and I love Owen. You wanted to tell me the truth. Here's my truth. I know you aren't quite ready for what I'm about to say. To me, someday is today. I'd marry you right this second and carry you across the threshold if it were up to me."

Riley's lips curled into a radiant smile.

"I would," Fallon said.

"I know."

"And, I know that you aren't ready for that. I can wait as long as you ask me to, Riley. I can even wait for you to move in here. Hell, if you don't want to live here; we can move into your...."

Riley pressed two fingers to Fallon's lips. "Stop," she said. She removed her fingers and kissed Fallon tenderly. "This is home," she said. "You're right; I'm not ready yet— not to walk down the aisle, anyway. You can carry me over the threshold anytime you like."

Fallon laughed. "Cute."

"I will be ready, Fallon. Not someday, one day."

"I hope so."

"One day," Riley said.

"So, you'll stay—here, I mean?"

"Yes."

Fallon let out a relieved breath. "Thank God." She pulled Riley into her arms. "Riley?"

"Hum?"

"I..."

"What is it?"

"I can't wait until it's one day."

Riley gripped Fallon tighter. *That might be sooner than you think, Fallon.* "Me neither."

CHAPTER TWO

TWO WEEKS LATER

*B*arb stared at Olivia blankly. She'd thought it was impossible for anything Olivia Nolan could say to surprise her. She'd been dead wrong.

"Say something," Olivia said.

"I don't know where to begin."

"You could come with me," Olivia offered.

"To Amsterdam?"

"Why not?"

"Liv, I don't want to move to another country. What about the girls?"

"We could all go."

"To Europe?"

"That is where Amsterdam is, so yes."

Barb shook her head, hoping it might clear the fog. "Why?"

"Why?"

"Why do you need to take a job in another country?"

"I don't *need* to; I want to."

"What about what I want?" Barb asked.

"*You* left *me*."

"We're back to this? Olivia, you'd left our relationship long before I took the position in Richmond."

"From your perspective."

"From *my* perspective? What other perspective is there? My God, Liv, you hadn't touched me in two years! What did you expect? Your life revolves around Dean! Jesus Christ, you called Dean before you called me when Summer went to the emergency room last year."

"He *is* her father."

Barb covered her face. "Well, I guess you made that clear."

"You know what I mean."

"Yes, I do," Barb replied. "As I recall, it's my name on the adoption papers. It was me rocking Emily and Summer through the night, changing their diapers, wiping their noses all these years. It was *me* you claimed to want to have a family with."

"I wasn't aware that we weren't a family. You made the decision to change that, not me."

"This is a circular argument."

"Which means?"

"Which means it has no end," Barb said. "At least, it has no good end." She took a breath. "Amsterdam. How close will you be to Dean?"

"I can't answer that."

"You can't, or you won't?"

"Does it matter?"

"No," Barb said. "I guess it doesn't. So, what now? I'm supposed to sit on my hands while you move my children across an ocean? That or I get to decide to come back to you?"

Olivia shrugged.

"You have to be kidding. What about the girls' lives, Liv? Their family and friends are all here."

"You're not coming," Olivia surmised.

"No."

"Then we let them choose."

"You want to ask our daughters to choose between us?" Barb felt sick. "Jesus, Liv."

"It seems fair."

"I guess it would to you."

"Well, what would you suggest we do?"

"As if that has ever mattered." Barb sighed regretfully. "I think the girls should stay with me."

"Is that right?"

"Liv," Barb softened her tone. "Do what you need to do. Whatever that is—do it."

"You think the girls will be happier in Richmond with you?"

"I don't know what will make the girls happy," Barb confessed. "Whatever that is, I assure you; I'll try to make it possible."

"And, what about me?"

There was no easy answer to Olivia's question. The question had been designed that way. In fact, Olivia's revelation had been intended to leave Barb with no good alternative. Barb wasn't certain what Olivia hoped to gain. Olivia always hoped to gain *something*. That lesson was one Barb wished she'd never had to learn. The worst part? She still loved Olivia. That made everything hurt more.

"I don't know, Liv. Maybe that's a question you need to ask yourself."

⁂

"Fawon!"

"In here, buddy!"

Owen bounced into the kitchen. "Where's Mommy?"

"Mommy went to see Grandma Andi," she told him. She delighted in Owen's insistence on calling Andi his grandmother. Grandma Andi and Grandma Ida, it was priceless.

Owen seemed to consider the information thoughtfully.

"Did you need Mommy?" Fallon asked.

Owen shook his head.

"What is it, buddy?"

"Can we go too?"

"Go where?"

"To Gwama's."

"You want to see Grandma Andi?"

Owen nodded.

"Owen? Is something bothering you?"

He shook his head. "Can we?"

Fallon tried to follow Owen's train of thought. He adored Andi. He hadn't seen Andi in a week. It didn't surprise her that Owen would ask about Andi. It was the way Owen was looking at her that perplexed Fallon. He seemed concerned. She would be happy to grant Owen's request, but Fallon hadn't the faintest idea where Andi and Riley were headed.

"I'm not sure what Mommy and Grandma are doing, buddy."

"I can call?" He posed his statement as a question.

"How about this? I'll call Mommy and see what she's doing."

Owen shrugged noncommittally.

"I'll call her right now, okay?"

Owen nodded and wandered out of the room.

What on earth is going on in your little mind? Fallon reached for her phone.

⚭﹒ℒ

"Are you sure you don't want to go somewhere?" Andi asked.

"Positive. I just can't believe you have beer in your refrigerator!" Riley said as she sipped from a bottle of beer happily.

"Thank Billie."

"You've been spending a lot of time with Nurse Steele lately."

"Don't you start," Andi cautioned.

"I didn't say anything," Riley reminded her friend. "Which makes me wonder why you are so quick to tell me I shouldn't."

"I know what everyone is thinking."

"What might that be?"

"That something is going on between me and Billie. It's not."

"Okay."

"Riley, it's not."

"I believe you."

"You do?"

"Why wouldn't I?" Riley held Andi's gaze for a moment. "Do you want there to be something?"

Did Andi want something more with Billie? Billie had become a close friend. She confided to Billie. She laughed with Billie. She learned from Billie. The last thing Andi desired was to risk a meaningful friendship because she was attracted to someone. She was grateful that her relationship with Fallon had endured after their affair. Andi wasn't convinced that was a gamble she wanted to take again.

"Andi?"

"I don't know," Andi answered honestly. "Billie has become a good friend, Riley. I'm not sure I want to risk that."

That sounds familiar. "Do you have feelings for Billie?"

What did that mean, Andi wondered? Why did people always ask if you *had feelings* for someone? Of course, she had feelings for Billie. If she didn't, she wouldn't invest time in their friendship. She had feelings for Riley too, and Ida, and Carol, and her sons. Feelings? The question Riley wanted to ask was, "are you falling in love with her?" Or maybe it was, "do you want to have sex with her?" Andi wasn't prepared to examine either question. "I care about her," she replied. And, there it was; the lame answer that followed the lame question. *I care about her.* That was code for, "I don't want to admit that I might be falling in love, and yes, I want to tear her clothes off and touch every inch of her." Andi's face flushed.

Oh, boy. There were times when what a person failed to say said everything. "You do realize that she's interested in you?" Riley said. Andi's heavy sigh tugged at Riley's heart. "I get it," Riley said. "I do. Just do me one favor?"

"What's that?"

"Don't close yourself off to a chance," Riley said.

"Riley…"

"Hey, I get it. I seem to remember you giving me and Fallon a few little nudges."

"That was different."

It was always *different* when it wasn't about you. "If you say so." Her phone rang. She was surprised to see that Fallon was calling. Immediately, her thoughts went to Owen. "Fallon?"

"Hey, sorry to bug you…"

"What's wrong?"

"Nothing is wrong," Fallon replied. "Owen asked if he could see Andi. Well, first he asked for you."

"Really?"

"Yeah. I don't know why. Usually, he's happy to be here with me."

Riley heard a note of sadness in Fallon's voice. "He *is* happy to be with you. Come to think of it, he was a little quiet yesterday after I picked him up."

"Do you think something happened at preschool?" Fallon asked.

"Maybe."

"Listen, I'll handle it."

"Can you hold on one minute?" Riley requested. She looked at Andi.

"What's going on?" Andi asked.

"Owen asked if he could see you."

"Me?"

"Yeah."

"Well, we can either go there or Fallon can come here; take your pick."

"Are you sure?"

"Sure, I'm sure."

"This is supposed to be our day to…"

"Riley, it's fine."

Riley nodded. "Fallon? Did you hear that?"

"Yeah, I heard it. How about I bring over something for the grill? I'll even cook it."

"Fallon says she'll bring something to cook," Riley told Andi.

"Good, tell her to pick up some beer too."

"Did she just ask for beer?" Fallon asked Riley.

"You heard that?"

"She is so far gone."

Riley bit her lip to keep from laughing. Andi might want to deny it, but the evidence of the way Billie Steele affected her was everywhere. "Yeah," Riley replied. "We'll see you in a bit."

Fallon laughed. "I see we agree."

"I love you too," Riley said.

Fallon kept laughing. "Tell Grandma we'll be there soon."

"I will."

Andi sipped her wine. "Should I ask what that conversation was about?"

"Probably not."

"That's what I thought."

❧ ❧

The last person that Carol expected to see at *Murphy's Law* at three in the afternoon was Beth. Beth Foster seldom wandered into the pub unless she was meeting Fallon. Pregnancy aside, Fallon's sister-in-law had never been much of a drinker. Beth sometimes joined Ida and Fallon for a causal lunch or dinner, but in all the years that Carol had known Dean's wife, she'd never seen Beth intoxicated — not once. And, she couldn't recall a time when Beth had strolled in by herself.

"Hey," Carol called out.

"Hi, Carol."

"How are you doing?" Carol asked.

"Not bad."

"Fallon's not here."

"Yeah, I know. "

Carol was curious. "Can I get you something?"

"Actually, I was hoping I could pick your brain about something."

"Me?"

Beth nodded. "You know Fallon as well as anyone."

"Well, I'm not sure I know her better than anyone."

"Maybe not, but you've spent a lot of time with her. And, you're objective."

Carol's curiosity swelled, along with a growing sense of concern. "I'd offer you a drink. Something tells me I might be the one who needs a few."

"It's not dire. I guess, I'm hoping you might have an idea how I should approach this with Fallon."

"Approach what?"

"Barb called me this morning."

"Oh, boy." Carol was tempted to reach for a bottle of tequila. "What happened?"

Beth shook her head ruefully. "Olivia has decided to accept a position in Amsterdam."

"New York?"

"No, Netherlands."

Carol felt sick. She wasn't certain which would be worse; Olivia moving closer to Fallon or Olivia moving across an ocean. "She's taking the kids to Europe?"

"They're staying with Barb."

Carol let out a sigh of relief. "That's the first sensible thing Olivia's done in years."

"Probably," Beth agreed.

"So, why do I get the feeling I'm missing something?"

"You have no idea how much I would like that drink."

Carol chuckled. "It can't be that bad."

"It's not—not really. Barb's looking to make a move too."

"Okay?"

"Here," Beth said.

"Here? Here as in Whiskey Springs?"

Beth nodded.

"Seriously?"

"Yeah. I was surprised too. She felt funny calling Ida or Fallon to talk about it."

"I get that. Calling your ex's ex, that could be a little uncomfortable."

"Beth," Carol waded deeper cautiously. "No offense, but I think how *you* feel about Barb moving here matters more than what Fallon or Ida think."

"I adore Barb," Beth said.

"Really?"

"That's surprising?"

"No, I like her too. I just thought maybe with everything that has gone down with Olivia, and then with Dean being..."

"With Dean being the girls' father?"

"Well, yeah."

"I think Barb and I have traversed what that means together for a long time. It surprised me a little that she'd want to move here."

"It surprises me too, although I suspect for different reasons."

"Emily and Summer need some stability. They need the support of family," Beth offered. "To be honest, I think Barb does too."

"And, you're not sure how Fallon will react?"

"Fallon's life is finally on track."

Can't argue with that. "Well, I can't pretend to know what Fallon will say," Carol admitted. "After the Cigar Club.... Well, I think it's safe to say her feelings for Olivia had changed a bit."

"I know."

"But I don't think that has anything to do with Barb and the kids."

"Maybe not. What about Riley?"

"Riley?"

"Yeah. Do you think she's going to enjoy having two kids who frankly think of Fallon as another parent around? I mean, Carol, I hate to say this, but Olivia has always behaved that way. I think it's the main reason Barb left her. She couldn't handle it anymore."

"I wish I could say I'm surprised to hear that. I am sorry. After the shit she pulled with Andi, not much about Liv surprises me."

"I don't even know how to start the conversation," Beth said.

"Just tell her what Barb told you. Come to think of it, tell her and Riley."

"Together?"

"Sure."

Beth sighed.

"Look, I get it. I think they might surprise you. Fallon loves those kids."

"I know she does. I also know that Owen..."

"If you're worried about Riley; I wouldn't."

"I'm not. I just... Fallon needs to concentrate on Riley and Owen. It's still new."

Carol offered Beth a compassionate smile. Fallon had shared a bit about Beth's reasons for moving in with Ida. It seemed Olivia's reach was far. She'd caused enormous pain and upheaval for the people closest to her, not the least of whom was Beth. Fallon had told Carol that she couldn't believe Dean had failed to ask Beth how Beth felt before agreeing to be Olivia and Barb's sperm donor. She confessed that she wondered if Olivia had consulted Barb, or if she had simply announced the plan. Ida and Andi had knocked back a few margaritas one night shortly after Olivia headed back to Washington DC. Carol recalled the uncharacteristic rise of Ida's voice when Ida explained that Dean had skipped out on several of Evan's events and games so that he could attend something with Olivia and the girls. It didn't take a genius to understand how that would have left both Beth and Evan feeling. Like second-class citizens; that's what Carol imagined. Riley was not Olivia. Carol though that a gentle reminder was in order.

"You know, I've spent a lot of time with both Fallon and Riley," Carol said.

"That's why I wanted to talk to you."

Carol nodded. "It might be new. It doesn't feel that way. They're probably the most solid couple I know."

Beth was surprised by Carol's observation.

"I'm serious," Carol said. "I think Charlie and I are a good match. And," she chuckled before continuing. "I think Andi's found her match. She might not think so." Carol grinned. "But, Fallon and Riley? I don't know, Beth. They've both been hurt so much in the past. I think somehow that gives them a different foundation than a lot of us have. Sometimes, I forget how young Riley is."

"I know what you mean."

"Just tell them," Carol said. "What about you? Do you think you'll stay here?"

Beth didn't know how to answer. "I honestly don't know."

Carol reached over and covered Beth's hand. "How about the strongest Virgin Pina Colada I have?"

"A virgin, huh?"

Carol cackled. *So much for the idea that Beth is innocent.* "Just remember, you only get to call it that once," Carol said.

It was Beth's turn to laugh. "Noted."

⚬⚬⚬

"Gwama!" Owen sprinted for Andi.

Andi couldn't help herself, she erupted in delighted laughter. "Well, look who's here!"

"Me!" Owen said.

"I see that."

"He insisted," Fallon told Andi. "Refrigerator?" She held up the six pack of beer in her hand.

"Perfect," Andi replied.

"Why don't you call Billie and ask her to join us?" Riley suggested. She forced herself not to laugh at the deer caught in the head-lights expression on Andi's face. "Is she working?" Riley asked.

"She was off at three."

"So? Call her," Riley said.

"I already have a date for this affair," Andi said. She lifted Owen onto her hip. He flashed her a toothy grin. "Did you miss me?" She asked him.

"Yep. Where's Biwwie?"

Andi rolled her eyes. "Is that the only reason you want to see me?"

Owen giggled. The last few times he had seen Andi, Billie had been in tow. "Biwwie's funny."

"She is funny," Andi agreed. "All right, I give up," she acquiesced. "I'll give Billie a call."

Owen clapped.

"Good thing you bought that beer," Andi told Fallon when she reappeared on the deck.

"Why? Finally developing a taste for it?"

"She's calling Billie," Riley explained.

"You don't say," Fallon grinned.

"Don't start." Andi shook a finger at Fallon.

Fallon held up her hands. "I wouldn't dream of starting what you aren't ready to finish."

Andi glared at her friend.

"I can call Biwwie?" Owen asked.

Andi's heart melted. "I'll call her, and you can ask her if she'd like to join us."

Owen clapped again.

"You are such a sucker," Fallon whispered into Andi's ear.

"Takes one to know one," Andi said. She took Owen's hand and led him to a chair where he could sit on her lap.

"Someone has *Grandma* wrapped around his finger," Fallon commented.

Riley smacked her gently. "Stop," she whispered.

Fallon was pleased with herself. She loved teasing Andi.

"I'm going to liberate a bottle of wine," Riley said. "And, Fallon's going to help."

Andi nodded her understanding, consumed with her task and Owen's attention.

"What did I do?" Fallon asked when they were inside the house.

"Go easy with the teasing," Riley advised.

"Why?" Fallon's forehead creased with concern. "Andi's okay; isn't she?"

"She is. I know you, Fallon. You love getting Andi riled up a little."

"She knows I'm kidding."

"Yes, but I think you might be missing something."

"About Andi?"

"Fallon..."

"What?"

"You know how things have been with Dave, and you know Jacob promises he's never getting married to anyone."

"Yeah, well, Jacob will sing a different tune when he meets the right guy. And, anyway, what do the boys have to do with me giving her a hard time about being Grandma?"

"More than you might think," Riley replied.

"Riley, I love you. If I am supposed to be following this, I'm afraid we are on different roads."

"I just think she might be worried that she'll never be a grandmother, or worse, she might not get to be a part of her grandkids' lives."

Fallon immediately felt horrible. Andi's youngest son remained distant. It continued to hurt Andi deeply. "Shit. Did she say something?"

"Not specifically. And, Fallon? I could be wrong about this—I could be."

"What?"

"I think she's falling for Billie."

"She's already on the ground," Fallon observed. "She just doesn't want to admit it."

"Maybe. Just take it easy today; okay? She's leaving in a couple of weeks to visit Jacob. I think she's feeling a little..."

Fallon didn't need Riley to explain. Andi was unnerved by everything. Andi was masterful at disguising her fears. "Say no more."

"Thank you."

"What did the two of you talk about before I got here?" Fallon asked.

"I'll fill you in later." Riley grabbed a bottle of white wine from the refrigerator and the corkscrew. "Grab some glasses," she told Fallon. "Did Owen say anything on your way here?"

"Other than singing about seeing his Grandma? No."

"Maybe he just missed Andi."

"Maybe."

"Mommy!" Owen bellowed when Riley emerged through the back door.

"Good God." Riley nearly jumped out of her skin. "What has you so excited?"

"Biwwie said yes!"

"That's great, sweetheart."

"Yep." He looked at Fallon and tugged at his bottom lip with his teeth.

"What's up, buddy?" Fallon asked.

"Fawon? You has a gwama?"

Fallon smiled. "I did," Fallon said. "Both my grandmas are in heaven now. Like Daddy is."

"Oh. Mommy has a gwandma."

"I do."

"I has…" Owen held up his fingers and tried to count. "I has…"

"You have a lot of grandmas," Riley said. "And, a grandpa too."

"You got a Gwampa, Fawon?"

"No, buddy. My grandpas are up in heaven too."

Owen frowned. He ran back to Andi.

"What do you suppose that's about?" Fallon wondered aloud.

"I don't know," Riley said. "Something tells me we're going to find out."

Fallon wondered when or if Owen would raise more questions about grandparents. She was curious to learn what had brought on Owen's questions. For the moment, he appeared content to command Billie and Andi's attention. Fallon watched those interactions with interest. Riley's earlier warning niggled at the back of her brain. She wanted to give Andi a gentle push, perhaps in the form of innocent teasing or maybe with a frank observation. Andi had guided Fallon to face her feelings for Riley. Fallon's entire life hadn't been upside down when she met Riley. Andi's currently was. Her divorce was due to be finalized at the end of the month. Fallon hoped that would provide Andi was some closure and solace. The strain that existed between Andi and Dave perplexed Fallon. Neither Jake or Jacob Jr. had made Andi feel guilty about her choices—her choice to ask for a divorce or her relationship with Fallon. Fallon couldn't understand why Dave insisted on being hurtful to his mother. And, she did know that Andi worried about the effect Dave's actions were having on Jacob. Jacob had yet to tell his father or brother that he was gay. That weighed on Andi's heart. She felt responsible. All of it made Andi reluctant to consider a romantic relationship with Billie. Watching the smile that graced Andi's lips as Owen entertained her and Billie confirmed Fallon's suspicion. Andi wasn't falling for Billie Steele. Andi was in love with Billie. Fallon was tempted to take a drive to Connecticut and confront Dave; throttle him if she had to. Did he have any idea how much pain he was causing his mother? Fallon took a swig from her beer bottle and flipped the burgers on the grill.

"What are you thinking?" Riley asked.

"I was wondering what Dave is thinking. She doesn't deserve his bullshit. It's my fault."

Riley rubbed Fallon's back. "No, it isn't."

"I wish I could believe that."

"I have no idea what his problem is," Riley said. "Neither does Andi."

"Me. His problem is that he thinks I'm the reason his parents divorced."

"Well, that is *his* problem."

"Which is causing problems for her."

Riley glanced over at Andi and Billie. Andi was laughing. Billie was looking at Andi lovingly. Owen seemed to be telling one of his tall tales. Riley smiled. "I wouldn't worry too much, babe. I think it will all work out."

"I hope so."

❧

"Gwama?" Owen tugged at Andi's hand.

"Yes?"

Owen looked over at Fallon.

"What is it Owen?"

"Fawon is a mommy?"

Andi was beginning to put together the pieces of Owen's puzzle. She smiled at him warmly. "You love Fallon."

"Yep. And you!"

"I love you too, Owen," Andi promised.

Billie sipped her beer, content to listen.

"What do you want to ask me?" Andi asked Owen.

His nose crinkled. He wasn't sure how to ask the question he needed answered.

Andi kissed him on the head. "You want to know if Fallon is your mommy," she guessed.

Owen smiled.

"Why don't you ask Fallon?" Andi suggested.

Owen's teeth gripped his bottom lip. He seemed to suddenly grow shy.

Andi gestured to where Fallon and Riley were standing by the grill. "How about this," she began. "I'll go get Mommy and Fallon, and Billie and I will finish cooking your hot dog."

Owen nodded. He grabbed Andi's hand before she could walk away.

"It's okay, sweetie," Andi promised. She kissed him again and made her way over to Fallon and Riley.

Owen looked at Billie.

"Grandma is right," Billie said. "You can ask Fallon."

He looked at the ground.

"You asked Grandma Andi, didn't you?" Billie reminded him.

Owen looked back up hopefully.

"See? It'll be okay," Billie promised.

Andi took a deep breath. "How about we trade?" She suggested to Fallon.

"Huh?" Fallon asked.

"Billie and I will take grill duty. You and Riley take mom duty."

Riley's gaze narrowed.

"I think Owen has something he wants to ask you," Andi explained.

"What?" Fallon wondered.

"That's for Owen to tell you," Andi said.

"Andi, if…"

Andi grabbed the spatula from Fallon's hand. "Trust me."

Fallon and Riley exchanged a confused glance.

"Okay," Fallon said. "Have at it."

"Don't look now," Billie whispered in Owen's ear. "I'm going to make sure Grandma doesn't burn my burger." Billie winked at Fallon and Riley.

Fallon suddenly felt nervous. What on earth was going on? "Owen?" Fallon asked. "Did you want to talk to us?"

Owen continued to toy with his lip.

Riley looked on with amusement. Fallon did the same thing when she was nervous. Owen mimicked nearly everything Fallon did. She sat down beside her son. Fallon crouched in front of Owen's chair.

"Grandma said you want to ask us something," Riley said.

Owen nodded.

"Go ahead," Riley encouraged him.

Owen looked at his mother. "Is Fawon a mommy?"

Fallon was confused. Riley immediately understood the question. "Is that what you want Fallon to be?"

Owen nodded.

Riley whispered into her son's ear. "You can tell her that."

Owen looked at Fallon. "Fawon, you be my mommy."

Fallon didn't think she'd be able to hold her position. In a million years, she would never have expected Owen to ask her to be his mother. "Owen..."

Riley clasped Fallon's hand and squeezed.

"I'd love to," Fallon replied, choking back tears.

Owen grinned from ear to ear. He hopped off his chair and ran toward Andi.

"Okay, Gwama!"

Andi laughed. "I knew it would be."

"Are you okay" Riley asked Fallon, as she helped Fallon find her feet.

"Riley, I..."

"You're a great mom, Fallon."

"I'm not..."

"To Owen, you are. I told you that before. You and I are the only parents he's ever known, Fallon. Andi and your mom? They're the grandparents he knows. This is his family."

Fallon felt herself wavering. "Riley..."

Riley looked over at Andi.

Andi nodded and whispered to Billie.

"Hey, Riley?" Billie called over. "Can you give me a hand getting the plates?"

"Sure." Riley placed a kiss on Fallon's cheek. "Go help Andi," she said. "Come on, Owen. You can help us find the ketchup." Owen ran toward the door.

Andi smiled at Fallon. "Are you okay?"

"I feel like I should have said..."

"Fallon," Andi directed Fallon to look at her. "Owen loves you."

"Yeah, but..."

"No. No buts. Just like he needed to call me Grandma, he needed to know that you are his mom. And, you are."

"Riley is..."

"Riley is your partner. Stop holding back."

"I never thought he'd..."

Andi kissed Fallon's cheek. "You're a good mom, Fallon."

"I hope I will be."

"You already are."

"Takes one to know one," Fallon offered. Andi's sad smile hurt Fallon. "You are, Andi. If I'm any good at it at all, it's because I had you and mom around to teach me—in different ways, but..."

"Thank you," Andi said.

"No," Fallon said. "Thank you, Andi—for everything."

CHAPTER THREE

It had always interested Fallon; the way life could change on dime. What seemed like an insignificant event or a forgetful moment to one person had the power to alter another person's world completely. As she sipped her coffee, listening to Owen sing one of his many songs, Fallon pondered that a single statement had changed everything. Her eyes fell on Owen. He spun while he sang his tune, falling in the grass with a thump. A moment could hold a lifetime within it. For Fallon, this was one of those moments.

Riley stood in the doorway watching Fallon from a distance. Fallon had remained uncharacteristically quiet the previous evening after Owen's question. At first, Riley was concerned. Fallon barely spoke through the dinner they shared with Andi and Billie. Owen played and laughed, delighting in the attention his antics evoked from his Grandma Andi and Billie. Owen had found a patch of mud to play in. That led Riley and Andi to wrangle him for a bath. Riley sensed Andi wanted to give Fallon and Billie some time alone. She didn't ask why. Andi had her reasons. She wondered what, if anything, had been said between Billie and Fallon during her absence. When they had returned home, Fallon had snuggled in Riley's arms. That wasn't unusual. Fallon's desire to *be* held accompanied by her marked silence was. Riley decided it was time to approach the events of the previous day with Fallon.

"You're out here early," Riley observed.

"It's too nice to be inside. Besides, Owen started begging for his bubbles at seven."

"Better bubbles than worms."

Fallon laughed.

"Fallon?"

"Yeah?"

"Are you all right?"

Fallon set down the coffee mug in her hand and smiled at Riley. "I know, I've been kind of distant."

"Not distant, just—quiet."

Fallon looked over at Owen. "I didn't expect him to ask me that, Riley."

"Does it bother you?"

"Bother me? God, no. It isn't something I ever expected to have. Well, maybe not ever, but not for a long, long time."

Fallon's admission surprised Riley. In fact, it hurt her a bit.

"Riley?"

"I guess, I'm a little confused."

"About what?" Fallon asked.

"Well, we were just talking about children the other day. I assumed…"

Fallon shook her head slightly.

"I mean, I assumed we'd be doing that *together*."

"I certainly hope you aren't planning to do it with someone else," Fallon joked.

Riley sighed.

"Riley, that's not what I mean."

"What *do* you mean?"

"It's different.; you and me deciding to have children together; that's not the same. And, before you tell me why I'm wrong, please listen to me."

"I'm listening."

"I worry sometimes."

"About what?"

"Owen had a father, Riley; a father who loved him very much from what I understand."

"Yes, he did."

"And, I don't want to intrude on that."

Oh, Fallon. "You aren't. You can't. He'll always know that, Fallon. But he will never *have* that with Robert. That isn't anyone's fault. He has *you*. He's had you since the moment you found us trudging through the snow."

Fallon smiled. She'd fallen in love with Owen immediately. On some level, she'd fallen in love with Riley too that night. Fallon wasn't a person who spent much time indulging in romantic fantasies about love at first sight. When she did take a moment to examine her relationship with Riley, her affair with Andi, and even her time with Olivia, it seemed obvious that if it wasn't love, there was a type of recognition from the moment she had met each of them. Something inside her had clicked, like a switch, a light that had been suddenly turned on. She tried to listen to Riley; her thoughts drifted to the crazy notion that perhaps love existed on some weird dimmer switch. Sometimes, it got turned all the way around the moment it flipped on. Most times, it turned gradually.

"Are you listening to me?" Riley asked.

"Sorry. I was." Fallon noted Riley's doubtful gaze. "I was. What you said—about Owen having me from that first night..."

"Yes?"

"He did. So did you, when I think about it."

"Fallon..."

"I hear you, Riley. Believe me; I couldn't possibly love Owen more, not even if I'd been the one to give birth to him."

"Yes, I know. Which is why I'm puzzled."

"I know he loves me. I never expected him to want me to be anything but Fallon."

"His playmate?"

"No, but maybe like the cool aunt."

"I think I understand."

"And, I still wonder where all of this came from."

"I'm not sure. Andi thinks it's from being with the other kids. She told me that Jacob came home once and dressed Dave up in her clothes."

"Why?"

"Because the two kids in his playgroup had sisters," Riley explained.

Fallon doubled over with laughter. "Maybe that's his issue. Maybe Jacob traumatized him."

"Stop it." Riley laughed.

"I guess it makes sense," Fallon said.

"That's not the only reason you were so quiet last night; is it?"

Fallon shook her head.

"I got the distinct feeling Andi wanted to give you some time with Billie."

"Probably."

"Want to tell me what that's about?"

"Billie and me... We've been friends since grade school."

"You mentioned that."

"I guess you could say that over the years we've kind of been each other's sounding board—about a lot of things."

"Like women?"

"Yeah, but not just that," Fallon said. "We both really wanted families."

"I'm surprised you two never... Did you ever..."

"No!" Fallon threw her hands up. "God, no."

"Billie's attractive."

"Yeah, but she's more like my sister, Riley."

"I get it. So? What had you upset?"

"Not upset," Fallon corrected Riley. "Just kind of, I don't know... I needed to process things."

"Besides Owen wanting you to be his mom, what might those *things* be?"

"Andi, for one."

Riley listened.

"She's in love with Billie, Riley."

"Yes, I know."

"Did she tell you..."

"No. I don't think Andi is ready to admit it to herself."

"Billie doesn't think she's good enough for Andi."

"That's the dumbest thing I've heard in a long time."

"Yeah, to you and me it is; it isn't dumb to Billie."

"What aren't you saying?"

"It's a long story."

"I have time," Riley countered.

Fallon nodded. "Billie was raped by her brother when we were kids, Riley. And that was my fault."

Riley froze. *What on earth....*

⁓

"Hi, Mom."

"How are things there?" Andi asked Jacob.

"Good. Pretty good. You're coming; right?"

"I'll be there."

Jacob let out a sigh of relief.

"Why wouldn't I be there?" Andi asked.

"I don't know. I thought maybe with Dad coming..."

"Jacob, your father and I are friends. That's not going to change."

"Yeah."

"What's wrong?" Andi asked.

"Mom?"

"Still here," Andi promised.

"I got a job offer after graduation."

"That's terrific."

"I don't know. It's in Los Angeles."

"And, that's a bad thing?" Andi asked. "You love the sun and the heat."

Andi's playful reminder lightened Jacob's mood slightly. "I don't know if I should accept."

"Do you want to accept?"

"It's kind of my dream job."

"But you're not sure."

"I looked for something closer to home. I..."

"Jacob," Andi stopped him. "You need to stop worrying about me."

"You're alone."

"Hardly."

"You know what I mean. At least, when you and Fallon were…"

"Fallon is still a big part of my life. "

"But you're in the house and there is…"

"Jacob, stop."

"Maybe you could move with me," he said.

Andi grinned. *Jacob, always worrying about me.* "I don't know if LA is the place for me."

"Why not? You love to tan, and you wouldn't even need to spray it on!"

Andi laughed. "Maybe you should have majored in advertising instead of graphic design."

"You could," he said. "I mean, what's holding you there?"

Andi took a deep breath. *What is holding me here?* "We'll talk when I get there. You're buying the beer."

"Beer?"

Andi chuckled. *Yeah, beer.*

❧

Andi was about to open a bottle of wine. She stopped, smiled, and grabbed one of the beers Billie had failed to drink. "Why not?" She carried it out to the deck. The sun was beginning to crawl beneath the tree line. The warmth of tan early September afternoon had given way to a soothing breeze. Andi reclined on a lounge chair and took a tentative sip from the beer bottle. "Not bad." The distant sound of a few birds singing their song filtered to her ears. She savored a breath of the crisp air and released it with a long, deliberate sigh. The week had proved more chaotic than she'd excepted. Who would have thought that her social life would improve after ending a marriage *and* a love affair? She giggled and took another sip of her beer. Jacob worried that his mother might be lonely. Andi had barely had an hour to herself in the last few weeks. The company of people she loved had eased Andi's loneliness. There were times when she felt incredibly alone; moments she wondered if the closeness she enjoyed with friends could eradicate her longing for the intimacy shared between lovers. She tried not to let her thoughts wander into memories — memories of Fallon beside her or of falling asleep in Jake's arms. She needed time; that's what Andi told herself, time to discover who she was.

Andi set aside the beer in her hand, let her head fall back against the lounger, and closed her eyes. How could a person banish memories? Should they? Each memory represented a time that had shaped who Andi was now. Was there any way to force memories into submission? She sighed. Three weeks earlier, she had collided with an attractive attorney at Murphy's Law; one of those passers-by that not so long ago Fallon might have taken home. A few margaritas and laughs later, Andi found herself standing in said attorney's room. She still found it difficult to believe she'd left with Ethel. Ethel? Ethel sounded more like a woman entrenched in Dora Bath's Biddy Brigade than a sexy lawyer — a sexy, *lesbian* lawyer. "Only me," Andi mused with a giggle. She inhaled another long breath as the memory of that evening began to play like an old movie. Ethel — what was her name again? Who would care? Ethel…. Ethel Gentry. "My God, that *is* awful! Thank God she liked to be called Dee. Why did she want to be called Dee?" Andi laughed and reached for the beer beside her. Here she was trying — actually *trying* to fantasize about the one time in her life she'd indulged in a one-night-stand, and she was obsessing over the woman's name. She took a sip from the bottle and set it down — *again*. Her eyelids fluttered and closed.

Dee. "Well, at least, that's better than Ethel." Andi hadn't paid any mind to Dee's presence at the pub that evening. She'd been engaged in a lively conversation with Riley and Ida. It was girls' night out. That meant a night that Fallon was home with Owen. Carol was behind the bar. Riley, and the Granny Brigade — Ida's name for her and Andi — got to get away, gossip, and guzzle. In fact, Ida had been giving Riley a lesson in the unspoken traditions of small town life.

At least, life in Whiskey Springs. Andi let her thoughts roam back to that evening:

"Fallon grumbled a little about our weekly date," Riley said.

"Yeah, well that comes with the territory—grumbling, I mean. She doesn't gossip, and she'd rather listen than gab. Grumble it is."

"I believe she told me about the three g's once; something about it being a prerequisite to small town living," Riley said.

"Told you that, did she?" Ida laughed. "That was her father's theory. I swear that man should've had a job writing damn handbooks. He had a rule for everything."

"Yeah, so he could break them," Andi commented.

Ida laughed. "Ain't that the truth! But, you know Fallon. I think she still believes his word like its testament."

Andi smiled. Fallon adored her father. He was her hero. "Probably so," she agreed.

Riley wasn't sure what to say. Fallon spoke about her father frequently. She'd seen pictures, of course. Outwardly, Riley thought that Fallon resembled Ida. It would be impossible to deny that mother and daughter shared more than good looks. They were equally charming and witty, albeit in different ways. Both Ida and Fallon were insatiably curious about everything. Riley concentrated on the straw in her drink, spinning it in slow circles, wondering what traits Fallon shared with her father.

"She's a lot like him," Ida said, intuitively knowing what Riley wanted to ask. "Smart. Too smart for her own good sometimes."

Andi chuckled.

"She is. Some of it is because she spent so much time with him, I think. Watch her when she drives the car. She taps the wheel, and she sings without realizing it's out loud." Ida's features softened as she spoke. "She hung on his every word," she told Riley. "That's why she loves this place so much, you know?"

Riley smiled. "I know."

"Can't say I blame her. Sometimes, I think I see him standing over there by that old jukebox. Other times, I swear I hear his laugh in the distance. He loved his old joint. That's what he called it. Not as much as he loved her, though."

"Or you," Andi interjected.

Ida howled with laughter. "I wouldn't be so sure of that. I think The Middle Ground was his mistress."

Riley pushed her drink aside. "I need to get home."

"Why? Did my daughter give you a curfew?"

"No. Owen wasn't feeling well when I left. To tell you the truth, I don't think Fallon was either."

Andi started to get up when Ida grabbed her arm. "I'll take Riley home. You stay and keep Carol company for a while."

❧

"Ida, you sneak," Andi muttered. Less than a minute after Riley and Ida had walked out the door, a tall, redhead had taken the seat Riley had vacated. Andi's lips turned upward playfully as she recalled meeting Dee:

"Are you saving this seat?"

Andi looked up at a pair of mirthful blue eyes. "There's a policy here," she said.

"Oh?"

"First come, first served. You leave, you lose."

"Sounds fair," the woman replied. She took a seat and extended her hand. "Dee," she said.

"Andi."

"Is that your real name?"

"Why? Does it sound fake?"

"No, but you do look like someone who might have a stage name. What I mean is, I thought you might be an actress or..."

"In Whiskey Springs? Hardly."

"It suits you," Dee commented. "Your name."

"Thank you—I think. Do you have a thing about names?"

"Well, my real name is Ethel—Ethel Gentry. I've always thought that sounded like some woman riding in a stagecoach, so yes, I do."

Andi laughed. "Are *you*? An actress—no, wait, let me guess, a comedienne?"

"Close, I'm an attorney."

"A lot of humor in that business?" Andi asked playfully.

"At times." Dee sipped from her drink and then gestured to Andi's. "You're running low. Can I buy you a refill?"

For a second, Andi thought she should decline the offer. Why should she? Unless she'd lost all of her senses, Dee was flirting. Andi wondered if she remembered how to flirt with a stranger. When was the last time she *had* flirted with a stranger? *Oh, God help me.* "Why not?"

"Ladies," Carol walked over. "Another round?"

"Please," Dee replied. "On my tab."

Carol's eyes twinkled with mischief. "Maybe Fallon will actually make a profit tonight." She winked at Andi.

Andi cleared her throat.

"Fallon?" Dee inquired.

"Fallon owns the pub," Andi explained.

"Is it normally slow?"

"No." Andi laughed. "I think Carol's referring to the fact that I normally have an open tab."

"Do you have a special relationship with this Mr. Fallon."

Andi coughed. *You could say that.* "*She's* my best friend."

"That would explain it. Well, I'm happy to contribute to the bottom line."

Andi felt her face flush. She was relieved when Carol returned with a fresh margarita. Maybe it would refresh her throat which had suddenly gone dry. *It hasn't been that long, Andi. What is wrong with you?*

"Just the way you like it," Carol said. "Heavy on the tequila and salt; light on the 'rita."

Dee grinned. "You're not a lightweight; are you?"

I guess we'll see.

⸎

Riley had been trying to process Fallon's revelation about Billie. Riley's hand softly traced the outline of Fallon's face as Fallon slept. Fallon tended to take everything on herself. She felt responsible for the world. It was one of the things that made Riley love her, and at the same time, concerned Riley. For some reason, Fallon seemed to think that she should be able to solve everyone's problems. Riley studied Fallon's features as Fallon slept. Fallon possessed the gentlest heart of any person Riley had ever known. Riley understood guilt as well as anyone could. She'd run through a million scenarios after Robert's death. The constant mantra of "what if" plagued her thoughts for months. There had to have been *something – anything* she could have done to change the outcome of that day. There was nothing, no answer, no solution, and no absolution. There was no sin for which Riley needed absolution. Sometimes, life happened. Part of life was loss. Part of life was death. And, part of life was change. "Oh, Fallon, how can I make you understand that you can't save the whole world, love?" Fallon would never change. Fallon was a caretaker by nature. Riley hoped that she might help Fallon to let go of her guilt. A person could give and guide without taking responsibility for the woes in the world. Riley had learned that.

"I love you," Riley whispered. She closed her eyes, her thoughts drifting to Billie and then to Andi. She missed her parents and her sister. She made it a priority to call each of them weekly. Family had taken on a new meaning for Riley. The family she'd been given had helped her to grow into the woman she was now. They stood beside her through some of the happiest and most painful moments in her young life. Family was more than a group of people created by circumstance and by happenstance. She loved the family she had been given. The family she was creating with Fallon filled Riley with a sense of pride, love, and possibility that continued to astound her. Fallon and Owen were her family. Ida was her family. Carol, Marge, even Pete and Dale were part of that extended family. And, Andi? Aside from Fallon and Owen, Andi had become the most important person in Riley's life. She was Riley's best friend; the best friend Riley had ever had. Andi was also Riley's guide, the person whose counsel Riley valued the most. Riley did know that Andi's choice to walk away from her affair with Fallon had hurt Andi more than she would ever admit to Riley. Andi had taken that step out of love for both Fallon and Riley. Riley knew that too. Andi was in love with Billie. Riley was sure of it. Billie was in love with Andi; everyone knew that. Riley prayed that the past wouldn't prevent her friends from finding happiness together in the future. Andi deserved to be loved. Billie deserved to be loved. Wasn't it time that they all had a chance to be happy? Riley opened her eyes and let them sweep over Fallon's sleeping form. She leaned in and kissed Fallon's lips sweetly. "It's time, Fallon—for all of us."

Heat crept over Andi's skin as she replayed her impromptu rendezvous. She'd never felt any inclination to seek a one-night-stand. Andi always believed that some things were best left to fantasy. Perhaps, that was the result of living in an unfaithful partnership for many years. It had taken Andi twenty-five years to engage in any physical relationship outside the boundaries of marriage. Traditional thinking told her that she should feel regret; she didn't. She'd felt alone in her marriage since its beginning. Loneliness left Andi feeling inadequate on more levels than she wanted to admit. Surely, there must've been something lacking in her. What other reason would Jake have to stray? Fallon had quelled those doubts, if only slightly. Fallon had opened her to possibilities. Andi wasn't attached to anyone now. She was a "free" woman; whatever that meant. The meaning of "free" seemed evident when Dee invited Andi back to the B&B she was staying at. Andi could accept. Andi wanted to accept. She was happy for Fallon and Riley—genuinely. Her joy at witnessing Fallon and Riley's relationship grow did not banish her feelings of loss. It wasn't easy watching Fallon wrap her arms around Riley's waist. There were nights when after they'd all shared a dinner, and Fallon and Riley left the pub hand in hand, Andi thought the wave of loneliness that encompassed her might swallow her whole.

Dee. Andi's lips twitched and curled at the memory. Standing in front of this elegant, attractive, assertive woman, Andi's skin tingled with anticipation and excitement. It was the sort of exhilaration that accompanied breaking the rules. After all, wasn't Andi about to do that? Okay, so maybe it was her stupid rule—no one-night-stands; no sex without any emotion. It didn't matter who had set the boundary. Andi had accepted the limit, and she was about to shatter that wall. It felt amazing.

⚜

"You're quiet," Dee observed.

"Am I?" Andi replied. "Is there something you wanted me to say?"

Dee's eyes flickered with desire. "No." Her hands pulled Andi closer, her mouth covering Andi's softly. "But," she whispered. "I'll do my best to break the silence—slowly."

Before Andi could muster a reply, Dee's tongue fluttered over hers making her knees buckle. What did Dee mean, Andi wondered? Did she hope that Andi would vocalize her approval? Did she intend to make Andi beg? *Oh, God.* That thought made Andi quiver with need. What was

Andi doing here? The sensation of Dee's fingertips skating over her throat as they meandered lower, banished Andi's question. She didn't care. Why didn't matter. Andi wanted to be here. She gasped when Dee began to unbutton her blouse. It'd been so long—too long since anyone had touched her. Andi's hands threaded into the waves of Dee's hair, deepening their kiss, imploring the woman touching her to continue—to take her. And, that is what Andi desired, to be taken. She had no desire to think, to evaluate, or to consider anything. All Andi wanted was to feel, to lose herself in another woman's touch. It seemed that Dee was eager to grant her unspoken request.

Dee tugged Andi's blouse open. She traced a delicate line from the hollow of Andi's throat to the swell of her breasts. Her gaze had fallen on Andi early that evening. Even at a distance, Dee could feel passion and curiosity emanating from the woman now standing in her arms. It wasn't Dee's style to engage in a hook-up. She briefly considered that Andi might be the living embodiment of a mythical siren; her call luring the unsuspecting stranger, conjuring lust from the depths of the most stolid soul. Andi wasn't merely sexy; Dee had struggled to name the quality that drew her to take a seat beside Andi at the bar. Was it confidence? Andi was poised. Beneath her assured exterior, Dee detected longing and hopefulness. Those were emotions that the attorney understood intimately. Stepping in front of judges and juries had forced Dee Gentry to appear in control, to convince anyone looking in that she had command of every situation— command of herself. In her business, someone was always seeking to strip her of that control. She pulled away and looked at Andi. Not Andi—Andi wanted to feel Dee's confidence. She desired that Dee dictate each moment they would share. The energy between them crackled. Expectation competing with apprehension could be intoxicating. It made Dee heady with lust. Her mouth crashed against Andi's, her intention was clear. *Your wish is my command—every, single one.*

Did Andi somehow lose track of the seasons? It seemed unusually hot for a September night. Dee's hands seemed to be everywhere all at once. Andi was naked— completely exposed, the breeze from an open window caressing her skin, and yet, Andi was sure she was on fire. She felt herself pushed backward toward the large poster bed. It was too high for her to fall onto. That momentary worry was put to rest when Dee lifted her onto the bed. Andi's nails raked lightly over the exposed flesh of Dee's back. No words passed between them. Involuntary moans, staggered breaths, and desperate sighs had replaced words. That was fine with Andi. She licked her lips when Dee's mouth took possession of her nipple. Faint pressure gradually increased, teasing Andi. Dee moved from one breast to the other, lavishing Andi's nipples with equal attention. Andi's hands pulled Dee's head closer, urging her to continue. Lust colored any hope of rational thought. It briefly occurred to Andi that she craved this moment. It felt primal, as if she'd never allowed herself the indulgence of pure, unbridled passion—not love, not emotion—lust and desire.

Dee's mouth moved lower, her tongue snaking out over Andi's stomach, circling Andi's belly-button and dipping lower. Andi held her breath. Her hands strayed to the bedspread beneath her. She gripped the material frantically. The faintest brush of Dee's warm breath caressing her center sent shockwaves through Andi's body.

Dee moaned against Andi's softness, unable to contain her excitement. Her hands drifted up to cup Andi's breasts. She rained kisses up and down the length of Andi's need—light and airy, breath barely touching flesh. A gasp from above tempted her to gently let her palms graze the tops of Andi's nipples.

"Jesus," Andi managed to gasp. An inaudible reply from below prompted Andi to lift her head. The sight that greeted her made her shiver with anticipation. Her head fell back again, and she closed her eyes, reveling in the warm caress that stoked her arousal.

Dee glanced up as Andi's back arched. She smiled inwardly. If Andi Maguire hoped that Dee would relieve the ache she was suffering quickly, she was in for a rude awakening. Dee intended to prolong the pain. Dee's muscles tensed with desire, and her center throbbed in desperation. She tasted Andi over and over, looking up occasionally to delight in the rise and fall of Andi's breasts. It should have been enough — watching. It wasn't. It wasn't nearly enough. Dee lifter her body, sliding against Andi inch by inch until their lips met again. "Tell me to stop," she said.

Andi nipped Dee's lower lip. "Do you want to stop?"

"No. If I don't, I'm afraid I might go too far."

Lust burned in Andi's eyes. *Too far?* Andi wasn't sure there was anything Dee could do that would constitute taking this adventure too far. What could too far be? "Unless you plan on trying to hurt me…"

Dee smiled. "Quite the opposite."

"Then do your worst," Andi said. *Please.*

Permission granted. Dee replied with a ravenous kiss. Her hands grasped Andi's hips, and directed Andi to kneel.

Oh, God. Andi's heart raced with excitement. She could feel Dee behind her, against her, and it sent a warm flood straight to her center. Dee's lips skimmed the length of Andi's spine. Andi bit her lower lip so hard, she tasted the tinge of blood it elicited. She felt Dee's hands caress her bottom and then reach around her to tug gently at both her nipples. "Fuck!" Andi cried out.

Dee pressed herself against Andi and played with Andi's breasts until Andi began to grind against her. She moved a fingertip to Andi's clit and played softly. Over and over, she circled the small point until Andi's legs began to tremble. Dee slipped her finger inside Andi and thrust deeply.

Andi's head fell forward, and her hands tugged at the bedding. Dee pressed another finger inside, and Andi cried out.

"Yes," Dee hissed. "You are so sexy, Andi. You have no idea; do you?"

Sexy? Andi wasn't sure if she was sexy, but she was turned on. There was something incredibly titillating about not knowing what to expect. As much as Andi enjoyed the intimate life she'd shared with Jake, and with Fallon; she'd always been able to read their body language. Lovemaking had often been playful, even adventurous; it had never felt salacious — unbridled. She barely knew the woman moving inside her. Not long ago, that would have prevented this liaison. Andi had no desire nor intention of turning back — not unless it was to indulge in the view Dee offered. She looked over her shoulder. *Jesus, that's hot.*

Emboldened by Andi's expression, Dee moved and placed Andi's hands on the headboard, forcing Andi upright on her knees. Dee pressed against Andi's back, her nipples hardening at the feel of Andi's flesh pressed against her. She cupped Andi's breasts again, wishing she could taste them. Tempting as it was, Dee had no intention of relinquishing control. Her palms brushed over Andi's nipples. She kissed the back of Andi's neck.

"Please," Andi begged.

"Please?" Dee asked. "I'm nowhere close to finished, Andi."

"Fuck," Andi groaned. It was a pathetic protest and she knew it. She didn't want Dee to stop — ever.

Dee chuckled softly. A lone fingertip moved to Andi's back, straight down her spine, lower, and lower, sliding gracefully over the wetness that continued to pool between Andi's legs. She teased Andi and grinned at Andi's futile attempt to prompt more. "Not yet," Dee whispered.

I might die here. Andi's heart pounded with such ferocity she feared it would knock her over. Dee would bring her to the edge of climax, and abruptly change her touch. One of Dee's hands tugged and toyed with Andi's breasts while the other taunted her center into a throbbing pool of need. She tried to turn in Dee's arms. Dee stopped her.

"That's not what you want," Dee said.

"Yes, it is."

"No, it isn't." Dee slipped a finger inside Andi and was rewarded with a throaty moan. "You want that."

Fuck. Andi did want that. Andi wanted to lose control of everything, of her thoughts, of her emotions, of her questions, and her protests. She didn't want love. She didn't want friendship. She wanted to feel lifted and jolted. She even wanted to feel used up. Questions had been plaguing her mind for weeks, emotions surfacing against her will. She'd tried to beat them all into submission. Nothing worked. Dee had momentarily transported her into a different world, one she'd fantasized about but had never dared tiptoe into. Now, she was immersed. She was drowning in her fantasy—happily drowning all her doubt, all her fear, and all her longing. Maybe lust could silence love, even if it were just for a moment.

Dee's arousal grew as Andi rode her finger. She couldn't recall any sight as erotic. Andi's hands gripped the headboard so tightly that her knuckles had gone white. Dee nipped lightly at Andi's back, sending a series of shudders through them both. She squeezed Andi's nipple.

"Oh, fuck!" Andi screamed as her release mounted.

Dee slipped two more fingers inside Andi.

The orgasm that ripped through Andi's body left her breathless and wordless. She quaked above Dee, who seemed unwilling to relent. Andi's heart lurched when Dee suddenly withdrew. A feeling of loss immediately gave way to unexpected excitement when Dee prompted Andi to lift her hips, and Dee slipped beneath her. The heat of Dee's tongue made Andi dizzy. She'd been happy to let Dee control their dance. Now, she needed more. She swiftly descended the woman beneath her, her mouth covering Dee's center. She felt Dee's legs begin to shake and smiled inwardly.

Together, they explored the other, Dee following Andi's lead, trying to concentrate on Andi's pleasure. Andi sucked gently on Dee's clit, sending them both into a frenzy.

Andi fell onto Dee and kissed her center softly before making her way back up the bed. She smiled at the woman she'd just met.

"You're amazing," Dee said.

"Not really," Andi said. Her body felt satiated, a sense of loneliness suddenly gripped her heart. Hopefulness sparkled in Dee's eyes; the idea that one day they might come together again. Perhaps, they could stay in touch. Maybe, just maybe their brief interlude would lead them to something deeper.

More than regret, Dee noted a strange recognition in Andi's eyes. Sex was a wonderful tool to avoid emotion, but in Dee's experience, the escape was fleeting. When it dissipated, a profound sense of longing took its place. She kissed Andi's lips softly. "Whoever she is, she must be amazing."

Tears gathered in Andi's eyes. How much longer could she deny it? "She is."

❧

Andi opened her eyes. They immediately drifted to the beer bottle next to her. She closed them again. She wasn't ready. She needed time. Billie deserved someone who could give her everything. If anyone deserved happiness, it was Billie Steele. Andi's heart fluttered perceptibly. She reached for the beer and sipped, wondering if Billie's lips might taste similarly. She set the bottle down. "Stop it, Andi." Maybe it was a good thing that she was going to visit Jacob. Maybe, just maybe, she could put this all in the proper perspective. Loneliness often made a person grasp for someone close. Perspective—that's what Andi needed. She steadied her breathing. "Billie…"

CHAPTER FOUR

THREE WEEKS LATER

A week had flown by. Andi had enjoyed every moment of her visit with Jacob; that was until he dropped the bomb on her that Jake and Dave were flying in for the weekend. Andi missed her younger son. She even missed Jake. She'd hoped that this trip might help her gain perspective. And, it had — just not the way Andi had hoped. Why she was determined to run away from her feelings for Billie Steele, Andi couldn't say. She hadn't envisioned herself falling in love with anyone so soon. She had resolved herself to the idea that love might never be part of her life again, at least, not romantic love. A week away had driven the truth home to Andi potently. She could try to avoid her feelings. She might try to deny them when she returned to Whiskey Springs. She would fail. As much as Andi wanted to run from Billie, she would never be able to. Seeing Dave complicated an already emotionally stressful situation for Andi. Dave continued to keep his mother at arm's length. And, Andi still had no idea why. She feared that if she entered into a relationship with someone, particularly another woman, Dave would push her away even further. If Andi decided to be honest with herself, if she came clean with Billie about her feelings, she would end up in a relationship. Billie Steele did not represent a passing fling or a one-night fantasy that Andi wanted to immerse herself in. Billie had become Andi's closest friend. She was the person Andi thought to call when something amused her or upset her. Just when Andi had thought she'd put the pieces of her life in order, everything felt upside down again. She lifted her phone and dialed a familiar number.

Ida startled when her phone rang. She looked at the caller and laughed. "Well, hello, stranger."

"I haven't been gone *that* long," Andi replied.

"True. It'd be stranger if one of my children were calling."

"Haven't heard much from Fallon lately, I take it?"

"Seems like I hear from Riley more. How's the visit?" Andi sighed.

"Uh-oh."

"Jake is flying in with Dave tonight."

"Good. That'll give you a chance to talk to him."

"I talk to Jake all the time."

"Very funny," Ida said.

"Honestly, I don't know what to expect."

"Want my advice?"

"That's why I called," Andi replied.

"Don't expect anything, and don't take any of his shit either."

Andi chuckled.

"I mean it," Ida advised. "Whatever is going on with that boy is not about you."

"I don't know, Ida."

"I do."

"I just can't understand it," Andi confessed. "We didn't raise him that way. He loves Fallon. He grew up with a gay uncle. How can he…"

"That's the question. You can't answer it. Believe me; they never get easier to understand," Ida said.

Andi sighed.

"That's not why you called me," Ida guessed.

"It is—partly, anyway."

"And, the other part?"

Andi sighed again.

"This isn't *Let's Make a Deal.* Are you going to make me guess?"

"I miss her."

"Billie?"

"Billie."

"And, that's a bad thing?" Ida wanted to know.

"I don't know."

"Sure, you do; that's why you called."

Andi laughed. Ida never minced words, and that *is* precisely why Andi called.

"So? What are you going to do about it?" Ida asked.

"I'm not sure I know what *it* is."

"You keep telling yourself that, and maybe one day you'll believe it."

"I'm not ready."

"No one's ready."

"You don't think so?" Andi asked.

"For love? Nope. I do not. Everyone thinks they are. Everyone pines away looking for it, praying they'll find it, and then when they do? They look for the nearest rock they can crawl under to hide from it."

"I never said that I was…"

"You don't have to," Ida interrupted Andi's protest.

Ida may not have raised Andi Maguire; she had watched Andi grow up. She loved Andi. She also respected and admired Andi. Respect, Ida gave freely. Admiration was reserved for those who earned it. She recalled Andi as a thoughtful, polite child who always seemed to smile. Andi had been in Dean's first, third, and fifth grade class. Ida was sure that Dean had developed a crush on his schoolmate by the time the two had been able to share a see-saw on the playground. She could hardly blame him, just as she easily understood why Fallon had gravitated to Andi. What had always impressed Ida about Andi Sherman, was that the polite, thoughtful child had remained polite and thoughtful throughout her teenage years and into adulthood. Graceful was the word that Ida had chosen to describe Andi. If Fallon was sensitive, and Dean was confident; Andi was graceful, or perhaps it was *grace-filled*. Andi tended to see the best in others, if not always in herself. Ida had rarely heard Andi raise her voice even amid frustration and anger. She took time to think through her words before speaking and when she did, she spoke calmly and confidently. What impressed Ida the most, however, was Andi's humility. Sometimes, humility could border on the cusp of insecurity. And, while Ida was sure most people would doubt Andi possessed much self-doubt, Ida could see evidence of her friend's vulnerabilities clearly.

"What are you afraid of?" Ida asked.

"I'm not sure."

Ida was sure that Andi knew what held her back. Andi simply didn't want to examine what drove her fear. "I think you are."

"I don't want to hurt anyone," Andi said.

"What about yourself?" Ida asked.

"I'm all right."

"You're afraid that you aren't enough for Billie."

The truth in Ida's statement pierced Andi's heart like an arrow; sharp and precise, it cut through her. "Maybe I am."

"That's not for you to decide."

"I don't think I can handle losing anyone else right now."

"Well, sometimes the fastest way to lose someone is to decide not to let them in."

"I wish I knew what the answer was."

"You know," Ida said. "You wouldn't have called me if you didn't. What would you tell the boys? What would you tell Riley, or Fallon for that matter?"

"It's not the same."

"It is," Ida disagreed.

"Do you take your own advice?" Andi asked lightly.

"I have to. Who else's can I take?"

"Gave up on Dr. Phil. Huh?"

"Dr. Pill, you mean. Everybody's an expert when they're in front of a camera."

Andi laughed. Ida had no time for television talk shows or self-help gurus. Fallon had bought her mother a book once about healthy living. Andi remembered how Ida had rolled her eyes, walked out of the room to return with a package of Oreos. She flung them onto the coffee table, turned on one of her soap operas, and reclined in her leather chair. Healthy living, she told Fallon and Andi, was all about balance. Andi giggled at the memory.

"Mom, just give the book a try. The guy speaks all over the world. Seriously, he even has a show…"

"A show?" Ida picked up the book and shook her head. "Dr. Blackworth Logan? What the hell kind of name is Blackworth Logan? Did you read this?" She asked Fallon.

"I heard about it."

Ida opened the book and started flipping through pages.

"What are you looking for?" Fallon asked.

"The disclaimer."

"What disclaimer?"

"The one that says, I'm not really a doctor, I just tell you that to sell a book."

"What are you giggling about?" Ida asked.

"Nothing. I was remembering something."

"Oh? Well, do you want another piece of advice?"

"We both know you're going to offer it either way."

"True. Stop remembering and start living, Andi."

"Ida…"

"The past has passed — period. Billie's here now."

"And, David?"

"David has his path. Whatever is going on with that boy, you'll have to trust he'll tell you when he's ready."

"And, in the meantime?"

"You live your life."

"Heard from Andi?" Carol asked Fallon.

"Not since she got to Florida," Fallon replied. "Owen made Riley call her the other day, though."

"He certainly is attached to his grandmas." Carol laughed. "Geez, Fallon, come to think of it; you could be his grandma."

Fallon glared at her friend.

"What? You could be."

"Stop talking."

Carol laughed harder. She looked up as Pete walked through the door. "You look like hell," Carol said. "You want a pitcher instead of a pint?"

"Might need one," he said.

"What's up?" Fallon asked.

"Didn't sleep much last night."

"Why are you here?" Fallon asked.

"Where am I supposed to be?" Pete bit.

Fallon's eyes darkened with concern.

"Sorry," Pete mumbled.

"Are you okay?" Fallon asked.

"Ask me after that pitcher."

Carol handed Pete a beer and followed Fallon into the kitchen. "What's up with him?" Carol asked.

"I'm not sure."

"But you have a guess," Carol said.

"Maybe."

"So?"

"I think he's feeling kind of lonely."

"Do you think he's pissed about Dale and Marge seeing each other?" Carol wondered.

"Not pissed. I think he feels like we all abandoned him."

Carol considered Fallon's observation. Things had changed in Whiskey Springs over the last year. Everyone suddenly seemed to be attached. Carol hadn't given it much thought, but Fallon's observation was spot-on. Evenings at Murphy's Law had been familiar for years. Carol and Fallon passed drinks over the bar to Pete and Dale. Andi would wander in and laugh at the pair's antics over a margarita. Ida would pop by and warn them all to stay out of trouble. Charlie would play sappy love songs on the jukebox in the hope that Carol might notice him. Eventually, she did. "I miss those days."

"What days?" Fallon asked.

"You know, when we were all here betting on which co-ed would take you home."

"Ha-ha."

"You know what I mean," Carol said.

"I guess I do. Do you really; miss it, I mean?"

"Sometimes," Carol confessed. "It's not like I think about it. I love Charlie, and I'm happy for you. Hell, I'm happy for Marge and Dale."

"Me too."

"But sometimes, if I'm honest, I miss the way it was a little. You don't?"

"I don't know. I miss seeing everyone, I guess. I wouldn't want to go back, though."

"Me neither. Weird, huh?"

"What's that?" Fallon wondered.

"All of us married."

"I'm not married."

"Might as well be."

Fallon rolled her eyes.

"Oh, come on, Fallon. You and Riley are more married than half the couples in this town."

"If you say so. I'm going to go check on Pete."

Carol watched Fallon's figure as it retreated back to the pub. *Now, what is that about?*

❦

Andi picked at the pasta on her plate; more accurately, she pushed it from side to side.

"Not hungry?" Jake asked.

Andi looked up, took a deep breath, and forced herself to smile.

Jake looked across the table at Dave. "Did you tell your mother your news?"

Dave's eyes grew wide.

"What news?" Andi inquired.

"Dave has a girlfriend," Jake offered.

"That's terrific," Andi said.

Dave shrugged.

"Isn't it?" Andi asked.

"Figured everyone else in the family had one. I might as well join in," Dave said.

Andi's eyes closed in defeat. *When will he let this go?*

"David," Jake warned their son.

Andi let out a long breath. "I'm happy for you," she said honestly. She set down the fork in her hand and pushed out her chair. "If you'll excuse me, I think I've had enough for one evening."

"Mom," Jacob Jr. grabbed his mother's hand.

Andi squeezed the hand holding hers. "I have an early flight tomorrow," she said. "Thank you for dinner," she thanked her ex-husband.

"Andi, wait," Jake jogged to catch up with her.

"What the hell is your problem?" Jacob asked his younger brother.

"What? What did I do?" Dave asked.

"Quit being an asshole," Jacob said.

"I'm not the one who was sleeping around. All I said was the truth."

Jacob shook his head with disgust. He'd always been closer to his mother than his father. Dave had always enjoyed a bond with their father. For months, Jacob had avoided telling his brother about his sexuality. He'd only found the courage to tell his father a few weeks earlier. That conversation had gone as Andi has assured him it would. Jacob Sr. had accepted his son's news with a smile and open arms. For some reason, Dave seemed hell-bent on making life difficult for everyone. Jacob had reached his breaking point.

He was tired of hiding, and he was sick and tired of what he perceived as his younger brother's selfish and childish attitude.

"The truth?" Jacob asked.

"Yeah. Everyone has a girlfriend, so why not me?"

Jacob took a deep breath and pushed his chair back. He threw the napkin that had been on his lap onto the table and shook his head. "Not everyone," he replied. He made his way to his feet. "I guess you can stop calling me too," he told his brother. "Unless you want to meet my boyfriend."

Dave stared blankly at his older brother.

"I don't know what your issue with Mom and Dad is. I didn't want to tell you because, frankly, I didn't want to feel the way I know Mom does. But, you know what? I don't. This is on you," Jacob said. "No one deserves your shit. I hope you treat that girlfriend of yours better than you do your family." With one last shake of his head, Jacob walked away.

ᏆᏎ ᏁᏚ

"Andi—wait!" Jake caught up with his ex-wife.

Andi stopped and turned slowly.

"Andi..."

"I can't listen to it anymore, Jake."

"I understand. He doesn't mean it."

"I'm not so sure about that. I *am* sure that he doesn't have the right to treat either of us the way he is."

"I thought he'd be excited to tell you about this girl," Jake said.

Andi nodded sadly. "Seems he's not thrilled about anything where I'm concerned."

"It's not just you."

"But it's worse with me," Andi said bluntly.

"Are you okay?" Jake asked.

"I will be."

"I miss you," he said honestly.

"I miss you too, Jake."

"Really?"

"Yes, really. Maybe not quite the way you miss me, though."

"So, I guess inviting you back to my room is a bad idea."

"Unless you want to ply me with alcohol — probably."

"Will that work?" He teased.

Andi laughed. "Honestly?"

He nodded.

Andi's smile failed to reach her eyes. "I wish it would."

"Are you sure you're okay?"

Andi leaned in and kissed him on the cheek. Jake's arms surrounded her and pulled her close. "Jake…"

"I do miss you; you know?"

"And, I miss you."

"Not the way I miss you."

"No."

Jake studied Andi's expression. "Who is she? Is it? A she?"

Andi's smiled brightened.

"It is," he surmised.

"What about you? Our son seems to think we all have girlfriends." Andi tried to change the subject.

Jake shook off the question. "Not all of us. No one special here."

"I find that hard to believe."

"It's true. There are… Well," he hesitated.

"I think I can get the picture."

"There isn't anyone — not really," he told her. "I think it might be time I try the celibate life."

Andi howled. She shook her head affectionately, and then kissed Jake's lips sweetly. "Let me know how that works out for you."

"I want you to be happy," he said. "Dave will figure it out, Andi. He will."

"I hope so. I can't keep my life on hold hoping he does."

"She must be pretty special," he surmised.

Andi placed a final kiss on his cheek. "I love you, Jake."

"I love you too."

"Let me know how celibacy goes," Andi joked.

"You're enjoying this."

"Maybe a little," she admitted.

"Andi?" Jake called after her. "I do; you know? Love you."

Andi winked. "Don't do anything I wouldn't do," she said lightly.

"Or anyone?"

"Goodnight, Jake."

"Goodnight."

"Mommy?"

Riley turned. "Yes?"

"Where's Momma?"

"Momma's at work, sweetie."

Owen grumbled.

Riley knelt down to Owen's height. "Owen?"

"I need Momma."

"You need Momma?"

He nodded.

"Can I help you?"

Owen shook his head.

"No, huh?"

Owen frowned.

Riley found it difficult not to giggle at the look of consternation on Owen's face. Lately, he had divided his *needs* between her and Fallon. She'd yet to determine his three-year-old methodology.

"I can call her?"

"You want to call Fallon?" Riley asked.

Owen stared at her.

"Sweetheart, I'm trying to understand."

"Momma," he corrected her.

Riley mentally slapped herself. It was hard keeping up with Owen's logic. There were still times when he called Fallon by her name. It left Riley uncertain how she should refer to Fallon. She watched as Owen lifted two fists to his eyes and rubbed vigorously. *Someone is tired.* One piece of the puzzle Riley had discerned was Owen's behavior when he was exhausted. Nights when Riley and Fallon were both home, Owen tended to make his way to bed giggling. On the occasions that Fallon was away at the pub, Owen's bedtime tantrums often left Riley wondering if she'd given birth to Damian. Her good-natured little boy morphed into a fit-throwing, hell-spawn. She took a gentle hold of his shoulders. "Sweetie, maybe we should get you ready for bed."

"No!"

"Owen," Riley gently cautioned the toddler.

"No! Momma!"

Do I call her? Riley was tempted to ask Fallon to come home. That would be a mistake, and she knew it. Giving into Owen would only encourage future outbursts. "Owen, Momma is at work. You know that."

Tears poured down Owen's cheeks. His body shook as he sobbed uncontrollably.

"Owen..."

Owen ran away toward his room.

"Shit."

❦

"Do you mind?" Fallon pointed to the barstool next to Pete's.

"You own it," Pete said.

"True."

Pete drank from the mug in his hand greedily.

"Bad day?" Fallon asked.

"Just a day."

"Yeah."

Pete turned his attention to Fallon. "You okay, Foster?"

"Yeah."

Pete laughed. "Let me buy you a beer."

"That'd be a change."

"You look like you could use one," Pete said.

"Thanks."

"Just sayin."

Carol caught the conversation and placed a frosty mug in front of Fallon. "He's not wrong. Maybe what you need is some liquid courage."

Fallon glared at her friend.

Carol held up her hands. "Hey, I'm only making a suggestion. You wouldn't be the first to get drunk and..."

Fallon's warning gaze stopped Carol's though in its tracks.

"Foster?" Pete asked. "Everything okay with you and Riley?"

"Why wouldn't it be?"

"Dunno. I ain't been on a date in a year. Just askin."

"Shit. I'm sorry," Fallon apologized. She took a swig from her beer mug. "Things are good," she said. "Really good."

"Good."

"Yep. It is — good," Fallon agreed.

Carol rolled her eyes. "Poets," she muttered.

"What?" Fallon asked.

"Nothing." Carol batted her eyelashes.

"That's what I thought." Fallon turned back to Pete. "Why don't you?"

"Huh?"

"Go on a date?" Fallon asked.

Pete shrugged. "With who?"

"I don't know. There's got to be someone you like."

"It's Whiskey Springs."

"So? Broaden your horizons," Fallon replied.

"Go to Jericho?" Pete laughed.

"Why don't you try that online thing?"

"What?"

"You know; online dating."

Pete considered Fallon's suggestion. "How do you meet someone on a screen?"

"I don't know," Fallon confessed. She'd tried once. Once had been enough for three lifetimes. That didn't mean that it couldn't work for Pete. "Couldn't hurt," Fallon offered.

"I don't know. Dale tried that once. He met her out at Esposito's."

"Really?"

"Yeah. She stalked him for like two months."

"Esposito's food isn't that good.

"Don't think it was the food she wanted again."

"No shit!" Fallon chuckled. *Dale, you dog.*

Pete held up his glass, touched it to Fallon's and took a long sip. "Then, he tried to set her up with me."

"Did you go out with her?"

"Nope. Don't like clingers," he answered.

"Clingers?"

"You know, hangers."

"Hangers."

"Jesus, Foster! You've had enough of 'em. Girls that won't let go."

"Oh."

"Guess you're done trying to shake 'em off, though," Pete said.

"Yeah, now I just worry she'll send me packing."

"Riley?"

Fallon nodded.

"You drunk?" Pete wondered.

"What?"

"Riley ain't goin' nowhere."

"I hope not."

"So? Put a ring on it," Pete suggested.

Fallon froze.

Pete fell over with hysterical laughter. "Aw, shit, Foster. You're all freaked out about gettin' hitched?"

"I'm not a trailer, Pete."

Pete kept laughing.

"Good thing," Carol interjected. "You and trailers have a complicated history." She wiggled a finger.

"That was a plow," Fallon said. "And, it was a freak accident."

"Oh, so that's what you're worried about?" Carol asked.

"What?" Fallon asked.

"You think marriage is a freak accident or something," Carol said. "And, it's going to cut you when you least expect it."

"No, I don't."

"Okay, so why are you so freaked out about asking Riley?" Carol challenged her friend.

"Holy shit! Foster, are you gonna pop the question?" Pete asked.

"Shhh," Fallon hushed her friends.

"Are you?" Pete whispered.

Despite all her misgivings, Fallon smiled.

"You gonna ask her on her birthday like Charlie did?" Pete wondered.

Carol gracefully shut down that notion. "That idea's been taken." She held up her ring finger.

Fallon smiled at Carol gratefully. Riley's birthday also happened to be her wedding anniversary. Fallon would never trample that memory. She sighed. "That's the problem."

"What's the problem?" Carol asked.

"When and how," Fallon said.

"That's why you're acting weird?" Pete asked.

"Weird is not new for her," Carol offered.

"Ha-ha," Fallon replied.

"Just ask her, Fallon," Carol suggested.

"I can't just ask her. You don't just ask that question. It takes planning and stuff."

"Stuff?" Carol laughed. "What *stuff*?"

"Rings, for one thing."

"She's got you there," Pete said.

"Riley doesn't care about that *stuff*, as you put it," Carol said.

"All women care about that stuff," Pete said.

Fallon gloated, raised her mug and clicked it against Pete's.

Carol rolled her eyes. "No, they don't."

"Oh, come on," Fallon said. "You would've said yes to Charlie if he just walked up to you and said, *marry me*?"

"In a heartbeat. Well, maybe in two. I like to make him sweat a little."

Fallon was about to make a smart comment when she noticed Billie heading toward the bar. "Hey."

"Hey," Billie greeted her friends.

"Just get off work?" Fallon guessed.

"Nah. I got home around noon. Couldn't sleep."

Fallon nodded. Billie looked like a lost puppy. *Someone is missing Andi.*

"Hey, Pete." Billie took a seat beside Fallon at the bar.

"Billie. How's Andi?" Pete inquired.

Billie shrugged. "Don't know. I haven't talked to her in a couple of days."

Pete looked at Fallon. "Jesus, we're pathetic," he said. "Carol!"

Carol startled. "What?!"

"Next round's on me. Then it's Fallon's turn to buy."

"Oh, you mean Fallon will buy you more free alcohol?" Carol asked.

Pete shrugged.

"I'll get the next round," Billie said. All eyes turned to her. "What? I'm not cheap!"

Fallon burst out laughing. Billie rarely drank more than one pint. She frequently bought rounds and served as a taxi driver.

Carol poured the group a round. *It's going to be a long night.*

Nearly two hours—that's how long Riley had been trying to comfort Owen. She'd grabbed her phone several times to call Fallon. Each time she'd set it back down. Owen was inconsolable. Riley couldn't understand what had caused the emotional outburst. "Owen, sweetheart, it's okay."

"No."

"Sweetie, Momma will be home in a little while." A thousand times—Riley guessed she'd spoken the same words at least a thousand times in the last couple of hours.

Owen flung himself into Riley's arms.

"Owen..."

"They come, Mommy."

"Who comes?"

"The bad guys."

"Honey, there are no bad guys coming."

"Yes," he disagreed.

"Sweetie, what bad guys?"

"The ones that take you."

Riley desperately tried to make sense of Owen's words. "Did you have a bad dream?"

Owen shook his head. "They come."

"Who comes, Owen?"

Owen crawled into Riley's embrace. "They take you."

Riley rocked Owen in her arms. "No one is taking anyone."

"Gigi says so."

"Oh, Owen." Gigi was a little girl in Owen's playgroup. Perhaps Gigi had shared a bad dream. "What did Gigi say?"

"They got her gwama—in the dark."

"Owen, no, honey. Gigi's grandma went to heaven."

Owen shook his head. "Gigi..."

"Listen, sweetheart, no one is going to take Fal—Momma. Okay? No one is coming to take any of us."

Owen held onto Riley tightly.

"How about you come sleep with me until Momma gets home?"

Owen nodded.

"Mommy?"

"Yes?"

"We call Gwama?"

Riley nodded. "We can try to call your grandmas."

Owen started to relax.

I just hope one of them answers.

⚜

Pete held up a finger, burped, and staggered to the bathroom.

"And, he wonders why he's single," Carol commented.

Fallon and Billie laughed raucously.

"What's up with you?" Fallon asked Billie when Carol stepped away.

"Nothing."

"Right. Missing Andi, huh?"

"We've been spending a lot of time together."

"Yeah, I noticed."

"We're just friends, Fallon."

"Uh-huh."

"We are."

"If you say so."

"Like Andi would ever give me a second thought," Billie said.

"What the hell are you talking about?"

"Never mind."

"No, I do mind."

"I'm not making a play for Andi."

"Maybe you should," Fallon suggested.

"Are you drunk?"

"I'm not drunk. Okay, maybe I am—a little, but that doesn't mean I'm wrong."

Fallon needed to tread carefully. She'd never seen Billie in love. There was no doubt that Billie Steele was head over heels in love with Andi Maguire. That was an affliction Fallon easily understood. Fallon feared Billie could not see Andi's vulnerability through the rose-colored glasses of love. Andi had fallen for Billie—hard. Fallon recognized the glassy-eyed gaze Andi would cast on Billie in the distance. She'd noted the hitch in Andi's breathing when Billie laughed. Andi worked to avoid her feelings. Fallon knew that too. And, she knew the reason—fear. Andi exuded confidence in most situations. That self-assuredness had always made Andi alluring to Fallon. Falling in love carried risk. When it came to love, Andi's confidence had been tested. Fallon couldn't help but feel partially responsible for her friend's apprehension. No matter how many times Andi reassured her, no matter how many conversations Fallon shared with her best friend, Fallon battled guilt. Andi had handled their parting as lovers with grace. The separation had left them both wounded. Fallon wondered if Andi realized that Fallon had struggled too. Fallon had Riley to guide her through it, first as her friend, and not long after, as her lover. Andi had made changes to her life that Fallon never envisioned. On top of it, Andi had faced rejection from her son. All of it added up to Andi's reluctance—a hesitancy to allow herself a chance at love. Billie faced the same challenge, albeit for different reasons.

"Billie," Fallon lowered her voice. "You need to tell Andi how you feel."

"I take it back. You're not drunk; you're insane."

"You love her. I get it."

"Yeah, I know you do."

"Come on, Andi's my best friend. We've moved passed that."

"Yeah, I know that too."

"Why can't you just be honest with her?"

"She's out of my league, Fallon."

"I didn't know we were playing baseball."

"You know what I mean. She thinks I'm funny."

"You are funny."

"Great."

"Andi finds funny attractive, Billie."

Billie chortled.

"I'm serious," Fallon said.

"Funny wears thin over time. Lots of women find me *funny*. Beautiful? That's a different story."

I'd like to beat the shit out of the people who made you feel this way. "Don't underestimate Andi."

"I'm not."

"Don't underestimate yourself then."

"Are we drinking or not?" Billie asked.

Billie was already buzzed. The few times Fallon had seen Billie slightly inebriated, Billie cracked jokes. Tonight, alcohol played a different role. It was time to change the subject. Billie was sore. Billie was scared. Fallon related to the latter.

"I'm sorry," Billie said. "I just don't want to lose her friendship. I don't want to jinx what we have now. I'm not you, Fallon. I'm no good at the romance thing. I end up looking like a gorilla on roller skates and sounding like a tone-deaf opera singer."

Fallon sniggered. Billie always made her laugh. She wished Billie wouldn't find such humor at her own expense. Why did people think Fallon was, "good at romance?" That was laughable. She tripped over herself a million times trying to express her feelings. Jinxing things? That was a notion Fallon related to. Riley and Owen had become Fallon's world. She would do anything to protect them and keep them close — anything. "Well," Fallon began. "You know what they say, Billie."

"What's that?"

"Beauty is in the eye of the beholder."

"Yeah? I've always lived by Joan River's theory."

"What's that?" Fallon wondered.

"The best birth control is to leave the lights on."

Fallon erupted in laughter. "You're a lesbian. You don't need birth control."

"Call it abstinence education, Fallon. I grew up with Republican parents. It's my redemption."

Fallon's laugh dwindled to a dull roar. *And, this is one of the reasons we all love you, Billie. I wish you could see that.*

❦

A sudden burst of light roused Andi from her sleep. She stretched to reach the phone. "Hello?"

"I'm sorry," Riley's voice came over the line.

"Riley?"

"Yeah."

"What's wrong?"

"Owen wanted to call you."

Andi looked at the time. *Midnight? Uh-oh.* "He's still awake?""

"Yeah."

"Put him on," Andi said.

"Gwandma?"

"Now, what are you doing still awake?" Andi asked playfully.

"You awake too."

Andi chuckled. *I am now.* "Did you have a bad dream?"

"You come home?" Owen requested.

"I'll be home tomorrow."

"You sleepy?" He asked.

"I am sleepy. Aren't you sleepy?"

"Gwandma?"

"Yes, Owen?"

"You come home, okay?"

"I'll be home before you know it, honey. I promise. You get some sleep and I will see you later today. How does that sound?"

"Okay." Owen handed the phone to Riley.

"Owen," Riley addressed her son. "I'm going to get a glass of water and talk to Grandma Andi for a minute; okay? You snuggle under the covers. I'll be right back."

"Mommy? Lights?"

"I'll leave a light on."

"Riley? What's going on?" Andi asked.

"I don't know." Riley sounded defeated. "Owen seems to think that when the lights go out, something is going to take the people he loves away. He made me call Ida too. And, he won't go to sleep without Fallon."

"Call her."

"I know; maybe I should. If I do, then he'll think…"

"Call her, Riley."

"You don't sound surprised by this."

"I'm not," Andi said. "Dave went through the same thing when he was about Owen's age. He'd crawl into bed with me every night when Jake was away. It lasted for almost four months. I had to call Jake in the middle of the night more times than I cared to count. It's how I found out… Well, let's just say I couldn't deny what Jake was up to after that."

"Oh, God. You're kidding?"

"I wish I were."

"It seems like it all started when he asked to call Fallon, Momma."

"Makes sense," Andi said. "Try not to worry, Riley. It's a phase."

"One of the little girls at playgroup told him bad people come at night," Riley explained.

"Bad things can happen anytime. But, you know, you can't see in the dark. It's a reminder that you don't always know what's coming. I think that's why kids often are afraid of it. It's their first basic understanding that there is an unknown."

Riley found herself letting out a relieved breath. "I'm glad you're coming home tomorrow."

"Why? Did Ida suddenly raise her babysitting fee from free?"

"No." Riley laughed. "We all miss you."

"I'm glad someone does."

"Oh no, things didn't go well with Dave, I take it?"

"The same," Andi replied. "I'll be glad to get home."

"Missing someone?"

"Maybe."

"Maybe you should give that someone a call."

"It's after midnight, Riley."

"Yeah, well, I have it on good authority she's up."

"What do you mean, you have it on good authority?"

"Carol texted me about an hour ago. Seems Fallon and Billie are keeping Pete company at the bar."

"You're kidding."

"Nope. I'll bet she's still there. Andi, you don't have to come here tomorrow."

"I'll see you sometime before the coach turns to a pumpkin."

Riley laughed. "Okay, Cinderella. Call her."

"Call Fallon, Riley."

"I will if you will."

Andi snorted. *So much for adulting.* "I'll see you tomorrow, Riley."

"Andi? Thanks."

"Anytime."

CHAPTER FIVE

*B*illie tripped on a divot in the sidewalk and collided with Andi. "Sorry."

Andi grinned. Billie was adorable. "New feet?" She teased gently.

"I probably could use a pair."

Andi's spirited laugh took Billie by surprise. She wrapped her arm around Billie's as they continued to stroll. "Thanks for making me go out," Andi said.

"I'm glad that you had time. I know you've had a lot to deal with lately."

Andi silently admonished herself. She liked Billie. She liked Billie more than she wanted to like the woman, and more than she was comfortably admitting aloud. Everything about Billie was refreshing. Andi stole a glance at her companion and her stomach immediately twisted into a knot. *Oh, God. I should run from this...*

"Hey... Are you okay?" Billie asked, not certain what to make of the expression on Andi's face.

"Just tired; I think," Andi tried to recover.

"Do you want me to take you home?"

Andi's mouth went dry. She was fairly sure that was because all the moisture in her body had traveled in a different direction. *Oh, my God.* She did want Billie to take her home. And, she wanted Billie to stay.

"Andi?"

"Not yet," Andi said. "Let's walk down by the pond like we planned."

"You know, it's okay if you're tired and you want to go home and relax. I won't be upset."

Andi stopped cold. She looked at Billie and took a deep breath. "Billie..."

"What? What is it?"

"I... Look, I..."

Shit. "Andi, I'm sorry."

"What? For what?"

"If it seems like I'm pushing or something. I guess it's pretty obvious how much I like you. I'm not Fallon. I'm not exactly all that terrific at..."

Andi pressed two fingers to Billie's lips. "Stop. I don't want you to be Fallon. You need to let that go." She felt Billie's trembling and wondered if Billie could sense hers. With a shaky breath, Andi spoke her truth. "I missed you last week."

Billie was stunned.

Andi blushed. "I did. I'm realizing just how much I missed you. I don't know if I'm quite ready for what that means. That's not about you or about Fallon. That's about me."

Billie nodded. "I don't expect anything, Andi—I'm happy with our friendship."

"Are you?"

"Yes," Billie answered honestly. "That doesn't mean I wouldn't like this to be something more. I would never..."

"Make a move?" Andi chuckled. *You are fucking adorable, Billie.* She leaned in and pressed her lips to Billie's cheek. "Let's take that walk," she whispered.

Billie swallowed hard and nodded.

Andi tightened her hold on Billie's arm, thinking how good it felt to be close to someone—no, not someone—to Billie. Her heart skipped erratically. Their friendship had been growing for several months. She'd taken to calling Billie nightly unless Billie called her first. Friends—they were friends, that's what she'd told herself. Hell, that's what she told everyone. Falling in love with anyone was not anywhere in Andi's plan, at least, not for a long, long time. *So much for that.* Andi suppressed a chuckle as the pond came into view. She was content to walk in companionable silence until they reached one of the benches poised at the edge of the water. She took a seat beside Billie, still unsure of what to say.

"Andi?" Billie asked.

"Hum?"

"Are we okay?"

Andi forced herself to take a nervous breath before turning to look at the woman beside her. *Am I actually going to say this here? Am I actually going to say this at all?* One more breath. "I don't know. I hope so."

"I meant what I said — about our friendship."

"I know you did," Andi replied. "The thing is, I don't think I want you to be my *friend*."

"I..."

"Billie," Andi hesitated. She closed her eyes and sighed. "I didn't expect to feel this way."

Billie's gaze narrowed in confusion.

"I'm falling for you," Andi said. She grinned when Billie's mouth fell agape. "Why does that surprise you?"

"Andi, you are probably — no, forget I said that — you *are* the most beautiful woman I've ever known. It's a little intimidating, to be honest."

Andi was flattered but also sad at what she perceived to be Billie's insecurity. She smiled. "Apparently, you don't see you."

Billie blushed furiously and shook her head. She'd never considered herself ugly. She'd also never considered herself particularly attractive. She worked long hours and often didn't take care of herself as well as she should. Late night meals and lazy days away from the hospital had conspired to add a few extra pounds to her physique. She knew she shouldn't, but she found herself comparing her looks, her body — her life to Fallon's. She'd meant what she said. As far as Billie was concerned, Andi was the most beautiful woman on earth. Of course, being in love with someone colored your vision. She knew that. And, she did love Andi. Billie knew that Andi had loved Fallon — been *in* love with Fallon. Fallon had always been confident with women, bordering on cocky at times. Billie had enjoyed the company of women. She'd even had a relationship for two years. The complimentary words she recalled from women always focused on how funny Billie was, how sweet, or how intelligent she seemed. Seldom had Billie been called beautiful, and she couldn't recall anyone referring to her as sexy. Andi and Fallon, on the other hand, turned heads wherever they went. Andi had been married to a handsome, successful doctor, and she'd had a love affair with a woman most regarded as sexy and alluring. Billie wondered how she could possibly measure up.

"What are you thinking?" Andi asked.

"Truthfully?"

Andi nodded.

"Can I wait to figure that out until my heart slows down a little?" Billie requested.

If Andi had possessed any doubt that she was falling in love, Billie's simple request banished it. A soft, hopeful smile curled her lips. She took Billie's hand and held it tenderly. "There's nothing intimidating about me," she said. "Billie, I don't know what to say. There's so much I'm just beginning to realize. I do know this much; I want to be more than the friend you have a beer with at the pub or take to a movie. And, the truth is that scares the hell out of me."

"Why?"

"Because falling for anyone was not in my plans. And, now?" Andi sighed. "I don't want what's between us to be an affair…"

"It won't be."

The confidence in Billie's declaration took Andi by surprise.

"I don't want to sleep with you. I mean, I don't *only* want to sleep with you. Oh, for Christ's sake! I can't even…"

"Shut up," Andi said.

Billie's eyes flew open.

"And just kiss me already," Andi requested.

Billie's body quivered as she moved closer to Andi. She wasn't falling. She had fallen. Andi made her laugh more than any person she'd ever known. Andi listened without judgment. For years, Billie had watched Andi at a distance. She imagined many people did. Maybe she was bias; love did that. She was confident many people shared the view that Andi Maguire was one of the most attractive women they'd ever seen. She was. Andi was striking. She was poised. She was sexy as hell. Simply put, Andi Maguire was the type of woman who conjured teenage fantasies—or lesbian fantasies, or...

"Billie?"

"Huh?"

Andi shook her head affectionately. She lifted her hands to Billie's face and guided Billie's lips to hers. A breath apart, she whispered. "Just kiss me."

Billie's eyes closed, colors swirling behind her eyelids when Andi's lips parted, inviting her to explore. She accepted gratefully, her tongue faintly brushing against Andi's. She heard a whimper. Billie couldn't be certain if it was hers or Andi's. It didn't matter. Nothing mattered. Andi's fingertips caressed Billie's cheeks as the kiss deepened. It remained tentative, but Billie sensed both passion and emotion lying in wait. Touch often spoke more volumes than the words that lined the shelves of great libraries. Words could sometimes cloud emotion, even diminish it. Words mattered; sometimes, there were no adequate words. For Billie, this was one of those moments. Andi wasn't ready to hear the truth. Billie would tell her silently. Her hands reached for Andi's.

Andi never wanted Billie to let go. It would be so easy to pull Billie closer, to whisper in her ear, "take me home." Andi was tempted to do just that. If a simple kiss could make her body hum and her heart race, she couldn't begin to imagine what Billie pressed against her would feel like. *Oh, God.* Andi forced herself to pull back. She steadied her breathing and let her head fall onto Billie's shoulder.

"In case you didn't know," Billie said. "I'm crazy about you."

Andi grinned. "I know the feeling." She savored a deep breath of the evening air and closed her eyes.

"If you want to go..."

"No," Andi said. "Let's stay a while."

Billie chuckled.

"What?"

"Nothing."

"You were hoping I'd ask you to take me home," Andi guessed.

"No, Andi… I…"

Andi laughed. "I do want you to take me home. That's why I think we need to sit here for a while." She felt Billie nod. "I don't have any intention of rushing this," Andi explained.

"Whatever *this* is?"

Andi tightened her hold on Billie's arm. *We both know what this is.* "I'm not going to lose you," Andi whispered.

Billie felt Andi's words lodge in her chest. "No, you won't," she promised.

Andi closed her eyes again. *I hope not. I don't know if my heart could take it.*

⁂

"I'd tell you that I don't want to know, but I do want to know. Get in here." Riley led Andi into the living room.

"Hello to you too."

Riley laughed.

"Where's the family?" Andi wondered.

Andi's question warmed Riley's heart. "Fallon took Owen down to the pond for a walk before she has to head to the pub."

"I'm sure she's heartbroken."

"Devastated. So? You sounded like you needed to talk. Coffee or wine?" Riley asked.

Andi snickered. "If I start with wine, I may not stop."

"Do you have anywhere you need to be?"

"No."

"You sound a little disappointed about that," Riley observed. "That wouldn't have anything to do with a certain nurse we both know; would it?"

"Can we get the wine?" Andi asked.

"So, it is about Billie."

Andi smiled.

"You're in love with her," Riley said.

Andi's eyes closed in resignation.

"Is that a bad thing?"

"No. I don't know. I don't know how it happened."

Riley chuckled and grabbed Andi's hand. "This is definitely a kitchen conversation — with wine."

Andi followed and claimed a seat at the kitchen table. "How did you know?"

"Seriously? I love you, but you are as bad as Fallon sometimes. You talk about Billie incessantly. The minute she walks into the room, your eyes go to her. You do realize she's head over heels in love with you too?"

"I know," Andi said. She let her face fall into her hands and sighed.

Riley poured them each a glass of wine and sat across from her friend. "Andi, why do I get the feeling you're upset?"

"I'm not upset. I'm terrified."

"Why? Billie's great."

Billie was more than great; Billie was everything. "I don't know how to explain this."

"Being in love? Good luck."

"It's not being in love; it's being in love with Billie."

"Have you told her?" Riley wondered.

"No."

"Why not?"

"Because I want to take this slowly."

"You sound like me. Good luck with that too." Riley raised her glass before taking a sip.

Andi sipped her wine. "Fuck me."

Riley burst out in laughter. "I'm sorry. I'm not laughing *at* you. I don't know why you seem determined to fight this."

Andi released a nervous breath. "I don't want to be without her, Riley. I don't think I can explain how different that is for me."

"I'm listening."

"I've had two relationships in my life. Neither involved the kind of commitment that most people search for. I was alone in both if you think about it. Neither were about fidelity."

"I know," Riley softened her tone.

Riley knew something that no one else did about Andi Maguire, not even Fallon. It had taken a long time to draw the truth from her friend. Andi was reluctant to confide in Riley when it came to her time with Fallon. Riley pushed gently. Eventually, Andi confessed that she'd stopped sleeping with her husband several months before her relationship with Fallon had ended. She explained that she'd tried to be intimate with him and found herself thinking about Fallon. It was the reason Andi knew she had to end her marriage; the reason she had to find herself again. Andi had given herself to someone completely. She'd never had someone give themselves to her completely. Billie represented that hope, and that was terrifying.

"She loves you, Andi," Riley said. "Really loves you. Let her."

"You have no idea how much I want to."

"It's not the way it was when you and Fallon started…"

"I know," Andi admitted.

"Fallon would tell you the same thing, you know?"

Andi did know. Fallon remained her best friend. It had taken time for them to fall back into a comfortable relationship. Billie had helped in that regard as well. "Riley…"

"What is it?"

"You'll think this is crazy."

"I excel with crazy," Riley said. "I live with Fallon."

Andi laughed.

"Tell me," Riley urged gently.

"Last night, I didn't want her to leave. I don't mean for the night. I mean, I wanted her to stay."

Riley recalled that feeling. She'd fought her desire to live with Fallon tooth and nail. She'd told herself they needed time. Waking alone, trying to fall asleep without Fallon had been torture. She finally gave up. Another week or month or year wasn't going to change how she felt. She didn't want to waste any more time.

"You'll get there," Riley said.

"I've never felt this way, Riley—not even with Jake. He was always gone. When I think about it, I was as much his mistress as the others. His life was his work. It still is. And, Fallon? Well…"

"There's something else bothering you."

"Billie," Andi said with a shake of her head. "She thinks she can't compete with them."

"Did she say that?"

"In so many words—yes. Why would she think that, Riley? My God, she's the best person I know."

Riley licked her lips and considered a response. She'd developed a close friendship with Billie. Andi's observation was correct.

"Did she say something to you?" Andi asked.

"Not to me, no. Fallon filled me in. She might've gotten a little tipsy the last night you were in Florida. She was missing you—a lot."

Andi smiled. She'd talked to Billie at the pub that night just as Riley had instructed her to. A few slurred words had amused Andi. "I missed her."

"Yes, I know."

"What did she say?" Andi asked. "I'm not asking you to betray her confidence or Fallon's. Well, maybe I am. I just want to know what I did to make her feel that way."

"You? Andi, you didn't do anything to make her feel the way she does. It's like how you feel about her."

"What do you mean?"

"Well, you want her—all of her; right?"

Andi nodded.

"But the people you've been with in the past—those relationships make it hard for you to believe that anyone can be what you need, even Billie."

Andi sighed. That was true.

"It's the same for her in a way. She's expecting you to look at her the way other people have, just like you're expecting any relationship you have to fall into those old patterns. You just said that she's the best person you know."

"She is the best person I know," Andi said.

"Are you attracted to her?" Riley asked.

"Are you kidding?"

"I think that's what worries her."

"What? Why on earth would that worry her? Jesus, I had to go home and get reacquainted with Max last night, and all we did was kiss!"

Riley's raucous laughter filled the kitchen. Max was Andi's pet name for her vibrator, short for "Maximus Relieficus," a tidbit Andi had shared after a few too many margaritas.

"I don't understand," Andi confessed. "What is she worried about?"

"I don't think many people have made Billie feel beautiful," Riley offered.

Andi was stunned into silence. Not beautiful? Andi couldn't take her eyes off Billie. Billie's eyes, Billie's lips, Billie's hips… *Jesus, Andi, get hold of yourself.*

Riley smirked. A rosy tint had risen over Andi's skin.

"She's gorgeous," Andi said.

"You see her that way. I don't think *she* sees herself that way. I don't know all the details. I just get the feeling she hasn't been with people who made her feel attractive."

Andi took a moment to process Riley's words. Billie often made jokes at her own expense. "What *did* she say?"

"Something like people find her funny."

Andi groaned. "She is funny. I think I'm beginning to get the picture."

"I thought you might," Riley replied.

"It's crazy; isn't it? What we let people do to us. What we do to ourselves."

"It can be," Riley agreed.

Andi understood Billie better than Billie might have imagined. While Andi had never looked at herself as gorgeous, she'd dealt with cat calls and whistles plenty over the years. She'd often been told she was beautiful. She'd also experienced the assumption that she was somehow dim; the stereotypical, blonde wife of a successful, wealthy surgeon. She was a pocketbook, not a professor. It had always bothered her. Billie had said she found Andi's looks intimidating. Ironic. Andi found Billie's intelligence and her dedication to her profession intimidating. Billie could speak about nearly any subject. She worked harder than anyone Andi knew. Billie saved lives. Andi wasn't certain how to measure up to that. What had she accomplished in her life?

"Andi?" Riley was curious where her friend's thoughts had traveled.

"Sorry. I was thinking how funny it is."

"What's that?"

"Here I am wondering how someone so smart and witty, someone who spends her days saving people's lives can be attracted to me, and she's worrying about the same thing for completely different reasons."

"Love can be that way."

"You didn't worry about that with Fallon; did you?"

"I worried that I would be too much for Fallon—that we would be too much for her."

"You are exactly what she's always wanted, Riley— you and Owen."

"I know. Sometimes, it's still hard for me to believe it's real."

"I understand that."

"You are really in love," Riley commented.

Andi's body trembled. Hearing Riley say it with such confidence brought it home. "I've never been so scared in my life," she confessed. "Never."

"I understand. The only way to stop being afraid is to love her."

Andi nodded.

"So, what are you doing here?" Riley asked.

"I wish I could run and tell her," Andi said. "She's working until Thursday."

"You could call her."

"Not to say, *I love you,*" Andi replied.

"No, but you could let her know that without saying it."

"How?"

"Call her."

"And say what?"

"Whatever it is that comes out. Trust me." Riley patted Andi's hand. "I'm going to go switch the laundry."

"She has you trained," Andi teased.

"It's ridiculous, I know; the whole laundry challenge she has — it's one of the stupid reasons I love her so damn much." Riley winked and stepped out of the room. "Call her!" She yelled back.

Andi looked at her phone. *Call her, huh?*

❧

"How are you doing?" Billie asked the mother of a young patient.

"I hate waiting. I hate feeling helpless."

Billie offered the woman an understanding smile. "She's in good hands."

"Do you have any children?"

"No," Billie replied solemnly.

"Do you think..."

Billie reached out and squeezed the woman's hand. "I've learned not to project the worst and to always expect the best," she said. "Kids are resilient. Dr. Corrigan will get to the bottom of it. He's relentless. If it's her appendix, they'll deal with it. If it's something else, they'll figure it out."

"She's in so much pain."

"I know. Sometimes, being here makes that seem worse," Billie offered. "It's the nerves. She needs to be here. This place is unsettling for an adult. For a nine-year-old? There's a lot of commotion and different faces. Try to relax as much as you can. You tell someone if you don't see me and you need something. Sometimes, I get pulled in fifty directions."

"Billie?"

"Yes?"

"Thanks."

Billie winked and made her way to the corridor. There couldn't be anything worse than watching someone you love in pain. Billie thought that was often worse than being the patient. Feeling helpless sucked. She felt her phone buzz and lifted it without thinking. "Billie here."

"Does someone else normally answer your phone?" Andi asked.

Billie laughed. She carried a hospital issued phone in her right pocket and her personal cell phone in her left. "I'm so used to answering the hospital phone... Force of habit; sorry."

"Don't be. I know you're busy."

"It's not too crazy here tonight—for once. How are you?"

Andi repeated Billie's question silently. *How am I?*

"Andi? Everything okay?"

"Yeah. Sorry. I know you have to work until Thursday. I was wondering if you might consider coming over when you end your shift."

Billie leaned against the wall. "I get off at seven in the morning."

"I know."

"Andi, are you sure you're okay?"

"I didn't want you to go last night." *There it is – the truth.*

Billie's heart fluttered. "I didn't want to leave."

"So, come over. I don't care if you want to fall asleep. I don't want to talk while you're at work. I just... I need to tell you..."

"I'll be there," Billie promised.

Andi let out a sigh of relief.

"Andi?"

"Yeah?"

"I...." Billie's thought trailed off when a page sounded through the emergency room. "Shit. I'm sorry; I have to run."

"Go."

Billie spoke without thinking as she hung up the phone and headed into a flurry of activity. "I love you."

Andi's ear remained pressed to the phone after Billie had disconnected the call. "I love you too, Billie."

❦

"Hey, Mom. I didn't expect to see you here."

Ida slid onto a bar stool. "Unless you're looking for a babysitter, this is the only way I *get* to see you."

Fallon rolled her eyes. "Quit being dramatic."

"Who's dramatic? I'm honest."

Fallon moved to make her mother a margarita. "Is this your way of telling me you miss me?"

"I wouldn't miss you if you called."

"Okay." Fallon held up a hand in surrender. "I admit it, I've been kind of out of the loop."

"More like out of this world." Ida chuckled. "I half expected the next time I'd hear from you would be with a wedding invitation."

Fallon coughed a bit.

"Something in your throat?" Ida teased.

"Drink," Fallon directed her mother as she passed her the margarita.

"Fallon, why are you suddenly pale?"

"I'm not pale."

Ida was enjoying her game immensely. "You're white as a ghost."

"I'm not."

Ida sipped through her straw and raised an eyebrow.

"Okay," Fallon gave in. "Maybe I've thought about it a little."

"*It?*"

"You know, asking Riley."

"It shouldn't be difficult to ask her anything; she lives with you."

"You're enjoying this."

Ida grinned. "Maybe," she confessed.

"How did you know?"

"That you want to pop the question? Fallon, I raised you. You're an open book."

"Great."

"That's bad?" Ida asked.

"It is if Riley has figured it out."

Ida's laughter lifted her off the stool.

"Why is that funny?" Fallon asked.

"Well, she's going to have to know if you plan to ask her."

Fallon grumbled.

Ida kept chuckling. "What are you so afraid of?"

"I just want to make sure it's the right time; that's all."

"There's never a right time." Ida took a long sip through her straw.

"Would you go with me?"

"Go with you?" Ida was confused.

"To pick out a ring."

Ida decided against a wisecrack. "Whenever you want."

"I don't know when yet."

"Well, assuming you remember how to use your phone; you can call me."

"Ha-ha."

"How *is* Riley?" Ida asked.

"Spending the evening with Andi—and wine. I think they were a full bottle in when I left." She chuckled. "Good thing Owen had plans for a sleepover with Beth and Evan. Which I hope goes okay. He's been a little…"

"He'll be fine. A change of scenery helps sometimes. Dare I ask why Riley and Andi need wine? Billie?" Ida guessed.

Fallon smiled.

"Does it bother you?" Ida asked curiously.

"Andi and Billie? No. I just hope Andi gives herself a chance."

"She will."

"You seem confident," Fallon said.

"I know her."

"I think I know her pretty well."

"You do, but you don't know her objectively."

"Because we were lovers?" Fallon asked.

"Yes."

Fallon's dislike of her mother's candid reply was obvious. Andi was Fallon's best friend—*best* friend. She would always love Andi, and she would never regret her time with Andi as a lover. Why did everyone seem to think that needed to change Fallon's ability to be objective? Why did everyone seem to think there would be lingering jealousy?

"Say what you're thinking," Ida directed her daughter.

"Why do you think that just because Andi and I were lovers, I can't be objective? I'm not a kid, Mom. I want her to be happy."

"I never said you didn't want her to be happy. I know how close you two are. I know how much you will always love each other. You're delusional, Fallon, if you think that you can see things clearly where Andi is concerned. This isn't easy for her."

"What? Falling for Billie? She deserves to be happy. Billie is crazy about her, and she can say whatever she wants; she's in love with Billie too."

"I don't doubt that either."

"What is it that you *do* doubt?" Fallon asked.

"It's not a matter of doubt. It's knowing Andi the way *I* know Andi."

"Like a mother."

"Yes," Ida replied.

"Go on."

"Andi's never had a stable relationship, Fallon. Stable financially? Yes. Stable emotionally? Not even a little bit."

Fallon felt as if all the air had been sucked from her lungs. She didn't enjoy examining the reality of her time with Andi. While she was grateful for that time, she also recognized that she'd been blind to what had developed between them. *Okay, maybe not blind.* She'd chosen to deny her feelings and Andi's. She couldn't regret that. All of it led to Riley being in her life. She also couldn't deny that Andi had fallen in love with her, and that had Riley not appeared, she would have had to face her feelings. Riley did appear, and that changed everything for all of them. She didn't want to consider that Andi's past relationships would cause her to hesitate pursuing something new with Billie.

"Do you think she's afraid to get involved with Billie?" Fallon asked.

Ida chewed on her straw for a second. "I think she needs more than she's ever had."

"Billie isn't one for affairs, Mom. I've known her for years. She doesn't play around; that much I can tell you."

"I'm sure that's true. You might not realize how scary this is for Andi. I don't think she expected to *want* a relationship with anyone for a very long time."

"Why not?'

Ida sighed and raised her brow.

"Because of me?"

"Not because *of* you. Because she loved you, Fallon. You do know that?"

Fallon nodded.

"It hurt her — walking away from you, having to walk away from Jake. You walked straight into Riley's arms. She had to watch — alone."

Fallon rubbed her brow. "I love her."

"I know, not the same way. She's loved twice, Fallon. Neither person could give her what she needed — not really. Billie *is* different. Andi knows how to handle infidelity. She knows how to handle someone who desires her…"

"I didn't just use Andi for sex, Mom."

"I know that," Ida said. "That doesn't change things."

"Billie's good for her." Fallon sighed.

"What?" Ida asked.

"Billie's also terrified of Andi."

"Terrified of Andi? Andi's sweet."

"It's not her sweetness that scares Billie," Fallon explained.

"Oh..."

"Yeah. She's got some insane idea that Andi could never be attracted to her."

"She said that?"

"Yep."

"I need another margarita," Ida said.

"Are you driving?"

"You can drive me," Ida said.

"One more, Mom."

"One more? Fallon, I can hold my liquor."

"Yes, you can. But I'm closing tonight, and I'm pretty sure Andi will be on our couch when I get home."

"What does that have to do with my margaritas?"

"Margarita," Fallon corrected her mother. "As in one. And, it means that I can't call Riley or Andi to drive you home."

Ida shrugged. "Make my drink, Fallon."

Fallon complied.

"And, tell me what this nonsense is about Billie. I'm going to have to sit that girl down too."

Fallon laughed. Ida took her appointed role as the town matriarch a bit too seriously at times. She meant well. Fallon wasn't sure why Ida thought she could impart wisdom to the masses. Had her life taken a different turn, Fallon was confident her mother would've ended up the president or maybe the leader of some small African tribe. She snickered.

"I don't know what's funny. Now, what is this nonsense about Billie being afraid of Andi?"

Fallon set her mother's drink down. "I'm not sure I'd call it nonsense. Billie hasn't always been with the kindest people."

"Go on."

"I know Billie pretty well."

Ida was curious. "Were you lovers?"

"No. We... Well..."

"Fallon?"

Fallon sighed. She and Billie had been close friends for most of Fallon's life. "Mom..."

"Fallon, what?"

"You can't tell anyone this. I mean it, not anyone."

"From your lips to God's ears."

"Mom..."

"I can keep a secret, Fallon."

"I know you can. It's just..." Fallon was tempted to join her mother and have a drink. She hadn't recounted the story to anyone except Riley—not a soul. She'd promised Billie that she would never share it with anyone. She also understood why Billie struggled with many things.

"Fallon." Ida's tone softened. Whatever Fallon wanted to share had clearly affected her daughter deeply. "Whatever it is, it can't be that awful."

"It is." Fallon sighed. "Jared... Mom, he..."

"Billie's brother?"

Fallon nodded. "We were fourteen."

"Go on."

"I guess he saw us kissing," Fallon explained. "We were kids, Mom. We were just kids. I'm not sure either of us knew what it meant."

Ida's skin erupted in tiny goosebumps. What hadn't Fallon told her?

"He..."

"Did he hurt Billie?"

Fallon nodded.

Ida fought to breathe. She'd known the Steele family her entire life. Billie's father, Jud Steele had attended school with Ida just as Billie had with Fallon. Ida remembered him as quiet. Vera Steele was a close friend of Dora Bath's, and a member of what Fallon called the Biddy Brigade. She was afraid to ask what might have happened as a result of Billie's older brother witnessing their innocent kiss.

Fallon's eyes welled with tears. She continued to carry guilt over the innocent episode that she and Billie had shared many years ago. Billie was her friend. They had been curious kids. The word lesbian hadn't even been introduced into their vocabulary. If she hadn't kissed Billie that day...

"Fallon?"

Fallon shook her head. She looked around the bar to ensure no one was close enough to hear. "Jared told Billie that he'd take care of it."

Ida's face drained of all color.

"He... Mom, he... He raped Billie."

Ida was sure she was going to throw up. Jared Steele was three years older than Billie and Fallon. He'd joined the Army after high school and had never returned to Whiskey Springs for more than a holiday visit. "Dear God..."

"It gets worse."

Ida braced herself.

"Billie told her mom. She... She blamed Billie."

Ida's eyes closed. "What the hell is wrong with people?"

"I don't know."

"Is that why Billie has never come out?" Ida asked.

"To the town? Yeah, I think so. It's also why she ends up with assholes."

"Explain."

"After everything happened, Jared told her that ugly girls sleep with other girls because no man would ever want them."

Ida's hand balled into a fist. "God damned..."

Fallon let out an uncomfortable chuckle thinking it was a good thing for Jared Steele that he lived far, far away from Whiskey Springs. It was probably a good thing for Billie's parents that they spent most of the year in Florida.

"I can't imagine how Billie dealt with that." Ida mused.

"She believed it for a long time. I think some part of her still thinks that, Mom—not about lesbians, but about her—that she's ugly. And, believe me, a few of the people she's dated didn't help in that department."

"Can I ask you something?"

"Sure."

"You're much closer to Billie than you two let on," Ida surmised.

Fallon smiled.

"But you've never…"

"No. Billie never felt like she could be herself. Being with me in public too much… I think it harkened back to that time when we were kids. I think that's all changing now."

"Because of Andi."

"Yeah."

"How do you feel about that?" Ida wanted to know.

"I think Billie is good for Andi."

"Do you think Andi is good for Billie?"

"I do. I just hope Billie's fears don't get in the way. She's had a crush on Andi forever."

"Sounds like you two had more than one thing in common."

Fallon laughed. "Fair. She still thinks Andi is out of her league."

"And, you're worried about how Andi will handle that?"

"Andi doesn't see herself like most people see her."

"No, she doesn't. She does know how people see her, though, Fallon. And, that hasn't always been easy for her. That old saying, 'don't judge a book by its cover?' Most people do it anyway. Have a little faith in Andi."

"I do."

"Mm. She might understand Billie better than you think she does. They'll figure it out."

"What did Andi tell you?" Fallon asked.

"Andi doesn't need to say a word to me. She's an open book."

"I just want her to be happy," Fallon commented.

"Which her?"

"Both of them."

※ ※

Fallon laughed at the sight that greeted her in the living room. Andi was on one end of the couch. Riley was at the opposite end, her feet resting on Andi's legs. "Guess they killed that bottle of wine." She moved to wake Riley when her phone buzzed. Fallon looked at the caller's name and sighed. She stepped into the kitchen to answer. "Beth?"

"Hey."

"Let me guess, Owen's up."

"He wanted me to call you."

"Put him on. Owen?"

"Momma, you come here?"

"Owen, I thought you wanted to stay with Auntie Beth?"

"I want you."

Fallon wasn't sure how to respond. Riley would likely try and calm Owen. Fallon's inclination was to hop back in her truck and go pick him up.

"Please, Momma?"

"Let me talk to Auntie Beth."

Beth came back on the line. "Hey."

"I don't know what to do."

"What does Riley think?"

Fallon sniggered. "I don't know. She's passed out on the sofa with Andi."

"Took full advantage of Owen's sleepover, huh? He can stay. I'll have him sleep with me."

"No." Fallon made her decision. "I'll come get him."

"Fallon, it's okay if you…"

"No, I'm not tired anyway. There's something about going from slightly buzzed to cold sober that wakes you up."

"I thought you were working?"

"I was. Long story."

"Are you okay to drive?" Beth asked. "Your mom's home. I can bring him…"

"I'm fine." Fallon hadn't had a drink in three hours.

"It's three in the morning, Fallon. He'll settle back down."

Yeah, but will I? "Maybe *he* will."

"Okay, I get it. Don't you think Riley will worry if she wakes up and you're not there?"

"I don't think anyone is waking up here anytime soon. I'll leave her a note. See you in a few minutes." Fallon started back toward the living room when her phone rang again.

"Stay home," Ida's voice instructed firmly.

"Mom?"

"Owen is fine."

"Mom, he…"

"Stay home, Fallon. I will bring him over in the morning."

"Mom…"

"I mean it. He needs to know that no one is going to disappear."

Fallon turned back to the kitchen and flopped into a chair. "He'll think I don't care."

"He knows you care. It's a phase that he needs to get through. Sometimes, you have to do things you don't want to do."

"Why is he so scared?" Fallon sounded despondent.

"Lots of change," Ida said. "That doesn't mean he feels insecure with you."

"That makes no sense."

"Sure, it does. He might be little; he's not stupid. Kids might not explain things the way we do. They do feel change. You did."

"Me?"

"When my father died, you went through an entire month where you would wander into our bedroom or Dean's. You'd want to call Grandma every night and every morning to make sure she was there. You were four."

"What did you do?"

"For the first week, I let you sleep wherever you landed. Then, I started putting you back in your bed. I let you call Grandma either before bed or in the morning. One day, you stopped asking. Your father heard your brother tell you that heaven wasn't real. They just put people in the ground." Ida groaned. "Who knows where he got that from? Probably watched some horror movie at a friend's house. I think he was scared, and he decided to share that with you."

"Good to know he was always thoughtful." Fallon made no attempt to disguise her sarcasm.

Ida sighed. She'd like to defend her son. She couldn't blame Fallon for feeling the way she did. "But Owen..."

"I think he might've heard Evan talking."

"Evan?" Fallon was confused.

"Mm. Evan and Emily were on the phone a couple of weeks ago when he was here."

"And?"

"Oh, I don't know, Fallon. They're both angry at Dean. Everyone leaves. I think that's the gist of it."

"Shit. Mom, I can come and..."

"No. Trust me on this one. We'll bring him over in the morning."

"He'll hate me."

"He'll never hate you. Being Mom isn't easy, huh?"

"No."

"I'd tell you that you'll get used to it, but that'd be a lie."

"I just don't want to screw it up."

"You will."

"Gee, thanks for the vote of confidence, Mom."

"We all do," Ida replied. "Go and get some sleep."

"I'm not tired."

"You will be."

"Yeah. I can come get him in the morning."

"No, I think Beth wants to talk to you and Riley anyway."

"To me and Riley? Why? Mom..."

"Relax. It's nothing earth-shattering. We can all have breakfast."

"I'm not going to win this, am I?"

"Nope."

Fallon grumbled.

"I'll see you in a few hours."

"Call me if he…"

"Goodnight, Fallon."

Fallon huffed. *I hate this.*

CHAPTER SIX

"**S**top pacing." Andi said.

"I'm not pacing," Fallon said.

"Oh, is this some new dance I've yet to learn?"

"I just wish she'd get here."

"You're going to wear a hole in the floor," Andi commented.

Riley walked into the kitchen and shook her head. "She's right."

"How can you be so calm?" Fallon asked her lover.

"Babe, Owen is okay."

"He's going to hate me, Riley."

"More than once," Andi agreed lightheartedly. "And, then he'll get over it."

Fallon hadn't slept all night. Aside from her concerns about Owen, she was curious what her sister-in-law wanted to talk about. Her head was pounding. Four cups of coffee, and Fallon still wasn't sure how she would survive the morning.

"Sit down," Riley told Fallon.

"You're really not worried?" Fallon asked.

"I'm concerned," Riley admitted. "But I trust the experts."

Andi laughed. "If you're referring to Ida and me, you might want to rethink that designation."

"Don't you start," Riley warned Andi. "Dave will figure it all out. You said it yourself, *he'll get over it.*"

"I hope so," Andi replied.

"Riley's right," Fallon offered.

"Oh?" Andi smirked.

"I see what you two just did," Fallon said.

"Relax," Riley said again.

"What do you think Beth wants to talk about?" Fallon asked.

"Who knows?" Riley replied. "Whatever it is, I'm sure it's not the end of the world as we know it."

"Let's hope."

⸎

"What do you mean you want to move?" Olivia asked.

"What don't you understand about that concept?" Barb shot back.

"I suppose, I think if you are willing to uproot our children, you might consider moving with me."

"Why would I do that, Liv?"

"Why wouldn't you? Europe offers opportunities for them."

"And, Vermont doesn't?"

"Not the same opportunities."

Sometimes, in fact, most times there was no reasoning with Olivia once she'd set her mind to something. Playing emotional tug-o-war with Olivia was nothing new. For the first time in their relationship, Barb recognized the game for what it was — Tug-o-war. Struggling with an emotional push-pull between adults was frustrating and painful. Barb was astounded that Olivia would involve their children. Emily and Summer had made it clear what they wanted. The girls' wish was to be closer to their family — to Fallon, Beth, and Ida. They needed stability and security. The opportunity to provide that existed in Whiskey Springs. "You mean not the opportunities *you* think matter," Barb surmised.

"Exposure to different cultures, first-rate education, the chance to travel — what do you find offensive about those *opportunities* for the girls?" Olivia challenged.

Barb wondered how she could reach Olivia. Had she ever connected with the woman sitting across from her? All the years they'd spent together raising their children, growing their careers—how was it that Barb suddenly felt she was looking at a stranger? Had she missed something? Perhaps, she'd chosen to ignore the signs of their relationship's doom. Did it matter? Barb's eyes searched Olivia's for something—any clue to indicate where they'd made a wrong turn. God help her, she missed Olivia. She doubted that she would ever love another person the way she loved Olivia Nolan. Looking at the woman she'd shared her life with for nearly a decade, Barb wondered who was looking back at her. She'd always marveled at the reality that strangers became lovers. Now, she realized lovers could also become strangers. It was heartbreaking.

"It's not offensive," Barb replied. "Is it what they need now, Liv? It is what Emily and Summer *want* right now?"

"They're children. Raising them isn't about what they *want*. I thought we agreed on that point before Emily came into our lives. Wasn't it you that said we should provide them with every possible opportunity?"

"It was," Barb agreed.

"Then what is the problem?"

"Liv," Barb paused, sighed, and offered her former partner a strained smile. "This move you're making isn't about the girls. It isn't *for* the girls. It's for you."

"It could be for all of us."

"How could it be when you never considered how any of us feel about it?"

"It's Europe, Barbara. It's not as if I am asking to whisk you all away to some war-torn country."

"No, it isn't."

"Then what is the problem?"

"You didn't ask," Barb said.

"I just did! My God, *you* left me!"

"Olivia, you'd left me long before I moved to Richmond. I was an afterthought at best in your life. I still am."

"This is ridiculous. You sound like Fallon."

Barb nodded. "It all leads back there, doesn't it, Liv?"

"Excuse me?"

"To Fallon. It all leads back to the fact that she said no."

Olivia's temper flared. "This isn't about Fallon."

"No. It's about you." Barb held back her tears. *It always has been, hasn't it?* "You can't be still," she told Olivia.

"What does that mean?"

"You're always looking for the next thing," Barb explained. "Somewhere to run. Someone to follow. That's not what the kids need, Olivia. They have their entire lives to explore the world. They're kids. They need structure. They need friends. They need the stabi..."

"Don't say stability."

Barb sighed.

"Stability isn't found in a place," Olivia said.

"No. It's found in the people that share a place," Barb said.

"I'm not a student in one of your classes."

"Do what you need to do, Liv."

"And, what will you do?"

"What the girls need me to."

⟞⟝

Fallon stared across the table at her sister-in-law.

"Fallon?"

"Barb wants to move to Whiskey Springs?" Fallon tried to process the information.

"The girls want to."

"I can't believe she'd do this," Fallon muttered.

Riley wanted to scream. Fallon's skin had gone ashen. It wasn't the idea of Barb relocating to Vermont that had shaken Fallon, it was the knowledge that Olivia would leave the girls behind for any reason she could control. Fallon had mourned the loss of her relationship with Olivia for years. It wasn't missing Olivia that presented her greatest demon. Riley knew that too. Until Riley's arrival in Whiskey Springs,

Fallon had believed that her chance at having children had passed her by with Olivia's exit. A short while ago, Fallon had been musing that she needed to spend more time with Owen. Perhaps she should take a week off? Maybe it would be best if she only worked afternoons until Owen felt more secure. Fallon would move heaven and earth for her family. Her family was an extended group of unlikely characters. Riley and Owen existed at its center. She didn't need Fallon to speak to know what thoughts passed through her lover's mind. What if Olivia had stayed longer? What if Emily and Summer had been their daughters? Would Olivia have made the same decision? Riley guessed that Olivia would. Olivia was a master at dressing up her decisions with flowery reasoning. From where Riley sat, Olivia Nolan resembled a used car salesman. Olivia could pitch her agenda to the staunchest resistance. She wondered what reason Olivia had given her wife for moving to Europe. It couldn't be discomfort with her minority status in Washington DC. That had been the argument Olivia waged to Fallon when she announced she would be accepting a job in the country's capital. Riley squeezed Fallon's hand.

"How are the girls?" Riley inquired.

Beth smiled gratefully. Riley possessed wisdom and grace far beyond her years. Her eyes fell to Riley's hand as it tenderly caressed Fallon's. She found herself thinking how grateful she was that Fallon found the younger woman, and that the family her sister-in-law would build would be with Riley Main, and *not* Olivia Nolan. Beth never trusted Olivia. Her lack of faith in her husband's best friend, and her irritation with the demands Olivia placed on Dean's time had created a deep rift in her marriage. She didn't share with Fallon nor with Barb her suspicion that Olivia Nolan's reassignment to Amsterdam was a deliberate ploy to be closer to Dean Foster. Who was she kidding? It wasn't a *suspicion*. She was sure of it. Her confidence in that assessment had brought her enough tears for them all. She would keep that observation to herself. At least, she would for now.

"The girls sounded all right," Beth said. "Actually, Emily sounded relieved to be with Barb. She went on and on about living here. To be honest, I think they all need the support; Barb most of all."

"I guess I don't understand why they don't just make the move," Fallon said.

"I think Barb wants to be certain that you and Riley are okay with that."

"Me and Riley? What do me and Riley have to do with it?" Fallon asked.

Riley grinned. She had yet to meet Barb. *I like her already.*

"Fallon, Barb knows how much Liv hurt you," Beth explained.

"Barb has spent lots of time here," Fallon pointed out.

"Yes. That was before you had a family. I don't think she wants the girls to intrude on that. You know how they are. They'll want your attention. You have a family now to consider."

"Emily and Summer are part of our family," Riley said flatly.

Beth wasn't surprised by Riley's statement. It did make her love the young woman even more.

"They are," Fallon agreed. "But Barb is right. Owen has to come first."

"Owen loves the girls," Riley said. "And, Owen also has to learn that we will all be here no matter who else comes along."

"I still can't believe Liv would take that job," Fallon said.

"Can't you?" Beth asked. "I'm sorry, Fallon."

Fallon groaned. "Don't be. I guess I'm the stupid one. I never thought she'd... Well, I never thought she'd put herself before the kids."

"Neither did Barb," Beth said.

"You don't sound surprised?" Fallon surmised.

"I wish I could say I am."

"Beth?" Fallon questioned.

"Oh, Fallon, my feelings toward Olivia are mine to deal with."

"You don't like her."

"Olivia is magnetic," Beth said honestly. "She's intelligent, funny, attractive, and she's engaging. Everyone sees that."

"Uh-huh."

"Everyone including Olivia," Beth said.

Riley sniggered. *That's the truth.*

"How do I explain this?" Beth said.

"Just say it," Fallon suggested.

"Olivia shines outwardly. Inwardly?" Beth took a deep breath. "I've laughed with Liv plenty over the years. It took me a long time to realize that while I was laughing *with* her; she was laughing *at* me."

"I don't think Liv…"

"It's true, Fallon. Everything with Liv is a competition—everything. It's a competition to be the center of attention. When she's no longer at the center—well, she finds someone who will put her there."

Riley's heart ached for Beth. Beth had kept Dean and Evan at the center of her attention. Dean had put Olivia at the center of his. Riley had never met Fallon's older brother. She didn't need to. The truth flashed in the glistening sadness of Beth's eyes. The center of Olivia's world was one person— Olivia. Riley understood.

"I'm not sure what I am supposed to do," Fallon confessed.

"Call Barb?" Beth suggested hopefully.

Fallon nodded. "She doesn't need my permission."

"No, but she does care about your feelings," Beth said. "And, yours," she told Riley.

"I appreciate that," Riley said. *More than you know.*

"I'll call her," Fallon promised. *I have no idea what I'm supposed to say, but I'll call her.*

❧

"Gwama?"

"Yes, Owen?" Andi replied.

"Does you have a Mommy?"

"I did have a Mommy."

Owen tipped his head.

"My Mommy is in heaven now," Andi explained.

"With Daddy?"

Andi smiled.

"Did you have a Daddy?"

"I did. He's up there too."

Owen frowned. "Gwama?"

Andi smiled more broadly.

"Can't you get anudder?"

"Another?"

"A Momma or a Daddy?" Owen asked innocently.

"Well, I sort of think of Grandma Ida as my Momma."

"She's Momma's."

"Yes, she is," Andi agreed. "But Momma doesn't mind sharing."

Owen concentrated intently for a moment. "Mommy has two."

"She does?"

Owen nodded. "Yep. Gram and you."

Andi's heart swelled. She pulled Owen onto her lap. "I do love your Mommy, Owen."

"Gwama?"

Andi chuckled. Owen was full of questions. "Yes, sweetheart?"

"Can Momma get one?"

Andi was confused. "Can Momma get one?" She repeated his question.

"Like me," he explained.

"Oh," Andi caught on. "You mean can your Momma have a baby?"

"Like me!"

Andi kissed Owen on the head. "What made you ask that?"

Owen grinned. "Evan gots two. Momma has one. She told me. Mommy too."

"Ahh... That's true."

"Can I?"

"Someday, I think you might," Andi said.

Owen huffed.

"Owen?"

"Evan's left."

Andi was beginning to see Owen's picture. "You mean that Emily and Summer left?"

"Yep. Evan's daddy left."

Andi sighed inwardly. "Not forever," she told him.

Owen frowned.

"Sometimes, people do go away, Owen. That doesn't mean that they don't love you."

"Like Daddy."

"Yes. And, like Evan's daddy too."

"Gwama?"

"Hum?"

"I can keep you?"

"Oh, sweetheart, you get to keep all of us."

"You left."

"I did leave for a little bit to visit my sons. I came back."

"Gwama?"

It took every ounce of restraint Andi possessed not to laugh.

"You get one?"

"Me? What should I get?"

"Me!" Owen giggled. "Like me!"

A roar of laughter erupted from Andi. "Oh, Owen." She held him close. "If your Momma and your Mommy have a baby someday, then yes; I will get another one, but there will never be another you, sweetheart. You will always be my one and only Owen."

"No, you get one!"

Andi laughed harder. "A baby?"

"Yep!"

"I don't think so," Andi said, still chuckling.

"You!" Owen shook with laughter.

Andi tickled the toddler in her lap. "You are silly."

"You silly, Gwama!"

"Maybe I am, Owen."

Owen cuddled up against Andi on the sofa. Andi stroked the soft curls on his head and closed her eyes. Her thoughts drifted to another little boy who once found comfort in her embrace. Insecurity had no age limit. The longer Andi lived, the more she understood that everyone searched for a place to belong. Owen's recent worries became clear to her. He'd heard Evan talking about his father, about his sisters. He'd likely overheard Beth and Ida discussing Dean and the new baby. And, she guessed that Owen had taken on some of the anxiety she felt about Dave, and likely had picked up on Fallon's fears of abandonment too. Children were emotional sponges. What kids struggled to comprehend in words, they intuitively understood. It reminded Andi that a person's mind sometimes clouded purpose. An attempt to justify, quantify, and qualify emotion often led a person to forget the purpose in things. The purpose to living was loving. Loving came with joy and grief. Loss heralded insecurity. Owen's innocent line of questioning opened Andi to a new understanding of Dave's behavior and of her private fears. She held Owen close and reveled in his affection. "I love you, Owen."

Owen looked up at Andi and grinned from ear to ear. "You get me!" He giggled uncontrollably.

Andi winked. "Thank God."

Riley walked into the bedroom to find Fallon massaging her temple in frustration. "Want to talk about it?"

Fallon looked up. "I'm not sure what I'm supposed to say."

Riley nodded. "What did Barb say?"

"More than I expected she would."

"Fallon?"

"I feel like shit, Riley."

Riley was confused.

"I should've distanced myself from Olivia a long time ago. I thought she was my best friend."

Fallon's disgusted chuckle sent shivers over Riley's skin.

"Hindsight is always 20/20," Riley offered.

"I should've seen it. I didn't want to see it. I keep wondering if I ever knew Liv at all."

"People change sometimes, Fallon."

"Do they? I don't know about that. I spent years thinking that I blew it—thinking it was my fault. I'd be with the girls and I'd feel jealous, Riley—jealous of Barb, not so much because she was with Liv, but…"

"I know why."

"How could Liv bail on the kids?" Anger poured off Fallon. "Who does that, Riley? She didn't want Barb to go with her. She didn't. Barb knows that too. Liv didn't get her way, and her response is to leave behind her family? How stupid could I have been?"

"How is Barb?" Riley asked.

"Better than I thought she'd be."

"But?"

"It's not just the kids who want to move up here. She's got a lead on a job in Burlington."

"At the university?"

Fallon nodded.

"Isn't that a good thing?"

"Maybe. I don't know."

"Why wouldn't you want Barb to move up here? You love Em and Summer. They love you and Mom, and we both know they miss Evan and Beth."

"It's not that," Fallon said.

"What is it?"

"I don't know, Riley. I want to focus on this."

"*This?*" Riley grinned.

"Me and you," Fallon explained. "Us—*our* family."

Be careful, Riley. Riley waited a few beats before exploring Fallon's explanation. Fear was a demon that every person had to do battle with. Insecurity was part of fear. Riley wanted to put at least some of Fallon's fears to rest. She reached out and took both of Fallon's hands. "I want you to listen to me," she said gently. "I love you. *This*, as you put it, you and me—our family—*this* is solid, Fallon. You need to trust that."

"I do. I just..."

"You do to a point. Some part of you keeps waiting for doom. I understand that. Believe me; I do. You had a bump on your head and I felt panic. What if you suddenly didn't wake up? It's ridiculous. I know it is. I understand that. It's my demon to face. Yours is different." Riley squeezed Fallon's hands. "Emily and Summer *are* part of our family. They love you. You love them. It doesn't matter how that came to be. Let me ask you something."

"Okay?"

"Someday—someday, when we decide to add to this family, will you love Owen less?"

"Of course not."

"Does what we have together mean that what you had with Liv or Andi means less to you?"

Fallon shifted nervously.

"Why does that make you uncomfortable?" Riley inquired. "The answer is no. We both know that. Maybe you saw Liv through rose-colored glasses. So, what? You still loved her. Maybe you and Andi were never in a committed relationship. You fell in love with her. We both know that too, Fallon. And, God knows you still love each other. Me being in your life doesn't change that. Just like I love Robert and I always will. That doesn't take away from my life with or my love for you."

"It's different. You already have to deal with Andi being..."

"I love Andi."

"I know."

"You're right. You don't have to see Robert. You don't have to watch us interact. But, Fallon, what if I had been divorced when we met? I understand that's a moot point; I still think it's worth making. The past is always part of the present, no matter how much any of us try to deny that. You can't let it dictate the present, though. I love Andi. I love Emily and Summer too. And, I'm sure I will like Barb. This isn't about *me*. You need to trust that we can endure the ghosts of the past — both of us."

No matter how much time Fallon spent with Riley, she continued to be amazed by Riley's wisdom. At thirty, Riley possessed an understanding of people and emotions that went far beyond her years. Some of that, Fallon knew, was the result of loss. Riley's grasp of life and relationships went beyond experiencing loss. Some people were born with insight — an ability to read people and situations, and to offer perspective on both. Ida said those people were old souls, people who had walked the earth many times in many forms. They carried their experiences in their DNA. For years, Fallon had found that idea amusing. The last couple of years had changed her perspective. Andi possessed that insightfulness. Ida did. And, Riley did. Fallon was surrounded by intelligent, fierce women who still possessed the ability to be vulnerable and sensitive to the needs of others. She smiled.

"What?" Riley wondered.

"You."

"Fallon, I'm serious."

"And, you're right."

"It's not about being right."

"Right again." Fallon kissed Riley's cheek. "Thank you."

"I didn't do anything."

"Yeah, you did. You set me straight. Not too straight, though."

Riley laughed. "You're impossible sometimes."

"Probably. Still love me?"

"More than anything."

"I just hope Barb can find somewhere to live. I mean, I could offer her part of my lot to build. Hell, they'd be close, and they wouldn't be on top of us. It's not like there's a ton of property here that would suit them, not in Whiskey Springs anyway. She will probably have to hire a builder if she's serious, and..."

"What about my house?"

Fallon's gaze narrowed.

"Well?" Riley asked. "I know it's not that big. She could still build, but it'd work for a while."

"Riley, that's your house."

"Is it? I thought we agreed this was our home?"

"You know what I mean."

"This is home, Fallon. I think we both know this is where we are going to make our home. That place is a house. It's a house that I happen to own—yes. It's not my home. And, why should it sit there empty?"

"You're serious."

"Why not? It makes sense."

"I could ask her."

"Ask her," Riley said. She hopped to her feet.

"Where are you going?" Fallon asked.

"I'm going to switch the laundry I started. You know, the batch that was covered in some kind of sticky red substance that I'm still trying to identify."

Fallon smirked with delight.

"Want to tell me what it was so I can avoid Google next time?" Riley asked.

"You didn't use Google."

"Want to bet?"

"I would have thought you would remember where betting gets you."

"I do. It gets me your laundry."

Fallon laughed. "You didn't use Google."

Riley pulled her phone from her pocket and opened her browser. "Let's see; 'sticky red substances on jeans.' Oh, let's see. Gum, stickers, ummm... Oh, here is my favorite on the list, 'is white goo in my pants normal?' So, not what I Googled."

Fallon erupted in laughter. "It doesn't say that." She grabbed Riley's phone.

Riley's eyebrow arched.

Fallon fell back on the bed as laughter shook her entire body. "Oh my, God."

"Not the question I asked. Give it up, Fallon. Where on earth do you find these things to wade in?"

"Why are you complaining? At least it wasn't white goo!"

"Good thing for us both."

Fallon snorted. It'd be easy to keep at this game. Fallon delighted in teasing Riley. The fact that Riley was using the internet to determine the various substances Fallon managed to get on her clothes amused her. Riley knew that Fallon enjoyed playing in the dirt. And, Fallon loved to make laundry interesting for Riley. Apparently, she'd succeeded. She pulled Riley down next to her. "It's clay."

"Clay? Are you making pottery behind my back?"

"No." Fallon's laughter had dwindled to light giggles. "Carol wanted to fix up the patio in their backyard."

"Yeah, I know. That's stone."

"Yeah, but Charlie and I put in red clay accents."

"Don't you have tools for that?" Riley asked knowingly.

Fallon held up her hands and wiggled her fingers.

Riley rolled her eyes. "You are worse than Owen."

"You think so?"

"Um-hum."

Fallon's heart fluttered. "I love you, Riley."

"Where did that come from?"

Fallon replied with a gentle kiss. "I love you," she repeated the words. Her lips meandered over Riley's neck.

"Fallon, I have to switch the..."

"I love you," Fallon whispered. Moment by moment, Fallon lost herself in the softness of Riley's skin. The simplest things drew her to the woman beside her — Riley's wit, Riley's warmth, Riley's tenderness. Laundry, family, dinner, yard work—simple, everyday events made Fallon's heart soar. She hovered above Riley, taking in the sight of the woman she loved. Why did she feel the need to say that over and over now? "I love you," Fallon spoke the words again.

"I love you too," Riley replied. A lone fingertip reached out and traced over Fallon's cheekbone. "I love that laundry is such a turn-on for you," she teased.

Fallon's lips brushed softly against Riley's forehead. "Everything about you turns me on."

"Is that so?" Riley asked.

"It is." Fallon's lips tasted Riley's. Her tongue delicately dancing with Riley's.

Raw emotion poured from Fallon. Riley could sense it filling the space between them. She felt Fallon's fears, desires, and dreams speak to her through the kiss they shared. Levity would not rule this evening's lovemaking. Desire would burn like embers beneath the crackling heat of unrestrained feeling. Riley would hear Fallon's questions in the unsteadiness of her touch. Gentle, hopeful, seeking and searching for sanctuary, that was Fallon. Riley would answer a resounding yes to every question Fallon hesitated to ask. And, Riley was aware of them all. Yes, she would submit to Fallon's touch, to Fallon's lust, to Fallon's longing. Yes, she would share the rest of her life with Fallon Foster. Yes, she would carry their children. Yes, yes, yes—the answer would always be, "yes." If only Fallon would find the strength to ask.

Strawberries. Fallon tasted strawberry syrup on Riley's lips. A hint of sweet, white wine tickled her senses when Riley's tongue brushed against hers. She loved the way Riley's lips tasted. Sometimes, Fallon caught a hint of Riley's morning coffee or note of the mint lip balm Riley always carried. It was all part of Riley, just as the light fragrance of mango from Riley's shampoo mingled with a faintly floral scent from her perfume. Every so often, Fallon would catch the scent of Riley's perfume in the air and a pleasant tingle would pass through her core. It reminded Fallon of the closeness they shared, of Riley waking in her arms, and of the way Riley's lips felt pressed against hers. Everything—Fallon wanted to give Riley everything. Nothing could ever be too much. She privately wondered if she could ever get enough of Riley. Fallon mused that Riley was her desert oasis. Fallon had been thirsty for so long, desperate to replenish all that she'd lost, and then there was Riley. Her thirst for the woman was insatiable. "Never enough," Fallon muttered.

"What?" Riley asked.

"I can't get close enough," Fallon said. "I can't stop saying it, Riley. I don't know why. I need you to know; I love you."

Riley caressed Fallon's cheek. She knew why, and tonight she intended to silence Fallon's questions—all of them. "Show me."

Fallon's pulse raced. She moved to pull Riley's sweatshirt over Riley's head. Riley sat up and removed it for her. "Jesus," Fallon moaned.

Riley reached over and pulled Fallon's T-shirt off. "Mmm," she agreed.

Fallon watched as the golden brown of Riley's irises danced liked a falling sunset. Mesmerized by Riley's ability to hold her gaze, Fallon's eyes stayed locked with Riley's as she deftly freed Riley of the rest of her clothing. A notable twinkle in Riley's eyes emerged that changed from golden brown, to hazel. "Yes?" Fallon asked.

"Did you forget?" Riley asked.

"Forget?"

"About turnabout, Fallon."

"It's fair play."

Riley raised an amused brow. "No. It's foreplay." She removed Fallon's bra. Her lips pressed to Fallon's briefly as her fingertips unbuttoned the fly of Fallon's jeans. Riley's mouth left a blazing trail from Fallon's throat straight to her waist. She glanced up, unzipped Fallon's jeans, and let her lips fall onto Fallon's thigh. One swift tug, and Fallon was laid bare.

How does she do that? Fallon was ready to slowly undress, and methodically explore Riley's body. In an instant,

Riley had turned the tables. *It's that turnabout thing. I should never have brought that up.* Fallon's thought disappeared at the warm sensation traveling over her center. Riley was wasting no time. *Dear God!*

Riley savored the taste of Fallon's immediate arousal. She teased Fallon's flesh, holding onto Fallon's hips and drawing her closer.

So much for foreplay. Fallon almost laughed. The steady throb that had taken up residence between her legs stopped her. "Jesus," she moaned. She indulged in the heart-pounding, muscle-clenching sensations Riley's tender exploration evoked. It would be easy to lose herself completely. She could close her eyes and let her fantasies wander. And, Fallon had plenty of fantasies about making love with Riley. Their short time together had thus far been filled with gentle playfulness and soulful lovemaking. Fallon wouldn't describe the intimate life she shared with Riley as timid; it was also not what she would deem adventurous. She hoped they would have a lifetime to explore the world together and all that it offered. Love happened without warning and without permission. Trust took time to build and a moment to shatter. Slowly, Fallon would open all the parts of herself to Riley, trusting that Riley would know anything and everything they might share was rooted in love.

Riley enjoyed the sway of Fallon's hips, and the expression of pleasure on Fallon's face that hinted at unspoken fantasies. Strange—Riley, thought it was odd that it was Fallon who worried about letting herself go. Fallon's fears were not founded on a lack of trust in Riley. Fallon worried that she might inadvertently offend Riley, that she might push for too much, too soon. That concern equated to every part of the life they shared. Short of lying, cheating, or abusing Riley or Owen, Riley was confident there was nothing that Fallon could share or ask to share that would frighten or offend her. Fallon Foster was the love of her life— *the* love of her life. Each moment, every relationship, all the joy and all the loss in Riley's past had led her here, not just to Whiskey Springs, but to this moment. Change often felt slow, but when the sand shifted beneath your feet, you had no choice but to follow the path it set. Resistance would swallow you whole. You either bent with the movement guiding you, or you were sure to fall where you stood. Riley understood that this moment passing between them would either cast them adrift or place them on solid ground. They needed to traverse this path together. Riley reluctantly lifted herself and coaxed Fallon to open her eyes. "Make love *with* me, Fallon."

Fallon brushed her knuckles softly over Riley's cheek. Her lips met Riley's lovingly. Her arms drew Riley closer, and she whispered. "I am always making love *with* you."

"It's not me who needs to remember that," Riley said. She let her fingers fall freely down Fallon's torso until they met the softness of Fallon's arousal. "Touch me," she said.

Fallon's breath hitched. She followed Riley's direction. "Oh, God." She sucked in a shaky breath.

"That's what touching you does to me," Riley said.

"Oh, God," Fallon groaned with excitement.

Riley nibbled on Fallon's earlobe. "You like it when I talk to you."

Fallon was positive she was about to lose consciousness. Like it? Fallon thought the sound of Riley's voice in the throes of passion was the sexiest thing she'd ever encountered. She'd never *ask* Riley to voice her desires. Secretly, she prayed that Riley would. Fallon searched for something—anything to say. The sound of blood swishing through her veins, and the thudding in her chest rendered her silent.

"Tell me, Fallon. Tell me what you want."

"Riley…"

Riley slowed the pace of her fingers. "Tell me," she directed more forcefully.

"Everything, Riley."

"Tell me."

"I want everything with you."

"What's everything?" Riley slipped a finger inside Fallon.

"Oh, God… Riley, I…"

"Tell me, Fallon. This? You want me to touch you like this? Or is that what you want to do to me?"

"Yes."

"Yes?"

"Yes, all of it. Oh, Jesus!" Fallon's flesh had become a quivering puddle of desperation. Half of her wanted to lift Riley over her. No, that wasn't what she really wanted. She wanted to be inside Riley. And, somehow, Riley knew it. She panted and tried to focus on touching Riley.

Riley grinned against Fallon's flesh. "I know," she whispered.

Fallon thrust two fingers inside Riley.

Riley cried out.

"Riley… was that too…"

"Perfect," Riley assured Fallon. "Show me, Fallon. Tell me."

Why was it so hard for Fallon to voice her desires? Riley loved her. "I want to be inside you." The words were spoken so quietly, Fallon wasn't sure she'd allowed them to pass her lips.

"You are," Riley pointed out the obvious.

Fallon moaned.

Riley moved to look into Fallon's eyes. "You want to be able to hold me and be inside me."

Fallon faltered.

Riley smiled and kissed her. "I want that too."

That was it. Fallon's body shook violently.

Riley pulled Fallon closer and held her as Fallon crested and fell again, and again, and then, again when Riley fell with her.

"Riley…"

"Shh," Riley cooed. Her lips parted and claimed Fallon's. "Marry me, Fallon."

"What?"

"I asked you to marry me."

Fallon pulled away. "You…. I… You…."

Riley giggled. "Don't you want to?"

"Well, yes…. I…. Riley…"

"So? Will you? Marry me, Fallon?"

Fallon smiled. "I thought I'd take you away and ask you at sunset or…"

"I don't need any of that."

"You deserve it."

"I have more than I deserve," Riley said. "I love you."

"I don't even have a ring," Fallon muttered.

Riley reached into the drawer of her night stand and handed Fallon a box.

"What's this?" Fallon asked.

"Open it and find out."

Fallon lifted the lid and lost her breath. "Riley…"

"It's Owen's birthstone."

"I know." Fallon stared at the simple band with three inlayed emeralds.

Riley swept Fallon's hair aside. "You don't have to be afraid to ask me anything."

"I'm not afraid. I just want it all to be…"

"Perfect?" Riley guessed. "Nothing is ever perfect, Fallon. We both know that. You said you want everything with me. For me, everything is being with you and Owen."

"Me too."

"You still didn't answer my question," Riley said.

"What?"

Riley laughed. "You know, a girl could get self-conscious. I seem to recall that I asked you to marry me."

Fallon's chest ached pleasantly. Her body tingled from the passion they'd just shared. She searched Riley's eyes. In her wildest dreams, Fallon never imagined anyone popping the question to her. "You never cease to surprise me."

"Still haven't answered."

"I'd marry you right now if I could."

"So, that's a yes?"

Fallon nodded. "Of course, it's a yes."

"Are you disappointed?"

"Huh?"

"That you didn't get to ask me?"

"No. I do wish I had a ring to give you."

"That bothers you."

"I told you, Riley. I want to give you *everything*. For me, that has always included a memorable proposal and a stunning ring for your finger."

"All I want, Fallon is for us to be together, to have a family together. I don't need things. I need you."

"I'm still buying you a ring."

Riley nodded. "Would you really marry me right now?"

"Yes."

"Good."

"Why? Do you have a preacher on speed dial or something?" Fallon teased.

"No. Besides, I still need to change the laundry before I can think about weddings."

Fallon's eyes fell to the ring in the box.

"I figured you would wear it as your band," Riley said. "I had it made last month."

"Really?"

"Well, I knew you wanted to ask. I wanted to be prepared."

"How did you know?"

Riley shook her head. "I love you, Fallon. It's a good thing you never wanted to be a spy because you can't keep a secret to save your life."

"Yes, I can!"

"Oh, you can keep someone's trust just fine. Hiding your agenda? Not so much." Riley reached back into the drawer and handed Fallon an envelope.

"What's this?"

"It's copy of a request for a quote on some engagement rings. Apparently when you sent the request online, you used my email address."

"Oh, shit."

Riley laughed. "It landed in my inbox."

"I'm sorry, Riley. I wanted to get some ideas before Mom and I went shopping, you know?"

"Why are you apologizing? I'm just relieved you said yes."

Finally, Fallon laughed. "No one will believe it."

"No one needs to know who proposed. Maybe we should surprise them all."

"What are you up to?" Fallon asked.

"Nothing." Riley feigned innocence. She kissed Fallon's nose. "I need to change that laundry."

"Riley?"

"Yeah?"

"Would tomorrow be too soon?"

Riley winked. "Right now, wouldn't be too soon for me."

Fallon lifted the ring from the box when Riley left the room. "You are one of a kind, Riley Main. Or is it Riley Foster? Oh, God! Am I Fallon Main? Oh. My. God... Am I a Mrs.?"

Riley stood outside the bedroom door listening to Fallon's endless stream of questions. "Priceless," she mused. "Not a Mrs. *yet*," Riley called back.

Fallon swallowed hard. *Holy shit! I just got engaged.*

CHAPTER SEVEN

THURSDAY

*A*ndi opened her front door. "Hi."

"Hi."

"You look beat," Andi observed.

Billie looked apologetic.

Andi leaned in and kissed her gently. "Come in here." She sensed Billie's nervousness and took the backpack from Billie's hands. "Can I get you something—other than sleep?"

"Andi, I… I realize I said…" Billie had been obsessing over her parting words to Andi on the phone. She'd debated whether to call and leave a message apologizing. Who apologized for saying, "I love you?" Billie did. She'd run through a million possibilities about Andi's reaction. Too fast, too much, that was it—what was wrong with her? Why did she become a clumsy fifteen-year-old whenever Andi was around? Here she was stumbling on her words—again.

"You worry too much," Andi said.

Tears were brimming in Billie's eyes. Exhaustion had paved the way for raw emotion, and every insecurity Billie possessed seemed determined to find its way to the surface.

Andi's heart ached. *You need to tell her.* She stepped up to Billie and cupped Billie's face in her hands. "I love you too."

What did she just say? Am I awake? I must have fallen asleep. Wake up Billie!

Andi grinned. "You are too much sometimes."

"I…"

Andi silenced Billie with a kiss. "Stop," she whispered. "You're exhausted."

Billie let out a long sigh. "I was so worried I blew it."

"Because you told me that you love me?"

"It's been a long time since I said that to anyone."

"I know." Andi caressed Billie's cheek with her fingertip. "I think you need some sleep."

"I'd rather be with you."

"What if I told you that I would like to lie beside you?"

Billie held her breath when Andi's lips pressed to her forehead.

"Tell me," Andi said. "Now that you're here, tell me again."

"I love you," Billie said.

"I love you too."

Billie shook her head, unsure how to process reality.

"Let me hold you," Andi requested.

"Are you sure?" Billie asked.

"That I love you or that I want to hold you?"

Billie chuckled nervously.

"Yes. We have a lot to talk about," Andi admitted. Her greatest concern at the moment was Billie's insecurity, something she understood fatigue enhanced. "Right now, you need to sleep. I get the feeling it ended up being a rough two days."

Billie's tears finally escaped.

"Want to talk about it?" Andi asked.

"We lost a seventeen-year-old boy," Billie explained. "Overdose. You'd think I'd be used to it. Watching his mother—I…"

Andi pulled Billie into her arms. "That's not you, Billie. You care about people."

"I try to put it aside," Billie explained. She clung to Andi. "His mother hit the floor. It's not like I haven't seen that before; I have. I just…"

"Shhh. Come on, let's go lie down. You need to rest."

"I need you," Billie whispered.

"I'm not going anywhere," Andi promised. She took Billie's hand and led her toward the bedroom. "Do you want something to change into?"

"I don't think your clothes will fit me," Billie tried to joke.

Andi bit her lip. "You might be surprised." She winked. In a few seconds, she'd retrieved a pair of baggy sweats and T-shirt."

"You wear this?" Billie smirked.

"Surprised?"

"A little."

"Mm. Reality might not be as exciting as you think," Andi said.

Billie's exhaustion made her ability to filter thoughts and emotions non-existent. She shook her head. "Trust me, Andi; everything about standing in your bedroom is exciting."

Andi laughed. *Adorable.* "I'm going to remind you that you said that one day."

"You won't need to."

"We'll see," Andi said. "If you want to grab a shower, go ahead."

"Nah. A shower will wake me up."

"Okay."

Billie started for the bathroom and suddenly turned back. "Andi?"

"Hum?"

"Thank you."

Andi winked. "Hurry up so we can climb into this bed."

Billie nodded and stepped into the bathroom. She leaned against the bathroom door when it closed. "Jesus... Could you act like a bigger flake?"

Andi chuckled while she turned down the bed. Being with Billie differed in every way from being with anyone she'd ever invited into her bed. It was strange when she thought about it. She was attracted to Billie. She'd been fantasizing about making love with Billie for days. All that mattered was that Billie was here. Andi would be content to be close to the woman she'd fallen in love with. It wasn't as if she'd never held Fallon, never had Jake crawl into her arms. She had. She'd enjoyed that closeness too. Like everything else in those relationships, that intimacy had come to exist as the result of passion. Passion sparked love. Now, love sparked passion. It prompted feelings that Andi was sure she'd never experienced. She closed her eyes when she heard the bathroom door close. With a deep breath, she turned and offered Billie her hand. "Come on."

Billie slid into the bed beside Andi and giggled.

"What?" Andi asked.

"I'm not sure."

"Okay?"

"We're not lovers."

"Not yet," Andi said.

Billie swallowed the lump in her throat.

"Well, look at it this way," Andi began. "By tonight, we'll be able to tell everyone we've slept together, and it will be true."

Billie laughed. "You're a little crazy."

For you. Andi opened her arms. "Come on, let me hold you for a while."

Billie slipped into Andi's embrace and closed her eyes. Andi's hand stroked her hair, and Andi's lips kissed her temple gently. Billie sighed in contentment. "You feel so good," she whispered.

"So, do you," Andi said. "Go to sleep."

Billie nestled closer. Andi's gentle caress relaxed her, and she drifted off.

Andi kissed Billie's head softly and closed her eyes. *Somehow, I am going to make you see how beautiful you are.* "I love you," Andi promised.

Billie's hold on Andi tightened.

God, it feels good to say that.

❧

Billie woke up unsure of where she was for a moment. She let her eyes open slowly and held her breath when Andi's eyes met hers. Andi smiled, and Billie's heart stopped for a second before pounding so furiously it hurt.

"Are you okay?" Andi asked.

"I can't believe I'm here."

Andi shifted in the bed and took Billie's face in her hands. "I love you, Billie."

Billie's eyes closed again at the softness of Andi's fingertips against her cheek.

The smile that curled Andi's lips came from deep within her soul. Happiness lit her eyes. She tried to recall a moment in her life when she'd felt similarly. Holding her sons for the first time was the closest she could come. A mother's love differed from the love shared between two people *in* love. Her eyes studied the peaceful expression on Billie's face, the laugh lines at the corners of Billie's eyes, the tiny freckle on her left temple, and the curve of her lips. Andi found herself mesmerized by the woman in her arms. She felt the embers of desire waiting to be stoked into a raging fire. She let them burn faintly. Emotions coursed through Andi like gentle waves crashing against the shore. Holding Billie close surpassed every spirited lovemaking session Andi had ever enjoyed. When she did touch Billie, Andi resolved that it would be reverently—tenderly and slowly. She kissed Billie's forehead and let her lips linger, tears forming in her eyes.

Billie tightened her hold on Andi. *Andi.* Andi Maguire was no longer a distant fantasy. Billie slowly pried her eyes open and looked at Andi. "What are you thinking?" Billie asked.

"I'm not thinking at all," Andi said.

Billie searched Andi's eyes for her meaning.

"I thought you'd wake up and I'd seduce you," Andi said.

Billie swallowed hard as her skin flushed.

Andi grinned. "I still want to," she said. "But... How do I explain this?"

"Is it me?"

"Yes, but not the way you're thinking," Andi said. "I'm in love with you, Billie—in a way that I'm not sure I've ever been before. I've known it for a while. I realized when I was in Florida that I couldn't deny it any longer. I hated not seeing you. Hearing your voice only made me want to be close to you more. I'm not used to that."

"Wanting to see someone?" Billie asked.

"No," Andi said. "I know what it's like to miss someone. I've always been content on my own. I've had to be."

"And, now?"

"I don't want to rush what we have," Andi replied. "It scares me, Billie."

"What scares you?"

How could Andi explain what she was feeling? She wasn't certain that she understood it herself. Now that Billie was in her arms, Andi was terrified to let go. She was tired of letting go. She wanted to hold on. She wanted to believe that the day would come when she would wake up and feel Billie beside her each morning. She wanted to imagine kissing Billie goodnight, and pouring her a cup of coffee in the morning. Andi wanted it all; she wanted everything life offered with Billie Steele.

"Andi?" Billie coaxed Andi to open her eyes. "Talk to me."

"I don't want you to leave," Andi whispered hoarsely.

"I'm not going anywhere," Billie said.

"I don't mean now," Andi replied.

Billie wiped a few tears that slipped over Andi's cheeks. "I'm not going anywhere," she repeated. "This is it for me, Andi. I won't push you. I won't rush you into anything. I know that you've been through a lot this last year. I know you're still struggling with Dave, and you're still finding your way. I want to be the person you trust to find your way with. That's what I want."

Andi's forehead fell against Billie's softly. "You are."

Billie let her lips brush against Andi's faintly. "I'm not going anywhere," she promised again.

Andi's lips claimed Billie's. An indescribable ache formed in her chest. Had she loved before? Not like this. She held Billie's face in her hands as their kiss deepened. *I'm not letting go this time.*

Billie's hands caressed Andi's sides, drawing her closer, praying that the connection they shared would last forever.

"I need you," Andi choked on her admission.

Billie opened her eyes. "I'm here," she said.

Andi shook her head; suddenly she felt terrified.

"Hey," Billie cooed. "Why are you crying?"

"I'm so scared, Billie."

"Shh... Don't cry. Please don't cry, sweetheart. Andi..."

"I'm sorry."

"You don't have anything to be sorry for," Billie said. She pulled Andi into her arms and held her close. "Talk to me."

"I don't want..."

"There isn't anything you can say that is going to push me away," Billie promised. "Not one thing. Not unless you are about to tell me you're really a man."

Andi laughed through her tears. "No."

"And, to be honest; I'm not sure that would change how I feel about you."

"Well, you can rest easy about that," Andi said. "Oh, Billie, I've loved two people in my life. Neither loved me the way I dreamed it should be."

"Andi," Billie began cautiously. "It's not my place to say anything about Jake or Fallon. I do know Fallon; better than most people realize, in fact. You weren't a fling to her. And, I don't know Jake all that well, but I saw the way he looked at you."

"I know they both loved me," Andi admitted. "That wasn't enough, though."

"You mean to be faithful."

"I do. Timing, circumstance, personality—it doesn't matter the reasons. The reasons don't change the reality."

"Do you trust me?" Billie asked.

"Yes, I do."

"But you're worried that I won't be able to give you that."

"No," Andi said. "I'm terrified that you will."

Billie was perplexed.

"What if I disappoint you? What if something happens and I lose you, and..."

"Andi," Billie's voice was firm but compassionate. "I'm not Jake or Fallon."

"I know."

"And, frankly, that scares the hell out of me."

"Why?" Andi wondered.

"You're not serious."

"I'm completely serious," Andi replied.

"I have eyes. Look at them. Look at me."

"I am looking at you," Andi said.

"You know what I mean. Fallon walks into a room and people pay attention. And, Jake? Come on, Andi; I'm a lesbian and I can see how attractive he is."

Andi smiled. The truth was on the table.

Billie sighed and shook her head.

"You're beautiful," Andi said.

"Sure, I am."

"Stop it," Andi demanded. "Please, stop. There isn't anyone in the world who holds a candle to you in my eyes," she said. "No one."

"You might change your mind when you..."

"Stop." Andi took hold of Billie's arms. She took a deep breath and let it out slowly. Billie harbored different insecurities from hers. "I'm not going anywhere either," she promised. "When I said that I need you, I meant that I need you in *every* way."

Billie's heart sped up so quickly that she gasped.

"Billie?"

"Jesus," Billie muttered. "I am a like a pre-teen puddle with you."

Andi laughed. It felt good to laugh. "Puddle, huh?" She let a fingertip trail over Billie's throat to the top of Billie's breast.

"Jesus Christ, you've barely touched me and I'm wet."

Andi's eyebrow arched.

"Oh, God. That was out loud; wasn't it?"

A giggle preceded Andi's kiss. "You are priceless, Billie."

Billie groaned, still feeling embarrassed. "And, here I thought I was a bargain."

"I love you."

"I love you too, Andi."

"Good. Now, show me."

❧

Fallon watched as Owen attempted his third somersault in less than a minute. She couldn't help but laugh. He'd discovered the trick at his playgroup and seemed determined to master it before he saw his friends again. Fallon wondered if he'd be able to stand. As expected, he reached his feet and promptly fell on his butt.

"You'd better take a rest," she said. "You'll end up like a Weeble Wobble."

"What's a weebie waw'low?"

"Weeble Wobble." Fallon laughed. "It's a toy that I had as a kid."

Owen pondered the answer. "Can I have it?"

"If you keep somersaulting, you will be one," Fallon laughed some more. "Except you *do* fall down."

Owen didn't understand what Fallon was talking about. "You do it," he said.

"A somersault?" Fallon asked.

Owen nodded.

Fallon scratched her brow. She looked over her shoulder for any sign of Riley. Once she was comfortable that the coast was clear, Fallon dropped to her knees.

Owen's grin stretched to his ears and he clapped. "Go, Momma!"

Fallon prepared to tuck and roll. The tuck was successful; the roll...

A crash sent Riley running from the kitchen. "What on earth?"

"Momma went boom."

Fallon rubbed her forehead; a small trickle of blood fell onto her hand.

Riley looked at the trickle on the side of the coffee table. "I'm almost positive I don't want to know."

"Momma's a weebie waw'low!"

Riley looked at Owen curiously and back at Fallon. "Are you all right?"

"It's just a little scratch."

"Let me see it," Riley said.

Fallon's hand remained fixed on her forehead.

"Fallon," Riley's voice grew insistent. She gently pried Fallon's hand away and shook her head. "Let's go."

"Go where?" Fallon asked.

"To the bathroom so that I can clean that up and see what it looks like."

"It's not that bad."

"Now, Fallon."

Fallon groaned. She went to find her feet and fell back.

"Weebie Waw'low!" Owen said, thinking Fallon's situation mirrored his.

Riley sighed. "Are you dizzy?"

Fallon nodded.

"Sit here."

"Where are you going?"

"To get a cloth and call Billie."

❦

Andi's head spun pleasantly. Billie's lips faintly teased her neck. Andi was sure she was about to explode. Her hands threaded into the soft waves of Billie's chestnut hair. Her singular thought left her wondering if she'd died and gone to heaven. "Billie," she whispered. "My God."

Billie's heart thrummed violently. She'd barely tasted Andi's skin and every cell in her body had come to attention. Her hand wandered steadily from Andi's hip, underneath Andi's shirt, delighting in the softness that greeted her touch. Her eyes wandered to find Andi's, and Billie lost the ability to breathe.

Andi marveled at the desire painting Billie's irises. Their light brown hue sparked with flecks of gold. Andi lost herself in Billie's steady gaze. The sensation of fingertips tracing the outline of her bra sent shivers up and down Andi's spine. She moaned when Billie's hands deftly unfastened the front hook. Billie's hands pulled Andi to sit, and without warning, Andi found herself sitting topless beside the woman she loved.

"Perfect," Billie rasped. She kissed the swell of Andi's breasts, journeying lower until her mouth met with a straining nipple.

Andi's hands pulled Billie closer, desperate to feel Billie's lips surrounding her breast.

Billie was happy to comply with Andi's unspoken request. Tiny sparks of pleasure erupted in her core when Andi moaned. She wanted to call out to Andi, to tell her how it felt to have Andi close, to taste her flesh; Billie would never relinquish her prize for that momentary indulgence. She was about to show Andi Maguire what it meant to be loved completely. She would touch every inch of Andi. She'd taste every inch of Andi. She would rock Andi gently for a moment, and then take Andi someplace she'd never dreamed possible. She'd whisper endearments and hold the woman beneath her close when the waves crashed over them.

A loud blare startled both women. Andi jumped and accidentally whacked Billie in the nose.

"Ow!"

"Oh, no!" Andi was mortified. "Billie, I'm sorry."

Billie started to laugh. "See who's calling," she said.

Andi groaned. *Andi, you idiot.* She glimpsed the number as she picked up Billie's phone. "Riley?" Andi asked.

"Andi?"

"Yeah." Andi looked over at Billie whose eyes were still watering from their brief collision. She stroked Billie's cheek. "I'm sorry, honey," she whispered.

"I'm interrupting something," Riley guessed.

Andi pulled Billie into her arms. She took a deep breath. "What's going on?" Andi wanted to know.

"Andi, don't worry about it..."

"If you're calling Billie's phone in the middle of the day; I can guess there's a reason."

"Fallon had a little accident," Riley replied.

"Is she okay?"

"I think so. She hit her head. I know if I suggest the doctor or the emergency room, she'll balk."

"If Billie thinks she needs to go; she'll go," Andi guessed.

"Yeah. I don't know if she needs to but if..."

"We'll be over in about twenty minutes," Andi said.

"Andi, seriously; I can call Ida."

"You can; you don't have to. We'll see you shortly."

"What's going on?" Billie asked.

"Fallon hurt herself. That's all I know. It's not life threatening. You know Fallon." Andi looked at Billie apologetically. "I'm sorry."

"For what? For Riley interrupting us or for that right hook?"

Andi groaned.

Billie grabbed Andi's arms, held them down, and kissed her gently. "Safety first," she teased.

"I'm not going to live this down; am I?"

"Already forgotten," Billie promised.

"This is going to be continued," Andi said. She claimed Billie's lips passionately. "You have no idea how much I want to kick Fallon's ass right now."

Billie laughed. "Well, let's fix her first." She pulled herself from the bed.

"Billie?"

"Yeah?"

"Stay here tonight. After Fallon is settled; come home with me. Even if we don't... I..."

"Let's go so we can come home."

Andi took a deep breath. *She's not going anywhere.*

"I just hope Fallon didn't almost cut something off this time," Billie commented.

"One can only hope."

Riley opened the door with the shake of her head.

"Where's the patient?" Billie asked.

"On the sofa."

"I'll see what I can do," Billie replied.

Riley looked at Andi apologetically. "I'm so sorry."

"Why? Did you beat her up and not tell me?"

"Not this time. This time it was the coffee table."

Andi put her arm around Riley's shoulder as they strolled to the living room. "I'll bet there's a story there."

"Yeah, she and Owen were doing somersaults."

"Obviously, unsupervised."

Riley rolled her eyes. "I need an extra pair of everything to keep up with those two."

"Imagine when it's three."

"Please..."

Andi laughed. "So, what's the verdict?" She asked when they reached the room. "I know the coffee table won. Is she going to survive?"

"Ha-ha," Fallon muttered.

Billie scratched her brow. "A couple of stitches would help it heal. And, Fallon, you really should get an x-ray."

"Why?"

"Because you could have a fracture. And, it wouldn't surprise me if you had a concussion. That's why."

"I'm fine," Fallon protested. Owen sat on her lap looking between the adults curiously.

"You *feel* fine," Billie said. "That doesn't mean that you might not have one."

"And, what are they going to do if I do?" Fallon argued. "They'll tell me to watch it. That's it. It wouldn't be the first time."

Billie tried again. "Yeah, I know. It's probably nothing at all. I'd rather know than guess it."

"Fallon, listen to Billie," Andi said.

"It's just a," Fallon continued to wage her protest.

"Would you give us a minute?" Riley requested.

Andi nodded. She looked at Owen. "Owen, why don't you show Billie your new truck?"

"Okay!" Owen hopped off Fallon's lap. He looked up at Billie. "Gwama got me a twuck." He smiled at Andi.

"She did?" Billie asked.

"Yep. A fiyah twuck!"

"Cool," Billie commented.

Andi cast her gaze at Fallon.

Fallon looked down and grumbled. No words needed. Andi's eyes said it all; don't give Riley any trouble.

"Fallon," Riley began.

"I'm okay, Riley."

"If Billie thinks you should get an x-ray, you should."

"Billie's being dramatic. She's probably pissed that I interrupted their…"

"Billie is here because she cares about you. Please, Fallon."

"Riley…"

Riley had to close her eyes to keep from crying. "Please, Fallon."

Fallon sighed. "Okay."

"Thank you."

"I really am all right."

"I'm sure that's true. Call me crazy; I don't want to take any chances." Riley kissed Fallon's forehead and started to leave the room.

"Where are you going?"

"To see if Grandma Andi will babysit for a while."

Fallon groaned. "This sucks."

Owen had grabbed Riley's hand and pulled her away. He was excited to show her the creation Billie had helped him make with his blocks.

Fallon pulled Andi aside. "I'm sorry."

"You should be."

"I..."

"You're a lot bigger than Owen, you fool. You should have moved that table," Andi said.

"You're not mad?"

"Fallon, seriously?"

"Yeah, but from what Riley said it sounded like..."

"It's okay," Andi assured her. "I'm glad you're all right, and so is Billie."

"I'm sure you would rather have been alone with Billie than babysitting."

"Billie's not going anywhere," she said. "And, Fallon? There isn't anything I wouldn't do for you—or Riley and Owen. You should know that."

"I do. You look happy," Fallon observed. "You're in love with her."

Andi had let go of Fallon. She was genuinely happy for Fallon and Riley. Fallon felt the same way for Andi. Nonetheless, a twinge of pain happened when you realized a person had truly moved on. She'd felt it. Now, it was Fallon's turn. Loving someone new would never exile the love you held for someone else. Andi leaned in and kissed Fallon on the cheek softly. "I love you, Fallon. Part of me will always love you. Yes, I'm in love with Billie. You already knew that, though."

Fallon breathed Andi in for a second. It was odd, the way love changed. She would always love Andi too. It seemed crazy, when she thought about it. Andi had taught her to love again. Without Andi, Fallon wasn't sure she would have found the strength to let Riley in. "Billie's a lucky lady," Fallon said, and she meant it. Andi was one-of-a-kind.

"Oh, I'm not sure I'd say that. If I can be honest, I can't believe it's happening."

"Yeah, I know *that* feeling."

"Do me a favor, will you?" Andi requested.

"Name it."

"Stick to using your feet for a while, and not your head."

Fallon laughed. "I'll try."

Andi winked and started to walk away.

"Andi?"

"Yeah?"

"I love you too, you know? I want you to be happy."

"I do know," Andi said.

❦

Andi forced herself not to laugh at the way Billie kept shifting her weight from foot to foot. "How tired are you?"

Billie's face flushed.

Andi finally lost all hope of holding back and laughed. "I was going to suggest I make us some dinner," she said.

"Oh." Billie chuckled nervously. "I'm acting like an idiot."

"Not at all. I'm nervous too. I'm the one who nearly sent you to the emergency room with Fallon; remember?"

"That was a pretty good blow," Billie teased.

It was Andi's turn to blush. "I'm sorry—about everything."

"Nah. I am."

"You?" Andi was confused.

"I don't want to screw this up, Andi."

"*This?* By this, do you mean us in bed or us together?"

"Is there an us?" Billie asked.

Andi took a deep breath. "I'm in love with you, Billie. I hope to God there is an *us* because I don't want to be without you. As for the other part..." Andi stepped forward and cupped Billie's cheek. "I don't want to disappoint you."

Billie fought to swallow. Andi's closeness left her breathless. Disappointed? Impossible.

Andi grinned. "I know what you're thinking."

"Do you?"

"I think so," Andi replied. "You think there is no way that I could ever do that."

"There isn't."

"I wish that were true."

"Andi, I knew I was in love with you long before you even gave me a second glance."

The sincerity in Billie's declaration touched Andi. "And, that's part of the reason I worry."

"You think that I don't see you clearly."

"Do you?" Andi asked.

"More than you think. I know you aren't perfect. I don't want you to be perfect, Andi. I don't expect everything to be easy all the time. The only way you could disappoint me is to lie to me. That's it."

"That won't happen."

"Then you have nothing to worry about."

Andi sighed. "Billie..."

"What is it?"

"I've never been afraid of being close to someone before."

"And, I've never felt safe before."

"We are certainly a pair; aren't we?"

"Maybe that's why we fit."

"Maybe it is." Andi kissed Billie softly. "What do you say I make us dinner? We can have a glass of wine and let the evening happen the way it's meant to."

Billie stood still, gazing at Andi, a pleasant ache in her chest whispering the truth to her. A truth she'd long given up on. She smiled.

"What?" Andi wondered.

"Dinner sounds great. What can I do?"

"You don't need to do a thing."

"Maybe shower?" Billie suggested.

Several flirtatious responses lingered on the tip of Andi's tongue. *Soon.* She kissed Billie again. "Take your time," she told Billie.

Billie started to walk away and stopped. "Andi?"

"Hum?"

"Thanks."

Andi's only reply was a bright smile that told Billie that she could trust the truth she felt. *This time it's for real.*

ᑫ. ℈

Andi stood beside Billie at the kitchen sink. Billie had insisted on helping clean up from dinner. Once they began the task, Billie fell silent. Andi glanced over and noted the trembling of Billie's hand. She removed the pot in Billie's hand and placed it aside.

"What are you...."

"That's enough," Andi said.

"Andi, I can..."

"There is one pot left. It can wait until tomorrow."

Billie stared at Andi blankly.

"Billie," Andi began cautiously. "Relax. What is going on up there?" She lightly tapped Billie's forehead.

"I feel like a fumbling teenager," Billie confessed.

"As I recall, I was the one who fumbled earlier."

Billie sniggered.

"See?" Andi winked at Billie. "Do you love me?"

"More than anything."

"Do you believe me when I say that I love you?"

"Yes."

"Then let me."

Billie swallowed hard.

Andi clasped the hand in hers and led Billie away. "I think there's still a catcher's mask in Dave's old room, if you want to grab it."

Billie laughed. "I'll take my chances."

Me too.

⁂

"How are you feeling?" Riley asked Fallon.

"You mean besides embarrassed and guilty?"

"Embarrassed I understand a little. Why do you feel guilty?"

"Oh, come on, Riley, my mishap completely fucked up Andi and Billie's day."

"It altered their plans."

Fallon stared at Riley.

"Okay, yes — they were..."

"Andi told you that?"

Riley nodded.

"Shit." Fallon groaned.

"I wouldn't worry about it too much. I think they'll make up for the lost time."

Fallon grimaced.

"Does that bother you?"

"No. I just prefer not to think about Billie and Andi — you know."

Riley's brow furrowed. "Fallon, does the idea of Andi..."

"No, it's not what you're thinking."

"What am I thinking?"

"That I'm jealous or something."

"Are you?"

"Billie's like... I don't know, we've been friends for so long. It's just... I don't want to think about Billie, you know..."

"Mm."

"What?" Fallon asked.

"You know, it's okay if it feels a little strange seeing Andi with someone new."

"It doesn't."

Riley debated for less than a second whether she should press this issue. Of course, it felt strange to see Andi with Billie romantically. Riley felt no insecurity. She imagined that it would feel strange for anyone to see their ex with someone new. The issue was that Fallon wanted to pretend because she called Andi an ex-*lover*, it somehow negated that feeling. "It wasn't easy for Andi, you know?"

"What's that?"

"Watching you and me together," Riley said.

"It's not the same."

"Why? Because you two weren't a couple?"

"Yes."

Riley shook her head. "So, that means that you don't feel anything for Andi at all?"

"I love Andi. She's my best friend."

"And, you were in love with her once."

"Riley..."

Riley held up her hands. "I've heard all your denials, Fallon. I know you love me. I'm not insecure. I wish you wouldn't be."

Fallon sighed.

"You need to trust me enough to be able to be honest about anything. I know that you don't want to be with Andi. She doesn't want that from you either."

"I want her to be happy, Riley."

"And, you think it's your fault that she hasn't been?"

"Not my fault, but..."

"Your responsibility?" Riley shook her head again. "I love you. You have got to let this idea that you are somehow responsible for everyone's pain go. You aren't."

"I hurt Andi."

"No. That's not how she sees it."

"But I did, and I hurt Billie."

"What happened to Billie was *not* your fault. Neither is what Andi has gone through. Andi is happy, Fallon."

"I just want..."

"I know." Riley took Fallon's face in her hands. "I love you, Fallon. I love Andi too. She's happy — really happy with Billie. You didn't ruin anything."

"Can I ask you something?"

"Anything; you know that."

"Do you think they'll make it?"

"Life is unpredictable. I don't know. I know the look in Andi's eyes when she talks about Billie. I feel it when I look at you. So, yes; I think that they'll make it."

"She deserves it. They both do."

"We all do, Fallon."

CHAPTER EIGHT

The room was dark. Andi went to flip on the light and Billie stopped her. She pulled Andi into her arms and kissed her soundly.

Andi clung to Billie, needing a tether. A simple kiss sent her soaring.

Billie's hands began to search Andi's form, traveling up and down Andi's back, pulling Andi closer steadily.

Andi could sense Billie's excitement, and she detected the waves of insecurity pouring off the woman she loved. She stepped back half a pace, reached over and clicked the light on.

"What are you doing?" Slight panic tainted Billie's words.

The smile that Andi offered Billie was playful and loving. She let a fingertip trace a pathway from Billie's temple, down her cheek, all the way to the top button of Billie's shirt.

Billie watched Andi's expression as Andi's gaze followed the trail of her fingertip. "Andi…"

Andi looked back at Billie and smiled again. Her palm found the softness of Billie's cheek. "I want to see you," she said.

Billie's breath caught and then sputtered. "Andi… I…"

A kiss silenced Billie's mounting protest. Andi's fingers began to deftly address the buttons of the denim shirt Billie wore. One by one, the buttons released as Andi steadily deepened their kiss. When she felt the soft material part, Andi whispered against Billie's lips. "I love you, Billie. I don't want you to shield anything from me."

Tears gathered in Billie's eyes. She closed them in a futile attempt to banish them.

A warm trickle brushed over Andi's lip as Billie's tears began to flow. She stepped back and lifted her hand back to Billie's face.

"I'm sorry," Billie choked.

"No," Andi said. "I told you; don't hold anything back. I don't want you to try to be anything or anyone but who you are. I don't want you to pretend to feel something you don't or hide something you're afraid to let me see."

"Andi, I…"

"Look at me."

Billie reluctantly followed Andi's direction.

Affection, admiration, and awe colored Andi's irises. "I love you. How many times do I need to say that for you to understand what that means?"

Billie's eyes started to close.

"Billie," Andi called. "Stay with me."

"Andi, there's… I…"

"Tell me."

"I've never let anyone…"

Andi tipped her head.

"God, how do I even say this?"

Realization jolted Andi. She caressed Billie's cheek. "You've never let anyone see you?"

"Not for years. And, it's not just that. I never… I usually am the one to…"

"Do you trust me?" Andi asked.

"Yes, and that's what terrifies me."

Tenderly, Andi claimed Billie's lips with hers. She didn't need to hear all the reasons, at least not now. Billie's cryptic words were an admission that somehow didn't surprise Andi. Billie was a giver. That was Billie's nature, and perhaps in some situations giving also served as her defense. Andi intended to open Billie to receiving the love she gave freely but struggled to accept. "Trust me," Andi whispered. "Let me love you, Billie."

Was there any choice? Billie tried unsuccessfully to swallow the lump in her throat. The tenderness in Andi's touch left her breathless. She would give Andi anything—everything. "Yes," she muttered.

Andi held back a chuckle, instinctively knowing that Billie was unaware the simple word had escaped her lips. She pushed Billie's shirt off her shoulders, watching Billie's expression as the shirt pooled in a heap on the floor. Her lips strayed to Billie's shoulder, placing light kisses over it and across Billie's collarbone, traveling methodically lower in a painfully slow descent until her lips hovered at the top of Billie's cleavage. Andi watched the rise and fall of Billie's chest as Billie struggled to inhale a full breath. Her hand reached around Billie's back and released the clasp that kept Billie's breasts concealed. Tingles erupted over her skin the moment Billie was revealed to her. "You are beautiful," Andi said.

Billie wanted to shout, *'No! I'm not!'* The sensation of Andi's warm breath caressing her nipple stopped her.

As if she could hear Billie's unspoken thought, Andi replied. "You are." She faintly brushed her tongue over Billie's nipple. Billie's body jerked in response. Andi pulled her closer, held her firmly, and continued her exploration until Billie had no choice but to fall into her. "You are," Andi repeated. She guided Billie to the bed, and straddled Billie's waist. "Look at me, love."

Billie pried her eyes open.

Andi pulled her shirt over her head, removed her bra and smiled at the immediate hitch in Billie's breathing. "I don't want to hide from you either."

Billie's hands sensually drifted from Andi's hips upward, as Andi's again found the softness of Billie's breasts. Billie was riveted to the sight of Andi looking down at her. The inclination to look away, to cover up, or to take command was washed away by the intensity of Andi's gaze. Andi's eyes reflected the emotions Billie felt—desire, love, hopefulness, and even a touch of apprehension. Billie stretched to trace the outline of Andi's lips with a fingertip. Andi sighed, and Billie spoke her truth. "I want you," she confessed.

"You have me," Andi promised. She lifted herself and unzipped her jeans, then Billie's, divesting them both of everything that separated them. She let her body fall softly against Billie's, her teeth tugging gently at Billie's lip. "You have me," she repeated her promise.

It seemed strange to Billie; she took what she thought might have been the first, full, deep breath in her adult life. She savored the feeling of fullness that spread from her lungs to her heart and exhaled gradually. "And, you have me," she told Andi.

No more words needed to be spoken. Andi felt the truth pass between them. She'd thought that she understood what it meant to love. Perhaps she did know what it meant to love — to be in love? Andi's chest ached with the gravity of the truth. The questions in her mind suddenly went silent. It felt as though everything in existence vanished except Billie. Nothing mattered at the moment, just Billie. The way Billie's flesh felt pressed against her — soft, warm, and yielding. The light scent that lingered on Billie's skin from the shower. Andi wanted to be closer. She searched Billie's eyes pleadingly. She'd made love before; hadn't she? Andi wasn't sure. The pull she felt toward Billie left her breathless, and they'd barely begun to explore each other. Shouldn't she be craving release? Wasn't this the part where she should beg Billie to touch her, to stoke the embers of arousal into a raging fire? Isn't that what was supposed to happen now? Andi's forehead fell against Billie's as she began to move against her lover erotically. It was intoxicating; the warm body beneath her, the first hint of wetness that brushed against Andi's thigh. She moaned. It was erotic, but it was much more. Andi didn't want to be released. She wanted Billie to hold her — to remain suspended in this time and place indefinitely. She wanted to feel Billie surround her. Lust hovered between them, but love tapered it. Andi wouldn't trade this moment for any in her memory or any she knew might come to pass. This moment was a promise, a realization, and a gift both given and bestowed. Andi's mother had once told her that there was one way to know when you were in love:

"When you get more fulfillment simply by giving, when that is the ultimate joy, then you'll know, Andi. That's when you've found love."

Andi swept a strand of hair out of Billie's eyes. She could say the words, "I love you," over and over and it would remain inadequate. Instead, she lowered her lips to Billie's, delighting in the hint of what Billie called *hoppiness* that lingered from Billie's beer. It was uniquely Billie. Andi's tongue danced with Billie's as her hand began to slip lower, descending to Billie's breast, cupping its weight; the tip of her finger grazing the tip of Billie's nipple lightly before pinching gently.

Billie moaned into Andi's mouth. How could she feel hot and still be shivering? It reminded her of battling a fever. Her body burned, her heart thrummed in her chest forcefully, and yet she felt herself shiver. She struggled to breathe. She opened her mouth to speak but two fingers pressed to her lips before any words could pass them.

Andi felt Billie's shudder. She kissed Billie softly. "Shh," she cooed. "I know." She placed her lips against Billie's forehead lovingly. "Let go."

Billie's hands trembled as they attempted to grip Andi's waist. Andi's mouth claimed hers passionately for a brief moment. Billie could feel Andi's breasts gliding against hers. It was perfect. Billie's head rolled to the side, and Andi bit gently on the exposed flesh. Billie sighed. Andi's touch was tender and insistent at the same time. For the first time in her life, Billie had no desire to resist the sensual assault of flesh against flesh. Andi wanted her. Andi didn't want to take her; she wanted Billie to, "let go." And, Billie wanted to. More than she wanted to give pleasure to Andi, she desired to submit herself to Andi fully, to allow Andi to wrap her heart and her body in all that Andi was offering. She would let herself go and trust that on the other side of physical ecstasy she would finally find release—the release of long-held fears and insecurity.

Curves and dips, long expanses of supple flesh quivered beneath Andi's fingers. She watched in rapt fascination as Billie's lips parted. Her mouth surrounded Billie's nipple faintly at first. She teased and tasted the peach flesh with the tip of her tongue, enjoying the gasps and gulps of desperation that escaped the back of Billie's throat. Had she ever seen anything as magnificent? *Billie.* It perplexed Andi; the notion that Billie could not see how beautiful she was. Andi's heart sputtered erratically. Longing stole the air from her lungs. Billie's body quivered beneath hers. She felt Billie begin to go rigid, as if she needed to flee. Andi pressed her weight against Billie and lifted herself to look into Billie's eyes. "Stay with me," she requested, lowering her hand to explore Billie's arousal.

Billie gasped and tensed.

"Billie," Andi called lovingly. "Look at me."

Billie's eyes met Andi's. Andi offered her a sweet smile of understanding, silently conveying the promise that Billie was safe.

Andi swept the same strand of stubborn hair from Billie's eyes, searching their depths with hers. Softly, her hand began to explore Billie's softness. She bit back a moan. She wanted to descend Billie's body inch by inch until she could make love to Billie tenderly, kissing her and tasting her into pleasure-filled oblivion. *Soon.* Billie needed her. Billie needed to see her. Andi wasn't sure what held Billie back, but she understood that it was her place to help Billie let go. Her fingers lovingly traveled the length of Billie's arousal, tenderly and lovingly she lifted them until Billie's body rose unconsciously to meet her touch. Andi could no longer hold back, she claimed Billie's lips hungrily.

Billie heard a moan pass between them, buried in the heat of the kiss they shared. Andi's fingers danced lightly over her, faintly then firmly, then faintly again. Fear evaporated as quivering gave way to quaking. The sound of Andi's voice in her ear brought Billie over a precipice she'd long avoided.

"I love you, Billie."

Billie gripped Andi's flesh. A primal cry of ecstasy echoed through the room.

Andi's arms immediately surrounded Billie just as Billie's whispered, "Andi," turned to desperate sobs. Andi held her lover close and rocked her gently. "Shhh. Billie," Andi cooed. "It's okay, sweetheart."

"I'm sorry. You must think I'm..."

"I think that you are the most incredible woman I've ever known," Andi said. "Let it all go. Whatever it is, Billie, let it go. I can handle it."

Andi's words gave Billie the permission she'd craved for years. She wept in Andi's arms, clinging to Andi like a life-line.

"It's all right," Andi promised.

With a deep breath, Billie began to pull herself together. She pulled back to look at Andi through swollen eyes. "Not the way I imagined our first time making love."

"Is that so?"

"Crying like a baby because you made me..." Billie blushed and fell silent.

Andi chuckled. Billie was adorable. She couldn't bring herself to say the word. "Billie," she began cautiously. "Was that the first time you had an orgasm?"

Billie nodded.

"Do you want to talk about it?"

"I do, but I think right now I owe you..."

Andi shook her head. "No." She pulled Billie back into her embrace. "If you don't want to talk about it right now, I'll understand. You can. And, Billie? You don't *owe* me anything. That's not how this works."

"I want to. I mean, I want to touch you."

"I want you to touch me," Andi admitted. "But we have all the time in the world. I'm not going anywhere."

Billie took a deep breath. *I know you aren't.* "I haven't talked about this for a long time."

Andi stroked Billie's back in encouragement. "Take your time."

"Andi?"

"Yes?"

"Just don't let me go, okay?"

"Never."

❦

"Do I want to know why you were holding gymnastics class in your living room?"

"Hi, Mom."

"Hi, Mom?" Ida huffed. "How are you feeling?"

"How did you know?"

"Fallon, few things fail to reach my ears."

"Riley or Andi?" Fallon asked.

"I called Riley this morning and she filled me in."

"Great."

"Quit moping. I didn't call you about your floor routine."

Fallon snickered. "No? Should I guess?"

"I called to ask you a favor. Riley couldn't do it."

"Is everything okay?'

"Everything is fine. Beth has an appointment with Dr. Sherbrooke at two. Evan has a soccer game."

"Okay?"

"I was hoping you could take Beth. I think she could use the moral support."

Fallon considered the request. "How come I get preggo duty and you get to be Soccer Grandma?"

"Because I *am* Soccer Grandma."

"You are also just Grandma."

"Can you?"

Fallon groaned. "Yeah."

"Honestly, Fallon it's not as if you have to get into the stirrups. You just have to drive her there."

"Uh-huh."

"You can meet us at the game afterward."

"What time do I need to pick up Beth?"

"One-thirty would be good."

"Okay."

"Cheer up. I'll take you all out to dinner after the game."

"Out of curiosity, what did Riley say?"

"Just that she had lunch plans and wouldn't be able to get to Beth in time."

"Huh." *I wonder what that's about?*

"Fallon?"

"Sorry, I'll be over later." Fallon looked at the phone. *Now, who does Riley have plans with?* Beth would be with Fallon. Carol was working. Marge would still be at school. Ida had Evan's game. And, Andi? Well, Fallon guessed that Andi was otherwise engaged. That meant Billie wasn't Fallon's lunch date either. *What is she up to?*

⋘ ⋙

"Can I tell you that I'm secretly glad Billie got called into work?" Riley admitted.

"So, am I."

"What? Why?"

"It was a trade-off. She gets the whole weekend off now."

"Think you can wait that long?" Riley teased.

Andi's face flushed; the kind of flush that signified happiness not embarrassment. "I can. I wish I didn't have to, but I can."

"I take it everything is on the table now?"

"It's strange."

"What's that?" Riley wondered.

"I feel a bit like a lovestruck teenager," Andi confessed. "Dreaming about happily ever after at my age? Seems crazy."

"I don't think so."

Andi inhaled deeply and let it out. "That's not why you wanted to see me."

"It is — partly, anyway."

"Um-hum. And, the other part?"

"I asked Fallon to marry me."

Andi's immediate reaction was a bout of laughter.

"Not the reaction I expected."

"I'm sorry," Andi apologized. "I have this vision of her face. There is no way she saw that coming."

"Neither did I."

"Explain."

"I know she's been concocting some master plan to propose. You know, Fallon. She can't hide anything. The more she tries; the more she gives it away."

"Accurate."

"I don't know, Andi. She holds back sometimes. I know she trusts me. It's like she doesn't trust herself."

Andi nodded. "Riley, can I say something without you taking it the wrong way?"

"Please."

"You have lived beyond your years. You're not a typical thirty-year-old. But the truth is, ten years more living does make a difference in a person's outlook. It's not just what you see when you look back. It's the road forward."

"I'm not sure I follow."

"Well, Fallon will be forty-one."

"And?"

"The clock ticks for all of us. It's not just about how many years we might have left to become mothers. It's that the ticking reminds us that what stretches out before us is likely only as long as what we see behind us."

"That's depressing," Riley said.

"No." Andi laughed. "It isn't. It's reality."

"What does that have to do with us?"

"Oh, more than you think. She's lived a bit. I think when Fallon looks back she sees some recklessness— indulgence. That road behind her is littered with faces, Riley—faces and experiences that came and went. Ahead? That's all you."

"I'm trying to understand."

Andi's thoughts traveled to Billie. "It's reverence," she practically whispered.

"What?"

"Reverence," Andi said.

"I don't want to be revered."

"No, not you—what she feels for you, what you represent in her life. It has gravity, Riley—permanence—as much permanence as anything can hold. She's never felt that before. In that way, we are very much alike. She needs to do what she can to convey that to you."

"Andi, there isn't anything she could tell me or ask me that would change how I feel about her. I don't want her to hold back anything or be afraid to tell me."

"It's not fear," Andi said. "Maybe it is, but not in the way you are thinking."

"That makes no sense."

"Oh, it does. Believe me; it does."

"Speaking from experience?" Riley asked.

"I am."

"So, you're afraid to share things with Billie?"

"Not afraid, no. I realized last night how much I've held back with everyone I've ever been with. Not just Jake and Fallon. Even when I had convinced myself I was being free; I was holding back."

"What changed?" Riley asked.

"Everything," Andi answered with a smile. "Billie. Knowing... It's funny when I think about it. I'd convinced myself that my marriage to Jake was forever. Looking back, I always saw its end. I felt its end. From the beginning, Riley, some part of me knew that we weren't meant to last my lifetime. I pushed it aside. I knew when Fallon and I started our affair that it had an end. It didn't prevent me from loving either of them. It didn't stop the hurt that came with the endings. But I knew the ending would come. I just didn't know when or who or how."

"And, with Billie?"

"It feels as though she's always been in my life. It's surreal, actually. I know there was a time when she wasn't—

not really. It was yesterday, for heaven's sake." Andi shook her head. "Don't get me wrong; I expect rocks in our road. I can't picture my life without her. I don't want to. The first forty-six years of my life passed in the blink of an eye. When I look back?" Andi chuckled. "Marrying Jake feels like a year or two ago. And, here I am being called Grandma."

"You're a young grandmother." Riley winked.

"Thanks, and an honorary one. But, Riley, I could easily be Owen's grandmother. I *could* be your mother."

"To me, you are."

"I know." Andi reached out and squeezed Riley's hand. "I feel the same way."

Riley's emotions began to bubble to the surface. "I hate that I hurt you."

"You didn't," Andi said. "Life hurts sometimes. That's my point. Oh, Riley, Fallon wants you to know that she sees the rest of the road with you. You know, technically, *she* could be Owen's grandmother. That's not lost on her. She knows how fast the next five, ten, twenty years will pass. It's not fear. It's knowing. I don't know how else to explain that to you. It *feels* different. I don't think Fallon expected to be thinking about having babies in her forties." Andi laughed. "Most of us don't. The clock is moving from ticks to tocks and it feels like we're just beginning our lives. It goes by so fast, Riley. One day, your kids are crawling onto your lap and the next they are off living their lives as adults. It just goes by so fast. When you finally realize that? You have a new appreciation for love—for life. Fallon's not afraid of you leaving, Riley. She knows one day, one of you will leave the other. And, she doesn't expect that to be a choice. That means more to her than anything else. I get that. It's not fear; it's reverence."

Riley closed her eyes and nodded.

"Not what you expected me to say?"

"I'm not sure what I expected." Riley looked at Andi. "It reminds me why I called *you*."

"You can always call me. Have you told your mother yet? About marrying Fallon?"

Riley shook her head. "I haven't told anyone. Neither of us have. Only you."

"Are you worried about what they'll say?"

"Not really. My parents will be supportive. Mary will probably freak a little, but that's Mary."

"And?"

"I don't know, Andi. Truthfully? I'd be happy to stand at Town Hall with you and Billie and not tell anyone until afterward."

"Can I ask why?"

"Because it's not about fanfare for me. I understand what you said—more than you might think. Most people would think I'm crazy; I'm sure."

"Why is that?" Andi wondered.

"I'd marry Fallon today and not have one second of hesitation."

"I don't think that's crazy at all."

"You don't?"

Andi shook her head. "No."

"I was watching her with Owen this morning.... Andi... I..."

"I understand," Andi said.

"I feel like I found home. Not just with Fallon. My old life... That's what it feels like—my *old* life. I loved Robert. I had fun with my friends. Somehow, when I look back, I realize I was always restless. I thought I was content. Something never fit. It's like I was so busy planning everything that was supposed to happen, I forgot to experience most of it."

A bright smile curled Andi's lips, and brightened her eyes.

"What are you thinking?" Riley asked.

"I know exactly how you feel."

"Sometimes, I feel a little guilty."

"About what?"

"Oh, I think about everyone in California. I'd like to see them. This is home. This is the place I miss when I'm away. This is my *family*. When I tell them? They'll want us to come out there, have a big wedding. That much I do know. I'm not going to do that."

"What does Fallon think?"

"I don't know," Riley confessed. "It won't be Town Hall."

"No, I don't imagine so. Are you okay with that?"

"I am. I know she wants something special. What I don't know is why she thinks I need more."

"She knows you don't need more."

"That makes no sense."

"Sure, it does. She wants to give you everything she can, Riley. Fallon's waited a long time to be able to give herself to someone, and to give someone all the things *she's* dreamed about. It's not because she thinks *you* need any of it. It's because she wants to. Let her."

Riley considered Andi's advice. It made sense when she took a moment to process it. She wanted to give Fallon everything Fallon desired. Fallon wanted the same thing. Ironically, the need to give sometimes led them both to lose sight of what the other *did* desire. "So, what you're saying is that sometimes the best thing you can give someone else is to receive what they offer."

"Something like that, yes."

"She was upset last night," Riley said. "That she interrupted your time with Billie."

Andi wasn't surprised. "I know she was. I told her she could thank me by staying on her feet and off her head for a while."

Riley laughed. "You might want to put that in writing."

"Probably a good idea," Andi agreed.

"She blames herself for…"

"Everything. Yes, I know. It's not that she blames herself. I think Fallon needs to believe she can make things better. She was that way as a kid. She hates seeing anyone unhappy. When she can't fix that, she feels like she's failed somehow. That's who she is, Riley. That's who she'll always be."

"I know, and I love her for it. I just wish it didn't eat her up so much."

"She'll be all right. She has you."

"Andi?"

"Yes?"

"Thanks."

"For?"

"I think you know."

"I love you, Riley. I love Fallon too. Don't ever forget that."

"I won't."

❦

The brisk September breeze did little to deter Owen's desire to get wet. Fallon watched as he stomped in a shallow stream with delight. "Your mother is going to kill me."

Owen flashed Fallon a devious grin.

"Are you trying to get us both in trouble?" Fallon asked him.

Owen shook with laughter and fell on his butt in the stream.

"Mommy's going to think I told you to do that."

Owen laughed harder.

"Owen, my boy, what am I going to do with you?" Fallon was ready to place Owen on his feet when a splash took her by surprise.

"You wet too, Momma!"

Fallon shook her head. "I'm going to be in divorce court before I even get married," she commented. "You know, this is not swimming weather."

"You siw'ly, Momma."

"I'm silly? You're the one sitting in the mud."

Everything Fallon said seemed to amuse Owen— everything. She'd decided to take a day away from the pub. When she announced at breakfast that she would have all day to spend with the toddler, Owen greeted the news by running through the house, screaming with excitement. Fallon had packed them a lunch and suggested they take a walk and have a picnic. Food was forgotten the moment Owen spotted the stream. Fallon had helped him skip a few stones and humored him with a search for fish and frogs. He'd spotted a few fish, and made a valiant, albeit ridiculous attempt to catch one with his hands. He was filthy. She looked down at the bottom of her jeans. Filthy was an accurate description for them both. She groaned.

"You know," she looked at Owen. "Your mother is going to make us *both* learn to sort out the laundry when she sees us."

Fallon's dire expression sent Owen into another fit of laughter.

"That's funny?" Fallon asked. "It won't be so funny when we're sleeping in the shed." She reached down to make another attempt at placing Owen on his feet and slipped, landing next to Owen in the stream. "Oh, great," she mumbled.

"Momma!" Owen fell into Fallon's side, laughing raucously. "You filfy!"

Fallon gave up and laughed. The happiness in Owen's eyes took her breath away. *Aw, who cares. Anything that makes you this happy is worth it, even laundry.*

⋰⋱

"Concentrate, Riley." Riley tried to focus on the words in front of her. Nothing worked. The words blurred together in squiggly lines that made her head hurt. She'd enjoyed a leisurely breakfast with Andi, and left feeling centered, even excited about the future. With her confidence high, and her spirits soaring, she'd picked up the phone and called her sister. "What were you thinking?" She admonished herself. True to form, Mary was Mary; the nagging, overly protective, always skeptical older sister. Love sometimes didn't taper frustration, and Mary could frustrate Riley unlike anyone on the planet. "Shit." The sound of the backdoor opening, and Owen's laughter filtered to Riley's ears. "At least someone is happy."

"Mommy!" Owen bellowed.

Riley winced.

"Momma's filfy!"

"Owen!" Fallon called after him. "Come back here and let me get your shoes off!"

Riley squinted against the mounting pressure in her head to bring Owen into focus. "Oh, my. What happened to you?"

Fallon stepped into the doorway.

Riley's eyes swept over Fallon. "And you."

"We had a little run in with the stream," Fallon explained.

"I guess I don't need to ask who won," Riley replied.

"Momma won!"

"I can see *that*," Riley commented.

"Owen, go into the big bathroom. You can play in some bubbles," Fallon told him.

"Kay!"

"Riley?"

"Decided on a swim?" Riley asked.

"More like fishing without a pole. Are you okay?" Fallon asked.

"Just a headache."

"You don't get headaches."

"I do when I talk to Mary."

"Oh, boy." Fallon walked over and shut Riley's laptop.

"Fallon, I have a deadline. And, some laundry to do, apparently."

"No, you don't. Not today anyway. You go lie down for a bit. I'll take care of Owen and me, and the laundry."

"And, my deadline?"

"Wasn't it you who said deadlines move?"

Riley huffed. "Not this one."

"Well, you're not going to get much done when you can barely keep your eyes open. Go. I'm serious."

"I need to…"

"You need to close your eyes for a while. I'll make you a deal."

"A deal? Does this one involve any major appliances?" Riley wanted to know.

"Only an alarm clock. I promise to wake you up in a few hours. Please? Take a rest for a bit."

Riley threw her head back against the sofa cushions. "Promise me you will wake me up."

"I promise."

"Momma!" Owen called out. "Bubbles!"

Riley pulled herself from the sofa. "Leave the laundry, Fallon. I'll take care of it later."

"Just go," Fallon said. She watched Riley disappear into the hallway and sighed. "I can only imagine what brought that on."

"Momma!"

"I know — bubbles!"

⁊ₑ ·ₑ₰

Owen followed Fallon's gaze as it moved from the laundry basket to the washing machine, and then to a heaping pile of clothes on the floor. "Why is this so hard for me?" She mused aloud.

"Bubbles, Momma."

"Huh?"

Owen pointed to the bottle of laundry detergent.

"Yeah, that does make bubbles."

"Yep. Like a baf!"

"I guess it is," Fallon agreed. "A bath for our clothes."

"Yep!"

"How did you get so smart?" Fallon asked playfully.

"Mommy," he replied seriously.

Fallon chuckled. "I have no doubt about that."

"Do I want to know what is going on in here?" Riley asked.

"I thought you were resting?"

"I was."

"How are you feeling?" Fallon wondered.

Riley looked at the chaos in the laundry room. "I *was* feeling better. What on earth are you doing?"

"Bubbles, Mommy."

"Uh-huh," Riley said.

"I've got this," Fallon said.

"What exactly *is* this?"

Owen pointed to the pile. "Pig Pen," he said.

Riley raised an eyebrow.

Owen grinned. "Momma's Pig Pen."

"No," Fallon corrected. "I said you looked like Pig Pen."

"You!" Owen pointed at Fallon and laughed.

"I look like Pig Pen?" Fallon asked.

Owen nodded.

"I took a shower!"

"Momma needs bubbles!"

Riley bit her lip to keep from laughing. Fallon might have showered, handling the dirty clothes had left a smudge on her cheek, dirt on her jeans, and a light brown film on her fingers. "Maybe I should throw you in with the pile," Riley said.

"Oh, ha-ha."

"You know, it might have been a good idea to start the laundry *before* you took that shower," Riley offered.

"Pig Pen!" Owen laughed.

"Whose side are you on?" Fallon asked.

Owen kept laughing.

"He's been laughing at me all day," Fallon said.

Owen grinned and wrapped his arms around Fallon's legs.

Riley gave up and laughed. Now, Owen was dirty again. "Honestly," she said. "Okay, you two... take it off."

"Take what off?" Fallon asked.

"Your clothes," Riley said. "You can leave the bare essentials on. Leave the pig pen on the floor. And, let's try this exercise in futility one more time."

Fallon groaned. "I'll be a prune before this day is over." She helped Owen undress and shed her T-shirt and jeans. "Okay?"

"Throw it all in the washing machine," Riley directed.

"I thought you were..."

"Fallon, we don't all need to shower again today."

"Fine." Fallon threw the dirty clothes into the machine.

"Momma, bubbles," Owen reminded her.

"I got it. I got it."

Riley shook her head and lifted Owen onto her hip.

"Where are you going?" Fallon asked.

"I'm going to put Mr. Bubbles here in a clean pair of pajamas while, you—Ms. Pig Pen, clean yourself up." She smiled at Fallon and started for the stairs.

Owen waved. "Bye, Momma!"

"Traitor," Fallon muttered. "I'm never going to live this one down."

Riley peeked back into the room. "Maybe by the time he's in high school." She winked and left the room again.

"He can do his own then!" Fallon called out.

"Your momma is silly," Riley whispered to Owen.

"Yep," he agreed.

Fallon had insisted that Riley take whatever time she needed to work. Laundry might not have been her strong suit; she could cook a mean burger, and according to Owen, Fallon was a mac and cheese master. True to her word, she'd made dinner, cleaned up, and led Owen to the bedroom for a story. Riley's deadline had provided Riley with an escape. Fallon was curious what had transpired between Riley and her older sister. It was strange when she thought about it. She was ready to marry Riley. She'd never met Riley's parents of sister, and Riley had yet to meet Dean. Fallon had spoken with both of Riley's parents on the phone, and even engaged in a virtual visit with Mary and Riley's niece a couple of times. Still, she was a stranger to them. She guessed that left unanswered questions in Mary's mind. She also understood that Riley had no desire to explain her decisions or feelings. Riley sought her sister's support and congratulations, not a barrage of questions. A barrage of questions could be exhausting. She should know. Owen had traded story time nearly an hour ago for what Fallon thought might end up a game of two-hundred questions.

"Momma?"

"Hum?"

"Gwama is your mommy?"

"Grandma Ida is my mommy, yes."

"Momma?"

"Yes, Owen?"

"You love Mommy?"

"Yes, I do. I love Mommy very much, and I love you."

Owen chewed on his lip thoughtfully. "Like Gwama and Biw'lie?"

"Yes, I love Mommy like Grandma loves Billie."

Owen smiled.

"How did you know that Grandma loves Billie?"

"She smiles."

"She smiles?"

"Uh-huh. Like you and Mommy."

"I smile with Mommy?"

"Uh-huh."

"Well, that's because Mommy makes me happy."

"Momma?"

Fallon sniggered. The question game had become Owen's favorite for the last month. "Yes?"

"I'm yours?"

Fallon's heart leapt into her throat. *Oh, Owen.* "I love you, Owen."

"I'm yours?" He asked again.

Riley had been standing just outside the room, content to listen to Owen question Fallon about everything and anything. She heard the emotional hitch in Fallon's voice, and detected the hopefulness in her son's. It amazed Riley—the way children processed relationships. Everyone needed to feel he or she belonged someplace. Everyone wanted to be loved. Owen was asking Fallon to be his. And, Riley didn't need to see Fallon's face to know how badly Fallon wanted to claim him as hers. She stepped into the room. Fallon looked up helplessly, and Riley smiled. She took a seat on the edge of the bed. "I think, Owen, the question is: do you want Fallon to be *yours*?"

Owen thought for a second and then nodded. "Momma's mine?"

"Fallon is your momma," Riley said.

Owen looked at his mother. "I'm Momma's?"

Riley's hand combed through the short wave of Owen's hair. "Yes, sweetheart," Riley said. "And, you are Momma's."

Owen smiled. He looked at Fallon hopefully.

Time stopped for Fallon. Owen silently implored her to answer his question. Why was she suddenly speechless? Owen had been referring to her as his momma for weeks. She loved it. She loved feeling that Owen *was* hers. Riley had assured her again and again that she would and should play the role of a parent in Owen's life. Fallon wanted to—desperately. Somehow, she felt that calling Owen her son was too much, not for her—for Riley and Owen. She felt Riley's hand gently squeeze her knee. Fallon took a deep breath, reached over and settled Owen between her legs. She kissed the top of his head and closed her eyes. "You will always be mine, Owen."

Owen smiled and snuggled against Fallon. "Cause we filfy, Momma."

Riley's laughter could not prevent tears from rolling over her cheek. Innocence was precious and honest. She cherished the perspective Owen had on life and the people he loved. Often, she mused that he taught her far more than she could ever hope to impart to him. "That is the truth," Riley agreed. "Thank goodness for all those bubbles."

Fallon rolled her eyes. "I did the laundry."

"Yes, you did," Riley agreed.

"I even folded it."

"I'm impressed."

"I just didn't put it away."

Riley smirked. It was Fallon's failure to put away her laundry that had led to their original bet, and to Fallon's foibles with laundry. It had become part of the fabric of their relationship—laundry. Silly and strange as it might have seemed to someone looking in, Riley understood that laundry represented a bridge between them. Neither had been sure how to proceed with the other. Looking back, Riley's feelings for Fallon had deepened almost immediately. She'd pushed them aside, brushed them off. She was in an unfamiliar place and Fallon was the one person who felt familiar. And, Fallon? Fallon had started falling in love with Riley almost immediately. Riley knew that. People often found connection in the mundane. Laundry had been theirs. Riley suspected it would always serve as a place for them to meet. When emotions bubbled to the surface, and insecurity knocked, laundry would remind them both that this was and would forever be home. Perhaps, to others it would seem silly. To Riley, banter over dirty clothes, washing machines, and laundry baskets represented love—falling in love with Fallon Foster and finding her way home.

"Well, I think it's time for someone to head to his bed," Riley said.

Owen groaned his protest and clung to Fallon.

"Nice try, Mr. Bubbles," Riley said.

He giggled.

"Go with Mommy," Fallon said.

Owen shook his head.

"Owen," Riley warned gently.

He looked at his mother.

"You want Fallon to tuck you in?"

"Momma," he corrected her.

"Momma can tuck you in," Riley said.

Fallon hoisted herself and Owen off the bed. "Did you get bigger after dinner?" She teased him. "I swear, you grew."

"No, Momma!" Owen laughed.

"Pretty soon you'll be carrying me," Fallon said as she left the room.

Riley shook her head affectionately at the pair. "Two of a kind," she mused. They were.

Riley collapsed back onto the bed. The day had presented her with a myriad of emotions. She had needed to talk to Andi. After their conversation, Riley felt she had the strength to call her family and tell them about her plans with Fallon. She'd called her mother first and been greeted with a simple, "if you are happy, that's all that matters." The sentiment was sincere. It was not the ringing endorsement that Riley had hoped for. She'd tried calling her father twice unsuccessfully. Finally, with a deep breath, she placed a call to her sister. Talking with Mary had reminded her why she sought Andi or Ida for advice and encouragement. Riley wasn't certain if that made her grateful or sad. Maybe it was a bit of both. She replayed the call for the umpteenth time that day:

"Are you telling me that Fallon asked you to marry her?"

"No. Actually, I asked her."

Silence hovered.

"Mary?"

"You proposed marriage?" Mary sought clarification.

"I did."

"Why?"

Did she seriously just ask me why?" Riley took several deep breaths, willing herself not to explode. "Why did I ask Fallon to marry me?"

"Marriage? Riley, you haven't even known this woman for a year."

"I know you have a point here. I don't know what it is."

"I just made it. My God, haven't you and Owen been through enough? I know you're lonely…"

"I'm not lonely," Riley countered.

"Then why the rush?"

"Who says we're rushing?

"Oh, so you plan on a long engagement?" Mary asked.

"I don't know. We haven't talked much about it."

"And, you don't find that strange?"

Riley was ready to reply that she found many things *strange*. The fact that she and Fallon had yet to start making wedding plans neither surprised nor concerned her. She suspected that Fallon was planning something, likely, some romantic gesture. "Why is that strange?"

"In my experience, when you get engaged there is usually excitement about planning."

"Well, this is *my* experience not yours." Riley reminded he sister.

"At least, that gives you time."

"Time?"

"In case you change your mind."

Anger simmered in Riley's veins. "That's not going to happen."

"Things change."

"Not this," Riley replied.

Mary let out a long sigh. "I know you think you're in love…."

A caustic chuckle preceded Riley's thought. "I don't *think* anything."

"You've had a lot of change, and I know that Fallon is good to you. I'm sure you feel secure there. Marriage is…."

"Why can't you be happy for me?" Riley asked.

"What? I'm only trying to…"

"Why can't you—for once—just say, 'Riley, that's wonderful?' Is that so hard for you?"

"Living with someone and marrying them are not the same thing, Riley."

"You don't think I know that?"

"I think you ran away."

There had been more than a handful of hurtful things Mary had said over the last year. Well-intentioned or not, her words often cut Riley to the core. Of all the opinions Mary chose to dress up as sisterly concern, this hurt most of all. Run away? Riley had faltered many times after Robert's death. She'd battled depression. She'd suffered sleepless nights filled with fear. She'd confronted anger that made her want to lash out. She'd wanted to *run away* many times. She never did. Her decision to move across the country had never been about avoidance. She needed something new. She needed to discover who she was again. She had. Along the way, Riley had created home. The longer she lived in Whiskey Springs, the more nights she slept beside Fallon, the deepening of the relationships she shared in the small town, reminded Riley that families—that *home* was not something you *found*. Home was a place you created by investing in the people you loved. It wasn't a place on a map. Home was knowing you belonged with someone. That extended beyond a lover. It encompassed children, parents, siblings, co-workers, and friends. Riley's home existed in Whiskey Springs because she chose to create it here. And, it was not always easy. She missed her parents. She missed her friends. She even missed Mary. Familiarity was not what drove Riley to settle on building a life in Vermont, and it certainly wasn't avoidance. Love was the reason.

"Riley?" Mary wondered if Riley was still on the line.

"I'm here. I heard you."

"Running into…"

"I don't know what to say," Riley said sadly. "I was crazy enough to hope you would be happy for me."

"I worry about you."

"No," Riley said. "You want me to do what *you* think I *should* do—what you believe *you* would do."

"That's not true."

"Yes, I think it is. The thing is," Riley steadied herself before continuing. "You can't know what you would do if you were me. You haven't lost what I have."

"That's my point. Loss…"

"Stop. I'm not here because I lost Robert. I'm not hiding from anything or anyone. This is where I want to be — where I *choose* to be. My life with Fallon isn't fallout, and it isn't someplace to shelter in place either. It's not always easy, Mary. We're not perfect. We don't always agree. God knows, we'll have our challenges. I know we will get through them."

"Riley, listen to me for a minute…"

"I've listened to you plenty. I know you aren't trying to hurt me. You do. This? This conversation hurts me more than any we've had. I love Fallon. Owen loves Fallon. She loves us. I don't need to explain that to you. Did anyone ask you to explain your marriage?"

"That's not the same…"

"Why? Because you don't like where I live, or you have an issue with who I live with?"

"Fallon seems lovely. I'm sure that you've made friends and…"

"You're not hearing me. You've never agreed with my decision to come here."

"Because you ran away from home like a teenager in crisis!"

Riley lost the will to fight. "No, I didn't," she said calmly.

"You did. You still are. This is like some kind of rebellion. You run three-thousand miles away and decide you're a lesbian…"

Ah, the truth comes out. "I never said I was a lesbian."

"What would you call it?"

"Does it matter?" Riley asked. "Do you think that because I'm with Fallon that somehow means my life with Robert was a lie? Maybe I was hiding back then."

"Were you?"

Riley sighed. "No."

"So, what? You're bisexual? Come on, Riley. Can't you see this for what it is?"

"I see things more clearly than I ever have."

"I wish you would think about…"

"Well, we all wish people would do what we want them to do. I wish you could accept me and my life without offering your opinion about either. That's not who you are."

"That's not fair."

"Life isn't fair sometimes," Riley said. "I need to go. Fallon will be back with Owen soon, and I have a lot of work to catch up on."

"Riley…"

"I'll talk to you."

"Riley…"

"It's all right," Riley said. "I think we both know where we stand. Give my love to everyone there." She disconnected the call.

Riley tried to banish the memory. "I guess it could have been worse," she muttered.

"What's that?" Fallon asked from the doorway.

"Did he go down?"

"Change the subject much?"

"I'm not. I just don't know what the point is in talking about it."

"For one thing, you don't tend to get headaches. I think there's a *big* point to talking about it. What happened?"

"What always happens," Riley said. "Mary still thinks I'm a thirteen-year-old kid. Maybe she just thinks that when I do something she doesn't agree with."

"Let me guess. That would be marrying me."

Riley pulled Fallon onto the bed with her. "No, Fallon; it isn't."

"I think it is."

"No. Mary has never agreed with my choices— certainly not any that led me here."

"To me?"

"To Whiskey Springs," Riley corrected her. "It doesn't matter."

"It does. She's your sister, Riley. It matters."

"Not as much as you think."

Fallon remained doubtful.

"I imagine it's a bit like how you feel with Dean."

"Maybe."

"You miss him. I know you do."

"Sometimes. I don't understand him, though."

"You're angry with him."

"How did this become about me?"

"I just think we have some things in common that we don't always talk about," Riley explained. "I love my family, Fallon. My family has been distant for much longer than I've lived here. The truth is, Robert and I barely saw any of them — even Mary. It was always tense. There's this need to ask forgiveness all the time with them. Mary thinks my parents owe her that. My parents... Well, they're friends, but that guilt... You can feel it. Mary hammered that with both of them. Me? She always sought to be my mother. Maybe because my mom had always been more like a friend to us both. Don't get me wrong, I love my mother. She's kind and she's honest. She's not the person either of us seek for guidance, more like for friendly support. And, that's okay. At least, for me it is. For Mary?"

"Maybe you should invite her to come visit," Fallon suggested.

"Here?"

"This *is* where we live. Invite her for Thanksgiving. Invite them all."

"I don't know, Fallon."

"I'm not suggesting it will fix everything. Maybe meeting all of us will help a little."

"Maybe. I'll think about it. What about you?"

"What about me?"

"Oh, I saw your face when Owen asked if he was yours."

Fallon took a moment to formulate her reply. "When we were down by the stream today, this older couple walked by. I don't know who they were. It kind of took me by surprise."

"I'll bet it's Mrs. Babcock's sister," Riley said.

"Mrs. Babcock has a sister?" Fallon asked. "How did I not know that?"

Riley shrugged. "Not really the point," she said.

"Anyway," Fallon went on. "The woman stopped to talk to Owen. You know him, he had to tell her all about his house, and the pond, and his grandmas."

Riley smiled.

"She looked at me, and said, *your son is a delight*," Fallon recalled.

"He is."

"He knows it too," Fallon said.

"Mm… I meant he is *your* son. Fallon? Look at me, please."

"Riley…"

"He is," Riley said. "You're his momma. We've talked about this. If you can't trust me on this point; you need to trust Owen. You're the parent he will always know. And, I wouldn't change that."

"Riley, I…"

"I wouldn't change that. Life happens. I couldn't concentrate on anything after I talked to Mary today."

"I know."

"Then I saw you and Owen walk into the house covered in mud."

"Sorry about that."

"Don't be. How do I explain this to you?"

"You don't have to explain anything," Fallon said.

"Maybe I need to explain it for myself. You know, I spent the morning with Andi."

"How is Andi?"

"In love," Riley said. "We talked about that. We talk about everything."

"Yeah, I know."

"I love her, Fallon. I love my mom and I love my sister, but I can't explain it. Andi's more like a mother, and a sister to me than Mary or my mom has ever been. Or maybe it's just she's the mom I need. I don't know. I just know that I can tell Andi anything and she's never going to tell me I should feel differently. She'll be honest, but she won't negate what I feel."

"No. That's not Andi's way," Fallon agreed. "It never has been."

"I told her, Fallon."

"Told her?"

"That I asked you to marry me."

Fallon nodded. "What did she say?"

"After she laughed?"

"She laughed?"

"She was picturing your face."

"Mmm. What did she say?" Fallon was both curious and concerned. While she and Andi had both moved on, Fallon wondered how it felt to hear that news.

"She wasn't surprised. I mean, she was surprised that *I* asked you, not that we wanted to get married. It's just…. You would think that I would be nervous to tell Andi that. I wasn't. Not even a little bit, Fallon. We talked about so many things today. I told her things I'm not sure I would tell anyone else except you."

"I'm glad you have her."

"I told her, Fallon."

"Told her?"

"To me, she's my mom."

"She feels the same way, Riley."

"Yeah, I know. I realized something while you were in the shower earlier."

"What's that?"

"Family is a choice, Fallon. It's always a choice. Home is a choice too. It's not something any of us are given—not really. It's something we create."

"You're pretty smart, you know?" Fallon said.

"I don't know about that. I do know that this is my family, and it's Owen's family. I wouldn't change that, not even if I could go back in time. I'm glad I had Robert. I am. Without him, I wouldn't be here. Maybe this is where I was supposed to be all along. I wish it hadn't taken that loss to find my way. But it does remind me that everything has purpose. It hurt today. Hearing Mary say the things she did — it hurt. Maybe I needed to hear that too."

"Why?"

"Because it reminded me what matters most."

"You need to write that novel," Fallon said. "You have a way with words, Riley."

"Mmm. And, you have a way with people. I love you, Fallon. I don't want to wait."

Fallon was confused.

"To get married. I don't want a big thing. I don't want fanfare. I just want you and Owen and the people we love. That's it."

"Then that's what we'll have."

Riley was surprised.

"What? You want me to argue? No argument here. I'm all about doing it before you change your mind."

Riley laughed. "Hoping I will?"

"Nope. Just locking it in."

"Well, I'm afraid you were locked in the moment you said yes."

"We all have our cross to bear," Fallon retorted.

Riley smacked her.

"Yours, I'm afraid is me." Fallon pulled Riley into her arms.

"Fallon?"

"Hum?"

"You're a great mom."

"I have great teachers," Fallon replied. "I do have a question."

"What's that?"

"Do I have to change my name?"

Riley laughed loudly.

"What? I'm serious!"

"I know," Riley said. "That's why it's funny."

Fallon grumbled.

"We'll negotiate," Riley said.

"You might want to rethink that. Last time you ended up with the short end of the stick," Fallon reminded Riley.

"Not a bet, Fallon—a negotiation."

Fallon's eyes gleamed with playfulness. She flipped Riley onto her back and grinned. "Okay, I start on top."

Riley giggled. "Bottoms up," she said, flipping them around. "Now, about your name…"

CHAPTER NINE

TWO WEEKS LATER

*C*ommotion—that was the best word to describe Murphy's Law at the moment. Pete had called Fallon and asked if he and Dale could use the pub for a party. Pete and Dale's desire to spend time at Murphy's Law was not surprising. Pete *or* Dale attempting to organize anything that bordered on an event was shocking. The impromptu festivities had half the town scratching their heads. Carol had joked that maybe the two finally decided to get hitched. Fallon had pointed out that Marge might object to any impending nuptials between her boyfriend and her brother. Carol had a few more guesses.

"Oh, I know!" Carol jumped up excitedly. "Pete's going on the wagon!"

"What wagon?" Fallon asked. "I think he's outgrown the Red Flyer."

"No! Maybe he's decided on sobriety!"

Fallon stared at Carol.

"What? You never know."

"Yes, because everyone announces sober living in a bar."

Ida shook her head at the muted rumbling in the pub. No one seemed to have any clue why they'd been summoned to Murphy's Law on a Sunday afternoon. "Now, what do you suppose this is all about?" Ida asked Andi.

"I haven't the faintest idea."

"She didn't tell you?"

"Fallon? Nope. I don't think she knows."

"Yeah, but what does she *suspect*?"

"I think where Dale and Pete are concerned, Fallon gave up on suspecting anything long ago."

Ida snorted. "Fair."

"Hi," Marge walked up to the bar.

"Hi, Marge," Andi greeted her. "Where's your other half?"

"He's still out with Pete, I think."

"What are those two up to?" Ida asked.

Marge's eyes fell to the counter and she blushed.

"Don't tell me, you and Dale got engaged; didn't you?" Andi guessed.

Marge's smile served as Andi's confirmation.

"That's terrific," Andi said.

"Thanks, but do me a favor, and let him announce it."

Andi crossed her heart. "Your secret's safe with me and Ida."

"For the next hour, it is," Ida quipped.

Marge giggled.

"How about a celebratory drink?" Andi suggested. "Ida's buying."

Ida coughed. "Which means it's on the house."

"Thanks," Marge said. "I think I'll stick with water."

"Nervous?" Ida asked.

Marge shrugged bashfully.

Andi studied her friend for a moment. She patted Marge's hand. "Nothing to be nervous about," she said with a wink. "When it's meant to be, it's meant to be."

"I hope so," Marge replied.

"I know so," Andi said.

"Oh, you two and your puppy dog love," Ida groaned.

Andi laughed. "Hey, you might be next."

"Ha!" Ida waved off Andi's statement. "The only thing sharing my bed these days is a three-year-old who kicks!"

"He does like to move around," Andi said.

"Owen?" Marge guessed.

"Yeah, I think Fallon's using some subliminal mind control on him," Andi commented.

"He's just like her," Ida said.

"Fallon kicks in bed?" Marge asked innocently.

Andi coughed slightly.

Ida patted Andi's back. "I don't think that's what she meant. But some habits are hard to break."

"Hey," Riley strolled in."

"Where's Owen?" Ida asked.

"Wherever his Momma is."

Andi smiled. "How's Fallon handling that?"

"Being Momma instead of Fallon? I think she's getting used to it—as much as any of us do. It's pretty much half and half these days. Half of the time he calls for Fallon and half the time he wants Momma."

"Which half?" Ida asked.

Riley laughed.

"I'll guess it's when he doesn't get his way with Mommy," Andi said.

"Bingo," Riley replied. "Or when he's tired. He seems to gravitate to Fallon at bedtime." Riley smiled at Marge.

"I'm missing something," Ida said.

Andi giggled.

"Okay, out with it, you three," Ida demanded.

Marge blushed again. Riley and Andi exchanged a smile.

"What is going on?" Ida asked again.

Marge looked at Andi. Andi understood the silent request. "I think Whiskey Springs might finally hit the 1000 mark this year," she said.

Ida's brow crinkled for a second, then she smiled broadly. "Andi! Did Billie get you pregnant?"

Riley and Marge burst out laughing.

"What are you laughing about?" Ida pointed to Riley. "Or is my daughter responsible for this?"

Riley held up her hands. "Not that I'm aware of."

Ida smiled. She reached over and embraced Marge. "It'll work out this time," she whispered.

"I hope so," Marge replied.

Ida tightened her hold. "Well, we'll all just have to keep saying and praying that it will; won't we?"

Marge nodded.

"Mommy!" An excited voice called out.

Riley turned to see Owen running toward her. "Where's Momma?"

Owen spun on his heels and pointed to the door. "Helpin," he said.

"Helping?"

"Yep. Daywul."

"Momma's helping Dale?"

"Yep."

"That could take a while," Ida commented playfully.

Marge smiled. "It might," she replied.

⚜

"What's up?" Fallon asked her friend.

"Do you think we could take a walk?" Dale asked.

"Are you okay?"

"Yeah. I just… Just before we go in there, I just…."

"Come on," Fallon said. "We'll walk up the hill."

"Yeah, but what about Owen?"

"I'm sure Riley and Grandma squared can handle it," Fallon quipped.

"You really love that; don't you?"

"What?"

"Owen calling Andi, Grandma," Dale said.

Fallon shrugged. "She loves it too."

"Can I ask you something?"

"Can I stop you?" Fallon replied.

Dale sighed.

"Hey," Fallon stopped walking. "What's going on with you?"

"I don't know, Fallon."

Fallon scratched her brow thoughtfully. She pointed to a big log a few feet away. "What's going on?"

Dale took a seat beside Fallon on the log. He struggled to answer her question.

"Dale?"

"Marge is pregnant."

"No shit! That's great!"

"Is it?" He asked.

"Isn't it?"

"I don't know, Fallon."

"I thought you and Marge were...."

"I love her."

"I'm not following. You love kids."

"Yeah. I never thought I'd have any, though. And, Marge? I don't know, Fallon. If this goes south, I'm not sure if she'll survive it."

Fallon sobered. She massaged her eyes, feeling a headache mounting already. Why did joy so often have to be tapered by fear? "You have to believe it'll be okay," Fallon said.

Dale sighed heavily.

"It's not just that; is it?" Fallon guessed.

"I don't know."

"You just said that you love her."

"I do," Dale admitted. "I guess I never thought I would."

"Would love Marge?"

"Would love anyone," he muttered.

"Why would you think that?"

"Because... I don't know. There's only two people I've ever trusted."

Fallon nodded. "Until now."

"Yeah. And, what if I lose her? I don't know. It was easier when I was pining over you."

Fallon smiled. She'd always known that Dale loved her. She'd also guessed that his feelings were misplaced. He trusted Fallon. Fallon knew his secrets and she was acquainted with his demons. She was also someone who was *safe* to love. She could never give Dale what he longed for. He knew that. She suspected that unconsciously, that was the main reason Dale had carried a torch for her over the years. "Probably so," she agreed.

"You knew?"

"Kinda' hard not to."

"Shit."

Fallon chuckled.

"I feel like an ass," Dale muttered.

"Why?"

"What kind of idiot falls for a lesbian?"

"Why does that make you an idiot?" Fallon wondered.

"Seriously?"

"I am serious. Shit—look at me."

"You have Riley."

Fallon beamed. "Yeah, I do. But I didn't always have Riley. I mean, look at my track record with love."

"What do you mean? You mean Andi?"

"That was a dead-end."

"Were you in love with her?" Dale asked.

Fallon took a deep breath and let it out slowly. "As much as a person can be when they know it *is* a dead-end."

"Yeah, but she loved you back. It's not like you go falling for people who'd never give you a second look."

"You don't think I care about you?"

"Nah, I know you *care* about me. You care about everybody."

"Not like I care about you," Fallon said.

"What if I'm wrong?" Dale asked.

"What are you talking about?"

"What if Marge is just with me because she was lonely?"

"I don't think Marge is that shallow."

"What if I suck?"

Fallon laughed. "At being a dad or at being a husband?"

Dale's face drained of all color. "How did you know?"

"That you proposed to Marge? You're not a hard puzzle to figure out."

"I didn't ask her because she's…"

"I know that," Fallon said.

"What if I do?" He asked. "What if I suck?"

"Don't ask me. I worry about that all the time."

"Huh?"

"Sucking at this whole thing. All of a sudden, Owen's calling me, Momma. And, then there's Riley…."

"Uh… Fallon? You guys are great together."

"Right now, we are."

"Are you having second thoughts about her?"

"Riley? No way," Fallon said. She rubbed her eyes again. "I don't want to let them down," she confessed.

"Yeah, I know the feeling. Are you going to ask her?"

"Ask her?"

"To marry you?" Dale clarified.

"I wanted to."

"But?"

Fallon said nothing. Only Andi knew that she and Riley were engaged.

"She's not going to say no."

Fallon nodded.

"What's stopping you?"

"Nothing."

"Riley ain't Liv, Fallon."

Fallon shook her head.

"Can I tell you something?"

"Something else?" Fallon quipped. "Is it twins?"

"Shit! I hope not."

Fallon laughed.

"Can I?" Dale asked.

"Go ahead."

"Liv wasn't good for you."

Fallon was surprised at the firmness in Dale's voice. He didn't sound angry or hateful. He did sound confident.

"She wasn't," he said again.

"Did you always think that?"

He nodded.

"Why didn't you say anything?"

"You would've thought it was me being jealous."

Probably true. Fallon groaned. "So, tell me now."

Dale hesitated.

"Dale?"

"Aw, fuck, Fallon."

"What?"

"Me and Pete saw her."

"Saw her?"

Dale shook his head. He'd wrestled his with guilt for years. He should've told Fallon years ago.

"Dale?" Fallon urged her friend.

"Fallon…"

"Just tell me. It's ancient history, anyway."

Ancient history or not, Dale was positive that what he was about to share would shake Fallon. Betrayal was never easy to accept.

"Dale!"

"Her and Dean," Dale said.

"What about Liv and Dean?"

"Fallon…"

"Oh, for Christ's sake, just tell me!"

"Me and Pete went out to the boathouse to drink a few beers, you know?"

"Uh-huh…"

"And, well… The thing is… See… We didn't know he was with Liv at first."

Fallon's gaze hardened. Dale's apologetic expression turned her stomach. She didn't need any more information. "Jesus…"

"I'm sorry, Fallon."

Fallon tried to breathe. Without warning she ran to a nearby bush and lost the contents of her breakfast. *How could they?*

Dale closed his eyes regretfully. *I'm sorry, Fallon.*

❧

All eyes turned to the door when Dale strolled through. Noticeably missing from his company was Fallon. He looked at four women gathered together near the counter apologetically.

"That doesn't look good," Ida commented.

"Where's Fallon?" Marge asked before anyone else had the chance.

"She took a walk up the hill," he said.

Riley waited for an explanation.

"Aw, shit," he said. "We were talking, and I ended up telling her something I didn't plan to."

Marge sighed.

"Care to enlighten us?" Ida asked.

"I don't think I should."

Ida's gaze narrowed.

Riley looked at Andi. "Could you..."

"We've got Owen covered. Go on," Andi replied.

Riley nodded her thanks and set out to find Fallon.

"All right," Ida said "Let's have it. What on earth could you have told Fallon that upset her? It isn't about this party of yours."

"I really don't think," Dale said. "It just... She pressed, and I told her."

"Told her what?" Andi asked.

Dale avoided Ida's gaze. "I told her about Liv."

"Liv?" Ida asked.

"You know, that Liv maybe isn't who she thought. It came up. You know? Just talking about things. And, I kinda' was pushing, I guess... You know, that she shouldn't be afraid to marry Riley. You know? Riley ain't Liv."

"No, she isn't," Ida said. "Fallon knows *that*."

"Yeah, but she didn't know about Liv and..."

"Oh, for Christ's sake! What could be so bad?" Ida asked.

Dale looked down at his feet. "Me and Pete saw her with Dean... you know..."

Ida froze.

Andi thought she was going to vomit. "Why would you tell her that?"

"It just... She pressed about Liv. And, anyway, maybe it's time she knew," Dale defended himself.

Ida covered her face.

"Ida?" Andi wrapped and arm around the older woman.

"How could he?" Ida asked.

Andi rubbed Ida's back. "I don't know," she said. "I really don't know."

⁓ ⁓

Riley trekked up the hill toward the house, hoping she would catch up to Fallon. A million thoughts passed through her mind she made the short walk. Marge had told Riley about her pregnancy and engagement a few days earlier. Of course, Riley had shared the news with Fallon. Fallon was elated. She adored Dale and thought the world of Marge. Both had suffered loss and disappointment, and both had struggled for years with loneliness. Fallon had poured herself into making the festivities at Murphy's Law special. Whatever had transpired between Fallon and Dale, it had to have been something completely unexpected to send Fallon off on her own. She would never want to spoil the day for either of their friends.

At the bottom of the driveway that led to the house, Riley spotted Fallon sitting on the front porch stairs. Fallon smiled at her. Riley picked up her place and took a seat on the stair. "Do I want to ask?"

"No," Fallon told her. "I'm sorry. I just needed a few minutes alone."

"Want to talk about it?"

"Liv slept with Dean." There, it was out.

Riley was stunned into silence.

"Yeah, that was my reaction. Well, right up until I puked."

"Are you sure?" Riley asked.

"Yeah."

"Oh, Fallon."

"I was walking up here, and I realized why it made me sick."

"I think that would make anyone sick."

"Maybe. The thing is, Riley, I can't say I'm surprised. That's the worst part."

"I'm sorry."

"No, don't be," Fallon said. "I'm glad Dale told me."

"Why *did* he tell you?"

"Oh, you know; he wanted to tell me about proposing to Marge. That led to me proposing to you. I think when I didn't answer, he thought that meant I was afraid to."

"And, that led to Olivia."

Fallon nodded.

"You could have told him—about us, I mean."

"I know. I wanted today to be about him—for him; you know?"

"I do."

Fallon cringed. "I shouldn't have taken off."

"Give yourself a break."

"The more I think about everything, the more the pieces fit," Fallon said. "The weird part is that I don't hate Liv. I just feel like she's a stranger. I'm not sure I ever knew her, Riley. I knew who I wanted her to be."

"People change."

"Do they? I'm not sure about that. I think people learn. Maybe they grow. I'm not so sure they *change*, Riley."

Riley took Fallon's hand.

Fallon shook her head. "Dean? I swear to you, Riley, if he were here? I don't know what I would do. He's my brother. Right now, I don't ever want to see him again."

"I wish there was something I could do."

"There is," Fallon said.

"Name it."

"This."

"This?"

"Yep." Fallon stood and pulled Riley to her feet. "I know that you already did this."

"Fallon?"

Fallon dropped to her knee. "But see, the problem is I've been wanting to do this for a long time."

Riley's heart sped up.

"I did need time to think. As soon as Dale headed back to the pub, I knew that I didn't want to wait anymore. He was worried about failing—as a dad, as a husband. I think about that sometimes, Riley. No matter what happens, I hope that you will always trust me—even when you might not like me all that much."

Riley smiled.

"I came all the way up here to get something, not to mope." Fallon reached into her pocket and pulled out a diamond ring. "This isn't how I imagined doing this. It might not be epic. It is real. I don't want to live in the past. The past is over. You're right about that. All of it—everything I went through with Liv, even what Dale told me today; it all led me to you. Or maybe it led you to me. It doesn't matter. I already know your answer. At least, I think so."

Riley laughed.

"Humor me anyway? Riley, will you marry me?"

"Yes, Fallon."

Fallon slid the ring onto Riley's finger and stood to face her. "Thank you."

"There's nothing to thank me for."

"There are a million things to thank you for," Fallon disagreed. "Starting with understanding that I needed to do this."

Riley leaned in and kissed Fallon tenderly. "Are you okay to go back to the party?"

"Totally."

"I am sorry, Fallon. I know how much hearing that news had to hurt you."

Fallon would never lie to Riley. "It did. But it doesn't matter anymore. Who knows? If I hadn't been with Liv, I would never have built this house. And, you would've had to sleep in Murphy's Law in the middle of a snow storm, and probably would never have forgiven me." She winked.

"That's one way to look at things," Riley said.

"It's all about perspective," Fallon replied. She started to lead Riley back down the path.

"Fallon?"

"Hum?"

"You do know someone is going to notice this ring?"

Fallon shrugged. "Want to bet who does first?"

"No."

Fallon laughed.

"Are you sure you're all right?" Riley wanted to know.

"Yeah, I am."

Fallon wrapped her arm around Riley's waist as they walked. She was still reeling from Dale's revelation. More than the feeling of betrayal, more than the disappointment that she felt, Fallon found herself musing that none of it mattered anymore. When she looked at the house she'd built at the top of the hill, she no longer thought about Olivia Nolan. When she considered family, building a family with someone, the only face she pictured was Riley's. Riley often said that she would never change her past, not even the unbelievable loss she'd endured. For the first time, Fallon understood that sentiment fully. If one thing had changed, it might have altered the life she shared with Riley. It was time to put the past behind her. Olivia and Dean were realities in Fallon's life. In some way, both would always be present. Some part of her would always love them both. And, if Fallon were to be honest, a piece of her would always recall the pain of their betrayal. Riley was pressed against her as they walked forward. Forward was the direction she needed to go.

"Fallon, you know; it's okay if you're not—okay, that is."

"Stop worrying about me."

"That will never happen," Riley told her.

"Thank God."

❧

"Maybe we should do this another time," Dale said.

"The hell you should," Fallon said as she entered the pub. All eyes turned. "Geez, who died? Can't a girl take a walk?"

Andi immediately noted a glimmer between Riley and Fallon's joined hands. She nudged Ida.

"We thought someone kidnapped you," Ida pulled herself from her funk.

"Aliens again, Mom?"

"With you, I wouldn't be surprised," Ida replied. "You're buying the first round."

"Because that's new," Fallon said. "How about we let Dale have the floor first?"

"Uhh…" Dale stammered. "Now?"

Fallon nodded.

"Uhh… Okay." Dale took Marge's hand and led her to stand in the center of the room. "So, it's like this: we wanted to see you all to let you know that me and Marge are getting hitched."

"About time!" Carol called out.

"Yeah… Well, the thing is… The day after I asked her we sort of found out we'll need an extra bedroom," he said.

"You're taking Pete in?" Carol cracked.

"Uhh… No?" Dale shifted nervously.

The crowd erupted in giggles and laughter.

"Marge is expecting," Dale clarified.

"Pete?" Carol teased.

"Huh?" Dale asked.

Marge kissed Dale's cheek and whispered in his ear. "They all know. They love to tease you."

Dale grumbled.

"Congratulations," Andi called out.

"So, that's my cue to offer a free round," Fallon said. "But since I'm feeling generous, I'll just make it a free afternoon."

"Anyone else knocked up besides Marge?" Carol called out.

"What?" Fallon asked.

"I'm just lining up the designated drivers," Carol explained. "Pregnant means sober. Look around. Unless you plan on giving Owen the keys to your truck, pregnant is our best hope."

Fallon looked at Charlie.

"Why are you looking at me?" He asked.

"Isn't it about time?" Fallon asked him.

"Time?" He asked.

Fallon nodded toward Carol. "I mean, hell—Dale's ahead of the curve."

Riley pinched Fallon's side. "Stop."

"Gwama?" Owen looked up at Andi.

"Yes?"

"What's pegant?"

Andi laughed. "Pregnant, Owen. That's when someone is going to have a baby—like your Aunt Beth."

Owen puzzled over the information. "You?" He asked.

"No, not me," Andi said.

"Momma!" He pointed to Fallon.

"What?" Fallon asked.

"Owen wants to know if you're pregnant?" Andi teased.

Fallon went pale.

"Oh, my God!" Carol started to laugh. "Fallon, you didn't tell me the rabbit died!"

The look on Fallon's face was priceless to all who knew her. Ida fell into a fit of much needed laughter. Andi and Riley followed, sending the entire pub into a chorus of levity.

Owen looked at Andi and Ida curiously.

"Your Momma is funny," Andi said.

Owen smiled proudly. He ran over to Fallon. "You funny, Momma!"

"You think so?" Fallon asked as she scooped him up. He giggled. "I'm glad you're amused," she said.

"Are you?" Charlie asked Fallon.

"Huh?" Fallon was confused.

"He wants to know if you've got a bun in the oven," Dale said.

A sardonic grin curled the corners of Fallon's mouth. "No, no," she said. "*I* do things the old-fashioned way."

"Oh, that'll be one for the record books," Carol commented.

Fallon's stern gaze did little to deter more amused chuckles. "Cute," Fallon said. She looked back at Dale. "I might have some news too."

"Holy shit! Riley's preggers?" Charlie guessed.

"No!" Fallon replied

Riley shook her head at the banter. The antics of the colorful residents in Whiskey Springs were part of what made it home.

"I asked Riley to marry me," Fallon announced.

"Actually," Riley said. "I asked you first."

"No way!" Carol yelled.

Owen looked at his mother. Riley smiled. "Momma and I are getting married," she explained.

Owen was still confused.

"It means you're stuck with Fallon forever," Carol offered. "And ever."

Owen bounced on Fallon's hip excitedly.

"Well, at least someone is happy," Fallon said.

Ida left her barstool. Riley extricated Owen from Fallon's grasp.

"I'm happy for you," Ida said as she embraced Fallon.

Ida cleared her throat and moved to kiss Riley's cheek. "You've got your work cut out for you."

"I like a challenge," Riley deadpanned.

"Good thing," Ida said.

"Hey! I'm standing right here!" Fallon reminded them.

"Well, then get behind the bar and help Carol fill our glasses," Ida suggested.

Fallon groaned and set Owen down. "Take Grandma Andi to play some songs," she said. "I'll help my remedial staff with the beer."

Ida let out a deep sigh. "Is she okay?" She asked Riley.

"I take it Dale told you," Riley said.

"He did."

"I think she is," Riley replied.

"She wasn't surprised," Ida surmised.

"After the last few months, no, I don't think so."

"I can't believe he'd do that, Riley. Olivia? I'd believe almost anything at this point. But Dean? To do that to Beth and to Fallon…"

"I'm sorry."

"Sometimes, Riley, you love your kids, but once in a while you don't like them much."

"I think that's true with everybody," Riley offered.

Ida nodded. "You'll do just fine." She squeezed Riley's hand. "I'm going to go see what Owen and Andi are planning to torture us with."

"Is Mom okay?" Fallon leaned over the bar and asked Riley.

"She will be."

"He told them, didn't he?" Fallon guessed.

Riley nodded.

"She'll have a hard time forgiving him," Fallon said.

Riley smiled. *I doubt she's the only one.*

The sound of rain pelting the window added to the feeling of peacefulness Andi felt. The steady rhythm seemed to beat in time with the sound of Billie's heart. Andi snuggled closer, breathing in the citrusy scent that lingered on Billie's skin. Billie had arrived at Andi's shortly after one in the morning, curious about the day's events. Andi had agreed to recap the everything that happened at Murphy's Law only if they could do it from the comfort of her bed. After a quick shower, Billie had crawled into the bed beside her. "Billie?"

"Yeah?"

"You don't seem surprised by anything I told you."

"I'm not."

Andi pulled away and propped herself up on an elbow. "You're not a fan of Olivia's."

"Not really."

"Can I ask why?"

"You're not either," Billie said.

"True. I never liked the way she tried to string Fallon along."

"Mmm."

"What?"

"I didn't care for the way she came onto you," Billie said.

Andi grinned. "She didn't make it halfway to first-base."

Billie laughed. "Don't judge me if I gloat—just a little."

"Never. Tell me," Andi said. "I get the feeling you *never* liked her much."

How should Billie explain her feelings regarding Olivia Nolan? Billie liked everyone. Billie had almost immediately disliked Olivia. She kept her thoughts to herself. It seemed that from everyone else's point of view, Olivia was likeable, even desirable. She couldn't deny that Olivia was physically attractive. Underneath her polished exterior, her witty retorts, and her seemingly selfless overtures, Billie sensed a fraud. Part of Billie's job was gauging people. Every type of person wandered into an emergency room. Every possible emotion and every imaginable agenda found its way into Billie's work life. One of the most common personality types Billie encountered was what she called "the manipulator."

For years, Billie had been a triage nurse. It had been her job to discern who needed care immediately and who could wait it out. She'd learned to read subtle body language; the way a person shifted in a chair. She would note their pupils when they answered a question, the crease in a person's forehead, or their inability to focus. There were a million indicators that gave clues as to a person's meaning, emotion, and their agenda. At the beginning of her career, Billie had often mistaken a manipulative person for someone genuine. Over time, she'd mastered detecting the difference. While Olivia seemed to charm the entire town—most of all Fallon—Billie waited for Olivia's true colors to shine through. It took much longer than she'd expected.

With a sigh, Billie answered Andi. "I never trusted her."

"Can I ask why?"

"A lot of reasons, I suppose. It comes down to knowing people. There are different kinds of people, Andi. There are nurturers. And, there are the fearful ones. There are also masters of resilience, masters of concealment, and masters at manipulation. Liv is the latter. She knows how to make you believe she fits into any and all of the other categories, and that is always so she can fulfill her agenda."

Andi wasn't certain how to respond. Billie's voice held no animosity. It sounded as though she were delivering a lecture on psychology.

"Did you suspect?" Andi asked.

"That Liv slept with Dean? No. It doesn't surprise me, though."

"I still can't believe it. I saw a side to Liv this summer I never thought existed. Don't get me wrong; I knew she loved to keep Fallon dangling, but I never thought she'd try and make a move on me. I'm still not sure what she hoped to gain. Was it just to hurt Fallon?"

Billie remained silent.

"Billie?"

"Hurting Fallon might have been a little bonus. You are hurt so you try to punch back."

"But?"

"I told you; Liv is a master manipulator. Everything she does has a purpose, Andi. It's calculated."

"So, touching me had some higher purpose?"

"From where she sits — yes."

"Like what?"

Billie sighed.

"Tell me, please."

"I think that she hoped if Fallon saw you with her... Well, maybe the jealousy Fallon felt would drive a wedge between Fallon and Riley. Maybe Fallon would step back from Riley."

"Oh, God. You're serious."

"She never expected Fallon to say no to her, Andi. When Liv announced she was leaving, she expected Fallon to fall in line."

"But she moved on quickly."

Billie chuckled. "Did she? Yeah, she jumped into a relationship with Barb, paraded Barb around, and then announced Dean would father their child."

"I'm not following."

"No? I'm pretty sure that Liv figured it would shock Fallon into asking her to get back together."

"Fallon wouldn't leave..."

"She almost did, Andi."

"What are you talking about?"

"Fallon. When Liv met Barb, Fallon came close to asking Olivia if they could try again."

"She never told me that."

"I know. I don't think she wanted to admit she missed her to you."

"We all knew she missed Liv."

"Yeah. But you all thought she'd stay the course."

"She did."

"She did," Billie agreed. "She faltered a bit, though. I think when she didn't fight for Liv, Liv upped the stakes."

"You mean when she and Barb decided to have the girls."

"I do. Ironically, it's that decision, and the decision to involve Dean that sealed Liv's fate with Fallon forever."

"You would think Liv would expect that."

"That's the thing about manipulative people; they never expect to fail."

"Sounds more like a narcissist."

"There is that," Billie said. "Liv has to be the center of everyone's world in some way. That's who she is. She wants what she wants, and she expects you to want the same thing. So, no—I'm not surprised that she'd play Dean too."

Andi collapsed into Billie's arms. "How could we all have missed it?"

"Because," Billie said, placing a kiss on Andi's shoulder. "Our friends are mostly nurturers. Fallon is. Ida, Carol, hell even Pete and Dale are when you think about it."

"And me?"

Billie scooted down to look into Andi's eyes. "You're a giver," Billie said. "And, you're resilient."

"I don't feel all that resilient."

"I know, but you are."

Andi stroked Billie's cheek. "All day, I kept thinking how happy I was that I'd be with you tonight."

"Here I am."

Andi closed her eyes.

"Andi? Are you all right?"

"So much better than all right," Andi said as she opened her eyes again.

"Yeah?"

"I'm happy, Billie."

"Me too. And, Fallon's okay?"

"I think Fallon is better than okay. I don't know. Somehow, I think learning what Liv did with Dean made her realize how lucky she is to be with Riley."

"Mm. And, what about you?"

"I told you; I'm happy—happier than I thought possible."

"I hope I have a little something to do with that."

Andi placed a sweet kiss on Billie's lips. "You have everything to do with it." She settled back into Billie's embrace.

"Do you think they'll have a big wedding?"

"Who? Marge and Dale or Fallon and Riley?"

"Either."

"At this point, nothing would surprise me."

"Really?" Billie asked flirtatiously.

"Probably not, but if you'd like to try, I'm game."

"Give me six hours and I'll take you up on that," Billie replied.

"Should I set the alarm?" Andi asked.

"Only if *you* need it."

Andi giggled. "I love you."

"I love you too."

Andi closed her eyes and let herself begin to drift away. *Maybe we'll all get that happy ending we've been hoping for after all.*

CHAPTER TEN

"**W**ell?" Fallon asked.

"She said she'd think about it."

"What about your folks?"

"Mom will be here," she said. "She's anxious to meet you in person."

"And, your dad?"

"Fallon, I'm not sure I want them all here at once."

"I thought your parents got along."

"They do. If Mary comes... It gets stressful—for me."

"Have your dad stay at your house."

Riley wasn't in the mood to argue. Fallon didn't mean to press; she knew that. Fallon was pressing an issue that made Riley uncomfortable. She preferred to deal with her family in small doses—small doses of time and preferably not all at the *same* time.

"Hey. I'm sorry. I'm not making things easy; am I?"

"Why is it so important to you that they all visit at once?"

Fallon drummed her fingers on the arm of the chair.

"Fallon? What aren't you telling me?"

"Nothing—honestly."

Riley folded her arms across her chest and waited. There was definitely something Fallon was not telling her.

"Okay! I thought *maybe*... Here's the thing... Well, if everyone is here... You know, maybe that would..."

"Fallon!"

"What?"

Riley laughed. "Just tell me what you're so afraid to tell me."

"I'm not *afraid*. I was kind of hoping to know who was coming for that weekend before I suggested it is all."

"Suggested what?"

"Well... Uggh..."

"Fallon, for heaven's sake..."

"I thought maybe we could get married that weekend."

Riley's jaw dropped.

Fallon's teeth clenched through a cautious grin.

"Married?" Riley asked.

"Yeah."

"As in have a wedding?"

"Umm... That was the idea."

"On Thanksgiving?"

"No. Maybe on Friday?"

Riley stared at Fallon. "You're serious."

"Yes?" Fallon's reply came out as a question. *I hope it's okay that I'm serious.*

"You want my family to come for Thanksgiving and spring a wedding on them?"

"I..."

"Where would we do this?"

"Here?" Another answer that ended up as a question.

"In our house?" Riley asked.

"Yes?" *Why am I answering her as if I am asking her?* "Unless you want to do it somewhere else... or maybe you don't want to..."

"Fallon," Riley began cautiously. "I do want to marry you."

"But?"

"I don't know. I hoped it would just be us — you, me, Owen, and maybe Andi and Billie or something. Maybe your mom and Beth and Evan — just family."

"Unless I'm missing something, I was suggesting we invite family."

"You know what I mean."

"Riley, if you don't want to..."

"I don't want anything to drizzle on my happiness that day — whatever day we choose."

"And, you think your family will?"

"I don't know."

"I don't want you to feel guilty later that they weren't here — to regret that," Fallon said.

"Can I think about it?"

"Sure."

Riley offered Fallon a half-hearted smile. "I'm going to get Owen in the tub."

Fallon nodded.

Riley leaned against the wall in the hallway. *Shit. She's disappointed. Way to go, Riley.*

❧

"Is that water I hear?" Andi asked when she answered her phone.

"Owen's in the tub."

"What's going on?" Andi asked.

"Fallon asked me to get married."

"Yes, I know."

"No, on Thanksgiving weekend. That's why she wants me to invite my family."

"Oh."

"Yeah."

"What did you say?"

"I asked her if I could think about it," Riley said.

"Oh."

"Yeah."

"Let me guess, she's disappointed," Andi surmised.

"She didn't say that. She didn't have to."

"What do you want to do?" Andi asked.

"I'd marry her this week if that's what she wanted."

"But?"

"My parents, and Mary's family... Andi, it's too much. I know she doesn't understand."

Andi hesitated to offer her observation.

"Andi?"

"I'm still here."

"Owen, no," Riley scolded her son. "Keep the bubbles in the tub."

"Multi-tasking or escaping?" Andi asked.

"Both? I don't know. I don't know what to do. I wish she could understand that I want this to be the happiest day of my life. You know? After Robert..."

"Tell her that."

"Tell her what?" Riley asked.

"What you just said to me."

"What did I say?"

"Riley, you need to tell her what will make it the happiest day for you, and why that matters. Just tell her."

"I don't want to disappoint her."

"The only way Fallon will be disappointed is if you don't marry her. She just wants to make you happy. And, she can tell that wasn't the result of her master plan."

"I don't know what to do. I want that moment to be with the people I'm closest to. I know it will hurt my folks if I don't invite them. It'll probably even hurt Mary, but..."

"Maybe there's a way to make it work out for everybody."

"Are you my fairy Godmother and didn't tell me?" Riley joked.

"I'm afraid I am fresh out of wands. I do have an idea."

"I'm all ears," Riley said.

"Well..."

❧ ❧

Riley hovered in the doorway to the bedroom. "Hey."

Fallon looked up from the book in her lap and smiled.

"You're reading?" Riley asked.

"I do that sometimes," Fallon replied cheekily.

"I'm sorry about earlier."

Fallon patted the bed. "You don't have anything to be sorry about."

"Yeah, I do," Riley disagreed.

"What did Andi say?" Fallon smirked.

"How did you know I called Andi?"

"Seriously? Owen never goes into the bath before seven, not unless he's been in the mud."

Riley sighed. "I need you to understand."

"You don't have to explain anything to me. I should've talked to you before making plans in my head."

"No. You wanted to surprise me with something special. I sucked the wind right out of your sails."

"It's okay, Riley. It doesn't matter to me when or where we get married. Honestly, I don't care who shows up as long as you *do*."

"Oh, I'll show up," Riley promised. "Fallon..."

"Riley, it's okay—really, it is."

"Can I please explain?"

Fallon nodded.

"I had the big wedding, Fallon. I thought that was the beginning to the rest of my life—the best day I'd ever have. And, it was… up until that day. It was just one day. For a few hours, it felt like my life was a fairytale—the perfect dress, the sun shining down on us, everyone's eyes glued to us on the dance floor. It was magical. It's taken me time to be able to look back on that day and feel happiness."

"I'm sorry you…"

"No, please listen."

Fallon nodded.

"Marrying you is different. Not just because it *is* you. Not just because Owen is part of it. It's different because I'm different. When I married Robert, I was caught up in the festivities. I dreamed about the music and the dress, the first song we'd dance to…"

"And, now?"

"I think about you," Riley said. "I think about slipping that ring on your finger, and then? Then I think about the next day, and the day after that. I loved Robert. I loved our wedding. I loved being married to him. But I didn't understand what marriage entailed the way I do now. I still saw things like a Hallmark movie, Fallon. I've never been happier in my life than I am now. That's the truth. I love my life here with you. When we speak our vows, I need that to be the happiest memory we've created so far. I don't want anything or anyone to take away from you and me. I love my parents. Mary's a pain in my ass. I love her too. They aren't part of my every day. I don't want our anniversary to remind me of anything stressful. I can't have another milestone like that. But I know this isn't all about me. It's about us, and I want you to have the wedding you've dreamed about."

Fallon smiled.

"What?" Riley asked.

"I never dreamed about weddings," Fallon replied. "It doesn't matter to me what or when or who or where, Riley. I told you; as long as you show up, it'll be the best day of my life — so far, anyway."

"Well, Andi had an idea."

"I'll bet she did."

"She suggested that we do something small before my family comes and do something larger while they're here."

"Get married twice?"

"I guess you could put it that way. They don't have to know…"

"I think Owen might give up the goods."

Riley laughed. "True. Maybe it could be a reception instead?"

"Do you think they'll be upset?"

"I don't know," Riley confessed. "My parents? No. I think they'll both understand. Mary? Well, no matter what, she'll have *something* to say. She's Mary."

"Is that what you want to do?" Fallon asked.

"I think so — yes."

"Any idea when you'd like to do this?"

Riley bit her lip. "Next weekend?"

Fallon's eyes grew wide.

"Is that too soon?"

"Next weekend... As in six days from now?"

Riley nodded. Fallon stared at her.

"Billie is off. Beth is due in a few weeks. If we wait, then," Riley began to explain her reasoning.

"Okay."

"Okay?"

"Yeah. Okay. I was just trying to figure out what I need to do."

"Find a Justice of the Peace?"

"That's easy."

"It is?"

"Yeah, Mom has been a JP for almost twenty years."

"You're kidding?"

"Nope. She hasn't performed a wedding in about five, though. Oh, unless you wanted someone else..."

"Do you think she would want to?"

"My mother pass up on the chance to marry me off? Seriously?"

Riley laughed. "Are you okay with this?"

Fallon kissed Riley softly. "Just don't tell Carol. The whole town will know, and I can't fit them all in the living room."

"Check. No telling Carol."

Fallon cupped Riley's face in her hands. "You're really going to marry me in a week?"

"Second thoughts?"

Fallon closed her eyes against a wave of emotion.

"Fallon?"

"No." Fallon's lips curled as she opened her eyes. "Now, I have to figure out what I'm going to wear!"

"Just make it low-cut."

Fallon erupted in laughter. "Is that your wedding fantasy?"

Riley shrugged.

"Noted," Fallon said. She laid back and pulled Riley close.

"Fallon?"

"Yeah?"

"Thank you."

"For?"

"For understanding."

"Riley, anyone brave enough to marry me, deserves endless understanding."

Riley giggled. "Oh, I think you might be underestimating what you've signed up for."

Fallon kissed Riley's temple and sighed with contentment. *Not even a little bit, Riley. Not even a little bit.*

Andi rolled over and answered her phone, expecting to hear Billie's voice on the other end. "I didn't think you'd be able to call."

"Mom?"

Andi snapped to attention. "Dave?"

"Yeah, it's me."

"Are you okay?"

Dave chuckled nervously. "Yeah. Sorry, it's late."

"No, no. What's going on?"

"Mom…"

"What is it, sweetheart?"

Dave's heart lodged in his throat. He had no intention of letting Andi know how much he missed her. A few beers had clouded his ability to control his emotions. He'd needed a dose of liquid courage to place the call. "Mom…"

"Dave, what is it?"

"Can I come home for a couple of days?"

Andi's brow furrowed with concern. "You don't ever need permission to come home."

"I was kind of hoping I could come up Thursday. I'll leave on Saturday, but I kind of wanted to talk to you."

"What about classes?"

"I can miss one."

Andi took a deep breath and released it slowly. "You can come here anytime. You know that."

"So, it's cool then?"

Andi couldn't help herself. She chuckled. "It's cool."

"Maybe we could, you know—have dinner together Thursday or something?"

"In other words, you'd like me to cook?"

It was Dave's turn to chuckle. "That'd be cool."

"I'll work on it," Andi promised. "Are you okay?"

"Yeah. I'll see you Thursday?"

"I'll be here."

"Cool."

Everything is cool. "See you then."

"Mom?"

"Yes?"

"I... Well... I'll see you."

"Travel safely," Andi said. She disconnected the call. "I love you too, David. I love you too."

❦

WEDNESDAY

Carol kept her gaze on Ida who was sitting at a table, scribbling in a notebook.

"What's Ida up to?" Charlie asked.

"Good question," Carol said. "I think it's about time I found that out." She strolled over to the table Ida was seated at and placed her hands on her hips. "Aa-hem."

Ida looked up.

"What are you up to?" Carol asked.

"I would think that's obvious. I'm sitting at a table, writing down some thoughts while I wait for you to deliver my lunch."

"Uh-huh."

"That shouldn't be difficult to figure out—even for you," Ida said.

"Uh-huh."

Ida set down the pen in her hand, closed the notebook, and leaned back in the chair. "What makes you think that I am *up to* anything?"

"I don't think it; you are."

"You've been watching too many spy movies."

"Oh, no."

"And, what *exactly* gives you this idea that I have a nefarious agenda?" Ida asked.

"I never said it was nefarious. Is it?"

Ida rolled her eyes. "Lunch in this place is always risky."

"Oh. Nice try. You never sit at a table. What are you hiding?"

"For your information, I am waiting for Riley and Owen."

"At a table," Carol pointed out.

"Was it reserved?"

"Since when do *you* sit at a table?"

"Since when do *you* allow a three-year-old to sit at the bar?"

Carol shook her head. "I'm watching you."

"You'd be better off watching that husband of yours." She gestured to the bar. "I think he just snuck a new ketchup bottle."

Carol growled. "Charlie!"

Ida sniggered. *Works every time.*

"Gwama!" Owen bolted through the door the moment Riley opened it.

"Well, look who's here!" Ida called out.

Riley walked up to the bar, giggling. "He's a little excited," she said. "Hey, Charlie. Why the long face?"

"He's in time-out," Carol said.

"Ohhh... What did you do?" Riley asked.

"He snagged the new ketchup when I wasn't looking," Carol explained.

"It wouldn't come out! Come on! Look at this thing." He held up the ketchup bottle on the bar for Riley's inspection.

"It's not empty," Carol said.

"It's almost empty," Charlie argued.

Riley loved Murphy's Law. She'd grown to understand Fallon's affection for the place. It was far more than a pub or a place to grab a bite to eat. It was a home away from home. Carol and Charlie, Ida, Pete and Dale, Andi and Billie, even the occasional visit from Dick Bath made the small establishment lively. It was the place where people gathered to drown their sorrows and celebrate their victories. More than that, it was the place where you could let your guard down, tell your story, and trust that the familiar faces you unloaded to could keep your secrets, hear your worst thoughts, and still love you.

Fallon referred to Carol as, *Commandant of Condiments*. For some unknown reason, Carol obsessed over using everything to its fullest. That included every bottle of ketchup and mustard that adorned a table. Riley guessed that the reason for Carol's seeming obsession with using every drop of everything stemmed from difficult times in her childhood. She doubted most people were aware of how rough things had been for Carol. Riley hadn't solicited the information. One afternoon, while she waited for Fallon to return from a fishing excursion with Owen, Riley found herself listening to Carol recount her childhood. The pub had been desolate that day. Sunshine and a warm yet a comfortable temperature had conspired to keep people away from indoor activity; everyone it seemed except Riley and Carol. The two had enjoyed a cold beer with their candid conversation. Within a few hours, Riley felt she'd gotten to know Carol far better than many of the lifetime residents in the small town.

Carol was regarded by most as a jokester. She was quick-witted and even-tempered, qualities that served a bartender well. After listening to Carol reminisce about growing up in Whiskey Springs, Riley understood that her friend had learned to laugh, and learned to roll with life's punches early on:

"Sometimes, I wonder what it would've been like to grow up here," Riley said. "Someplace where everyone knows you."

Carol smiled. "They *think* they know you."

"What do you mean?"

"People know what you look like. They call you by name. They know where you live. They seldom know *how* you live."

Riley listened curiously.

"Take me for instance," Carol said. "Everyone knew my parents. And, everyone liked them. What wasn't to like?" Carol grinned. "They were good people—both of them. My father worked as a salesman most of his life."

"He was on the road?" Riley guessed.

"Mm. You could say that. He should've been a truck driver. He would've made more money."

"Not the best salesman, huh?"

"He couldn't sell you a bar of gold for a dollar," Carol said. "But you'd never have guessed that looking in—not even if you came to dinner at our house. Oh, no. When we had company, it was a grand affair. That's what my Nana called it. And, the house was always pristine. I think that hides what's missing. It wasn't sparsely furnished, but we never had anything new. My mother could take the oldest, rattiest piece of furniture and make it shine. She could sew together two pieces of old clothing and make it look like it came off the rack at Sax. It never did, though. It didn't even come out of the thrift store. I think I wore more than one old pair of curtains as a blouse." Carol laughed. "I'm not complaining. I learned to use everything to its fullest. And, I learned to appreciate everything I was given. But there were times I wished I could have what my friends did. There were times I wondered how no one knew that most nights we ate canned vegetables and potatoes from the garden. My parents were too proud to accept help. We managed. We never let anyone know that we had to *manage*."

Riley smiled at Carol. She picked up the nearly empty ketchup bottle, unscrewed the cap, and peered inside with one eye. "Looks like it's good for at least another burger or two," she said.

"See?" Carol looked at Charlie. "Thank you, Riley. It's nice to have *someone* who understands the value of things around here."

"I understand the value!" Charlie said.

"Use a knife next time," Riley whispered in Charlie's ear. She winked at Carol and made her way to Ida.

"Don't go bailing her out," Ida said to Riley. "She's been snooping."

"Carol?"

"Of course, Carol. You know her."

"She should be the writer," Riley offered. "She's got more stories than Mother Goose."

"Yeah, only hers aren't about giants and golden eggs. Well, maybe a giant..."

There's more truth to that than you know, Riley thought.

Ida passed the notebook she'd been writing in across the table. "You can take a look at that and let me know what you think," she said.

"Now?"

"Well, before Saturday if you could."

"I'll see what I can do," Riley quipped.

"What's going on Saturday?" Carol wondered. She placed a sandwich in front of Ida.

"Mommy's gettin' married!" Owen said.

"Yes, I know, Owen. That's exciting," Carol said.

"Yep!"

"You two are up to something," Carol looked between Ida and Riley.

"Has life gotten *that* boring here?" Ida asked.

"I'm not bored. I'm *observant.*"

"You're nosy," Ida replied. She took a bite from her sandwich.

Riley stifled her laughter.

"And, *you* are avoiding the question."

"There was a question?" Ida asked.

"Why's Saturday important?" Carol inquired.

"I get to hold a w'ring," Owen said proudly. "Momma says."

Carol's gaze narrowed. "Oh, my God! You're eloping! You are; aren't you? Are you going back to San Diego? It can't be Vegas. That's way too gauche for Fallon's taste. Unless... She likes Elvis…"

Riley gave up all hope of holding back and burst into an animated guffaw.

"Why is that funny?" Carol asked.

"I'm sorry," Riley managed to say through ongoing laughter. "The idea that we would ever have an Elvis impersonator marry us…" Riley doubled over onto the table laughing. "Oh, God, my sides hurt."

"Who's El'bis?" Owen asked innocently.

Ida covered her face. "I give up."

"What? So, it's not Vegas? Fallon said she was taking the weekend off. Come on, you have to tell me! Where are you running off to?" Carol asked.

Riley caught her breath. She looked over at Ida. "You do realize it's hopeless?"

"Probably," Ida agreed.

"What's hopeless?" Carol asked.

"Keeping a secret in this place," Riley said. "Sit down," she instructed Carol.

"Why am I sitting?" Carol asked.

"Just sit," Ida said.

"Okay… I'm sitting."

"No," Riley began. "Elvis will not be attending my wedding." She winked at Owen. "In any capacity," she told Carol. "And, no—we are not running away to elope."

"Well, something is going on," Carol said.

"Ida is marrying us on Saturday at home," Riley said.

Carol tipped her head as she processed the information. "Uh-huh. So, no Elvis—Ida."

"Right," Riley said.

"You're getting married here?" Carol asked.

Riley smiled.

"On Saturday?"

Riley nodded.

"How do I not know this?"

"You know it now," Ida said. "So, keep it quiet."

"You didn't want anyone to know?" Carol was confused.

Riley suddenly felt terrible. Carol was one of Fallon's closest friends. She was, if Riley thought about it, part of their family. *What was I thinking?* One of the things Riley had wanted to avoid was a big affair. Marrying Fallon was about being married, not having a wedding. Looking at Carol, Riley wondered if she'd thought things through enough.

"I get it," Carol said. "You just want it to be the two of you."

Riley sighed regretfully. Weddings had a way of hurting feelings. She'd learned that the hard way. When you invited one person and failed to invite someone who'd been in that same circle of friends, someone was bound to be offended. She'd mulled it over long before she'd asked Fallon to marry her. If they invited Carol and Charlie, they would need to invited Pete and Dale. She should invite Marge. And, what about Andi's boys? Dave would likely take a pass. Jake was as close to Fallon as anyone she knew. He still called at least once a week. And, then there was Barb and the girls; they were family. As Riley went through the list, one person led to another and pretty soon she'd had at least thirty names, not including any of her family or friends back home on the list. In her estimation, a wedding either had to be limited to immediate family or opened up to a wide community. No wonder people ran off to Vegas. "Right now, Vegas sounds like a good option," she muttered.

"Hey, don't worry," Carol assured her. "My lips are sealed."

And, your feelings are hurt. Riley tried unsuccessfully to smile. "I didn't want to say anything until we had all the plans in place," she said.

"Riley, it's okay. It's *your* wedding. You don't owe anyone an explanation," Carol said.

"No, you don't," Ida agreed.

"I get to hold w'rings!" Owen bounced in his chair.

"Yes, you do," Riley agreed.

"You can come," Owen said to Carol.

"Oh," Carol began. "I think I might be working that day, little man. You know, your momma's going to be busy."

Owen frowned. Carol was his friend. Sometimes, he went to Carol and Charlie's house. He loved the pair. He looked at his mother curiously. She'd told him that Saturday would be a party with the people they loved, and he would get to carry the rings she and Fallon would give each other. And, after that? After that they would have a cake. Why wouldn't Carol and Charlie be there? They were always at celebrations. He even got to go to their wedding.

Riley smiled. *This is ridiculous.* "Carol, we just haven't finished making all the plans. It's a last-minute thing." She reached over and took Carol's hand. "And, I think Fallon would want to be the one to tell you our plans. So, do me a favor, and when she does; play dumb?"

Carol grinned. "Promise. I need to go say goodbye to Charlie before his lunchbreak is over." She clapped. "Ooh! I'm so excited!"

Riley threw her head back.

"Now, why did you do that?" Ida asked.

Riley gathered herself and shrugged. "Because... I've been selfish."

"What on earth are you talking about?"

"I have been," Riley said. "We both know Fallon wanted something bigger—not huge, but we both know she had bigger plans."

"Fallon wants this day to be special for *you*."

"Yes, but it should be special for *us*." Riley glanced over her shoulder at Carol. "We can't leave everyone out," she said. She turned back to Ida. "We can't." She shook her head. "I don't want to."

"What about your family?" Ida said.

"This is my family," Riley replied. "I guess we have some revisions to make, huh?"

"Are you sure about this?"

"Yeah, I am. I need to call..."

"Call my daughter. I'll help Owen pick a few songs."

"Are you sure you..."

"Go on," Ida said. She turned to Owen. "Your mother is one of a kind, Owen."

He grinned proudly.

"What do you say we liven up this place a bit?" She pushed back her chair and held out her hand. "Something tells me we'd better dust off our dancing shoes."

❧

"Riley?" Andi guessed who had been on the phone.

"Yeah."

"Uh-oh. What's wrong?"

"Nothing. She wants to expand the guest list.," Fallon explained.

Andi laughed.

"You're not surprised, are you?"

"No," Andi replied.

"It's too big for the house."

"Well, you could have it here."

"At your house?" Fallon was shocked.

"Why not? I have the space."

"Andi, I can't ask you..."

"You didn't ask me; I offered."

"I don't know. She mentioned doing it at Murphy's."

Andi nodded.

"At a pub?" Fallon groaned.

"You love that place," Andi said.

"It's not the place I imagined getting married."

"Fallon?"

"Yeah?"

"Why don't you use the gazebo in my yard? Honestly, we can put something together that will be nice. How many people is she thinking?"

"I don't know. When we counted it ended up around thirty-five."

"That's not very big," Andi pointed out.

"No, but you and I both know that in this town, thirty-five will be fifty — at least.

"That's still small," Andi said. "And, it's easily accommodated out there. Then, you can have a reception at the pub. You own it," she reminded Fallon. "If you can close it down for the Cigar Club, you can shut it for your wedding."

Fallon groaned. "It's not just that."

"What is it?"

"Her family is going to hate me."

"I doubt that."

"Really? She's not asking them to come. She's not asking any of her friends. That was okay when it was just us. Now? Andi, we can't lie about this. It's not even three days away!"

"Well, you could offer to fly them here," Andi suggested.

"What?"

"It can't be that difficult to get hold of her family. Call them and offer to fly them here for the weekend."

"From California?"

"Why not?"

"It's two days from now!"

"Move it to Sunday," Andi said.

"How can you be so calm!"

"I think you have dramatic covered for both of us."

"I'm not dramatic!" Fallon protested.

Andi held her forefinger and thumb a hair apart.

Fallon sighed. "Maybe we should postpone things."

"That's what I just suggested."

"You know what I mean!"

"Fallon, I don't think Riley wants to wait."

"Yes, but *Riley* is the one who now wants to invite half the town."

"See? There's the dramatic."

"What if they say no?" Fallon asked.

"Who? The town or Riley's family?"

"Very funny."

Andi reached over and clasped Fallon's hand. "If they say no, you can look in the mirror and say you tried."

"What if Riley gets mad at me for inviting them?"

"She won't."

"How do you know?"

"Because I know her," Andi said. "And, I know you. Deep down she wants them here, Fallon. She's afraid they'll say no. Maybe, just maybe they'll surprise you both."

"And if they don't?"

"You tried."

"You'd really let us do it here?" Fallon asked.

"Do you need to ask that?"

"I just mean… I don't want you to feel weird…"

"I don't." Andi put the thought to rest. "I love you, Fallon. Maybe this talk is long overdue. There's a lot I've never said to you that I should have."

"Andi, you don't…"

"Listen for a minute." Andi took a deep breath, hoping to steady her emotions. "Riley is more than a friend to me."

"I know that."

"I know you do. It's funny when I think about it. She's the me I wish I'd been at her age. She's also the daughter I'd always hoped I'd have. You know, Jake and I tried for years for another baby. Once—actually, not that long ago; we thought we were successful. It wasn't meant to be. Twenty weeks into my pregnancy, I lost my little girl."

"You never told me that."

"The only person I've ever told that to until now is Billie."

Fallon smiled. "Not that long ago?"

"Not really," Andi said. "Jake was in high school."

"I'm sorry, Andi."

"Don't be. It hurt. It hurt a lot, if I'm honest. If it had worked out... Well, we might not be sitting here right now — either of us."

"True."

"I don't regret what we shared, Fallon. I never will. I told you once that some part of me fell in love with you. That wasn't the truth. I fell in love with you."

"I know," Fallon admitted. "I loved you too, Andi."

"I believe that," Andi said. "And, maybe if I'd admitted it sooner... But neither of us did, Fallon. That assured our relationship would have an end. I don't regret that either. I still love you. It's not the same. I love you more than I did before we became lovers, not just differently — more. *You* are my best friend in this world. Just like, I think I'm your best friend."

"You are."

"I would never have had the courage to be with Billie if we hadn't been together."

"I know the feeling."

"I'll bet you do." Andi smiled warmly. "There isn't anything I wouldn't do for you and for Riley."

"That goes both ways, you know?"

"I do. Can I give you a piece of advice?"

"Please."

"Stop worrying about disappointing Riley. Someday, you will. In some *small* way you will. You'll lose your temper, or you'll react to something without thinking. Maybe you'll forget a milestone, or you'll raise your voice with one of your children. You will. You'll never lose her as long as you're honest. And, you'll never disappoint her by doing something because you love her. Trust me, Fallon. I would tell her the same thing. I was married for a lot of years. No marriage is perfect. No family is tidy. And, I'm not talking about your laundry."

Fallon chuckled.

"Relationships and families are messy. You do the best you can to accept the people you love as they are and help them become who they want to be. That's all you can do, Fallon. If I've learned anything in my life, that is it."

"Can I ask you something?"

"I don't know. What is it?" Andi teased.

"Do you see yourself with Billie? I mean, ten years from now — is that what you see?"

Andi considered the question for a minute. "I'm not sure how to answer that."

"Honestly?" Fallon suggested.

Andi grinned. "That's not what I mean. I'm trying to learn to live in the present. I spent too much time looking back or looking forward. I can tell you this; I don't see myself without her. I can't imagine I would ever make a choice to be without Billie — not ever."

"You both deserve to be happy."

"Happiness is an interesting term," Andi offered. "I used to aspire to be happy."

"And, now you don't?"

"I wouldn't say *that*. I know that happiness lasts for a short time. No one can be happy all the time."

"Another life-lesson?" Fallon asked with a wink.

"Something like that. I want to be whole. I want to be loved, and I want to be able to love someone and not feel alone when they leave."

"Andi..."

"That's not about you, Fallon. I made my choices in the past. I told you; I don't regret those. I don't. When Billie leaves for work or to see you — when she's apart from me, I know that she's still *with* me. *That* is different. It sounds corny, but I feel it. She's always with me."

"Nah, it's not corny. I get it."

"I'd give her anything I could to make her happy. So, I understand how you feel about this wedding. I do."

"You're really okay with us getting hitched here?"

"More than okay," Andi promised.

"What about Dave?"

"What about him?"

"He's not exactly my biggest fan these days. He gets here tomorrow; doesn't he?"

"He does. He's leaving on Saturday," Andi said.

"Worried?" Fallon guessed.

"More like curious," Andi said.

"It'll be okay. I'm sure he misses you."

Andi surprised Fallon with her response. "I've no doubt that he misses me. I could hear it in his voice. He doesn't *want* to miss me, though."

"Are you going to tell him about Billie?"

"I think Jake likely did that for me."

"You told Jake?"

Andi shrugged. "Like I said, we were married for a lot of years. We didn't part in anger."

"How did Jake take that news?" Fallon wondered.

"He likes Billie."

Fallon laughed. "Everyone likes Billie."

Andi smiled.

"Are you worried that your relationship with Billie will create a bigger rift between you and Dave?" Fallon asked.

"Sure," Andi admitted. "But that won't come between Billie and me."

"What if he has an issue with it?"

"David needs to learn the same thing I told you."

"Which is?"

"You don't have to like everything about someone just because you love them. You *do* have to learn to love people for who they are, not who you want them to be."

"Think he'll understand?" Fallon asked.

"I don't know. Billie is part of my life. And, that's not going to change."

Silence hovered for a few moments. Fallon took a sip from the glass of wine Andi had poured earlier. Her eyes fell onto Andi as Andi sipped from her glass thoughtfully. Her heart clenched. "Thank you," Fallon whispered.

Andi looked at her quizzically.

"For loving me," Fallon clarified. "Even if I am a first-class ass sometimes."

Andi snickered. "But a first-class ass who makes a mean margarita."

"Everyone needs something to fall back on," Fallon quipped.

Andi laughed.

"I love you, Andi."

Andi reached over and squeezed Fallon's hand. Love changed sometimes. One thing Andi did believe, when you loved a person, no matter what life threw at you, you would never stop loving them. Fallon was meant to be her best friend. They'd landed where they'd both longed to be. Relationships, just like people, played different roles in life. Sometimes, relationships and people played many roles in a person's life. Fallon was a star on Andi's journey; someone who would always be present, even at a distance, guiding Andi in some way. The relationship she had shared with Fallon had been a bridge for them both. It led them across the rocky waters of change to the solid ground both craved. Andi would be forever grateful for the woman beside her. She smiled. "I love you."

ᨕᨘ᨞

The house phone rang. Only one person ever called the house—Dean. Ida steadied herself before answering.

"Hi, Mom."

"Dean."

"Is Beth there?"

"No, she isn't."

"I thought she'd be back by now."

"She's spending a little time helping Riley this afternoon."

"She mentioned that Fallon's getting married this weekend. Why didn't Fallon call me?"

Ida took several deep breaths. "Why didn't Fallon call you?"

"I would've thought she would."

"Mm. I want to ask you something. And, I want you to tell me the truth."

"Okay?"

Ida repeated her deep breathing patterns. She was in no mood to have a heart attack, and approaching the subject of Olivia Nolan with her son was the one thing she feared might send her into cardiac arrest. "Did you sleep with Olivia?"

"What?"

"I asked you if you slept with Olivia when she was living here in Whiskey Springs."

"Why would you ask me that?" Dean shot.

"Did you?"

"Where did you hear that?"

"Does it matter? I want you to tell me the truth."

Dean sighed. "It was an accident."

"An accident? You accidently fell on top of Olivia in the boathouse, and just happened to be naked at the time?"

"How did you find out?"

"I don't think that matters. It suffices to say that *you* are not the only person who knows about the boathouse as a getaway."

"Does Beth know?"

"I didn't think it was a wise idea to tell your pregnant wife that you'd cheated on her. You two have enough problems."

Dean sighed with relief.

"Fallon knows."

"You told Fallon?"

"No. And, don't ask me how she did find out. It doesn't matter."

"It was one time."

"Was it?"

"Mom, please..."

"Mom, please? You have got to be kidding me, Dean."

"You don't believe me."

"About which thing? That you only did it one time or that it was an accident?" Before Dean could answer, Ida continued. "No, I don't. I don't know what to believe."

"Liv was upset. Fallon had just told her she wouldn't move. It just happened."

Ida bristled. The old boathouse hadn't been in use for anything except the occasional teenage party or a place for a couple to sneak away and have sex in years. That was it. Everyone who'd lived in Whiskey Springs any length of time knew that. It was bad enough that Dean was lying to her. Now, he seemed to think he could play *her* for a fool as well. "Do you think that when you pass seventy you suddenly become stupid?"

"What?"

"I asked you if you think I'm stupid. Maybe you think I've gone senile."

"It's the truth."

"You took Olivia to the boathouse to *comfort* her?"

"We took a walk. She was upset."

"And, *you* were married," Ida replied.

"It just happened."

"That might work with some people, Dean. It doesn't work with me."

"Are you going to tell her? Beth, I mean?"

"Not immediately, no."

"But you are going to tell her, aren't you?"

"My guess is that she already suspects," Ida told her son. "But, I'm not planning on giving her confirmation. I would advise that you do before someone else does."

"Fallon..."

Ida's disgust escaped with a caustic laugh. "Your sister isn't that mean-spirited."

"Taking her side, huh?"

"Her side? What side would that be?" Ida asked. "She didn't choose teams, Dean. She chose Liv. You betrayed her. Sides? There are no sides. Fallon would never betray you that way or Liv, for that matter."

"But she'll tell my wife..."

"Fallon won't say a word to Beth. I'd stake my life on that. She would never want her to feel the way she did when she found out."

"I made a mistake."

"You made a decision," Ida countered. "And it wasn't the first one that has torn this family apart."

"Don't ask me to regret my daughters."

Ida's head started to pound. "I would never expect anyone to regret Emily and Summer," she said. "As far as I knew, the girls are Barb and Liv's. You helped them. Wasn't that the plan?"

"They're still my daughters."

"And, Barb?"

"Barb is a good parent. I never said she wasn't."

"But she's not *their* parent. Is that what you're saying?"

"No. They just happen to have an extra."

Ida was at a loss. "Be careful, Dean."

"I never intended to hurt anyone."

"I wish I believed that," Ida said.

"Mom…"

"I have go. I have a lot to get done before Saturday."

"Tell Fallon I…."

"Right now, Dean, I think it's best if you let Fallon have some space."

"I'd like to…"

"If you care about your sister at all, leave this. This weekend is the most important in her life. Don't spoil it for her."

"Will you tell Beth I called?"

"She has her cell phone. You can call her anytime."

"I don't want to disturb her if she's out…"

"You do what you think is best. I'll tell her you called."

"Mom, I…"

"I need to go. You be safe," Ida said. She set the phone down. "Oh, Dean—what were you thinking?"

CHAPTER ELEVEN

*A*ndi wondered what gave children the idea that parents have the answers to all of life's problems. Dave had arrived at the door that afternoon sporting a sheepish grin. When Andi moved to hug him, he'd held onto her. It reminded Andi of when he was a toddler seeking comfort from a nightmare. He'd regaled her with stories about his friends and shared a few tidbits about his studies. For a couple of hours, Andi had felt a sense of normalcy return between them. They'd moved their conversation to the living room after enjoying a snack at the kitchen table. The topic quickly moved to Dave's girlfriend, Becky, and the fact that she wanted to meet Andi. He grew quiet, looking up at his mother, silently imploring her for an answer to whatever dilemma existed in his heart.

"Do you think you can you love two people?" Dave asked softly.

Andi's eyes glistened. "What are you asking me? Can you love two people, or can you be *in love* with two people?'

"What's the difference?" Dave asked his mother.

"There's a big difference, David."

"So, who were you in love with? Dad or Fallon?"

Andi let the question roll through her mind for a few seconds. "Love changes sometimes," she replied.

Dave shook his head.

"It does," she continued. "I'm not the same person I was when I met your father."

"Because you're a lesbian now?"

Andi laughed. "I'm not certain that is such a recent evolution. And, I'm not sure I'd label myself anything. I'm in a relationship with a woman. That doesn't mean I never loved your father."

"That makes no sense."

"Why not? Because your father is a man, and Billie is a woman?"

"And Fallon."

"So, if I started seeing a man, you would be comfortable with that? What's your question?" Andi asked.

"I don't get it."

"I don't get what it is that you can't understand," Andi confessed. "I met your father when I was still a kid. I fell head over heels for him, and I was in love with him for a long time."

"Then you met Fallon."

"Fallon's not the reason your father and I grew apart. I know you want to believe that. She's not."

"So, you didn't love her? You just slept with her?"

Andi pressed down her anger. "I loved her. I still love her. Just like I still love your father. I'm not in love with either of them. Someday, you might understand."

"No way. I love Becky. That's not changing."

Andi smiled. "I hope it doesn't," she said honestly. "I hope, Dave, that you've met the person you are meant to travel your lifetime with. Believe me; I hope that's true. Love happens," she continued. "Relationships take work. People grow. Life is unpredictable. Sometimes, you fall out of love without even realizing it happened."

David silently studied his mother.

"Go ahead and say what it is you want to say," Andi told him.

"I don't want you to tell everyone about you—you know..."

Andi's jaw tensed. "I know that."

"But you're going to anyway," David guessed.

"I'm not ashamed of who I am. And, I'm not ashamed of my relationship with Billie. I've never asked you to lie about who you are, who you love, or how you feel. I would've hoped you'd give me the same courtesy."

"Mom, Becky's parents aren't going to understand. Her dad's a pastor, you know?"

"I'm sorry."

"So, that's it?"

"My life with Billie has zero bearing on Becky's parents," Andi said. "Zero. I want you to be happy. If you love this girl, I support you with all I have. If you're asking me to pretend I am someone that I'm not; if you're asking me to put Billie in a corner; you are in for a disappointment."

"Should I expect a wedding invitation?" He asked bitterly.

Andi brushed off her son's sarcasm. "I think that's a bit premature," she said.

He laughed. "You'd marry her?"

"I might."

"That's great, Mom. Seriously? What about me?"

"What about you? It sounds to me as though you've found someone you'd like to share your life with. So, have I."

"So, I just have to deal with it."

Andi took a deep breath. "I love you, David. This entire conversation is about what you want for your future. I have a future too."

"Yeah…"

"I'm not a moment to moment part of your future. That's another way life changes. You don't need me the way you once did. That's the way it should be," Andi told her son.

"Do you really love Billie?"

"I do," Andi replied.

"Are you going to live with her?"

"I hope we're headed that way."

"But you don't know?"

Andi steadied her emotions. The tension in the room was making her slightly nauseous. "I know that I want to be with Billie, and I know that I want that to be for the long haul. I'm not going to rush her. I'm not going to press you to understand. I'm also not going to justify what I feel or what I'm hoping for. That's all I can tell you."

"Does she have to be there when Becky meets you?"

"No, but don't ask me to lie."

David nodded and looked at the floor. He remained silent for a minute before meeting his mother's eyes again. "Would she want to be?"

Andi's gaze narrowed with confusion.

"Would Billie want to meet Becky?"

Andi smiled. "I'm sure she would."

"I would have thought she'd hate me," he said.

"No one hates you, sweetheart." Andi was positive she saw tears welling in her son's eyes.

"Do you?"

"I love you," Andi said. "Nothing you say or do will change that."

"Can I think about it?"

"What's that?"

"Who should be here when I bring Becky home to visit," he explained.

Andi nodded. "You let me know."

⬥

"You're quiet," Fallon observed.

Billie shrugged. "Andi's spending the afternoon with Dave."

"And, you're worried that will change things between you and Andi?"

"No," Billie replied. "I'm not."

"But you are worried about something," Fallon surmised.

"I don't want to come between Andi and the boys."

"You aren't."

"Could have fooled me."

Fallon considered how to reply. Anyone who knew Andi at all was aware that her sons were her pride and joy. Dave and Jacob had been the center of Andi's world. Fallon hadn't spent much one-on-one time with Andi in months. She'd met Andi for lunch the previous day while Billie was at work. Lunch had been followed by a long walk, and an overdue conversation. Fallon hadn't planned on sharing her discussion with anyone, not even with Riley. It wasn't because her time with Andi held any secrets. It had been the first time in longer than Fallon wanted to admit that she and Andi had spoken openly—completely openly. Billie was worried about hurting Andi. There was only one thing Billie could do that would hurt Andi deeply.

"You aren't the reason that Dave has issues."

"No," Billie agreed. "Andi being with any woman is. I know. But that woman is me now."

"True."

"Why do I get the feeling Andi said something to you about this?" Billie asked.

"Andi and I had a long talk yesterday," Fallon replied. "A long overdue talk."

"I know; she told me."

"I'm sure she did. Listen, Billie; Dave and Jacob were the center of Andi's life for years."

"Were?"

Fallon nodded. "*Were.* She loves them. You are the person she needs in her life the most. Trust me on that."

Billie sighed, feeling a sense of guilt. "I hate seeing her hurt."

"I get that. You aren't the cause; David is the cause. Andi needs you, Billie. She needs to know you are there for her no matter what happens with Dave."

"I am."

"Can I give you one piece of advice?"

"Please."

"Make sure she knows that you won't let anything come between you—not anything."

"Dave is her son, Fallon."

"And, you are her partner."

"What if he never comes around?" Billie asked.

"I think he will," Fallon said.

"He didn't with you."

"It's different," Fallon commented.

"Is it?"

Fallon took a deep breath. "I loved her, Billie."

"Yeah, I know."

"I was in love with her," Fallon admitted. "At least, part of me was."

"How can part of you be in love?" Billie asked. The entire concept of loving someone part-way made no sense to her.

Fallon grinned. "That question is why *you* are the person who belongs with Andi."

"Uh-huh."

"I'm serious."

"Fallon…"

"Yeah?"

"I want Andi in my life. I don't want to be the cause of pain for her, though. Even if that isn't about *me*. Her kids are everything to her."

"Sure, they are. They have lives of their own now, though. So, does Andi. *You* are the center of that life. Don't forget that. And, don't be afraid to remind David of that either."

Billie was surprised by Fallon's advice.

"I'm not kidding," Fallon said. "You fight for her no matter what," she advised. "Andi doesn't need someone willing to let her go. She needs someone willing to hang on no matter what."

Fallon's words hit Billie forcefully. "You know, sometimes I wish I could have been the one to have everything with her," she told Fallon.

"Who says you can't?"

"I think the time has passed for some things," Billie said.

"I wouldn't be so sure that the time has passed for anything where you and Andi are concerned," Fallon replied.

"You're not following…"

"Sure, I am," Fallon said. "You're talking about the boys. Give it time, Billie. You might be surprised at the family you end up having. Don't underestimate Andi."

"I don't."

"Good. Don't underestimate yourself either."

"Fallon?"

"Yeah?"

"That must've been some talk you two had."

"It was."

***

"You've been quiet all day," Beth said.

"I'm sorry," Ida said. "Fallon's got me handling some last-minute details for Sunday. Now it's on Sunday," she griped.

"Mm. Somehow, I don't think you've been avoiding talking to me because of the wedding."

"I'm not avoiding you in any way," Ida said.

Beth lifted her brow.

"I'm not."

"What happened when Dean called yesterday?" Beth asked.

"Nothing important."

Beth shook her head. "How is Fallon handling it?"

"What?"

"That Dean slept with Olivia."

"You knew?" Ida was stunned.

"No, not until the other day."

"How did you find out?"

"I overheard Riley and Andi."

"Oh, Beth...."

"It's okay," Beth said. "It's not like I didn't suspect it for years."

Ida felt sick. "I'm sorry."

"For what? It's not your fault, Ida. It's not Liv's either — for the record. He made a choice. Now, I've made mine."

"You're following through with a divorce," Ida guessed.

"I am."

"This is the last thing you need right now."

Beth smiled. "Actually, I feel better."

Ida's eyes narrowed to slits.

"I do," Beth said. "He's always tried to convince me that I was insecure. I started to think that maybe he was right. It's a relief," she said. "I know I'm not crazy. And, I know that I can trust what I feel. I'm okay, Mom. Honestly—I am. I'm more concerned about you and Fallon."

"Don't be," Ida said. "I think Fallon's feelings on the subject are similar to yours."

"And you?"

"I love my son."

Beth smiled.

"I don't like his behavior, and I have to admit; I find myself wondering who he is lately."

"I understand," Beth replied.

"I'm sure you do."

"I hope this won't…"

"You are part of this family. A far as I'm concerned, you and Riley are my daughters as much as Fallon."

"You felt that way about Liv once."

Ida massaged her eyes in frustration. "I did," she said. "Right now, I'd prefer it if I never had to see her again."

"Yeah, I know the feeling."

"Have you talked to Barb lately?" Ida wondered.

"Earlier today."

"How is she doing?"

"Anxious for Liv to leave, I think, so that the girls can get situated."

"She's still planning on moving here at Thanksgiving?"

"That's the hope. Liv leaves for Amsterdam that Saturday. She doesn't want the girls to have to move to Richmond for a month and then here. One move is enough."

Ida shook her head.

"What are you thinking?" Beth wondered.

"I can't believe the upheaval those two have caused this whole family."

"Well, at least, we all have each other. And, we have something to celebrate this weekend. I'd rather focus on that."

Ida nodded. "I can't argue with that."

Billie was startled by the sensation of her phone buzzing in her pocket. She answered Andi's call with concern. "Are you okay?"

The sound of Billie's voice always brightened Andi's world. Billie was worried about her. "I'm good," Andi promised. "Are you still with Fallon?"

"Yeah? Do you need to talk to her?"

Andi laughed. "No. I still have her number."

"Ha-ha. I didn't expect to hear from you until later tonight."

"Well, I wasn't sure I'd be calling before then either. Dave suggested I invite you to have dinner with us." Silence. "Billie?"

"I don't think I heard that right."

"What did you hear?" Andi asked.

"I heard you say that Dave wanted me to come for dinner."

"That's what I said." Silence again. "Billie?"

"Ummm. Andi, are you sure that's a good idea?"

"He asked. And, yes, I think it's an excellent idea."

Billie sighed nervously.

"Unless you don't want to," Andi said.

"I want to. I don't want to make things worse."

"You won't."

"How can you be so sure?"

"You can't."

"How do you figure that?" Billie wanted to know.

"Unless you plan on throwing me onto the kitchen counter and playing with kitchen utensils, I think we'll be fine."

Billie's face flushed.

Fallon tried unsuccessfully not to snicker. Andi had a colorful sense of humor at times. She could easily imagine what might be said on the other line.

"Are you sure?" Billie asked.

"I'd love for you to grab the spatula, but maybe another night would be better."

Finally, Billie laughed. "What time?"

"Come over whenever you finish with Fallon. How is she, by the way? Having a meltdown yet?"

"Nah, I think mine kept hers in check."

"I'll see you in a while."

"I'll be there," Billie promised.

"I guess you have plans later after all," Fallon said.

"I have time."

"It's okay, Billie. We can finish our drink and go."

"Anxious to get home?" Billie asked.

"Maybe a little."

"I get it."

"I'm sure you do. Just remember what I told you."

"Which part?" Billie wondered.

"Don't let Dave come between you and Andi."

"I just hope he doesn't try."

"Me too. No matter what—you hold your ground."

Billie nodded. "Maybe we could have one more drink."

"You'll be fine."

"It's not me I'm worried about."

⁍⁌

Fallon climbed into the front seat of her truck, closed the door, and closed her eyes for a moment. She couldn't decide if she was eager to get home to see Riley or if she'd like to avoid it a while longer. Should she tell Riley that Riley's parents would be arriving tomorrow? At first, Fallon had planned to surprise Riley. She'd even worked out a plan with Carol. The more she thought about it, the more Fallon began to think she should let Riley prepare. Both Brenda and Doug had been quick to accept Fallon's invitation to fly to Vermont for the wedding, and both had insisted that there was no need for Fallon to pay their way. Fallon insisted. Bringing Riley's family would be part of her wedding present. Andi was right; Riley *did* want her family there. When Fallon had made the call to extend the invitation to Mary, she gained an understanding of what had held Riley back.

Mary's reception to Fallon's call and the reason for it had been cordial, although not close to what Fallon would consider warm. If Fallon could feel the strain three-thousand miles away over a phone line, she could only imagine what it felt like for Riley. It was ironic. Neither Dean nor Mary would be at their wedding. Fallon was still reeling from Dale's revelation. The knowledge that her brother had slept with Liv didn't shock her. Perhaps, that was the reason it made her sick to her stomach. What surprised Fallon most was that Olivia's betrayal hurt far less than Dean's—again. She was relieved that he would be unable to attend her wedding. Her relief helped her to understand Riley's reluctance to extend an invitation to Mary. *We are quite the pair.* She started the engine and moved to pull out of the parking lot when her phone blared through the cab. Without thinking, she answered it.

"If your selling something, I'm broke," she answered, expecting a quick retort from any one of a number of people.

"I doubt you have much interest in what I offer anymore."

That voice—Fallon bit her lip gently. "What do you want, Liv?"

"Hello to you too, Fallon."

Fallon made no reply.

"I hear congratulations are in order," Olivia said.

"Thank you," Fallon said evenly.

"Did you think that you might have called to let us know?"

"Apparently, you *do* know."

"Because your brother told me."

"There's a shocking revelation," Fallon bit.

"I can see we have some things to discuss."

"Not really."

"I think we do."

"You would."

"Starting with how you think it's fair to exclude your goddaughters."

Fallon gripped the steering wheel with her right hand. "It happened quickly."

"I see. It is a weekend event, isn't it? You're going to punish them because you're angry at me? Or is it about Dean?"

"I'm not punishing anyone. Emily and Summer are welcome to visit whenever they want. That's never changed," Fallon said.

"As long as it's not with me," Olivia guessed.

"If the girls would like to come up for the weekend, they are more than welcome. They can either stay with us or Mom."

"I see."

"Is there anything else you needed?" Fallon asked.

"Don't you think we should talk about this?"

"*This*? Would that be the way you behaved this summer, the fact that you are skipping out on the girls, or is it ancient history you'd like to discuss?"

"I know you're hurt…"

"I'm not hurt."

"Fallon, I know you heard that Dean… Look, it was a long time ago. You'd ended it with me, and…"

Fallon laughed. "Of course, it's my fault that you fucked my brother. I apologize, Liv."

"For once, could you give up the martyr act?" Olivia yelled.

"Oh, I'm no saint. I'm pretty sure I never slept with Beth, though."

"You've had an affair."

"Don't," Fallon warned.

"Don't? Don't what, Fallon? So, you sleeping with someone else's wife is okay…"

"Don't. Leave Andi out of it."

"Defensive much? Are you sure it's Riley you should be marrying?"

"This conversation is over."

"That's always your answer, isn't it?"

"Goodbye, Liv."

"Fallon!"

"If the girls want to come up here, let Mom know or have Barb call me. Otherwise? Do me a favor and stop calling me."

"So, that's it? Ancient history it is. Do you hate me that much?"

"I don't hate you, Liv. I'm not sure I know you well enough to hate you."

"What is that supposed to mean?"

"Exactly what I said. I'm not doing this with you. We've both made our choices. I'm happy with mine. If you aren't? Well, I can't help you with that. I'm not sure who can," Fallon said. "I need to go. Let us know about the girls."

"You mean, have Barb call you."

"That will be fine," Fallon said. She hung up and tossed the phone aside. "Unbelievable." Fallon took a few deep breaths. Her momentary disgust vanished. Olivia was, as Fallon had said, ancient history. She meant what she said; they'd both made their choices. Fallon was content with where all of those choices had led her. She smiled. "Time to go home."

Dave gauged the interaction between his mother and Billie curiously as Billie handed Andi a beer.

"You hate beer," Dave observed.

Andi shrugged. "Some things grow on you," she said with a wink. She scrunched her face after taking a sip. "Like a fungus."

Billie laughed. "It doesn't taste like fungus."

"How do you know?" Andi asked.

"I've seen plenty of fungus," Billie said.

"Do they make you taste test it in the ER?" Andi asked playfully.

Dave's laughter surprised them both.

"It's an IPA, Mom," he explained.

"What does that mean to me?" Andi asked. "Incredibly Putrid Ass in a bottle?"

Dave snorted. "Give it to me, and I'll get you a glass of wine."

"You're not twenty-one," Andi reminded him.

Dave stared at her.

"Oh, fine!" Andi handed her son the bottle of beer. "There's a bottle of chardonnay in the fridge already open," she told him.

"Got it. Do you need anything?" He asked Billie.

Billie shook her head. "I'm okay with my bottle of Incredibly Putrid Ass; thanks."

"Yeah?" Andi asked. "You're brushing your teeth before we go to bed."

Billie's eyes flew open, and she spewed beer across the room.

Dave laughed harder. "Don't sweat it," he told Billie. "Becky won't come near me when I've been drinking it either."

Now, Andi's jaw fell.

Dave rolled his eyes. "I'll get your wine—and a paper towel." He gestured to the spray of beer that had landed on the coffee table.

Billie and Andi looked at each other. "Umm," was all Billie could manage.

"Don't ask me," Andi said. "I'm not going to argue with it, though."

Dave strolled back into the room, handed Andi a glass of wine, and sat down in a chair. He looked into his beer bottle for a minute before speaking. "See… The thing is," he began. "I sort of never thought Mom would be with anybody but my dad."

Andi was stunned.

He looked up, smiled sadly at his mother, and then turned to Billie. "And, then I met Becky." He sighed. "Her parents would make me pray if they saw me with this bottle," he said. He took a sip. "If they ever found out we've had sex…"

Andi choked on her wine. Billie rubbed her back gently.

"Sorry, Mom." Dave blushed. "Anyway, I guess I just didn't want one more thing; you know? One more thing they could find out and have a reason to try and break us up."

"What does your girlfriend think?" Billie asked gently.

"About which thing?" Dave asked.

"Any of it," Billie clarified.

"She doesn't think like they do. I mean, she grew up that way; you know? She worries they'll disown her. They sort of don't talk to her older sister anymore," he said.

"Why is that?" Andi inquired.

"She married a black guy," he told her.

Andi wanted to scream. "Dave…"

"I know! It's fucked up!" He looked at Billie. "Sorry."

"Nah, it *is* fucked up," Billie agreed.

Dave sighed heavily. "Then Jake told me—you know, about him. Well, he sort of yelled at me."

Andi smiled.

"It took me a few weeks. I told Becky, and she said that I needed to call him. She talks to her sister every couple of days. Her parents don't know that, though."

Billie took a sip from her beer bottle and set it aside. "Listen, Dave, I get it. When I say, I get it? I mean that *I get it*."

He looked at her as if to implore her for an answer.

"My parents," Billie began. "They're a lot like that— a lot like that. They talk to me. They *know* about me. They choose to pretend I'm someone else. They're in Florida now. They've probably already heard the buzz about me and your mom. I haven't had the guts to call them in weeks," she admitted.

Andi reached over and took Billie's hand. "Billie, you don't have to…"

"I know," Billie said. She smiled at Andi and looked back at Dave. "I tried for a long time to pretend or to hide who I was. My brother is the golden boy. To them, he is anyway. They've caused issues for him too. I don't need to talk to him to know that. I can't tell you what to do. I can tell you that trying to be someone you aren't for anyone else will only make you miserable in the end, no matter how much you love them."

"That's kind of what Becky's sister said when she visited us last week."

Andi held Billie's hand tightly as she addressed her son. "Let me guess; that's when you decided to call me."

He nodded. "I'm sorry, Mom." His eyes met Billie's for a second and he looked back down.

Billie recognized the expression in his eyes—shame, fear, guilt—all begging for someone, anyone to see and to offer some hope. "Dave," she addressed him.

He reluctantly met Billie's gaze. "I don't have any right to say this to you."

"Go ahead," he told her.

"Look, I spent a lot of time feeling the way I suspect you do now; scared that I'd end up alone somehow. I get it. But, you know, you can't make anyone accept you. That includes them accepting the people you love. If they can't accept who you are, and the people and things that matter to you, that's their loss; it isn't on you. I wish I had figured that out when I was your age."

"When did you figure it out?"

Billie glanced at Andi. "A while ago," she said. "I'm just learning how to live up to it, though."

He nodded.

"Billie's right," Andi offered. "Being right doesn't always make things easier."

"Mom?"

"Hum?"

"Never mind," Dave mumbled.

"What do you want to ask me?" Andi wondered.

"Did you always know? Like Jake? Did you always know you were... You know..."

Andi grinned. "That's a good question," she said. "I haven't given much thought to *what* I am," she admitted. "I don't know, Dave. I think if people spent more time worried about *who* they want to be instead of *what* other people might like to call them, they'd be a lot happier. Maybe that's a cop-out."

"It's not," Billie said. She held Andi's gaze, thinking how lucky she was that Andi loved her.

"So, you're not a lesbian?" Dave asked.

"You can refer to me any way that makes you comfortable," Andi replied. "I'd prefer you thought of me as Mom."

Dave chuckled nervously. "I think I get it. Would it be okay if Becky came home with me for Thanksgiving break?"

"You're welcome to invite anyone," Andi said. "But if you choose to come home for the holiday weekend, you should know that Billie will be here as well."

Dave nodded. "I figured."

"Are you all right with that?" Andi asked.

He nodded again. "I'm not really an asshole," he told Billie.

"I never thought you were," Billie said.

"Seriously?" His surprise was evident.

"Well, I thought you were acting like an asshole. I never thought you were one. I've encountered my share of assholes."

"Kind of like fungus?" He joked.

Billie laughed. "Kind of."

"I didn't think you'd be home for a while," Riley commented when Fallon walked through the door.

"Andi called and asked Billie to come over for dinner."

"With Dave?"

Fallon nodded.

"Wow."

"I know. I hope it goes well," Fallon said.

"Everything okay?" Riley detected something off with Fallon. She wasn't sure what it was. "Second thoughts or something?"

Fallon laughed earnestly. "Hoping that I'll let you off the hook?"

"Not a chance. Something is up; I can tell."

"Liv called me."

"Oh, Fallon…"

"To ask me why I didn't invite the girls to the wedding."

"Ugh."

"Mmm. I told her they're welcome and she can arrange it with Mom or have Barb call me."

"I'll bet that went over well."

"Mm-hum."

"Are you okay?"

"Yeah."

"Are you sure?"

"Yep."

"Is there something else bothering you?" Riley asked.

"Where's Owen?"

Riley smirked. "Out with it."

"Okay, here it is…."

"I'm listening."

"We need to drop Owen off with Mom after lunch tomorrow," Fallon said.

"Why?"

"So, we can go to the airport."

"Why are we going to the airport?"

"Ummm…" Fallon grinned guiltily.

"Fallon…"

"Uh… Because your folks are flying in from Vegas."

Riley stared vacantly at Fallon.

"Riley?"

"I thought you just said my parents were flying here."

"Yeah, because I did. Your mom was headed to meet your dad tonight, so they could fly together."

"To come here," Riley tried to understand.

"Uh-huh."

"To Whiskey Springs."

"Ummm... Yes?" *Why am I always answering her with questions?*

"My parents are coming here."

"Right."

"Tomorrow."

"Yes."

"And, we're picking them up at the airport."

"That's the plan."

"How did my parents decide... When did my parents..."

"Ummm... After I called and invited them to the wedding."

Riley shook her head as if trying to clear cobwebs.

"Please tell me you're not mad," Fallon said.

"Mad?"

"That I invited them."

Riley sighed. "No," she promised. She led Fallon to the sofa. "No, I'm not. I'm just surprised."

Fallon failed to meet Riley's gaze.

"Fallon, I'm not upset," Riley said. She lifted Fallon's chin with a fingertip. "I'm surprised," she repeated. "And, I love you for doing it."

"They should be here. I was going to surprise you tomorrow, but then I thought, if I were you, I'd want a head's up."

Riley moved to kiss Fallon gently. "Thank you."

"I called your sister."

"I figured. Let me guess; not enough notice?"

"Something like that," Fallon said.

"Thank you for trying."

"I'm sorry about Mary."

"Don't be."

"I know you two have your issues, but I also know you love her."

"I do. I'm not devastated that she declined," Riley said.

"I understand."

"I know you do."

"Riley?"

"Yeah?"

"We're really getting married."

"Yes, I know."

"Sunday."

"That's what I hear."

"You're making fun of me."

"No," Riley said. "You are adorable sometimes."

"Adorable or annoying?"

"That too."

"I am?"

"Only occasionally."

"You're having fun right now, aren't you?"

"Maybe a little," Riley confessed. "I'm glad you're home."

"Me too. Seriously, where's Owen?"

"Your mom picked him up about an hour ago."

"Really?"

"Normally, I wouldn't send our son off with a strange woman, but since she will be my mother-in-law in a few days, I thought I'd give it a try."

Fallon nodded. Riley was immensely pleased with herself. "Is that so?" Fallon asked.

"Yep."

One quick swoop, and Riley was over Fallon's shoulder, headed straight for the bedroom.

"What are you doing?" Riley protested through a fit of giggles.

"Putting you in time-out."

"In our bedroom?"

"That's the idea."
"Are you going to tie me down too?" Riley asked.
"Only if you ask nicely," Fallon replied.

CHAPTER TWELVE

SATURDAY

Whiskey Springs was a far cry from San Diego, and not just when you stopped to count the miles that separated them. Riley's mother had heard many tales from Riley about the people in the small town whom she considered friends. Nothing had prepared her for reality. The most striking difference between Whiskey Spring, Vermont and San Diego, California was the contentment evident on Riley's face. It would be impossible to deny the warmth that emanated from the people Riley spent her time with. If Brenda had entertained any lingering questions about Riley creating a life in small-town, New England, the last two days had banished them all. Lively conversation seemed to drown out the sound of the jukebox. She was happy to sit and take it all in.

Fallon took a seat next to Brenda. "They're an animated bunch. I hope we haven't scared you too much."

"Oh, it'd take a lot more than this," Brenda promised. "It was nice of Andi to offer her home to you tomorrow."

"That's Andi."

"You two are close as well?"

Fallon shifted a bit. "She's my best friend."

"I get the feeling it hasn't always been that way," Brenda said.

"It has been for longer than I sometimes want to admit," Fallon replied. "If you're asking if it was ever more than that; it was."

"It's always a relief when you can be best friends with your ex."

"I think so," Fallon said. "I've never thought of Andi as my ex, though. We both found the person we were meant to."

"I can't say I identify with that, at least, not yet. Speaking of my ex-husband, have you seen him?"

"Last I saw, he wandered outside with my mother. She'll return him eventually. I can't promise what condition he'll be in, but…"

Brenda laughed. "He might give her a run for her money."

"I'd love to see that."

"Thanks for letting me come," Dave said.

"Don't thank me; thank Fallon," Andi said.

"I will."

"You know, you are welcome to stay for the wedding tomorrow. She won't mind."

"Actually, I'd really like to," Dave said. "I feel like I owe her an apology."

"I don't think Fallon expects you to be sorry."

"But?"

"She's been part of your life since you were small," Andi told him. "You spent a lot of time with Fallon over the years."

"Yeah, I know."

"I think it hurt her to know that you were so angry with me. She blames herself."

"Why?"

"Because she cares about you, and she cares about me. And, because she knows that I love you and your brother more than anything."

"I'm sorry, Mom. I didn't mean to be an asshole."

Andi wrapped an arm around her son. "Most of us don't. Somehow, we still manage."

"Thanks." He chuckled.

"You're welcome."

Dave's eyes scanned the room. Fallon was sitting with Riley's mother. Riley was attempting to wrangle Owen from spinning in circles by the jukebox. Billie and Carol were talking in the corner quietly. Dale was dancing with Marge, and Pete was sitting a few seats away sipping on a pint of beer. "I thought at a rehearsal dinner you were supposed to rehearse?"

"They are," Andi said. "For the reception."

⁓

"Worried?" Ida asked Riley's father.

"About Riley?"

"About Riley and Fallon getting hitched."

"No. Riley's always had a good head on her shoulders. She likes adventure but she's not reckless."

"Mmm."

"Are you worried?"

"Me?" Ida waved off the notion. "I'm just relieved someone is finally willing to take her off my hands."

"Oh, somehow, I imagine Fallon's had her share of chances," Doug offered.

"She has. Never took the bait, though. Came close once. Thank God, she threw that one back."

"That would be Olivia?"

"Heard the name, huh?"

"Riley mentioned it."

"I'll bet she did."

"Not a fan?" He asked.

"I was—once. We all were."

"She's your granddaughters' mother?"

"She is. She and her wife, Barb had Emily not long after they met. My son..."

"I heard," he said. "They seem like great kids."

"Emily and Summer? Oh, they are," Ida beamed. "They'll be moving here in a month."

"Riley mentioned that last night."

"It'll be nice to have all my grandchildren nearby," Ida said.

"I can imagine."

"I'm sorry. That was insensitive of me."

"No, no, not at all. It would be nice to have more time with them—Riley and Owen, I mean. It can get stressful when we're all together."

"Really? You all seem…."

"Mmm… You haven't met our older daughter."

Ida smiled. "Mary."

"Mary. She means well."

"But?"

"Mary, Mary quite contrary—emphasis on the contrary."

"I think I follow."

"You know, we thought it'd be easier with two."

Ida laughed. "So, did we."

"How'd it work out for you?"

"It's had its ups and downs," Ida replied. "Lately, it's been a lot more in the downward direction."

"Never easy."

"No, and it never ends."

"Can I ask you something?"

"Can I reserve the right to drink afterward?" Ida asked.

"I'll even buy."

"Oh, a cheapskate, huh? Don't worry, it's on the house when it's family. Come to think of it, that's half this town."

"How does she stay in business?" Doug wondered.

"Oh… That's a story for the bar, my friend."

"Huh."

"What did you want to ask?"

"How did you handle it—when you found out Fallon was... You know..."

"A lesbian?"

Doug nodded.

"There wasn't anything to handle as far as I was concerned."

"It didn't worry you?"

"Oh, sure it *worried* me. This is small town America. I know the rest of the country thinks we're all progressive over here in New England. Trust me; we have our share of backwoods bigots."

"I'll bet. And, now?"

"Oh, Fallon's been out most of her life. And, Riley? Well, I wouldn't worry about Riley. Like you said, she's got a good head on her shoulders. They'll be fine."

"Do you mean as a lesbian couple?"

"Oh, if I had to guess, that will be the least of their obstacles," Ida said. "And, before you ask; I'm as sure as I can be that they will get through it all."

"I'm glad to hear that. Now, about that other story..."

"For this, we drink," Ida replied.

SUNDAY MORNING

The fragrant aroma of coffee and flowers filtered through the house and filled Riley's senses. She stretched and pulled the sheet tightly to her chin. Fallon had protested when Riley hopped into Andi's car after their impromptu rehearsal dinner. Not much was rehearsed except Carol's ability to mix drinks; something she had mastered long ago. It had been an evening filled with friends and family, and one that Riley was immensely grateful Carol and Andi had thrown together. Hearing the sound of animated laughter and watching as her parents engaged with the friends she'd grown to love in Whiskey Springs had been a salve for Riley's soul. She'd called her older sister early in the day. The call had left Riley feeling raw and self-conscious. Was she selfish? Perhaps, she was. Whiskey Springs was her home. Fallon would be her wife in a few short hours — her wife. "My wife." The sound of the words curled the corners of Riley's mouth, a smile edging its way onto her sleepy face.

She still had no idea what to expect from the day ahead. Details didn't matter to her. She trusted Andi. Andi and Ida had made nearly all of the arrangements. Andi had even coerced Dave into helping set up for the wedding, and to stay another night. Fallon had been delighted. Jacob was in the middle of a project and wasn't able to fly home. Riley had caught the shimmering tears in Fallon's eyes when Dave came over to tell her he'd like to stay for the wedding. Fallon adored Andi's boys. Riley had witnessed Jacob's affection for Fallon over the summer. Dave's reaction to Andi's relationship with Fallon and his parents' divorce had not only hurt Andi deeply; it had left Fallon feeling responsible and guilty. When Dave tried to apologize to Fallon, she had brushed it all off as though it never happened. Riley recognized a lightness in Fallon's step afterward. That was until Andi announced that Riley and Brenda would be spending the night at her house. Riley wished she had a camera to capture Fallon's wounded expression.

"Why?" Fallon asked.

"It's tradition," Andi told her.

"Nothing about this is traditional," Fallon replied.

Andi shrugged. "We have things to do in the morning, Fallon."

"Like what?" Fallon wanted to know.

"You'll see when you get to my house."

"Why can't you tell me now?"

"Because it's a surprise. That's why."

"I don't like surprises," Fallon said.

Andi shrugged again. "I'll refrain from comment."

"Ha-ha." Fallon looked at Riley. "You're not really sleeping at Andi's; are you?"

"It's one night," Riley said.

"Why?"

"It's only one night," Riley repeated.

"I don't have to like it."

Riley kissed Fallon's cheek. "Owen is so excited. He will love having you to himself tonight."

"Oh, I get it. You think he'll crawl in our bed, and you need your beauty sleep."

"That's a bonus."

Fallon huffed. "I'm not going to win this argument."

"Not likely," Riley agreed.

"Call me in the morning," Fallon said.

"Good God," Andi chimed. "You are pathetic. It's only a few hours."

"I'm pathetic? You might as well have a leash on Billie!" Fallon returned.

"I don't think we've been together long enough for bondage games, Fallon," Andi deadpanned.

Fallon's eyes grew as wide as saucers.

Riley howled with laughter. "You are both nuts," she said.

The details of the day ahead were unimportant to Riley. She had to admit, she was glad that they had expanded the guest list. As much as Riley desired something simple, she would've missed the chance to share the happiest day of her life with the people she loved. Today, she would promise her future to Fallon. That promise was something that deserved celebration. When the festivities ended, she would fall into Fallon's arms. "What's better than that?" Riley mused.

"Whatever it is, I doubt my coffee will compete," Andi's voice echoed in the doorway.

Riley pried her eyes open.

"Good morning, sunshine," Andi said.

Riley sat up and accepted the steamy offering from her friend. "You're the best," she said.

"How are you feeling this morning?" Andi asked.

"Relaxed," Riley replied. "Excited, but relaxed. Weird, huh?"

"I don't think so."

"Is my mom up yet?"

"She left with Ida about twenty minutes ago to do an errand."

"Do I want to know?" Riley asked.

"Don't ask me. Ida wouldn't tell me what it was."

"Is Billie here?" Riley wondered.

"She's out back with Dave taking care of some things."

"What *things*?"

"You'll see," Andi said. "I should go check on them."

"They seem to be getting along," Riley observed.

Andi was thrilled that Dave seemed to enjoy Billie's company. She was still tentative regarding how long things would last. "They are. I just hope things hold when he goes back to school."

"They will."

"I hope so," Andi said. "Love does strange things to people sometimes."

"I thought you told Fallon it was too soon for bondage games for you and Billie?" Riley quipped.

Andi laughed. "I did say that, didn't I?"

"Yep."

"She brings the worst out in me sometimes," Andi teased.

"She definitely brings out your inner comedienne."

"That too. Drink your coffee," Andi advised.

"What can I help with?" Riley wanted to know.

"Nothing. Relax this morning. This is your day to enjoy. But, you might want to call Fallon."

Riley raised a curious brow.

"She called me at six o'clock."

"Oh, God. I'm sorry."

"Don't be. Billie took the phone and told her to go back to bed."

Riley giggled.

"She called again at seven and said she wasn't Sleeping Beauty."

"I'll call her."

Andi nodded and started back toward the hallway.

"Andi?"

"Yeah?"

"Thanks."

Andi's only reply was a wink.

❧

"How's Riley?" Fallon asked when Ida and Brenda walked in.

"Sleeping, last I knew," Brenda said.

"Sleeping? She was still asleep when you left? How can she be sleeping?"

"Most people do sleep," Ida said.

"It's nine already!"

"Heaven forbid anyone sleeps past the crack of dawn on Sunday," Ida replied. "Not everyone was up at five a.m., calling the entire town."

"I didn't call the entire town; I called *you*."

"Yes, I know."

"I can't believe she's still asleep."

"Fallon, Riley's not a nervous wreck like you are," Ida offered. "Why *are* you so nervous?"

"I don't want anything to go wrong is all."

"What could go wrong? Dear God, don't tell me you messed up the laundry again and have nothing to wear. She was gone one night!"

"Very funny," Fallon said.

Brenda found the entire scene amusing. Fallon couldn't sit still. She was fidgeting more than Owen did on a long car ride.

"Gwama!" Owen ran into the room. He hugged Ida and then Brenda. Then he frowned.

"What's wrong?" Fallon asked him.

"Is Mommy coming?" He asked.

"Mommy's at Grandma Andi's, remember?" Fallon said.

Owen made his way to Fallon and climbed onto her lap. "Gwama can come here."

"Grandma is busy with Mommy right now, buddy," Fallon explained. "Remember? We're going to Grandma's in a little while for the wedding."

"I get the w'rings!"

"That's right," Fallon said.

Ida marveled at the sense of calm that swept over Fallon the moment Owen was present. His needs and his questions came first. She watched as Fallon pulled Owen close and he nestled against her in contentment.

"Maybe you can call Mommy," Fallon suggested. "I'll bet she's awake by *now*."

Owen grinned.

Fallon grabbed her phone, pressed the contact, and handed it to him.

"Mommy!"

❧

"I was just about to call you."

"Mommy!"

"Owen?"

"Hi, Mommy."

"Good morning, sweetheart. What are you doing this morning?"

"Sittin' with Momma."

"Oh? How is Momma?"

Owen studied Fallon. "She's gwumpy."

"She's grumpy?"

"I'm not grumpy!" Fallon's voice carried in the background.

Riley chuckled.

"Gwama's here," Owen told his mother.

"Grandma Ida and Gram?"

"Yep. Mommy?"

"Yes, Owen?"

"Can you come home now?"

"Oh, sweetie, I will see you in a few hours at Grandma Andi's. You get Momma all to yourself this morning. And, you have two grandmas to entertain."

Owen grinned. "Okay! Here's Momma." He handed Fallon her phone and jumped off her lap. He grabbed one of Ida's hands, one of Brenda's, and started to pull them toward his room.

Fallon rolled her eyes. "Whatever you said did the trick," she told Riley.

"Grumpy, huh?" Riley asked

"I'm not."

"Nervous?"

"A little," Fallon admitted.

"Want to talk about it?"

"It's standing in front of everyone. I'm better one on one."

"Fallon, you are great at speaking in front of people."

"At a bar, maybe."

"Just do what the experts advise to ease your nerves."

"What's that?" Fallon asked.

"Picture everyone naked."

"That is a terrible idea, Riley."

Riley laughed.

"I'm worried about messing up my vows in front of everyone. I don't want to picture my mother naked. And, I'll be looking at *you*. There is no way I will keep things straight if I picture *you* naked."

"That's probably a good thing," Riley quipped.

Fallon chuckled. "How are *you*?"

"Looking forward to seeing you."

"Really?"

"Of course."

"Do you have any idea what they're all up to?" Fallon wondered. "They're plotting something; I know it."

"No doubt," Riley agreed.

"Go snoop."

"What?"

"You heard me; go snoop!"

"Oh my God, you are worse than Owen. I'm not snooping. I can see it now; I'm going to have to hide your Christmas presents in the forest."

Fallon laughed. "Maybe." She sighed. "I miss you."

"You'll see me in a couple of hours."

"What are you wearing?"

"What does it matter if you're going to picture me naked anyway?"

"Riley! Stop. I cannot picture you naked at the altar."

"We're not getting married at an altar. We're standing under a gazebo."

"Ha-ha."

"Relax," Riley said. "Enjoy the surprises, Fallon."

"I can't believe you're so calm."

"Why wouldn't I be? I'll be with you."

Fallon closed her eyes. Riley always knew what to say. "For a long time," Fallon said.

"That's the plan. I'll see you in a little while. Have fun with Owen."

"He wants you."

"No. He can tell you're nervous and he's not sure how to help. Enjoy the rest of the morning, Fallon. Carol will be there in a while, won't she?" Riley asked.

"Around ten-thirty."

"Trust me. You'll be here with me before you know it."

"Riley?"

"Yeah?"

"I love you; you know?"

"I certainly hope I know. I'll see you in a bit."

"Okay."

"And, I love you too."

Riley placed her mug in the dishwasher. A crashing sound followed by a high-pitched yelp sent her sprinting toward the back door. The only thing that registered was Billie on the ground. She opened the door and ran over to kneel beside Andi. "What happened?"

"Damn rock," Billie grumbled.

"I must've missed it when I put the runner down," Dave said. "Shit, I'm sorry, Billie."

"It's not your fault. It's the damn rock's!" Billie griped.

"Can you stand up?" Andi asked.

Billie nodded. Andi and Dave helped her to her feet. She winced the moment her foot touched the ground.

Andi frowned. "Let's get you in the house."

"Nah, I'll be fine in a minute."

"Did you hit your head too? You're a nurse, for God's sake!" Andi said.

"Seriously," Billie began. "Just let me sit for a minute. I think I just twisted it."

Andi's doubtful gaze made Riley giggle.

"I'll get some ice," Riley said.

"I'm okay!" Billie protested.

"You're delusional," Andi muttered.

"I'll get the ice," Riley repeated. She turned to make her way back to the house. After a few paces, she looked up and stopped cold. In her rush to reach Billie, she'd failed to notice the display that had taken shape in Andi's backyard. "Oh, my God..."

Billie and Andi exchanged a smile.

"We were almost done setting up when a rock decided to land me on my ass," Billie said.

"I'm sorry," Dave apologized again.

"Don't be," Billie offered. "I'll be fine."

Andi raised her brow a tad higher.

"Like you said, I'm the nurse; I should know," Billie told her.

"I give up," Andi said.

"There is no way I am missing my chance to dance with you later," Billie explained. "So, don't get any ideas."

Andi shook her head and made her way to Riley.

"Andi," Riley could barely speak. "What did you do?"

"Me? Nothing. I made some calls and gave them my credit card. Billie and Dave did all this — with a little help."

Riley shook her head in disbelief. In her wildest imagination, she couldn't have envisioned the transformation to Andi's yard. White wooden chairs lined either side of a makeshift aisle. Every chair that stood along the aisle was adorned with a small spray of flowers that included blush and yellow roses, burgundy calla lilies, and eucalyptus. The gazebo was draped with a cream-colored ribbon, and floral sprays were attached to each corner. Underneath her feet, Riley noted the runner that led from the backdoor to the gazebo was a deep burgundy that complimented everything perfectly. "Andi," she whispered again. "This must have cost a fortune."

"Oh, I wouldn't say that."

Riley turned to Andi. "I don't know what to say."

"You don't need to say anything. Consider it my wedding gift."

Riley's arms surrounded Andi. "You did too much."

"Riley, I could never do *too much* for you or for Fallon." Hearing Riley begin to sniffle, Andi rubbed soothing circles on her back. "Finally hitting you, huh?"

"Yeah." Riley pulled back.

Andi wiped a few tears from Riley's cheeks. "It's your day — yours and Fallon's. I want it to be special."

Riley was unsure of what to say. "I'll get that ice."

Andi nodded. Riley needed a moment alone. So, did she.

"Is Riley okay?" Dave whispered to Billie.

"She's okay," Billie said. "She's getting a reminder of how much your mom means to her."

Dave watched as his mother tried to conceal her emotion. "Is mom crying because of Fallon?"

"Not the way you're thinking," Billie said. "Not at all. Riley and your mom—well, let's just say I think you have an honorary big sister."

Dave looked over at his mother who was standing a few feet away. He nodded.

"Dave?" Billie wondered what was going through his mind.

"I'm going to go see if I can help Riley," he announced, giving his mother and Billie a moment alone.

"Andi?" Billie called to her lover.

Andi took a deep breath, turned and smiled.

"You okay?" Billie wanted to know.

"I'm not the one waiting for ice," Andi pointed out.

"Are you sure you're okay?"

"Completely," Andi said.

"Why do I think I'm missing something?"

"Just two good feet," Andi said. She kissed Billie's cheek. "I'll check on the ice."

"How much ice do you people think I need?!" Billie chuckled. "This is going to be a long day."

⁓

Ida peeked into the living room. Fallon was sitting in her favorite chair, her head back and her eyes closed. "Napping?"

"No. Practicing," Fallon replied.

"Your vows?"

Fallon nodded.

Ida walked over and put a hand gently on Fallon's shoulder. "I have something for you."

Fallon opened her eyes. "What is it?"

Ida handed Fallon a small box. "Open it."

Fallon looked at her mother curiously before opening the lid. "Mom..."

"I know you bought a band for Riley. I thought you might rather give this to her."

"Mom... This is the diamond from your ring, isn't it?"

"It is. The sapphires are from Riley's grandmother's ring."

"How did you..."

"Oh, I have my ways," Ida said. "Earl owes me a few favors. I popped over there yesterday. He dropped it off last night."

"Earl Leland?"

"He does own the only jewelry store in this town," Ida reminded her daughter.

"That's why you went outside with Doug last night," Fallon guessed.

"Don't feel obligated to use this one. If you'd rather give her the band..."

"Obligated? Mom, I don't know how you managed to get this done so quickly."

"Well, after you called and invited Riley's parents, I made a call to Brenda."

"You did? How did you get her number?"

"I have my ways. I thought she might have something she wanted to give you for Riley, and I didn't want to step on any toes. She mentioned that she had the sapphires from her mother's anniversary ring. I suggested we combine them. She sent me the size and a photo. I went to Earl that afternoon. He said he'd make time to get it done."

"What did you do to earn that favor?" Fallon asked.

"I got him out of a slew of parking tickets when I was mayor. Probably kept him out of divorce court too."

"How many favors did you buy as mayor?" Fallon asked.

"I never kiss and tell."

"There was kissing?"

"Only a little ass now and then," Ida said. "Mine, that is."

Fallon laughed.

"Listen, I need to get Brenda back to Riley." Ida said. "Do you need me to come back and help you with anything?"

"Carol's coming in a bit, and last I checked, I can dress myself."

"But do you have anything clean to wear?"

"Funny. Thanks, Mom." Fallon stood and embraced her mother. "I love you."

"I love you too, Fallon. You're a pain in my ass sometimes, but God knows, I love you."

"Thanks, I think."

"Momma!"

"Another corner heard from," Fallon noted. "Yes?"

"Can we go?"

"In a little while," Fallon said. "We have to get dressed first."

"Now?"

"A soon as Gram and Grandma Ida leave," Fallon promised.

Owen turned on his heels and ran back toward his room, nearly tripping Brenda on his way.

"He's a little anxious to get things started," Brenda said. "He showed me his shoes three times."

Fallon laughed. "He loves those shoes for some reason."

"They're shiny," Ida offered.

"I had to make him take them off last night. He came home and put them on immediately," Fallon said.

"Don't fight it," Ida advised. "Do you need anything before we go?"

"Can I bring a cheat sheet?" Fallon asked.

"You'll be fine," Ida said.

"Vows?" Brenda guessed.

"I just hope I don't forget anything."

"No one will know if you do," Ida reminded Fallon.

"I'll know."

"Well, you'll have the rest of your life to fill in those blanks," Ida said. She kissed Fallon on the cheek. "See you in a couple of hours."

"Or sooner," Fallon said.

"A couple of hours, Fallon."

CHAPTER THIRTEEN

WEDDING TIME

*R*iley held her breath as Andi zipped the back of her dress. "I think I'm bloated."

"You look gorgeous," Andi said.

"Why am I nervous all of a sudden?"

"I think that's normal."

"Is she here yet?" Riley asked.

"She's downstairs," Andi replied.

Riley held her breath again.

"Keep holding all that air in, and you will be bloated," Andi teased. "And, she looks amazing too."

"Oh, God. I think I might throw up, or maybe I have to pee. I think I have to pee."

Andi laughed. "Relax."

"I swear, I wasn't this nervous the first time. Why am I so nervous? I was fine this morning."

"I think what you're feeling is anticipation," Andi offered.

"Is she nervous?"

"No, it seems you two have had a bit of role reversal. I think Owen gave her something to take her mind off her nerves."

A faint knock landed on the door, and Riley held her breath again.

Andi chuckled and went to open it.

"Someone wants to see his Mommy," Ida said.

Andi knelt down to Owen's height. "I think Mommy could use an Owen hug." She opened the door wider. "Someone is here to see the bride," she said.

Riley turned just as Owen barreled through the door and straight for her. "Well, look at you," she greeted him.

"Mommy! I got my shoes. See?"

"I see."

He pointed to the tie around his neck. "A gold tie! See? Momma did it."

Riley played with the tie and smiled at Owen. "Momma did a great job."

"Yep. Momma looks pwetty."

"I'll bet she does."

Owen grabbed Riley's hand. "You come now?"

Riley giggled. "In a few minutes. How about you come sit down while I get my shoes on?"

"Okay!"

"We'll come back in a few minutes," Andi said.

"Thanks," Riley replied.

"You help Mommy," Ida instructed Owen.

"Gwama?"

"Yes?"

"I get w'rings?"

"I will get the rings from Momma; I promise," Andi told him.

Owen grinned and nodded.

"It's all about the rings and the shoes," Ida commented as the pair left the room.

"How's Fallon holding up?" Andi asked.

"I think she could use a minute."

"Alone?"

"With you."

Andi nodded. She squeezed Ida's hand as they descended the stairs.

Fallon and Billie looked up at the sound of familiar voices.

"Jesus," Billie muttered.

Fallon sniggered softly. She could hardly blame Billie for the expletive. Andi looked radiant. Fallon had seen a picture of Andi's dress. It was simple. Riley wanted simple everything to be simple. Riley had chosen Andi to stand beside her. Andi's dress was floor length, burgundy, and gathered slightly at the waist. Her hair was braided in the back, allowing a few tight curls to frame her face.

Andi's eyes held Billie's as she reached the bottom of the stairs. "I'll take that as a compliment." She leaned in and kissed Billie softly. "And, you look amazing." Andi wiped a smudge of lipstick from Billie's lips. "Not quite your color," she teased.

"The lipstick?" Billie asked.

Andi laughed. Billie's cheeks had deepened to a warm pink color. Andi adored her—everything about her. Billie was dressed in a black fitted suit that Andi would describe as delicious. She pressed a palm to Billie's cheek. "Yes, the lipstick. Everything else is perfect."

"I thought this was *my* wedding day," Fallon said.

Andi stepped back and let her eyes sweep over Fallon as if she were inspecting her.

"What? You don't like it?" Fallon asked.

Andi shook her head. If she didn't know that Fallon was serious, she would have laughed. Fallon made a striking appearance. She'd chosen to wear a double-breasted women's tuxedo. She left the crisp, white shirt unbuttoned at the top of her cleavage. Andi had seen Fallon dressed similarly for a few charity events over the years. Today, Fallon's hair had been styled half up/half down. Andi knew that Carol had planned to visit Fallon's to help her get ready. Fallon's makeup was flawless, enough to complement the formal occasion, and still barely noticeable. Riley would be left breathless again. "Riley may pass out before she gets down that little aisle we made."

"Why? Is she nervous?" Fallon asked.

"Well, she has been holding her breath a bit. When she sees you? We might have to resuscitate her."

"So, I look okay?"

"You look beautiful, Fallon," Andi promised.

"Billie?" Ida called across the room. "Can you give me a hand with something for a second."

"Be right there."

"Just be careful, hop-along," Ida said. "We don't need any more injuries."

"Yeah, yeah. I'll see you in a bit," Billie told Andi.

"You will," Andi said. "So?" She asked Fallon. "Are you ready to tie the knot?"

Fallon nodded.

"I'm happy for you, Fallon."

"Me too. I think Billie almost peed herself when she saw you."

Andi's spirited laughter filled the house. "Don't make me laugh."

"Why?"

"Getting out of this dress to pee is a lot harder than getting out of your tux."

"Too bad Billie's injured."

"Huh?"

"I'll bet she'd have fun cracking that puzzle."

Andi burst out laughing again. "I told you to stop making me laugh."

"Thanks," Fallon sobered. A lighthearted moment was exactly what she had needed.

"You're welcome," Andi said. "Seriously, though, no more making me laugh until this ceremony is over."

"Scouts honor."

Andi rolled her eyes. Fallon had never been any kind of scout unless you considered spying on girls, girl scouting. "I need to go wrangle your future wife. Do you have the rings?"

"Yeah, but..."

"Fallon, I'll be with Owen until he walks down the aisle to you and Billie. He won't lose them. Now, hand them over."

Fallon reached in her pocket and handed Andi the rings.

"Thank you. Now, go find Billie."

"Andi?"

"Yeah?"

"Tell her... Well, tell her I can't wait."

"I'll let her know."

❦

"Don't hold your breath," Andi advised Riley.

"I think I'm passed that."

"You haven't seen Fallon yet," Andi whispered.

"Oh, God," Riley muttered.

Andi heard Pete start to play the guitar softly and knelt down to Owen. "Now, you take the rings and walk to Momma and Billie; okay?"

"Yep!" Owen replied.

"Take your time," Andi told him.

"Okay, Gwama!"

Andi kissed him on the cheek and gently patted his butt. "Go on, just like you practiced." She turned back to Riley. "You ready?"

Riley nodded. She'd opted to walk the short trek alone. When her father asked who would be giving her away, Riley had explained that she wanted to give herself to Fallon. She'd done the traditional walk with her father once, and it had meant the world to her. Marrying Fallon differed. Understandably he'd been curious.

"What do you mean it's different?" Doug asked.

"Not for the reason you might think," Riley replied. "I loved Robert, Dad. I was young."

"You're still young."

"Maybe. I don't feel young most days. I know what I want. Marrying Fallon isn't about traditions or weddings — not for me, and not for her. It's about making a promise."

"And that's different from the reason you married Rob?"

"Yes and no. Look at you. You're on your second marriage."

"True."

"Was it the same for you when you married Lisa as it was when you married Mom?"

"Not even close," he admitted.

"When Fallon and I decided to do this — to get married, I told her that I wanted it to be just us — me and her, Owen, Andi, Billie, and Ida. It wasn't because I wanted to leave anyone out. I just... I wanted it to be about Fallon and me. I didn't want anything to cloud that."

"I think I understand," Doug said.

"When I walk to her, I want her to know that I didn't ask anyone's permission. I didn't need anyone's blessing. I want to spend the rest of my life with her. I want her to feel that."

"She's a lucky woman, Riley."

"No," Riley disagreed. *"It's me and Owen who hit the jackpot, Dad. Believe me; it is."*

Andi had already made it halfway down the short aisle when Riley came back to the present. She inhaled a long, deep breath, exhaled it slowly, and stepped through the door. The first thing that captured her attention nearly caused her to stop in her tracks. Fallon was whispering to Owen. She couldn't see Owen's face, but she could tell Fallon was attempting to calm his excitement. There were a million reasons Riley had fallen in love with Fallon Foster. Fallon's tenderness topped the list. She smiled when Fallon directed Owen to look her way. Owen grinned from ear to ear. He turned back to Fallon. "Mommy's pw'retty too!"

"She sure is," Fallon agreed. Fallon's eyes met Riley's, and she remembered to heed Andi's advice. "Breathe," she muttered.

Riley defined elegance. The dress she wore hugged her curves — not too tightly — just enough to enhance her figure. Fallon wasn't sure if the dress was a light gold or ivory. Since when did she care about colors? She shook away the thought. Riley's eyes twinkled with amusement, as if she were able to hear Fallon's every thought. Mirthful, joyful, loving eyes glistened with a hint of gold when Riley smiled. Fallon could drown in Riley's gaze and die happily. She took a brief second to take in the sight before her. Riley's hair fell freely over her shoulders in long spiral curls. A faint gold shimmered on her eyelids, highlighting the soft brown and gold of her irises. Before Fallon could complete her next thought, Riley was standing next to her.

"Hi," Riley greeted Fallon.

"Hi."

"Want to get married?" Riley asked.

Fallon nodded. Riley took her hand just as Ida cleared her throat.

"All right," Ida called for everyone's attention. "I can't think of any place I would rather be today or any ceremony that could mean more to me to perform." She cast her gaze in Carol's direction. Carol handed Andi a large glass vase filled with colorful sand. Andi passed it to Ida. "I want you to look behind you," Ida instructed Fallon and Riley. "Everyone here has a small vial. Hold them up."

"When they arrived, each was given a little bit of sand to add to this vase."

Fallon and Riley turned back to Ida curiously.

"Oh, you thought if you asked *me* to marry you, I'd let you off the hook. Not a chance. I'm going to offer you a little wisdom before you take your vows," Ida told them.

Light chuckling filtered through the air.

Ida reached behind her to a small table, put down the vase, and picked up a large stone. "Hold out a hand," she told Fallon. She placed the stone in Fallon's hand and covered it with Riley's hand. "I'm sure that you've heard people refer to marriage as a rock, as a foundation. It is. It's the foundation of a life shared. But don't be deceived by that feeling in your hands right now. That solid weight that you have grown to trust that brought you here." She picked the vase back up from the table. "That rock you're holding in your hands is made of millions of grains of sand. Your marriage is made of more than just the two of you, more than your children, more than any one person, place, or thing. It's millions of memories. It's endless experiences that have passed and have yet to come. It's the pressing together of the people you have both loved, and all those who have given their love to you. As solid and as foundational as it feels, never forget the fragility that created your marriage. It will be your ability to remain fragile, to cherish the tiniest grain of sand that will ensure your marriage remains the foundation of both your lives."

Fallon bit her lower lip gently as her mother removed the stone from her grasp and set it aside. She felt Riley's hand fall into hers again and squeeze gently to calm her. Ida enjoyed teasing the people she loved. She reveled in spirited banter. Underneath Ida Foster's sense of humor, and occasional unsolicited observations, existed the most thoughtful person Fallon knew. She loved her mother beyond words. She respected the wisdom, the candor, and the compassion of the woman who raised her. It occurred to her—not for the first time—that she was surrounded by powerful, beautiful, selfless, compassionate women. She'd had the privilege to be nurtured by one as a child, and to be loved by a woman who'd reminded Fallon that letting go was sometimes part of holding on. And, she was about to commit the rest of her life to Riley Main. Riley's intellect, her gentleness, her playfulness, and her ability to see the best in everyone and everything had captured Fallon's imagination and her heart. If a person could claim to be blessed, Fallon was sure it was her.

Ida offered Fallon a knowing wink. "Fallon, I will assume you have *something* you'd like to say to Riley."

Fallon nodded and turned to Riley. She hesitated for a second.

"Take your time," Riley whispered.

"You know, I've practiced this—a lot," Fallon admitted. "Listening to Mom, I'm not sure there are any words that can sum things up better than she just did. I know that we've both traveled a road that made us question if we could love again. And, I know that we've both found home in more than just each other. I do know that. We've been given so much—people who love us unconditionally, people who stand by us through the best and the worst life offers. I know that, and I'm grateful for every person that led me here. That's the truth. But you—Riley, you are the center of my life—the most important person in it. You're not only the person I choose to promise to be faithful to or to live with forever.;

you're the person I trust with the uncomfortable truths of my past, and the deepest desires I have for our future. I love you more than I ever thought it was possible to love another person. You take care of me — and, before anyone chimes in, I don't mean my laundry."

Riley giggled along with everyone present.

"But the laundry is a big bonus," Fallon chimed.

Riley laughed.

"I also understand that I'm not marrying one person. I'm making a promise to my *family*. I hope you know that I fell in love with Owen too. I wish I could have seen his first step and heard his first word," Fallon confessed.

Riley's eyes filled with tears.

"But if I had, he wouldn't be Owen, and you wouldn't be the Riley that was brave enough to drive her car in a Vermont snow storm. Believe me, I have thanked God a million times that your car crapped out on the side of the road."

Another round of laughter.

"Well, it's true!" Fallon defended herself. "I can't promise you that I'll never make you angry or frustrated. I know I already have, and I will a million times more in the future. I can tell you that you are in my thoughts with everything I do. Owen, and anyone else who comes along will always come first in my life — always. You make me laugh more than anyone I've ever known. And, I've laughed a lot over the years. Being able to make someone laugh when all they want to do is cry is an enormous gift. You've given that to me time and time again. You're the writer, Riley. You have a way with words. You do. I'm better with numbers, and maybe, margaritas. I hope that I tell you enough, that I show you each day that you are my world — you and Owen. I never thought I'd get to be someone's Momma. Every night when he asks for me, every time I hear you tell him to find, *Momma* — I swear to you, it's like hearing it for the first time. I will do my best to live up to the gift Owen has given me too. No matter what is ahead, I will love you through it — always.

I love you, Riley. There's nothing on earth I want more than to be married to you." Fallon exhaled forcefully.

"Riley?" Ida looked to her future daughter-in-law.

"Fallon, you *do* have a way with words. You're the most generous person I know. You would give someone your last dime and go hungry, and never once regret that decision. I knew that the night you led me to Murphy's Law in the snow. I've thought back to that day often. I fell in love with you that night. I know people might think that sounds impossible. It isn't. I remember you walking through the door without a hat, snow capping your hair in fluffy white flakes. I didn't think about it—what I felt when you looked at me. Now, I know what that feeling was. You were walking through the door, and I was the one coming home. I've come home. This is the place I was meant to find. You are the person I am meant to walk through life with. There isn't an ounce of doubt in my heart or my mind about that. Owen chose you, Fallon. That first morning when we shared breakfast, he adopted you as *his* Fallon. It was only a matter of time until he realized what I already recognized; you are his momma. I know there are moments when you think that takes something away from him, from Robert. Robert would adore you. I don't need to ask him to know that. I did ask him once. And, he sent me the sign that I knew he would. *You* are the person intended for us in this life. Everything in my life led me to you.

I can't wait for tomorrow. I feel that way every morning when I wake up and every night when I crawl into bed beside you. I know that I can face anything with you beside me—anything." Riley took a deep breath. "One day, we are going to add to our family," she said.

Fallon smiled sweetly, her chest clenching at the words.

"And, I want that as much as you ever could. You are an amazing partner. You're also an incredible parent. I *will* confess that before that happens, I'd like you to take a few laundry lessons."

Fallon snickered.

"And, maybe *not* play with so much dirt and worms," Riley teased. "That's a small price to pay for sharing life with the best person I know. You've taught me more about love than you realize. There's no safer place on earth than in your arms, and at the same time no place that makes my heart beat faster."

Fallon blushed.

Riley giggled. "That's the truth," she said. "Loving you makes my heart ache, and my pulse race, and my world seem suddenly brighter. Every part of life that we share matters to me — our friendship, being your lover, our friends, our family, and our children — every part, every moment — everything. I can't promise you perfection. I can't promise you there will never be questions between us or problems that we'll face. I know there will be. I can promise you that I will love you enough to see each one through to the other side, and that every day for the rest of my life I will remind you that I love you, and that I am yours. There's nothing more in this world that I want either than to be your wife. And, Fallon? For me? This day is about far more than a lifetime. It's about home. And, home is something you carry with you forever. I love you."

"Who knew you were both poets?" Ida teased lightly. "Are you ready to make this official?"

"Please," Fallon said.

Riley laughed.

"Always have to have a comeback," Ida quipped.

"Fallon, do you take Riley to be your partner, your lover, your best friend, and your wife? Do you promise to love her, cherish her, respect her, be faithful to her, and offer her your friendship and devotion for the rest of your lives?"

"I do," Fallon said.

"Riley?" Ida called for Riley's attention. "Do you take Fallon to be your partner, your lover, your best friend, and your wife? Do you promise to love her, cherish her, respect her, be faithful to her, and offer her your friendship and devotion for the rest of your lives?"

"I do," Riley replied.

Ida nodded to Billie. Billie handed Owen Fallon's ring for Riley. "Give this to Momma," she said.

Owen took a few steps toward his parents. He handed Fallon Riley's ring.

Fallon surprised everyone by placing him between them. She looked down at him and smiled. "Owen, when I put this ring on Mommy's finger that means that I'm promising you and Mommy that I will always be here for both of you. You can always come to me — no matter what ever happens. If you have a bad dream, or you have a question, or you just need a hug — you can always come to me, and I will always be there."

Owen smiled.

"And, no matter what you ever say or do, I will always love you, and I will always be your Momma. Do you understand that?"

"I get to keep you," Owen said.

"You get to keep me," Fallon agreed.

Owen flashed Fallon a toothy grin and tilted his head back to look at Riley.

Riley smiled at him, leaned down, and kissed his forehead. "We love you, Owen."

"Yep! Can I get the ud'der w'ring now?"

Fallon and Riley laughed.

"Rings and shoes," Fallon commented to Riley. "In a minute, buddy. One at a time, okay?"

"'Kay!"

Ida's emotions threatened to overflow. Fallon's inclusion of Owen shouldn't have surprised her. She was sure that Fallon had planned it. An enormous sense of pride in her daughter swelled in her heart. Riley was right; Fallon was the most generous person Ida knew as well. She wiped the corner of her eye and continued with the ceremony. "Fallon, place the ring on Riley's finger and repeat after me. Riley, I give you this ring as a symbol of my love, my fidelity, and my commitment to our life together, now and forever."

"Riley," Fallon began as she slid the wedding band on Riley's finger. "I give you this ring as a symbol of my love, my fidelity, and my commitment to our life together, now and forever."

"Riley," Ida began. "Do you have a ring for Fallon?"

"I do."

"Go see Billie," Fallon whispered to Owen.

Owen scurried around her to Billie and accepted the ring. He bounced back to Riley. "Here, Mommy. You get a w'ring too."

"Thank you, Owen," Riley said.

He nestled against his mother as Riley took Fallon's hand.

"Riley, your turn," Ida said. "Fallon, I give you this ring as a symbol of my love, my fidelity, and my commitment to our life together, now and forever."

Riley started to slip the ring onto Fallon's finger. "Fallon, I give you this ring as a symbol of my love, my fidelity, and my commitment to our life together, now and forever."

Fallon exchanged a smile with Riley.

"Fallon and Riley have promised to share their lives with respect, love, and devotion. May they be blessed with more laughter than tears, with the strength to overcome life's obstacles, and with friendships that support them along their way. And now," Ida said, a grin creeping across her face. "It's my pleasure to pronounce Fallon and Riley legal and loving spouses."

Fallon released the breath she hadn't realized she'd been holding.

"That means you can kiss your wife, Fallon," Ida said.

Fallon leaned closer and captured Riley's lips with hers. Riley's hands lifted to hold Fallon's face as the kiss continued softly. Fallon didn't want it to end—ever. She savored the moment, forgetting anyone else was present. "I love you," she told Riley when she found the strength to break their kiss

"I love you too."

Fallon bent over and scooped up Owen. "And, I love you," she told him.

"Momma!" Owen squealed.

Fallon shrugged and moved Owen to her left hip. She took Riley's hand. "Well, Mrs. Foster, what do you say we go celebrate?"

"Lead the way."

The sound of *Brown Eyed Girl* barely managed to break through the laughter at Murphy's Law. Brenda had been content to sit at a table and observe the festivities. Owen had been dancing with Emily, Summer, and Evan in the center of the bar since the jukebox had begun to play. The only exception being when he would run to Andi, Ida, or one of his mothers in an attempt to pull them along. He was thriving in Whiskey Springs; that much was obvious. Hearing Riley and Fallon speak their vows had moved her deeply. Watching them as they danced together, witnessing the look of happiness in Riley's eyes, and hearing the sound of her laughter when Fallon would whisper into her ear, cured every misgiving Brenda had about Riley's decision to make a life in Whiskey Springs. In her experience, it said a great deal about a couple when they could be content to go their separate ways in a crowd and remain secure that they were still together. Fallon had made the rounds in the opposite direction from Riley, mingling and accepting congratulatory hugs. Riley had been sucked into the kids' dance marathon repeatedly, and had disappeared for a few moments with Andi. The air in the pub pulsed with more than happiness. The energy that crackled everywhere radiated love. These people loved each other—all of them. Riley had said that she'd come home. Brenda could easily understand the feeling. She made her way over to Fallon and gently grabbed Fallon's arm. "Thank you, Fallon."

Fallon was puzzled.

"For making sure Doug and I had the chance to be here," Brenda said.

"I'm glad you made it. It means a lot to Riley — and to me." Fallon's attention turned to Riley in the distance.

"You know, I'm sure you think Mary is a bit of a bitch. She can be difficult, but…"

Fallon looked back at her mother-in-law.

"She and Riley have always been opposites. Mary likes to think she's Riley's caretaker. Riley let her for most of their lives. The truth is that Riley was always everyone's caretaker. She's the peacekeeper."

Fallon wasn't surprised.

"That doesn't surprise you; I take it?"

"No," Fallon replied.

"Mm. Riley's always been adventurous, not reckless, but open to new things — curious. I was surprised when she and Robert bought their house in San Diego."

"Why?"

"Oh, they were both that way; interested in the world and determined to experience all it offered," Brenda said. "I think she stayed local because of Mary."

Fallon sighed. She didn't need Riley to tell her that Mary's absence hurt. She felt Brenda offer a gentle squeeze to her arm in acknowledgment.

"I'm sure she's disappointed that Mary chose not to come," Brenda offered. "But I'll bet she's also relieved."

Fallon was curious.

"I told you; Riley is the peacekeeper in our family — the mediator. She's been doing that for years — chief consoler, expert negotiator, and CEO of keeping calm."

Fallon laughed.

"When Doug and I split, Mary went off the rails. She was incredibly angry at us both. We waited until the girls were older to part. Who knows if that was the right decision? The funniest part? There was no anger between *us*. Riley took the news in stride. Mary? You'd think we'd delivered a nuclear bomb on her life. For her, I guess it was."

"Riley mentioned that Mary still has a tough time with your divorce."

"All these years later," Brenda said. "There isn't one get together that she doesn't find an opening to comment on how we ruined the family."

"Riley doesn't feel that way," Fallon said, unsure of what else she could offer.

"No. Like I said, Riley and Mary are opposites. Riley has always been wide-eyed with wonder. She came into the world that way. She would wander away from me to explore anywhere we went if I didn't keep hold of her. Mary?" Brenda chuckled. "She was happiest when she had hold of my hand and her father's. No... Riley's always been driven by a need to experience life. Mary wants to feel secure. I'm not sure how much Mary picked up on as a kid. Riley was aware of Doug's affairs early on. She'd cajole me out of a funk, make me laugh. Sometimes — I hate to admit this; I think Riley was more the adult in our relationship. She's always been able to understand that people are who they are. You don't always understand the people you love, not even your kids. Sometimes? Sometimes, I look at one of the girls and all I can see is Doug, or even myself. Other times?" Brenda shook her head. "Other times I wonder if I was inseminated by pod people."

Fallon laughed. She'd heard Riley make a similar comment about Owen once.

"They come through you; they are not you," Brenda said.

Fallon liked Riley's mother immediately. She reminded Fallon a great deal of Andi. That wasn't surprising. It explained why Riley gravitated to Andi so easily. Brenda's admission that Riley often took on the role of the adult in their relationship made perfect sense. With Andi, Riley had found a mentor, someone who treated her as an adult, but understood Riley's need to have a parental presence in her life. Without thought, her eyes moved to Andi and Ida in the corner.

Brenda's gaze followed. "Ah, the other set of grandmas. Owen is lucky."

"He is," Fallon agreed. "He has a lot of people who love him."

"So, it would appear."

"Brenda?"

"Yes?"

"In case I haven't been clear, I love Riley and Owen."

"You don't say?"

"What I mean is; I hope you know that I want you to be part of our lives — not just on FaceTime."

"I appreciate that. You should go find my daughter," she suggested.

"Actually, I think maybe she'd like to see you," Fallon replied. "She's stuck with me from here to eternity. And, between you and me? That isn't her favorite flick."

Brenda's animated laughter pulled Riley's gaze to her mother standing with Fallon. Riley looked at Carol. "Now, what do you think they're up to?"

❧ ❧

"You promised me a dance," Billie said.

"You can barely walk."

"I made it through the wedding. I can make it through one song."

Andi studied Billie for a moment. For some reason, the idea of dancing with Andi seemed to be the only thing on Billie's mind. Andi wasn't certain what was driving Billie's determination. She would love to sway to the music in Billie's arms. She didn't relish the thought of Billie in pain, and Billie *was* in pain. She'd caught Billie wincing more than once. She'd even entertained the idea of ushering Billie to the car and driving her to the emergency room. There was no way Andi was going to win that battle, at least, not today. "Why is this so important to you?" Andi asked.

"Why don't you want to?" Billie countered.

"I don't like seeing you in pain," Andi replied. "Don't try to tell me that you aren't. I know you. I understand why you insisted on making it through today; I do. What I don't know is why you are determined to stay on that foot when it is clearly causing you pain."

Billie was growing frustrated.

"Billie?" Andi asked.

"I never have."

"You never have? I don't understand."

Billie sighed.

"Danced with me?" Andi asked.

"Danced with anyone that I wanted to—not in public."

Andi was stunned.

"I know; I'm pathetic."

"Not at all," Andi disagreed. "I'll tell you what; you let me pick the song, and I will dance with you."

Billie brightened.

"But when the song ends, we are leaving."

"We can't leave, Andi. It's Fallon and Riley's..."

"Fallon and Riley know that you're hurting, just like I do. They love you—*not* just like I do," Andi teased. "They do love you. I love you, Billie. It hurts me to see you in pain."

Billie nodded her agreement.

"Thank you," Andi said. She kissed Billie on the cheek and started to walk toward Fallon.

"Where are you going?" Billie asked.

"I need someone to tap the jukebox for me," she said. "Wait here."

❧

"Hey, Mom," Riley greeted Brenda. "I hope you're having a good time."

"Your friends are wonderful," Brenda said. "I can see why you fell in love with this place—and, with Fallon."

Riley beamed with happiness. "It is a pretty amazing place, isn't it?"

"I'd say so. Listen, I'm sorry about your sister."

Riley nodded. "Me too. Can I be honest?"

"You're relieved she's not here."

"I know; it's awful."

"It's not. This is your day. You deserve to enjoy every second of it," Brenda said.

"Thanks."

"Oh, Riley, I'm so happy for you, and so glad that Fallon called us. Although, I think your father might have a little crush on your mother-in-law."

Riley roared with laughter. "I think his wife might have something to say about that."

"I wouldn't be too sure about that."

"Oh, no. Is that the real reason she didn't come with Dad? He said she had a commitment she couldn't break. Is he okay?"

"He's fine," Brenda assured Riley. "And, don't you dare tell him that I let anything slip."

Riley pretended to zip her lips.

"Riley?"

"Yeah?"

"I hope you know that you and Fallon are welcome to visit whenever you like — me or your father."

"I know. It goes both ways, Mom. I know you're not coming for Thanksgiving now. You know, you're welcome anytime. This holiday season, I just... I really want to be..."

"Home?"

Riley nodded.

"I don't blame you."

Andi hated to interrupt Fallon. Fallon was in the middle of a conversation with Dale, and Andi wanted to give them time. She also wanted to get Billie home sooner than later. "I'm sorry." She laid her hand on Fallon's arm.

"Hey." Fallon was happy to find Andi standing beside her. She'd barely spoken to Andi since they'd arrived at Murphy's Law. "Dale, would you…"

"I need to find Marge anyway. By the way," he said. "You both look fantastic."

"Thanks, Dale," Andi said.

He nodded. "See you later. Congratulations, Fallon. Riley's terrific."

"Yeah, she really is," Fallon agreed. She waited a beat and turned to Andi. "He's right; you look fabulous."

"Thank you," Andi said. "Who knew you cleaned up so well? Thank God for Riley's laundry skills."

"Cute," Fallon said. "Listen, Andi… Everything you did for us—I need you to know that it means a lot to me. I never expected any of that."

"Well, I know you. You'd do it for anyone. You wouldn't do it for yourself. And, Fallon? You deserved to have a memorable day."

"You know, spending the morning with you—Well, I don't know if you realize how much that meant to Riley."

Andi couldn't reply. She didn't expect most people to understand the bond that she shared with Riley. People came into your life for reasons that often weren't meant to be explained. Riley's arrival in Whiskey Springs had changed life for more people than Fallon. Andi had spent some time with Brenda alone. Riley's mother was engaging, witty, and sincere. She'd traveled a similar road to Andi; save falling in love with a woman. She had also recognized that amid the affection evident between Riley and her mother, there was a sense of distance brought on by more than the number of miles that separated them. Sometimes, Andi entertained the idea that people created what they needed to create with people in their lives. She missed her sons. Perhaps, Riley filled part of that void. It might have been true that she filled a similar space in Riley's world. Their friendship ran deep, much as Andi's did with Ida, and in some ways Fallon's with her. Love took on many forms. One thing that Andi had come to believe; love, however and whenever it appeared in your life was meant to be accepted and nurtured, not questioned. It demanded gratefulness not skepticism. In Andi's heart, Riley had become her daughter. A late adoption, perhaps, but that is what she *felt*. And, Riley felt the same way. Andi had felt a range of emotions throughout the day. She wasn't ready to examine any of them.

Fallon sensed unease from her best friend. If anyone could understand Andi's reluctance to talk about her feelings, it was Fallon. She guessed that more than the wedding, Andi was confronting the depth of her feelings for Billie. Admitting that you loved someone was always a big step to take. Inviting them into your life was another. Fallon suspected that Andi had crossed yet another threshold today. Billie wasn't a stepping stone in Andi's life. Billie was the person Andi wanted to stay. More than her bond with Riley, or the time she spent with Dave; more than watching Fallon take the proverbial plunge—Andi's realization that she wanted to be with Billie forever had rocked her. Fallon knew Andi as well as anyone ever had. Andi wasn't ready for that revelation. Fallon understood that too. Ready or not, life had changed for them all. She smiled at Andi. "Billie almost passed out when you walked down the stairs today."

"Eh, it was probably the painkiller I gave her."

"There was nothing *painful* in her expression."

Andi rolled her eyes.

"You had the same look on your face; you know?"

"What look is that?" Andi asked.

"The way you looked at her when you walked down the aisle—you looked like you wanted to crawl inside her."

"I love her."

"Yeah, I know. Let me guess; you want to get her out of here."

Andi glanced over to where Billie was and shook her head. "She's determined that we dance."

"Yeah, I know. She's been looking forward to that all week. She's been listening to sappy country songs for days." Fallon sniggered then sobered. "Andi, Billie has never..."

"She told me."

"She told you that she's never asked a woman to dance?"

Andi shook her head. "She told me she's never danced with someone in public; not someone that she wanted to dance with."

"Yeah. She's shy. Always has been."

"She can barely stand. She's in so much pain, Fallon."

"No pain would stop me from dancing with Riley," Fallon said.

"It's your wedding day," Andi reminded her.

"True. I think you underestimate today for you and Billie."

"I'm not sure that I..."

"You know what I'm talking about. Dave's spent most of the night talking to her. You haven't let your eyes stray from her for more than a few minutes. Mom even commented on that. Dance with her, Andi. You have no idea how much it means to her."

"Actually, I do," Andi said. "That's why I came over here. I need you to play one of those sappy love songs on that hunk of junk in the corner. I promised her *one* dance, and then I'm taking her home."

"I'll take care of the music. You grab gimpy," Fallon said.

Andi shook her head affectionately. She leaned in and kissed Fallon's cheek.

"Thank you," Fallon whispered. "For everything."

"Thank you, Fallon."

"Andi?"

"Hum?"

"Let her take care of you too."

Andi was puzzled. "You're used to taking care of everyone else. Sometimes, I think Riley *could* be your kid. Billie needs to take care of you too."

Andi nodded. "I will."

"Good."

❧

Andi led Billie to the small dancefloor. "Don't try anything fancy," she warned her lover.

One song faded into another, and Billie immediately recognized the tune. "You played this?"

"Oh, I have it on good authority that you were listening to this on repeat."

Billie blushed.

Andi listened to the words as she swayed with Billie. "It is stronger than it's ever been," Andi repeated the words softly.

Billie pulled Andi closer. She let her cheek press against Andi's and closed her eyes, savoring the sound of the music and Andi pressed against her. She sighed.

"Billie? Are you okay?"

"Never been better," Billie promised.

"You might feel differently when you put that foot up later."

Billie pulled away to look at Andi. "I'd live in traction for a year to have this dance with you."

Andi was positive she'd never felt anything close to what she did at the moment. She lifted her hands to Billie's cheeks. "You have the rest of your life to dance with me," she promised.

Andi's words left Billie speechless. They were spoken without reservation or hesitation. She pressed her lips to Andi's and whispered against them. "I love you."

Andi closed her eyes and lost herself in Billie's kiss. *I love you.*

❧

"How are you doing?" Fallon asked Dave.

Dave kept his focus on his mother and Billie. "She's not like I thought."

"Billie?" Fallon asked.

"No, Mom."

"She's happy," Fallon said.

"Yeah."

"Be happy for her," Fallon advised. "If anyone deserves it, it's your mom."

"It's just weird."

"What's that? Your mom with Billie?"

"Seeing her happy," he said. "I never realized how lonely she was until I saw them together."

Fallon's heart twisted slightly. "Like I said, she deserves it."

"Fallon?"

"Yeah?"

"Riley's pretty hot." Dave snickered at Fallon's blush.

Fallon laughed. "Keep your eyes off my wife," she told him with a wink.

"Dude, you're married," he said.

"Do I look like a dude?"

"Not from where I'm standing." Riley's voice came from behind Fallon.

"Oh, look; it's my *hot* wife."

"I won't ask where that came from," Riley said. She held out her hand. "I think you should dance with your *hot* wife."

Fallon offered Dave a shrug. "Duty calls," she said. "I have to obey her now."

Riley let go of Fallon's hand and pinched her. "There was no promise to *obey*."

"No? Where's my mother?"

"Let's go," Riley said, pulling Fallon toward Billie and Andi.

"Left you alone, huh?" Ida asked Dave.

"They're all a little crazy," Dave observed.

"Yep," Ida agreed. "Better crazy than lonely," she said.

"Do you think Mom and Billie will get married too?"

"Oh, I don't know," Ida said. "In this family, anything is possible."

∽ ⋅ ∼

Fallon carried Owen into his bedroom and laid him down on his bed. He grumbled when she tried to take off his shoes. "What is it with these shoes?" She laughed.

"You know, your mom offered to take him for the night," Riley commented.

Fallon continued to undress him. "For once, I wish he'd wake up. He's like dead wood." She laughed. "He's exhausted."

"He had a busy day," Riley said. She handed Fallon a pair of pajamas for Owen.

Owen groaned in protest when Fallon tried to sit him up. Fallon managed to pull his shirt over his head, and Owen grabbed hold of her in his sleep. Fallon held onto him tightly.

"Fallon?"

Fallon's tears finally escaped. She felt Riley's hand on her shoulder. "I need you both here tonight," she said.

"Bring him into our room, Fallon."

Fallon swiveled to look at Riley. "Riley, I didn't mean that I…"

Two fingers pressed to Fallon's lips to silence her, then moved to the curls of Owen's hair. Riley smiled. "I promised you forever, Fallon. Believe me; I will need you and want you to make love with me countless times. Tonight, you need to know that we are *home*—all of us. Today wasn't only about me and you. Your mother was right about that."

"Are you sure?" Fallon asked.

"Positive. You *will* have to help me with this dress, though."

"In that case, I think we might want to leave Owen here."

"Is that so?"

"As tired as I am, if I unzip that dress…"

"Fallon, are you coming on to me?"

"Definitely."

Riley laughed. "What if I told you that I'm exhausted, and I would be happy to sleep beside you tonight?"

"You want me to control myself, *and* you want me to undress you?"

"I want you to *unzip* me," Riley corrected her.

"Uh-huh."

"I'll make you a deal."

"Another deal?"

"Yes, and this time we will both benefit."

"I'm all ears."

"I promise to wear this dress one night soon when Owen is with one of his grandmas, and you can unzip it slowly then."

Fallon's pulse quickened. She was ready to suggest again that Owen sleep right where he was when he opened his eyes and rubbed them.

"Momma," he whined.

"Hey, buddy. It's late," Fallon said.

He wrapped his arms around her neck, and Fallon melted. "Do you want to sleep with me and Mommy tonight?"

He nodded and let his head fall onto her shoulder.

"Sucker," Riley teased.

"Mm. I intend to see the completion of that deal *soon*."

Riley turned. "Just start the zipper for me. I'll get changed while you finish getting him dressed."

Fallon pulled the zipper of Riley's dress down a couple of inches. "*Soon*, Riley," she whispered in Riley's ear.

Riley shivered. *Not soon enough.*

CHAPTER FOURTEEN

A MONTH LATER

Owen raced into the living room. "Momma!"

Fallon nearly fell over at the state of her son. "What on earth..."

"I made cake."

Fallon cocked her head to one side. Cake? Owen was covered from head to toe in what Fallon assumed was flour. He'd helped Andi bake a cake the day before. That's all he had talked about since. He was going to be a cook just like his Grandma. Earlier, Riley had been in the kitchen making a list of the things she needed to do for Thanksgiving. The list included baking a cake for Beth's birthday. Beth had missed celebrating *her* birthday because she was in the hospital giving birth. They'd made plans to throw a party for Beth on Sunday. It would be a celebration combination. They would formally welcome the newest addition to Whiskey Springs, a little girl named Hope, and Beth could blow out the candles on her birthday cake. Fallon was almost positive that Beth would need a pick-me-up by then. Barb had arrived on Saturday to start moving into Riley's old house. Olivia was due to arrive on Thanksgiving morning with the girls. She would fly out on Saturday to Amsterdam to begin her new job, and what Fallon could only imagine would be her new life. Spending two days with Olivia Nolan was not high on anyone's list of priorities in their extended family—least of all Fallon's or Beth's. A party gave everyone something to look forward to.

Fallon stroked her cheek. Owen was immensely pleased with himself. "A cake, huh?" She asked.

Owen nodded. "Come see!"

Oh, I'm almost positive I don't want to. Fallon nodded. *Why do I think I'm going to have to master the laundry sooner than later?* "I'm right behind you," Fallon told him.

⌁

"Are you sure that you want to have everyone at your house?" Andi asked Riley.

"Why not?"

"Why not? You want to entertain Liv in your home?"

"Not really," Riley confessed. "I can think of a few things I *would* like to do. That's not one of them. I'll be damned if she ruins this holiday for any of us."

"We can have it at my house. It's neutral ground," Andi offered.

"No. You hosted our wedding. I'm hosting Thanksgiving."

"I'm not going to win this, am I?"

"Not this one," Riley said.

"It's a lot of people, Riley."

"Which is why you are helping me cook."

"That's fine as long as someone else cleans it up," Andi commented.

"That's the plan. Both the boys are still coming?"

"As of now."

"Nervous?" Riley asked.

"About Dave bringing his Bible-thumping girlfriend to a dinner attended by a flock of lesbians? Maybe a little."

Riley laughed. "He didn't say *she* was Bible-thumping. He said that her parents were."

"I hope there's a difference."

"I thought that things were still on track with you two?"

"They are. He calls a couple of times a week. To tell you the truth, I think he talks to Billie more than he talks to me these days." Andi laughed.

"Mm."

"What?"

"Nothing."

"What?" Andi asked again.

"Just wondering when you two are going to make things a bit more *permanent.*"

Andi sighed.

"Hey, I'm teasing."

"I asked her to move in."

Riley stopped walking and looked at Andi. Andi's bashful grin made her chuckle. "When did this happen?"

"Last night," Andi replied. "I'm probably crazy," she said. "I hate it when she goes home, Riley. I mean it. It feels so...."

"Empty?"

"That's a good way to describe it."

"You're not crazy," Riley said. "What did she say?"

"She wants to be sure that I'm sure."

"Are you?" Riley asked.

"I am," Andi replied. "This is not a conversation for the grocery store."

"Well, let's get a move on then. We can discuss it over wine in my kitchen."

"How many bottles do you have?" Andi asked with a nervous chuckle.

"My wife owns a bar. The supply is endless."

Andi laughed. "Thank God for Fallon."

∽∾

"What on earth happened in here?" Riley asked.

"Hi, Mommy!"

Andi stepped into the kitchen and gasped. "Good thing she has an endless supply," she whispered in Riley's ear.

"Owen wanted to bake a cake," Fallon tried to explain.

"Is he the filling?" Andi asked.

"Ha-ha. I was making the beds in the spare room," Fallon offered. "He seems to understand that eggs and flour are needed."

Owen grinned proudly. In addition to the white dust that covered him and the kitchen, there was a bowl of cracked eggs on the island, shell and all. "I helped, Gwama!"

"I see that," Andi said.

"Like you," he said. He held up a finger. "F'wour, egg, water..." He stopped and tapped his forehead. "Miw'lk! Momma, I need miw'lk!"

Riley covered her face and laughed.

"You need a bath," Andi said. She looked at Fallon. "Tandem, perhaps?" She teased her friend. Fallon was covered now as well.

Fallon groaned.

"He was alone for five minutes!" Fallon said.

"I helped!" Owen repeated with pride.

"Yes, you sure did," Riley said. She tried not to laugh at Fallon's forlorn expression. The kitchen *was* a mess. It looked a bit like someone had dropped a flour bomb in the middle of it. And, Riley couldn't deny that the scene was the last thing she'd expected to find. The expression on her son's and her wife's faces made any hint of irritation vanish. These were the moments that Riley knew she would remember for the rest of her life. This mess was a memory. She and Fallon had been married just under a month. Riley had never been happier. Little moments like this reminded Riley why she loved the life they shared. Every so often, her eyes would fall to the band on Fallon's finger. Now, its glimmer had been dulled by a fine, white sheen. "Why don't you take Mommy to the bathroom and you two get cleaned up from all your hard work," Riley suggested. "Grandma and I will put things away."

"We got to bake it," Owen said.

"Well," Riley began. "Auntie Beth's birthday party is on Sunday. That's still five days away. Four sleeps, Owen. On Saturday, we'll bake a special cake together. How does that sound?"

He considered his mother's offer.

"Owen?" Riley asked.

"But I can help," he said.

"You do help," Riley promised.

Owen seemed doubtful.

"You know what?" Andi interjected. "I think you could help Mommy by giving Momma a bath."

Owen grinned. He looked at Fallon. "You filfy, Momma."

"I'm filthy?" Fallon asked.

"Yep," he said. "You s'posed to bake it. You not s'posed to wear it. Gwama says."

Fallon's jaw dropped.

Andi and Riley both erupted with laughter.

"That's it," Fallon said. She threw Owen over her shoulder. "Bath time!"

"Momma!" He giggled uncontrollably.

"Nope," Fallon said as she headed down the hallway. "I'm gonna mix *you* up in the tub."

"I's not a cake!" Owen laughed harder.

"Riley!" Fallon called out. "You and Grandma get the eggs. I'm gonna make an Owen treat!"

"Momma!" Owen shook with laughter.

"Those two," Andi commented. "God bless you."

Riley looked at the kitchen. She took out her phone and started snapping pictures.

"What are you doing?" Andi asked.

"Documenting the crime. I may need leverage in the future."

Andi snorted. "God help Fallon."

THANKSGIVING DAY

There were few things that Fallon enjoyed more than a lively gathering with her friends. The smell of turkey in the oven, coffee on the burner, and autumn leaves were on the short list. She savored a sip of the coffee in her cup and inhaled the brisk autumn air. A sprinkle of color remained on several of the trees in her yard. Most of the leaves had fallen, creating blanket of, red, gold, and orange on the ground. "I really need to rake this yard."

"Your reinforcements will be here in a few hours," Riley commented. She handed Fallon a sweatshirt. "Put that on."

"It's not that cold out," Fallon said.

"You're not a penguin," Riley replied.

Fallon set her coffee aside and slipped on the sweatshirt. "Do you need my help with anything?"

"No," Riley said. "Nothing more to do for a while."

"Talked to Andi this morning?" Fallon wondered.

"Just now."

"How's everything there?"

"So far, so good. Dave got there late last night. Billie's not there yet. She had to work until seven."

"She's going to be wiped," Fallon said.

Andi said she was heading home for a few hours to sleep.

"Mmm."

"What?" Riley asked.

"I just wonder how Andi feels about that."

"She hates it."

Fallon turned to Riley curiously.

"She asked Billie to move in."

"What? When?"

"The other day."

"What did Billie say?"

"Something to the effect of, *let's see how it goes this weekend before you decide,*" Riley replied.

"Oh no."

"Mmm."

"Is Andi upset?"

"I don't know if upset is the right word."

"Hurt?"

"No, more like frustrated."

"Billie doesn't want to hurt Andi's relationship with Dave."

"I know, but she might injure Andi's feelings in the process."

"I'll talk to her."

"Don't," Riley warned.

"Why not?"

"Because, Fallon, Andi told me that in confidence. And, they need to work this one out without anyone interfering. That includes you and me."

Fallon muttered.

"Fallon, I'm serious. They'll work it out. What about you?"

"Me?"

"Yes, you. You didn't have to invite Olivia for dinner."

"I'm not letting her spoil things, Riley. Before you say anything, if I didn't invite her, she'd find a way to do that. If not for me, then for the girls or Barb."

Riley nodded. Fallon had spent two days helping Barb unpack. "You haven't said much about what you and Barb talked about."

"There's not much to say," Fallon said. "We didn't talk about Liv much. They'll do their dinner and come over for coffee. The kids can play together. Liv can behave. If she acts like an ass, I'll throw her out on hers."

"My hero."

"I don't think any of us have the energy for Liv's drama," Fallon said bluntly. "Barb's okay. Beth is okay. Me? I'm a lot better than okay. They will be too. She'll behave for the girls' sake. It's one afternoon. She'll spend the day with Emily and Summer tomorrow, and then she'll be an ocean away from us."

"Fallon..."

"Oh, I know; she'll be an ocean closer to my brother. I don't care, Riley. I know you think I do. I don't. It hurts to know that they both lied to me. I admit that. Things have turned out better than I'd ever dared hope for me. Believe it or not, I hope they both find happiness. That doesn't mean I want either of them to be a daily part of my life."

"I know."

"I have my family," Fallon said.

Riley kissed Fallon on the cheek.

"Where are you going?" Fallon wondered.

"I want to make sure our son isn't trying to help again."

"Well, maybe he'll decide to try laundry the next time."

"Oh, Lord. Owen!" Riley called out.

Fallon laughed.

ᏪᎯ᎐Ᏺ

Andi set a cup of coffee on the table in front of Becky.

"Thank you," Becky said.

"You're welcome."

"Where's Billie?" Becky wondered.

Andi braced herself. "She had to work until seven this morning."

"Oh."

"She'll be over in a few hours," Andi offered.

"Dave talks about her a lot."

Andi was both surprised and curious. She sipped her coffee slowly.

"I'm glad she's a lesbian. Otherwise, I might be worried," Becky joked.

Andi choked and coughed.

"Sorry," Becky apologized with a giggle. "Was that inappropriate?"

"No." Andi chuckled. "You took me off guard."

"He told you about my parents. I know; he told me."

"He cares a great deal about you," Andi told her son's girlfriend.

"He worries too much," Becky said. "I can't change who they are. That goes both ways."

Andi smiled. Becky displayed a maturity that Andi admired. "Well, neither Billie or I want to make you uncomfortable."

"Me?" Becky shook her head. "My aunt is a lesbian."

Andi was stunned.

"He didn't tell you that?"

"No."

"Probably because I haven't seen her since I was a kid. I think that's what freaked him out the most. My father doesn't speak to her. My sister talks to her. I haven't gotten up the guts to call her yet."

"May I ask why?"

"My parents forbid us to see her. My sister is... Well, they don't talk to her. They do talk to me. I guess I feel like I need to choose sometimes."

Andi's chest tightened. "That has to be hard."

"It is. I'm close to my mom. Closer than I am to my dad. I don't think he's close to anyone—not really. He's wrapped up in his church." Becky sighed. "I'd like to say that I don't care if they know about Dave and me, and well..."

"That his mother is a lesbian?"

"I guess. I'm sorry."

"It's okay. I don't take it personally."

"Please, don't. I just want to get through the next year at school."

Andi understood. "You don't need to explain, Becky."

"Yeah, I do. I never wanted to come between you and Dave."

"You didn't."

Becky was doubtful.

"You didn't."

"I hope that Billie isn't avoiding coming home because I'm here."

Andi tried to smile. *I wish Billie would come home.*

⌘

"Dave?" Billie answered her phone.

"Where are you?"

"I'm at home."

"At your place?"

"That's what I said."

"Why didn't you come home to Mom's?"

Billie sighed. "I wanted to give you all some time together."

"Without you? Jacob thinks I told you not to come."

"What?"

"He's pissed at me—again. He took off a few minutes ago. Pretty sure he went to Fallon's already."

"Dave, I just thought you all might want some family time."

"I don't get it," he said.

"What?"

"You basically live with Mom. That makes you family. You stayed at home when I was here last month."

Billie sighed.

"I thought we were cool."

Billie couldn't help but chuckle. "We are *cool*."

"Becky wants to meet you. She and Mom are in there, and they probably both are pissed at me that you aren't here."

"Your mom is not pissed at you," Billie assure him. *Me, I'm not so sure.*

"Can't you just come home?"

"Your mom is expecting me to get there around noon."

"So, what?"

"I need to rest a little before Fallon's."

"And? Sleep in your room here."

"You're not going to let this go."

"Dude, I don't need everyone pissed at me."

"Okay, *dude.* I'll be there in a bit."

"Hurry up." He hung up the phone.

Billie laughed. "Well, let's hope she's happy to see me."

❧ ❧

Andi's heart stopped for a second when Billie walked into the kitchen.

"Hey," Billie said. She wasn't sure what she saw flickering in Andi's eyes. Was it anger? Maybe it was confusion. Or perhaps it was—before Billie could complete her next thought, Andi's arms were around her. She closed her eyes and held on. "I'm sorry," Billie said.

Andi didn't let go. "I don't want to miss you anymore, Billie."

"I'm home," Billie said. She heard Andi's sharp intake of breath. "Assuming you still want this to be my home."

Andi pulled away slightly and smiled. "Do you need to ask that?"

"No. Maybe I'd just like to hear it."

"I want you here," Andi said. "With me. Is that clear enough?"

Billie smiled. "Completely."

"I am curious; what made you come home?"

"Dave."

"Dave?"

"Mm-hum. He called me."

"When?"

"About half an hour ago."

"What did he say?" Andi wondered.

"He wanted to know why I didn't come *home.*"

Andi smiled.

"I felt a bit like a teenager being scolded," Billie said.

Andi laughed. "Billie, he cares what you think of him."

"He said that?"

"No. He didn't have to. I can tell. But, Becky might have mentioned it this morning."

"Really?"

"Why does that surprise you? He talks to you more than he does to me."

"I don't know."

Andi moved a step closer and wrapped her arms around Billie's neck. "You're like his cool new stepmom."

"Don't we need to be married for that?"

Andi shrugged lightly.

"Someday, I might ask that again," Billie said.

Andi caught her meaning. "You don't need to ask me anything for this to be your home."

"I know," Billie admitted.

"Do you want to go lie down for a couple of hours?" Andi asked.

"Alone?"

"I wish I could join you."

"Too much to do?" Billie guessed.

"No."

"The kids?"

"No."

"Why can't you come with me then?"

"Because you need rest, and I want *you*."

Billie swallowed hard. "I can sleep later."

"Is that so?"

"Totally." Billie grabbed Andi's hand and tugged.

"You do realize that Dave and Becky are home?" Andi said. "You have to be quiet."

"I'll bite my lip."

Andi laughed. "Not if I bite it first."

"Jacob?" Fallon looked out the window. "Riley?"

"Yeah?"

"Did Andi send Jacob over here for something?"

"Not that I'm aware of."

"Shit."

"Why?" Riley looked out the window. "Uh-oh."

"I hope no one's bleeding," Fallon said.

"I doubt it. Andi would've called."

"If she knows." Fallon went to the door.

"I'll be in the kitchen if you need me," Riley said.

"Just hide the knives." Fallon stepped onto the porch. "You're early," she called out.

"Is that okay?" Jacob asked.

"You know that you don't need an invitation."

"Will Riley care?"

Fallon folded her arms across her chest. "What happened?"

"Dave's a dick."

"Why is Dave a dick?"

"He told Billie not to come home."

Fallon waited for an explanation.

"Mom was upset this morning. I could tell. That's because Billie didn't come home after work. She went to her place instead."

"And you think Dave told her not to come home?"

"He did! Billie is always at Mom's."

"Let's go inside," Fallon said.

"Why aren't you pissed?" Jacob asked. "Can't you or Riley talk to him?"

"Right now, I think it's you that needs to get some things straight," Fallon said. "Come on. I'm sure Riley started another pot of coffee." She led Jacob into the kitchen.

"Hi, Jacob. Do you want some coffee?" Riley asked.

"Sure." Jacob looked at Riley. "Did you talk to Mom?"

"Not in the last hour," Riley said. "Why?"

"She was upset this morning," he told her.

Riley nodded. She put the carafe of coffee on the table and directed him to sit. "What makes you think she's upset?"

"She was," he said. "Dave's home with his girlfriend, so Billie went to her place."

"And?" Riley asked.

"What the hell, Riley? He shouldn't be asking Mom not to have Billie over."

"What makes you think he did?" Riley asked.

"Come on, why else wouldn't she come!"

Riley leaned back against the counter.

Jacob looked at Fallon. "You guys are on his side?"

"There's no side," Fallon said. "Maybe you jumped to a conclusion."

"I don't think so."

"I know that Dave hurt you," Fallon said. "You had every right to feel that way. He's trying, Jacob. Why don't you give him the benefit of the doubt on this one?"

Jacob shook his head.

"Fallon?" Riley began. "Would you go help Owen get dressed?"

Fallon nodded. She leaned into Jacob's ear. "Listen to her," she advised.

Jacob reluctantly met Riley's gaze. He'd grown close to her over the summer. Right now, her expression reminded him of his mother.

"Dave's not the reason Billie went home instead of to your mom's."

"How do you know?"

"I know," Riley said. "She wanted to give you all time as a family."

"That makes no sense."

"Maybe not to you. It makes sense to Billie."

"I don't get it."

"I know. Fallon's right; give your brother a break."

"I don't like seeing Mom hurt," he said.

"Neither do I."

"Is she okay? Mom, I mean? She tells you everything."

"She tells me a lot," Riley agreed. "Not everything. Have a little faith, Jacob—in your mother and your brother."

"I don't want her to be alone again."

Riley nodded. Jacob was extremely close to his mother, and equally protective of her. Fallon was still his hero. Riley had worried that he might dislike her, seeing her as the reason for the demise of Fallon and Andi's relationship. Over the summer, those worries had been put to rest. By the time Jacob had left for his last year of college, she'd come to view him as a little brother. Riley was confident he shared that feeling. He never referred to Andi as *his* mom. He always called her, Mom, as if he and Riley had always shared her attention. Jacob had not been able to come home for Riley and Fallon's wedding. While he may have spoken to Dave, heard about the weekend from Andi, and talked about it with Fallon and Riley; he didn't witness the interaction between his younger brother and Billie. Billie's friendship with Dave had continued to grow, much like his relationship with Fallon had flourished over the years. Billie didn't only love Andi; she cared for the boys. Her decision to give the family space had not been made out of fear. Andi knew that. It still hurt Andi. Riley was confident it would work out. She wasn't sure that Andi, Billie, or the boys saw what both she and Fallon could see; they had already begun to create a family. Riley and Fallon were an extended part of that.

"Have a little faith," Riley told him again. "Your Mom loves Billie. They'll work it out. Finish your coffee and help me with this dinner. You come to my kitchen, you get put to work."

"You know, you sound just like her."

"Who?"

"Mom."

Riley shrugged.

Jacob laughed.

"What's so funny?"

"Now I know what it's like to have a nagging older sister."

"Shut up and grab a towel," Riley said.

How had they managed to fit this many people into the living room? Riley's eyes scanned the group affectionately. Jacob had started to snooze in Fallon's favorite chair. Evan had promised Owen he'd help complete a Lego project. They'd disappeared into Owen's room nearly an hour ago. Beth sat on the sofa with Ida, cradling Hope to her chest. Andi and Billie sat at the other end. Billie's head was quickly making its way toward Andi's shoulder. Fallon had headed off to the kitchen to start a pot of coffee—something that by the looks of it, more than one person desperately needed. And, Dave and Becky had claimed spots on the floor. Both seemed to be listening to the conversation in the room with interest. Riley found that amusing. In the last twenty minutes, she'd heard more about breastfeeding and diapers than she'd heard since Owen was a baby.

The sound of a car pulling up silenced the room.

Ida patted Beth's knee. "Don't worry, there are plenty of pies to throw at her if she misbehaves."

"Oh no, I worked hard on those pies," Andi said. "Find something else."

Fallon appeared from the kitchen and opened the front door. Emily and Summer bolted through the door in search of Evan and Owen.

"Hi, Aunt Fallon." They both rushed by her.

"Don't stop on my account," Fallon said.

"Fallon," Olivia greeted her.

"Hi, Liv."

"How's married life?" Olivia asked.

Fallon smiled and looked at Barb. "Hey, Barb. Come in."

"You didn't answer my question," Olivia noted.

"Didn't see the need."

"Fallon," Oliva pulled her former lover aside before walking in. "Let's not do this today; okay? Let's just play nice for a few hours."

Fallon nodded her agreement. She held the door open for Olivia.

"Hello, Liv," Riley said.

"Hi, Riley. Congratulations, by the way," Olivia said cordially.

"Thanks." Riley moved to Fallon's side when Olivia approached Beth and Ida. "Maybe she'll be on her best behavior."

"Mm. Today, maybe," Fallon said.

"After today, you won't have to deal with her for a long time."

"One can hope."

SUNDAY

"Didn't we just do this?" Andi asked Fallon.

"Yep."

"Why are we doing this *again,* again?"

"Because we're gluttons for punishment?"

"I'll accept that."

"How's married life?" Fallon poked.

"I'm not married."

"Do you mean anymore or *yet*?" Fallon quipped.

"Where's Riley?"

"You're blushing."

"I don't blush."

"You do now," Fallon observed,

"Isn't there supposed to be free drinks at this thing? Where's the owner?" Andi asked.

"Okay, I get it; lay off."

"Thank you," Andi said. "Seriously, Fallon, did you invite the entire town?"

"No, I left the Biddy Brigade off the list."

From where Andi was standing, it appeared that Dora Bath's entourage were about the only people left off the guest list. "Does Beth even know these people?"

"Hey, this is a big deal, Andi. We finally hit the 1000 mark in Whiskey Springs."

"Ummm.... Unless I'm mistaken, we hit the 1003 mark."

"Huh?"

"If Hope is the 1000th resident, that makes Barb, Emily, and Summer 1001, 1002, and 1003."

"Oh, shit. I don't think I can fit three more candles."

Andi laughed. "I hope you have fire insurance."

"Hey, where is Billie?" Fallon asked. "I thought she had the weekend off?"

"She did."

"Uh-oh."

"I guess the flu is sweeping through the nursing staff. She went in for a few hours. She'll be here around seven."

"How are things with the boys?"

Andi's spirits immediately lightened. "Great. I think Dave's in love."

"Kind of seems that way," Fallon agreed. "Maybe the next wedding will be his."

Andi smacked her — hard. "Stop speaking."

❧

Beth smiled when she saw Riley approaching.

"Want me to take her off your hands for a few minutes?" Riley offered to hold Hope.

"Are you sure you don't mind?"

"Mind?" Riley took charge of the infant. "She's so precious."

"She is," Beth agreed.

"How are you doing?" Riley asked.

"Do you mean after Liv's visit?"

"There is that."

"Surprisingly well," Beth said. "I'm happy Barb's here."

"You are?"

"Yeah. Evan's thrilled to have his sisters close, and honestly, Riley? Barb is about the best friend I've got. We've been steering through a shitstorm together for a long time."

"Does Barb know about Liv and Dean?"

"She knows."

"I don't know how Olivia can face any of you."

"Oh, I think Liv sees things one way—her way," Beth replied. "She's the center of her world. So, she expects to be the center of all of ours."

"Maybe now that she knows she's not, everyone will get a break," Riley said.

"I hope so. For the first time in forever, I feel like I can breathe."

"I understand."

Beth watched as Riley cooed to the infant in her arms. "Have you and Fallon thought at all about adding another one?"

Riley's smile gave away her heart, if not the answer.

"She'll be a great mom," Beth said.

"She already is," Riley replied.

"MVA three minutes out!"

Billie groaned. "So much for seven o'clock."

"Billie!" A voice called out.

"On my way!" *So much for birthday cake.*

Andi was growing worried.

"I'm sure she got held up at work," Riley offered.

"Yeah."

"Andi, Billie's okay," Riley said. "You know how it is there. If they got busy, she probably couldn't call."

"I know."

"She'll call. It's only eight o'clock."

Andi nodded. "I know you're right. I just have this sinking feeling."

Riley understood. Life seemed to have hit its stride, not just for Andi and Billie. Fallon and Riley, Andi's boys, even Beth and Barb seemed to finally be happy, or at least, they believed they had the chance to be happy. It wasn't unusual for Billie to get stuck at work. That much, Riley did know. "She's okay, Andi. I know it."

Andi nodded again.

"Come on, let me buy you a margarita on Fallon's dime."

"Isn't that your dime now?" Andi asked.

"Half of it anyway."

"Never let it be said you're not a big spender," Andi replied.

Riley laughed, glad to see that Andi was beginning to relax.

Andi sipped her margarita and laughed. Fallon had challenged Dave to a game of darts and lost badly. It was a first, and it was a first that thoroughly delighted everyone in attendance. "I wish Billie could've seen that," she commented just as her phone buzzed. "Speak of the devil!"

"Told you," Riley said.

Andi stepped away from the bar. "Hey, you. Are you all right?" Andi strained to hear Billie over the noise. She stuck a finger in her ear. "Billie?"

"Can you hear me?" Billie asked.

"I can now. It's loud in here. Dave just handed Fallon her ass at the dartboard." She heard Billie sigh. "Billie? What is it? What's wrong?"

"I shouldn't be telling you this."

"Telling me what? You're scaring me. What's going on?"

"It's Olivia, Andi."

"Olivia? Liv is in Amsterdam."

"No, she's not," Billie said. She took a deep breath. "Andi," she hesitated. "Liv's dead."

"What are you taking about?"

"They brought her in two hours ago. MVA. That's a…"

"That's not possible. She flew to Amsterdam yesterday."

"No. I don't know what happened. All I do know is that they found her in her car. She'd been there a while, Andi. I know the State Police are on their way there now to make the notification. I can't get ahead of them. I thought you should prepare…"

Andi felt sick. "How am I going to tell Fallon?"

"I don't know, but I think you should tell her before they get there. I'll be there as soon as I can."

"Billie…"

"I'm okay," Billie promised. "I just wish I was there with you."

"So, do I."

"I love you, Andi."

Andi was sure she was going to be sick. "I love you. Drive safely. I mean it, I can't…"

"I'll be there in one piece as soon as I can."

Andi closed her eyes.

Riley made her way over when she saw Andi put her phone back in her pocket. "See. She's fine."

Andi took a moment to steady herself. She turned to Riley. "I need to talk to you and Fallon privately."

"Andi?"

"Don't ask me here. Billie's okay. I need to talk to you and Fallon."

Riley suddenly felt ill. Something was wrong. She nodded. "We'll meet you in the kitchen."

"Now?" Fallon asked.

"Fallon, please," Riley said.

"Okay! What can be so urgent that…"

"Fallon."

Fallon groaned, but followed Riley. The moment she caught sight of Andi, her heart plummeted. "Andi?"

Andi's smile ached with sorrow. "Fallon," she started softly. "Billie called."

"Is she okay?"

"She got caught at work," Andi explained. "Fallon, she… They…"

"Andi, what is it?"

"It's Liv," Andi said. "I don't know why or how or…"

"Liv?" Fallon tried to understand.

"Fallon, I don't know how to tell you this. The State Police are on their way here now."

"What? Why would…"

Riley needed no more information to know what Andi was about to say. She wrapped an arm around Fallon's waist in support.

"Liv's dead, Fallon," Andi said.

Fallon's knees buckled.

"All I know is they found her in her car. That's all Billie could tell me."

"She's in Amsterdam," Fallon said.

"I'm sorry," Andi said.

"A loud wail came from outside the kitchen."

Fallon immediately recognized Barb's voice. She bolted for the other room. Riley and Andi followed, their arms entwined. Ida was guiding Barb into a chair. Riley was grateful that Marge and Dale had agreed to go back to Riley and Fallon's with the kids earlier. "This can't be happening," she said.

Andi found herself at a loss.

Fallon whispered something to Barb and then stood to her full height. She found herself face to face with a familiar pair of eyes. "Greg," she greeted her old friend. She'd known Trooper Greg Molloy since grade school.

"Fallon," he said. "I'm sorry to have to deliver the news."

"I don't understand." She pulled him aside. "Liv left yesterday for Amsterdam."

"She was supposed to," he said.

"What do you mean?"

"That's how we found the car," he explained. "She didn't show. Your brother called it in."

Fallon's jaw tensed.

"She never returned her rental car. We put it out as a possible stolen vehicle or missing person. Local cops spotted it off the beaten path near Essex Junction."

"And, Liv?"

"Fallon, I can't tell you any more than that. She was in the car, unresponsive. I'm just the one who makes the notification. I imagine the detectives will be in touch when they finish at the scene."

"Detectives?" Fallon wasn't following. "For a car accident?"

"That's all I know, Fallon. I'm sorry."

"I'm sorry. I just…"

"I know. I am sorry."

Fallon nodded.

"What did he say?" Riley asked.

"Not much." She turned to Riley.

"What now?" Riley asked.

Fallon was about to answer when Billie walked through the front door.

Andi met Billie halfway across the pub and embraced her. "You have no idea how happy I am to see you."

"Yes, I do," Billie said.

"Are you okay?" Andi asked.

"I'm more worried about everyone else." She beckoned to Fallon to meet them in the kitchen.

"Billie," Fallon said. "I'm sorry. I can't imagine how that must have been for you."

"I'm okay," Billie promised. "What about you?"

"I don't know," Fallon answered honestly. "I'm not sure I believe any of it's real."

Billie nodded.

Fallon held her gaze. "What aren't you supposed to tell us?"

"Fallon…"

"Billie, Greg Molloy just told me to expect a visit from detectives. What the hell happened?"

"I don't know. Fallon, her injuries weren't consistent with a car accident. I've been doing this a long time. It looked like…"

"It looked like what?"

"Like someone beat the shit out of her," Billie said.

"What are you saying?" Andi asked.

Billie kept her gaze locked with Fallon's. "I don't know what happened to Liv," she said. "It didn't look to me like she hit anything. It looked like something hit her — repeatedly."

"This can't be happening," Riley said.

"I hope you're wrong," Fallon said.

Billie closed her eyes.

"Fallon?" Riley called for her attention. "What do we do now?"

"There's nothing any of us can do," Fallon said. "We take care of Barb and the kids. I can't worry about the rest. None of us can."

"Fallon…"

Fallon wrapped her arm around Riley and smiled as best she could at their friends. "There's nothing else for us to do," she said. "We take care of our family. We take care of each other. That's all we can do."

Billie nodded her agreement.

"Fallon," Riley stopped Fallon from following Billie and Andi out of the room. "Do you really think someone would hurt Liv?"

Fallon didn't know what to think. "I don't know."

"Are you all right? Stupid question…"

"No," Fallon said. "But I will be. We all will be. We have each other." She led Riley out of the room. She made herself a silent promise. "And, nothing will change that. Not Olivia's life or her death—nothing."

TO BE CONTINUED IN
AFTER HOURS